A Dark Inheritance

Erme Lander

Cover images – Author's own
Elementary Gothic Script – Bill Roach,
www.dafont.com

ISBN 978-1-9997453-1-8

To Suzanne for the editing,
despite her "not doing" vampires.

More frog than princess, Erme Lander lives in Gloucestershire with two children and a mad cat.

The Vampire Duology

A Dark Inheritance
A Dark Infection

The Medici Chronicles

The Lion of Ackbarr
Blood Lore
Medici of Ackbarr
Blood Debt
War Lord of Ackbarr

Lord of Dust
Death's Touch

Sasha
Willow

Table of Contents

Wolf

I

The car lights picked out trees above her as she drove along the country lanes, ghostly white in the darkness. An unsettled feeling, of someone watching her, holding her tight. Always dark, always dusty, a grittiness covered the back of her throat, making her want to cough. The smell of herbs strong in her nostrils. Trapped and with no way out.

She drifted onwards, the ground moving, her legs unable to keep up. The moon between the clouds outlined the leaves that swayed in time with her head. The swaying she couldn't stop, whatever she tried, no matter how hard she tried, aware on some level it couldn't be right. Swayed and fell, never stopping. Rain fell while she looked at a punctured tyre, cool on her hair and the cool hands clasping hers. Kept hold and wouldn't let go, unable to move, unable to escape.

Engines rumbled, vibrations underneath her, flowed through her, past her. The note of the engines changed, higher, into a whine, into a scream. Her own scream in her head while the engines droned on and on. Her vision blurred, a smell of rain, a cool breeze, stuffiness. The noises dimmed, the vibrations slowed. Dark, warm and airless, she spiralled into a deeper pit away from the dreams.

Tina

Chapter 1

Tina woke in the daylight, tucked up in the same bed as yesterday, the sheets and quilts around her chin. Her head hurt when she looked around, her neck felt bruised, her arm, her wrists... her face... She ached all over when she sat up.

Last night, she remembered him leaning over her. He'd drunk her blood, sucked it right out of her. A helplessness started to rise. There were dark bruises on her wrists, she could see the shape of his fingers where he'd held her.

Tina began to shake. No friends, no family, no going to the authorities. She didn't know where she could be – certainly not England, they'd spoken another language while she'd been lying there unable to move. If she believed what he'd said, everyone thought she was dead, everyone she loved. Tina put her head in her hands and winced when they came into contact with the side of her face. She'd never been hit before, the casual violence had shocked her, all her confidence shattered in seconds. He'd picked her up and hadn't found it difficult despite her struggling, his complete lack of emotion... She'd been nothing more than... She shied away from the thought.

She was trapped here on her own, with a madman and his helper. Tina stopped herself, not a madman - a vampire. Her hands crept up to touch her neck, it was a little swollen on one side and it felt bruised with two indentations, the proof it had happened. A vampire and his servant. Shit. Tears streamed down her face. For a long time she sat holding herself, not thinking of anything.

After a while the tears ceased. Thirsty and with a sticky face she looked around. A tray with food and water sat on the table like yesterday. Smearing her arm across her eyes, she swung her legs off the bed and stopped. Her sleeve smelt of him, giving rise to memories of him pinning her against the bookcase. She pulled off the shirt and threw it onto the bed. Sniffing and with her arms wrapped around herself, she crept to the door and tried to open it. Rattling the handle she tried again, not quite believing it was locked. Something cracked further inside and she lost all decorum, thumping, kicking and screaming at the door and the same quiet smothering silence answered when she stopped, no-one came.

Tima stared at the door, solid and ages old, its refusal to move a testimony to her helplessness. Empty and with bruised toes, she slumped back on the bed. Automatically she picked at the food, not tasting anything and drank most of the water. Still wearing only her underwear she wandered the rest of the room. Her prison. The place where she would be fed and watered like a cow, waiting until milking time. Hysteria threatened and with hands over her mouth she forced it down.

There was little in the room, a few pieces of heavy old fashioned furniture, a chair and the bed. The windows were tiny panes of leaded glass, the opening too small to climb out off. Tina looked out over the mountains, a heart-breaking view of freedom - something she no longer had. Below the castle, a cliff plummeted at least a hundred feet and her stomach lurched at the drop. No way out, even if she could fit through the window.

Hiccupping, she went back to the table and finished the water. The room was cool, the sun wasn't coming in through the windows yet. Cold hands, she shivered and rubbed her arms. Tina curled up under the covers and remembered him picking her up. He must have undressed her too, she almost threw up at the thought.

She hugged herself tight, ignoring her aches and bruises as she tried to convince herself that if she woke, she'd be back home with Jo bouncing on the bed, chattering and laughing. She gave in to tears again, the waves washing over her, soaking the pillow and sheets. Slowly she tired herself out and a calm built up as though rising from a deep pond into the light. It spread through her, echoing the silence of the castle. She was determined to get out, back to Jo and her family, back to her old life. Whatever it took, however long it took. She fell asleep with the thought that eventually this would be nothing more than a bad dream.

The sun shone warm and red on her eyelids, she couldn't open them and didn't want to. She stayed curled up, cocooned in the heavy blankets with the smell of dust and old wood filtering through as one by one her senses switched on. A bad dream, Tina muttered to herself and turned over, unable to stop memories of the previous day rising from her subconscious.

Reluctantly she became aware of a man's voice, the words were hazy and running into one another, none of them made any sense. China clinked as he put a something down and a thread of sleepy irritation ran through her at the interruption. She reached back for the detached woolliness and almost grasped it, losing it again as she heard the feet walk away on a wooden floor and a door clicking shut.

It was the signal to wake properly. In the silence Tina opened her eyes and the room blurred into existence. Clean white sheets and a thick duvet were snuggled up to her cheek. She had the old childish feeling of not wanting to break the spell before the school day began - if she moved then she would be awake and have to pay attention. Her eyes began to focus on objects further away and saw wood panelling, a matching door and old-fashioned wall paper. A small table was next to her bed and an aroma of food came from the covered dishes sitting on the tray. Her body wanted to stay snuggled up in the warmth and with eyes closing, her brain agreed. In a minority of one her stomach rebelled, urging her to wake and grumbling, Tina gave in. Her head span as she pulled herself up and closer to the table to investigate. There was beef soup in one dish, small fancy nibbles in another. A water jug, glass, napkin and spoon all neatly presented as though for an invalid or guest.

Tina's hands shook as she realised how hungry she was and almost without thinking, she tucked in. The food helped the dizziness and she drank most of the water. Her brain felt lethargic as though she'd slept too long. She rubbed a sore spot on her neck and yawned, running her hands through her hair.

Having eaten, she became more curious about her surroundings, she didn't recognise the room or the bed. Pulling the covers off, she discovered she was only wearing her shirt and her jeans had been carefully placed on the end of her bed. Her bleary mind struggled to think, she couldn't remember much after getting into her car the previous evening. Minding her fragile head, she bent to look underneath the bed to find her shoes and found there was nothing on the wooden floor apart from thick dust and a chamber pot. Her socks were nowhere to be seen either. She pulled her jeans on, tucked her shirt in and padded across the room to the window.

Unheard, her dreaming mind shrieked that this was a replay of yesterday's drama and that she'd missed this opportunity to escape. Brilliant sunshine over the mountains greeted her. An uneasiness twisted further as she attempted to work out how she'd got here, there was nothing like this place where she came from. Tina looked at the room, a passenger in her own head with no recollection of coming in last night, and none of getting undressed. Absently she scratched her arm and found a small mark, as though a bug had bitten her, she frowned and scratched it again.

Fuzzily she reasoned she might have had an accident and been brought here as it looked like an old hotel, or private mansion, everything on a larger scale than normal. Patting her pockets, she couldn't think where she'd put her phone. Remembrance hit - it had been on the car seat next to her last night. With the memory, she made the fragile decision that her car would be outside and she'd go and find it. She opened the door into the corridor and started to call out to see if anyone was close by but felt muted by the deep silence pressing down. It had an odd feeling, similar to some of the National Trust houses she'd been in, as though very little ever disturbed it. Timeless, it made her want to move quietly in case she woke something.

The corridor stretched out on either side, the sun lighting up warm patches on the floor. Grey stone walls and similar deep windows faced her as she looked out at the large inner courtyard, the stonework chilly under her fingers. Everything had a neglected feel, dusty and decayed. The curtains framing the windows had once been luxurious, now they were thick with spider webs and thin from the appetite of moths.

She chose a direction and walked. Thick dust

coated the edges of the floor and she kept to the middle, not wanting to dirty her feet in this strange dream. After a short distance the corridor turned and carried on, mirroring the courtyard's boundaries. In front of her was an archway and a large staircase ran around the outside of the next room. Tina peered over the stone banister, careful of where she put her fingers. Several suits of armour, weapons and pictures below, all covered with the same dust and spider webs. Paint bubbled on the walls high up and at the bottom were a huge set of double doors.

She crept down, the stairs creaking in the silence. At the bottom she stopped and listened, wriggling her toes on the stone tiles and looked at the other doors she'd not noticed from the top of the staircase. The others were smaller, this must be the way out. She pushed at one of the double doors, winced as it squealed and slipped through the smallest gap, leaving it open. More steps led to an open space before a gatehouse. A fresh breeze brought with it the smell of a warm day and the sound of leaves, making a change from the dusty quiet confines of the building. Tina couldn't see her car anywhere and she stopped, momentarily stumped.

The large entrance of the gatehouse was open, the doors pushed back into the shadows. The sound of the trees almost pulled her through the courtyard, stepping lightly on the warm flagstones. Coming out from underneath, she was greeted by a mountain panorama, gorgeous in its rugged isolation.

It was late afternoon, the sun had passed the middle of a warm day. The long tufty grass trembled on the sides of the road, bleached by late summer. The brilliant sunshine dimmed and she shivered in sympathy as she looked up and saw dark clouds gathering. Tina squinted and gazed around, she must be dreaming this place, there could be no other explanation for her being here. Leading down the hill, through the trees below her was the only road, no other signs of civilisation could be seen in the wide view. She turned and saw the castle behind her. Grey and forbidding it crouched solidly, dominating the landscape.

Befuddled, she began to walk down the road, rubbing her face. She should be feeling anxious, she couldn't get past the cotton wool in her brain. Her bare feet slapped against the tarmac. It was rough, scuffing her toes and warm from the heat of the day. She felt tears coming into her eyes, this couldn't be a dream but if she wasn't dreaming…

Tina woke, the fragile calm shattered and with tears spilling over from the beginning of her nightmare yesterday. She pulled a sheet off the bed and tucked it round herself as she walked to the window. There were no shadows outside, it must be about noon. Another hot day, she could hear crows and see what looked like a buzzard circling high up. Listlessly she wandered back to the bed rubbing her sticky face and stopped. Footsteps were coming down the corridor and someone was whistling a jaunty tune, jarring with her captivity.

The lock clicked and Wolfie stuck his head warily round.

"You bastard!" Before Tina could think, she'd shrieked and flung the water jug at him. He swore and ducked behind the door as the glass and dishes followed the jug. Realising her intent before she did, he whipped around and grabbed her before she could run barefoot over the broken crockery.

Wolfie wrapped Tina in his arms and held her, refusing to let her go. She hit what she could reach and fell to pieces again. Despite her resolutions not to trust him, he was another human in this monstrous place and had been kind. She heard him talking into the top of her head, repeating himself until she'd calmed down enough to respond.

"I'm sorry," he muttered. "I didn't realise it would be different for you. I didn't think you came from a different place to me. Different expectations, different circumstances. I knew what would happen to me and wanted it. I'm sorry."

"You wanted him to...?" She couldn't finish the sentence.

"Yes." A calm acknowledgement. "I knew what he was years before he needed to feed from me. It felt right." He shrugged as well as he could with his arms full of her.

"And you let him?"

"Yes." She stared up at him, unbelieving as he continued, "I'm happy to talk as much as I'm allowed but there are two things you need to know. First, I'm sworn to his Excellency, I can't betray him in any way. Certain things I can't talk about, no matter how much you ask, until he allows me to. The second is that I can not and will not help or allow you to escape. If I find out any plans you have then I will stop you. Do you understand?"

"What do you mean you can't do these things? What's stopping you from helping me? You know I don't want to be here. I want to go home, be with my family, with Jo."

Wolfie shook his head. "I'm sworn Tina. Body and soul to his Excellency. I literally can not say or do certain things. You'll understand more later but please take my word that I will try and stop you if I find anything out."

No help from the monster's servant, she'd have to do this on her own. Before the helplessness rose again she took a deep breath, stiffening her resolve. Wolfie hadn't had to tell her about himself, he was helping her in his own way.

"Look, are you hungry? Do you want to get dressed? Not that I mind cuddling half naked women…" He trailed off and grinned at her sheepishly. She rubbed her face, still upset and now embarrassed at her lack of clothing. He gave Tina a final squeeze and let her go. "I'll get a broom and sweep up while you get dressed," he said. "I'll leave the door open, don't go near it till I've swept. Don't want you adding cut feet to your collection of bruises."

Tina slowly got dressed and calmed herself. There must be a way out of this place, she had to stay focussed and keep her eyes open. Her head felt clearer than yesterday, less fuzzy. She watched while he swept the sherds up and followed him along the corridor. She eyed him as they walked and a nasty thought struck her about this man who'd both helped capture her and had also been reassuring her.

"Wolfie." He raised his eyebrows, waiting. "Your name, does it mean anything?" He frowned, not understanding. "What I mean is, before last night, I hadn't realised about vampires." She stumbled over the word, "being real. What I mean is are you…"

He frowned, then laughed as he followed the way her mind worked. "Am I a werewolf…. with this hair?" He ruffled his bright red hair. "No! His Excellency calls me Wolf. Everyone else – Wolfie. Apparently, I'm friendly, faithful etc. etc." He rolled his eyes. "It's a nickname given to me by the Count. You'll probably get one in due course."

She shuddered at the thought, "Your accent's changed as well, it's not as thick."

Wolfie had the grace to look embarrassed, "Yes. I knew I wouldn't be able to answer all your questions. His Excellency wouldn't let me tell you the truth until he'd met you. It was the only thing I could think of doing, I thought it might make it harder for you. Sorry."

Could he really not do certain things? Tina peered at him and said, "I prefer your current accent, it's easier to understand."

"I know someone who talks like that, can't understand a word of what he says when he gets excited." Wolfie grinned and then shifted apprehensively, "You may feel a bit odd for a few days, he gave you a sedative while he brought you here. So you'll need to take it easy."

Tina nodded, she'd been right, had known something had made her confused and muzzy-headed. A thought occurred to her and she stopped on the stairs. "Just a sedative?"

Wolfie flinched. Tina stared harder at him and he looked increasingly uncomfortable until he finally muttered, "I think he mentioned Ketamine."

"That's a fucking date rape drug!" She leaned against the bannisters for support, hand over her eyes and forced herself to keep breathing. No wonder she'd been so docile yesterday, so accepting. Despite being in a strange place with a gap in her memory, nothing had fazed her.

He waved his hands, "I can't apologise for what he's done. I can only do so much if he forbids it and yesterday, I couldn't do anything." She glared at Wolfie standing opposite her and he went pale under his tan. "I didn't touch you while you were unconscious, just made you comfortable after he'd brought you in. I don't need stuff like that…"

Wolfie looked relieved as she slowly nodded. He continued to talk as they walked down the stairs, "Look, I'll explain as much as I can. If it helps, I didn't want to deal with you while you were asleep, it felt wrong but I didn't have much choice." She scowled, he thought it was wrong. If she was going to have her jeans taken off by a man, then she wanted to be awake to appreciate it.

They reached the kitchen and she sat next to the fire and warmed her feet. She watched him flick through utensils as he made tea and buttered toast. It felt an age since she'd last been here, only yesterday afternoon but so much had changed. Swallowing her anger she gave way to curiosity, "Don't you ever object to having no choice in what you can do?"

"It's rarely a problem. He tends to have his reasons for doing things but before you ask, no, I didn't like yesterday." Tina shook her head, unable to comprehend why anyone would give up so much freedom.

Finally, he sat in the chair opposite her with his own plate on his lap. "Before I say anything else, I've been told to tell you that you may go through any doors that are unlocked and none that are locked. Fairly obvious." He shrugged, "I'm having to go without a number of things during daylight hours - I don't have the keys any more. So don't get any ideas about knocking me out to find them. His Excellency doesn't need keys anyway so locking yourself away from him won't work either." While he spoke, he ticked things off his fingers, licking the butter running off his toast.

"Don't think about setting light to the place. I know the castle is a complete fire hazard with all the old wood and stuff but the authorities won't come anywhere near here. The only thing we can do if there's a fire is to retreat to the courtyard and watch everything burn around down our ears." He eyeballed her and jerked his head, "And someone else won't be too happy either." Tina shivered from the veiled threat, there was no way she was going to provoke the owner of man and castle, at least not for the moment.

"We don't get much in the way of visitors here and when we do, you'll be kept out of sight for the time being. Anything you think you need or want, let me know and I'll get it sorted. Some things won't be allowed, I'll have to pass others through His Excellency first. There will be some parcels arriving in the next few days for you. Clothes - I had to guess what you might like." He looked at the ceiling briefly while he thought, "I think that's about it. Any questions?"

Yes, what about her daughter, what about being kidnapped, drugged and being in the same place as a monster who'd bitten her? She pushed them down, she had to know more about him maybe he'd let something slip without realising, "What brought you here? In the first place?"

Wolfie hesitated, clearly thinking through what he could say, "I didn't come here immediately. I was young when we first met, about eight or nine, I think. I was starving at the time, I came from a poor family. They couldn't cope with feeding or dealing with me. I met his Excellency in a street, in the dark. I remember him looking at me and asking whether my family would miss me. Of course, I was a street wise little bastard, wouldn't go anywhere near him. I'd heard about boys being taken off by men with a fancy to them."

Wolfie slumped further into his chair, making himself more comfortable, "But he brought me round over a number of days, kept finding me, talking to me and feeding me. I think it was the food that convinced me and eventually I agreed. Only he didn't take me to a fancy hotel and rape me as I'd half expected. He brought me back here, to a small town close by. Gave me to a family who brought me up and educated me. Not that they were happy, having to do this to a gutter rat like myself."

His face had slackened while he remembered, "I was vile, constantly mis-behaving and stealing. The only person who could make me do anything was His Excellency. Despite all that, I did think I'd gone to heaven. When I found out what he was, it felt right for me to offer myself. He made me wait, sent me away to live in different places and learn new things. Constantly learning. Still am." He sighed, "After a number of years he allowed me to take my place here and here I've been ever since."

"So, you've been brain-washed." Tina was certain of it now, no one would voluntarily give up so much freedom.

"No!" He protested, "You don't see, I was starving. He looked after me, helped me. I wouldn't have survived without him."

Tina decided to leave it, the nineteen seventies hadn't been that bad, he must be exaggerating. She wanted information, about him, the Count, the castle, anything to help her escape. "What about these people who've been watching me, the Count talked about them - who are they?"

"People? Oh… you mean other vampires. The Count's known about you for some time, quite a few have. It's to do with a blood or a genetic element or something, they can't help themselves. There are rules though, they have to wait until the person is a certain age and they've hopefully had children by that point. There aren't many like you, do you see? Anyway, after you hit forty you were considered fair game. His Excellency's been planning this for a while. He's snatched you from…" He paused, his face twisting and carried on "from under the nose of another vampire, he'll be smug about it for weeks." Tina blinked and shook her head, very little of that had helped.

Wolfie smiled at her confusion and suggested she go and explore the castle. "Don't do too much though," he warned. "You'll get tired easily at the moment, from the Count feeding and the sedative. Some parts of the castle don't have electric lighting, so if you want to investigate then you'll need a lantern. Do you mind spiders?" He saw her shudder and laughed, waving at a long slender stick tucked into the corner, "We've got rather a lot. You might want to take that with you, for the cobwebs."

He'd relaxed while talking to her and appeared unworried about the possibilities of her escaping. Tina took him at his word and wandered out trying to look casual. She checked the main doors to the courtyard, they were unlocked but the main gatehouse wasn't. The outer courtyard was shady, weeds straggled in the corners and edges. On one side there was a huge wood store, mostly empty. Several large buildings were on the other side, she guessed they'd been the old stables. She checked, those doors didn't open either.

Inside the castle, she found her way through to the inner courtyard and peered in at the windows, seeing little in the gloom. She worked out that the library, dining room and another large long room accounted for three out of the four sides. The other had a dark corridor along it, Tina could see even less through those windows. Above her was a covered walkway and she imagined ladies using it long ago to take air when it rained.

Tina sat on a step, thinking about her situation in her sweaty smelly clothes and dirty bare feet. There had to be a way to get out. She would have to plan this carefully and without letting Wolfie discover what she was doing although she knew he'd watch her, he'd made that clear. She ignored what he'd said about other vampires, positive the police would protect her once she'd got out but the question lurked around the corner of her brain - who would believe her? Vampires were supposed to be fictional.

She scuffed a flagstone with a bare toe, what would her daughter be doing now? Running around, playing at school? Then it hit her, Jo would be upset and crying, thinking her mother was dead. She buried her face in her hands, allowed herself to cry quietly for a time, then wiped her face, determined to keep looking for a way to escape.

Tina found the bathroom from the day before, counted her bruises and looked at her discoloured cheek in the tarnished mirror. With nothing else to do, she bathed and washed away the reek of sweaty fear. Her feet were disgusting from the dirty floors, she had no deodorant and her clothes were not nice. With no other options, she pulled them back on and went to explore.

She tried various doors along her corridor. They opened onto similar bedrooms to her own, mostly with more dust and spider webs. Every window once cleared of grime showed the same scene of untamed mountains and forests. The leaded glass was old and delicate, distorting the view. In the coolness inside the castle walls, she peered out at the brilliant sunny day, the wind blowing incessantly against the panes.

She rolled up the bottoms of her jeans, not wanting to get them dirtier or have anything run up the inside. The bedrooms were dark, wood panelled and old-fashioned, fireplaces in everyone. Tina inspected each piece of furniture carefully, looking for anything that might help. She found nothing, it all gave the impression of having not been used for a long time. Someone, she suspected Wolfie, had done the minimum of housework in her room before she came.

Wolfie was right about the castle being a fire risk, there was so much old and dry wood panelling. Although she wanted to escape, she guarded her lantern, even with the threat of the Count not being happy, she didn't want to get caught with no way out. The rooms downstairs had high ceilings with enormous fireplaces, they'd be difficult to heat in winter but were merely cool on this warm summer's day. The floors were also tiled and fairly clean. Upstairs she walked on bare boards, her feet cringing from crunching things in the dust. Despite the obvious lack of use, she didn't hear or see any mice. Dead flies, insects, woodlice, yes – but nothing bigger.

The servant's quarters where Wolfie had the kitchen and his bedroom were smaller and cosier. Tina found Wolfie's suite of rooms by accident while exploring and he laughed when she stuck her head round the door. It was a mess, worse than Jo's, clothes, magazines and books were scattered everywhere. He also had to Tina's surprise, a television. He offered to bring it into the kitchen and find programs in English for her. She declined, wanting to look further.

She crept into the library, not sure what she would find after last night. It looked as quiet and dusty as the rest of the castle and nothing apart from the light, had changed. The Count's paper was on the table, unreadable in a foreign language. Tina could smell him as she stood next to his chair, could see his imprint left in the padding. She shivered and moved away quickly. Streams of sunlight lit the interior as she climbed onto the balcony and ran her fingers across the books.

Tina re-found her room, padding along the dim quiet corridors. She would explore everywhere she could in the next few days, she was bound to find something that would help her. Weary, she decided to lie on the bed for a bit. Closing her eyes she drifted off, dreaming of Jo and what she would say when she saw her next.

Chapter 2

Tina heard a shout behind her and turned to see a man run out from the gatehouse. He reached her, panting through words that didn't make sense, until she realised he wasn't speaking English.

"I'm sorry, I don't understand you."

He paused and spoke in an accented English, "My apologies, is this better? You must come back." He pointed at the castle and the clouds, "It will rain, we will get very wet." As if summoned by him, the first drops came down followed by a sharp gust of wind. She hesitated, the smell of cool rain hitting warm tarmac reminding her of some memory she couldn't grasp. In her sleep she twisted, burying her face in the musty pillow. Not this again, she didn't want to be reminded of this, she should have run, should have tried to get away despite knowing she couldn't have done anything differently at the time.

Any recollections slid away and the dream took over, instinct making her run as the heavens opened. He grabbed for her arm, helping her towards the gatehouse. Panting, they stopped under its shelter.

"I am Wolfie. You are?"

She had to concentrate to understand his accent, she was sure he'd said his name was Wolfie. She tried to think through a fuzzy brain. "Christine – People call me Tina."

"You must come back inside. I have food for you."

Tina glanced back at the road, it was chilly now the sun had gone in and streams of water ran across the gatehouse floor. The view of the valley below had all but disappeared in a sheet of mist. He noticed her shiver, took his jumper off and offered it to her. She took it and hesitated, part of her shouting that something wasn't right and then put it on as the wind gusted again, blowing the rain into her face.

"Here, we run!" He grasped her arm again. The shock of the cold water on her bare feet made her gasp as they splashed through the puddles to the castle. He laughed at the downpour as they reached the main doors, shaking the rain from his red hair. She stopped just inside and looked back at the storm. It appeared determined to stay for the afternoon.

"Come inside." Wolfie was waiting for her.

Tina had the nagging feeling she'd missed something and yet her brain refused to think for her. "My car. Do you know where it is?"

He shook his head. "I am sorry, I do not know. I have been told to look after you. Will you come in? Please?" She hesitated, it seemed right to do as he'd asked and nodded. He closed the rain out, the heavy door clicking shut in the quiet of the castle with the finality of a prison cell.

Wolfie led her through a smaller door in the entrance hall, opposite the big doors, down a number of corridors and into a kitchen. Despite the bare stone walls and the quiet of the castle around them, it was cosy. A Ray-burn or Aga against one wall, several comfortable chairs close by, rugs on the floor. The dreamlike feeling rose again in the warmth, fraying the edges of her rational brain.

He invited her to sit and put a kettle on. The stove warmed the air and chased the chill away. Her jeans and bare feet started to dry and she folded the long arms of his jumper up around her wrists. She noticed a few minimal nods to modern living, electric lights mixed with candles, copper saucepans and a radio chatting to itself in a foreign language. A small window on one wall let the light in. The effect was warm and friendly, somewhere to sit and talk on a long winter's evening. Tina watched Wolfie while he pottered, he looked about her own age, in his forties.

"Tea? English tea?"

She jumped as he spoke, "Yes, please." Her whole thought process was fuzzy, she couldn't attach any urgency to her situation, could only plod through one thought at a time. "How did I get here? I don't remember."

Wolfie fiddled with a teaspoon while he waited for the kettle to boil, "I do not know, you will have to wait until his Excellency has arrived, he will let you know why. He will be here later."

The overlay of fudge in her brain accepted this explanation, underneath it was a different matter but she couldn't translate the urgency into action. Tina tucked her feet under her and grimaced at the colour of them. "Who?"

"The Count. He owns the castle, you will meet him later. He is busy at the moment."

Distracted by the state of her feet she asked, "My shoes are missing. Have you seen them?" He shook his head, looking apologetic and passed the tea mug. Aware she wasn't getting the right answers to her questions but finding it difficult to think what the correct answers or questions might be, she dug deep and found another with triumph, "You don't happen to have a phone, do you?"

He looked at his own mug. "I am sorry, I can help very little." This was hopeless, she squashed the impulse to roll her eyes both at him and her own laboured thought process. She gave up asking and hoped this Count would be more helpful, she was sure there'd be some rational explanation for being here.

The fire crackled in the quiet and Tina searched around for another subject and asked inanely, "The cakes are good. Did you make the food in my room too?"

He cheered up, his smile lighting his whole face. "I enjoy cooking, it is good to cook for someone else."

"What about the Count?" Wolfie waved a hand dismissing the comment, that was different. His English had improved as they spoke and he had the ability not to be threatening, despite his dreadful accent. She frowned to herself, or maybe this was just part of the dream.

He saw her picking at her dirty feet and waved in their direction. "Do you want to freshen up?" At a loss for further conversation, Tina nodded in relief at the suggestion. She felt grubby with the dirt and dust and it would be good to wash, despite not having clean clothes. Then she could confront this Count, sort out why she was here and demand to be taken back.

Wolfie led her through the maze of rooms at the back of the castle. He pointed out the old servants' quarters, the library and the dining room as they passed. Up the staircase and along another corridor a short way. All the doors looked the same to her, he opened one.

"Here, it will be a bit old-fashioned for you but it works. Can you find your way back to the dining room?" Seeing her nod, he continued, "Good, I will have food waiting when you have finished."

Tina smiled at his obsession with eating, struggled out of his jumper and gave it back. He grinned as she thanked him, slung it over his shoulder and walked off, leaving her to go into the bathroom.

He was right, it was old-fashioned. A free-standing bath stood in front of her with the taps coming out of the wall and above were a few shelves with various pots on. The labels looked old, she couldn't read the writing when she checked. An open cupboard held a pile of folded towels. She took one, half expecting moths to fly out and was almost disappointed when nothing did. They were clean but well worn.

Tina washed her feet, the water steaming in the cool room. She felt stale all over as though she'd not bathed for several days. There was no lock on the door and she eyed it. Wolfie didn't appear the peeping tom type but even so… she peeked around to make sure he wasn't in the corridor. Leaving the towel within reach, she undressed and slid in. The hot water was blissful, she washed swiftly and lay back feeling it was criminal not to relax in it.

She woke with a start in the cooling water. How long had she been asleep? She hurriedly dressed, wondering if Wolfie would come looking for her. There was an old mirror close to the window. Tarnished, she couldn't see much in it, just as well being one of life's pear shapes. She'd never lost the weight she'd gained since she had Jo, despite her daughter having had her tenth birthday recently. A desk-bound job and turning forty hadn't helped either. Her neck still ached, she could see a slight swelling but nothing else.

Wiping the mirror, Tina felt a wave of guilt hit her. Why hadn't she remembered her daughter? Looking at herself, she was so tired, what had happened? There was a gap in her memory, a blank space. She hadn't been hit on the head, she couldn't find any bruises. She'd not drunk much last night either, and yet she felt hung over. Tina rubbed her face, she'd enjoyed last night, lots of laughter and fun but she could remember nothing after leaving.

She reassured herself that Jo would be safe, just worrying about her not coming back. Tina had left Jo with her grandparents, a rare treat for all of them. She didn't go out often in the evenings on her own, not since her divorce several years ago, she'd been too busy working. Her parents would be concerned, they'd have called the police and would be looking for her. She must have been missing at least a day. She needed to contact them, to let them know she was all right and that she'd be back soon.

Opening the window, she noticed it was coming into early evening. The rain had stopped and gave a freshness to the air. The sun shone through gaps in the cloud, starting to turn the mountains pink. The air blew a clear space into her brain for the first time. Steven, her ex-husband, would spoil Jo rotten in her absence. She wanted to sort out where she was, and how long it would take to get home. Irritation ran through her and she chalked it up as another thing to say to this Count. Tina determinedly walked back to the main entrance instead of the dining room, wanting to look again for her car. A tiny wail came through that it was too late and was swallowed by her sleeping brain.

Wolfie appeared as she tugged at the door. She asked, "Why is it locked?"

He shrugged, "I always lock the doors in the evening. Would you like me to open them?" She nodded, he produced the key and opened it. The main gates were still pulled back, framing the valley and trees below. Her resolve wavered at the sight and she asked, "Where's the nearest town?"

"There is a village about ten miles from here."

"So, you have transport?"

"Yes. My car is in the stables, with the Count's. I do not have the key at the moment, he has them, I will get it later for you."

Tina kicked herself for not asking earlier, he could have taken her back. "What about contacting people – they'll be worrying."

A pause while they both looked at the darkening sky. "I have told you, I can not do anything. Please, wait a little longer and my employer will be able to explain." He shifted, "You are hungry? I have food waiting."

The tide of rebellion ebbed at her inability to influence him and she asked, "You'll leave the door unlocked?" He nodded and after a moment she followed him to the dining room.

The dining room was large and imposing, built to impress the peasants. Chandelier were suspended from the ceiling, candles sat on the long wooden table in the centre and tall electric free standing lamps tucked beside the armchairs towards the edges of the room. The careless mix of old and new as though someone wanted the convenience of modern technology but couldn't be bothered to finish the job.

The candles gave a warm glow in the darkening room and the fire, lit more for comfort than warmth, flickered softly in the background. The food was good and despite her stomach being tight with worry, Tina ate far more than normal, making the decision to enjoy it now and restart her hopeless diet when she got back. The meal helped focus her mind further, the cotton wool in her brain giving way.

Wolfie talked while they ate and it felt strangely normal to be conversing with this man she didn't know. Although he had a thick accent, his English improved and came easier as he spoke. He'd been born in Scotland in poverty she found out, and the Count had adopted him as a child. He now dealt with all the Count's business and was a trusted employee.

"Does that include dealing with women waking up here, not knowing where they are?" Tina couldn't help herself.

His face darkened, "No, it is not normal." Wolfie changed the subject and he asked about Tina's life, her work as an accountant and about Jo when she mentioned her.

The room dimmed and an uneasiness stole over Tina, it added to the veiled worry she felt about Jo. She tried to ignore it, shivered and noticed Wolfie watching. They'd finished eating, he stood and said he would clear the dishes and introduce her to the Count shortly. She stifled a sigh of relief, finally a chance to speak to someone who would help her. She couldn't stay here much longer, everyone would be worrying. At least she should be able to phone and let them know she was all right. With her clearing brain she'd dismissed Wolfie as lovely but useless.

He loaded a tray, refused her help with a smile and left the room. Tina moved towards the fire, seeking the comfort of its warmth and light in the dusky room. She tried to convince herself that she felt chilly and failed - the feeling refused to leave her. The shadows felt darker, the entire room had an edge to it, a predatory stillness Tina recognised from the nights she'd spent trying to settle Jo.

She hoped Jo would be asleep by now, she had a habit of night waking, calling and saying she was frightened, leading to tears if she was left. The amount of times Tina had sat up with Jo, half asleep while she tried to settle and convince her everything was all right. Having the same strange feeling here made her shiver. Tina had always put it down to the night, a thread of disquiet running through her. She rubbed her neck, positive it came from inside the castle.

Wolfie hadn't come back yet. Tina made a decision and followed the feeling out of the room. In the corridor, the library doors had been opened and it was dim inside, like the dining room. She could hear the crackle of a fire and the lamps were on. In the quiet she heard a faint rustle of a page being turned over. Hardly breathing, Tina moved towards the door, bare feet moving lightly on the cold tiles.

Tina woke with a lurch, gasping at the lurid details of her failure to act plastered before her again. She couldn't have done anything differently, she knew that now with the new information of her having been drugged but it didn't stop them being etched onto her brain.

It was dark, shadows in the room. The uneasiness twisted her stomach and ran over her skin, she'd not had this feeling since last night, since before she'd met the Count. Had he woken now it was night time? She shivered, she didn't know where the lights were in her room or if there were any. She kicked herself for not checking, she had to start thinking every action through with such a monster around.

Footsteps sounded in the corridor outside and she froze as they came closer, it was a long stride. Her breath came faster, feeling her heart start to race. He couldn't be coming here, not in the dark. Somehow the idea of him being close to her when she couldn't see him was worse than anything she could imagine. Tina swung off the bed and into the middle of the room to give herself the chance to move. She opened her eyes wide, trying to see in the blackness and to her embarrassment, whimpered as the door opened and the lights clicked on.

Wolfie looked at her from the doorway,

curious to see her so obviously panicking. Tina leant against a corner of the four poster bed in relief and tried to control her shaking hands - it wasn't him.

His first words brought the panic back. "He wants to see you."

Tina's mouth sagged open. "No." She backed away, knowing she had nowhere to run to.

"Don't worry, he's fed twice in two days…" Wolfie trailed off as he realised it didn't sound as reassuring as he meant it to be. "He's just not likely to need any more at the moment."

"I can't." Agitated, Tina wrapped her arms around herself. "I really can't do it."

"You're going to have to. Don't let it frighten you or let him frighten you. If you don't go to him, he'll come here. What's worse?"

He could come here. This room, prison though it was, was her sanctuary. "I can't." She repeated, her eyes shut and tears started leak out.

Wolfie's voice became firmer, "You must. Here, take my hand. See? Wipe your face, here's a handkerchief. You can't let this beat you. I don't think anything will happen. He's testing you, to find out what you'll do. Chin up and face him down. Don't be impolite, he'll react to that but show him you will do something, even if it scares you. He'll respect you for it."

In the distance the bell rang. Still holding her hand Wolfie walked her down the corridor and stairs to the library. Tina went with him, her steps reluctant, her passiveness a hangover from the previous day. Before they entered, he squeezed her hand hard and released it so she could walk in of her own accord.

The Count sat in the same chair, a book in hand. He took his glasses off, shut the book and stood. Such simple actions from one such as himself, almost human. She waited near the door and clenched her own hands behind her back, trying to control herself.

"Ms Johnson." Tina inclined her head stiffly in acknowledgment. He continued, "You are well?"

"Yes." Her voice was little above a whisper. He waited patiently until she realised what he wanted, "Your Excellency."

"Good." He looked past her, towards Wolfie. "I have need of your skills in the office."

She twitched aside as the Count moved towards them. A vampire, she could feel the panic rising. Feeling sick, Tina forced herself and asked softly, "Please Your Excellency." He stopped next to her and looked down. She barely came up to his shoulder, she focused on his clothes, trying not to look at his face. He had a soft deep red velvet jacket on. It fitted beautifully but was worn on the elbows and cuffs. It begged to be touched. She kept her eyes on it, thinking it reminded her of a tiger's pelt, the warm heavy softness that made you want to forget the predator beneath and cuddle it. Shaking the thought out of her mind she looked up, stomach tight with nerves, "May I have my shoes back?"

"No." His voice was brisk, "No shoes mean you are less likely to escape or at least, not escape far." A corner of his mouth twitched and he walked out.

Wolfie followed and grinned at Tina, pleased with her. "There's some food in the kitchen if you want it."

Alone, Tina let her breath go. Deep breath in. Out. That hadn't been what she'd wanted to ask but at the sight of him, any determination she'd had about confrontation had died. She'd felt helpless like last night. Tears prickled behind her eyelids and angry, she forced herself to think. He mentioned an office. Offices meant phones, computers and communication with the outside world.

She slipped out of the library, looking for them and followed at a safe distance. She saw the monster put his hand on a door that had been locked earlier in the day and it opened onto to a corridor. Wolfie went to go through first and paused as the Count touched his hair. Tina saw the flash of Wolfie's teeth as he smiled and the door clicked behind them. She gave them time to move away and gently tried the handle and found it locked.

Chapter 3

In the kitchen the next morning, Wolfie announced, "You'll be pleased, I've got some clothes for you." He placed a large parcel into her arms.

"How did you know the right sizes?"

"Don't throw anything!" Wolfie pretended to cower, "I checked the sizes on your clothes while you were unconscious on the first day. They should fit."

She didn't care, some things no longer mattered in her desperate need for clean clothes. "Thanks, I was beginning to wonder how long I could cope with these." Tina saw his grin flash and his hand wave before his nose.

"I didn't like to say. There's the washing machine when you're ready." She laughed and clutched her parcel tightly.

In her room she stripped off her dirty clothes with relish. Little things made a big difference at the moment. Clean clothes and more importantly, clean knickers. Anything that could make her help her stability in this new world would help. The new clothes were similar but didn't fit so well, the perils of ordering over the internet she assumed. Wait - how had they arrived? Postman? Out here? Tina decided to ask Wolfie later. The only things missing were deodorant and shoes.

Over the following days, she explored the unlocked parts of the castle thoroughly. It was compact, with more rooms than it felt it should have. Dusty corridors opened onto rooms, most of which looked as though they'd been unused for many years. Armed with a candle lantern and a stick to push past the cobwebs, she went through drawers in the old furniture, searching for anything that might help.

Tina explored the three sides of the castle around the large courtyard. The fourth had the corridor along which the Count had walked to his office. Looking beyond this from windows in the top storey she could see another smaller courtyard, at a different angle to the main one and she realised the only way to it could be through the corridor.

They talked while doing the minimal cleaning Wolfie deemed necessary and she helped to cook their meals. She could understand his obsession with food now, she'd been constantly hungry since she'd been brought here. Tina found he had a dish washer as well as a washing machine, fridge and freezer. He certainly used enough plates and dishes to warrant having one. It felt strange to have some of these items in the castle and not others. Wolfie shrugged, telling her that there was no way he'd do the washing up if he didn't have to and asked if she'd prefer to scrub her own knickers out by hand. He admitted he liked computing but was unable to during the day, due to the office being behind the locked doors.

Wolfie was grumpy at times, unable to follow his normal routines and he didn't like Tina questioning his supposed lack of freedom. She asked what his name had been before and he refused to tell her. Said it didn't matter, he'd been Wolfie for so many years that he no longer thought of himself as anything else.

She soon got to know when he'd been forbidden to talk about a subject. Wolfie was generally open to the point of over sharing although she wasn't sure if it was normal for him or due to having someone new in the castle. The barriers would slam up when she asked about certain subjects and he'd end up shrugging, unable to talk further, frustrating both of them. He acknowledged the uneasy feeling she had when the Count was awake and told her it would fade when she'd got used to him. When another vampire came near, she would notice it again.

Tina kept an eye on Wolfie's routine and noticed he slept odd hours. His main sleep seemed to be from dawn to late morning, with a cat nap during the afternoon. Most of the night she assumed he stayed awake with the Count. Tina also woke in the late dusk with the feeling of Kalmár waking and she would lie with the lights on, sweating until she fell asleep again. He'd not summoned her since but it didn't stop the panic, forget being locked up, something unnatural was around and she knew it was there.

She began to dread the nights and any time where her brain could be left to ruminate on her fate. Tina's sleep was punctuated with reminders of her first meeting with the vampire, leaving her jerking into wakefulness and crying. How could she not have known how wrong it all was and yet who could have known? That point where she'd stopped in the library doorway and stared in delight at its magnificence. Such innocence and her mind ran away immersing itself in her living nightmare.

Tina had a pang of book envy at her first sight of the library, it was two stories high, a balcony running around most of the room and more bookcases above. Books covered the walls, magazines and newspapers on desks. It spoke of a life where money was no barrier to learning but again, there were dust and cobwebs, parts of it neglected. No need or expectation here to keep things clean for the sake of it.

All this was taken in and forgotten as Tina caught sight of the man sitting by the fire. He saw her as she peered around the doors and immediately stood, placing his paper and glasses on the table nearby.

"Good evening." His deep voice carried in the silence, there was no need to speak loudly. He waited while Tina came into the room.

She smothered a sigh of relief. Being here in this castle, without knowing why or how she'd arrived, had unnerved her to the point where she'd expected a caricature out of a horror movie in a dinner jacket and cape. Instead, this man looked intelligent, well-educated, and very expensive. Such innocence... how could she have known?

"I am Kalmár. You have been looked after well?" He looked over her shoulder and she partly turned to see Wolfie hovering near the doors, darting nervous glances at both of them.

"Yes."

"Good. You may leave." The veiled order was directed at Wolfie and he left, pulling the doors closed behind him. The Count turned to her, "Please," and gestured towards a chair opposite him.

His accent was odd and with strange stresses on certain sounds, it almost swallowed others. She could understand him but English was clearly not his first language. His hair was grey and his eyes were dark in the dim room. Coming closer, Tina noticed how tall he was, taller than Wolfie – she barely came up to his shoulder. Despite being expensive, his suit looked in a similar state to the rest of his castle, worn and with threadbare cuffs.

As Kalmár folded his length into his chair, she became aware that the chair indicated was far too big for her, its mate fitted the Count perfectly. She could either curl up into the back of it or perch on the edge and dig her toes into the dusty rug underneath. Uncomfortable, she chose to perch. With the tattered shreds of the unknown drugs still confusing her, she worried inanely about being in this isolated spot, about her daughter and unsure why she'd been brought here.

"My name is Christine Johnson." Her voice sounded too loud in the quiet room. His dark eyes watched her over steepled fingers without comment, signet ring flashing in the firelight. She tried again, softer this time, "Thank you for looking after me. I'm not sure what happened but I'd like to be taken home." She smiled through her embarrassment, "I appear to have lost my shoes somewhere."

"You do not remember?"

Damn, he looked amused at her attempts to take control of the situation. She attempted to curb her irritation, conscious her nerves would make her snap. "I remember getting in the car to drive home last night and I remember waking this afternoon but not much in between. My family will be wondering where I am and worrying… please?" The last word she said quieter, his stillness unnerving her further.

He sighed and said briskly, "That is a shame. Unfortunately we cannot take you home Ms Johnson, it would disturb your family as I believe they are in mourning. A red Nissan was found burnt out close to your home. The remains of the owner and the car match your particulars perfectly." He paused, his eyes gazing into hers, a smile curving the edge of his mouth. Tina stared at him as the words penetrated her mind, the room felt darker, the candles dimming.

"They think I'm dead?" Her brain tried to assimilate the idea and gave up, it was too big a concept. The words flooded out of her instead, "I need to speak to them, I need to tell them I'm alive.

They'll be upset." Kalmár hadn't moved. She perched in her chair, bare toes spread into the dust underneath and demanded, "How come the body fits mine? They do testing these days you know, what about dental records? DNA? Why did you bring me here? What right do you have to do this to me and my family?" His silence chilled her as the thought sank in, if this were true, no-one would look for her. No-one would know she'd been kidnapped.

"DNA and dental records are not a problem, they can be dealt with if you know the right people." His careless tone left her in no doubt that he did indeed know the right people.

"Why me?" Controlling her anger, Tina looked at her hands, twisting them together in her lap, this was a madman she was dealing with. A rich and well-connected madman but a madman nevertheless. He couldn't be serious about faking dental records, she had to humour him until she managed to get out of here. There was a road leading from the castle, she'd get out somehow. The part of her with future knowledge sighed, nothing had been left unlocked since that evening and the landscape was empty of human inhabitation, even the aeroplanes trails high in the sky appeared to avoid the space above the castle.

She tried humour, "After all, if you wanted a cleaner, the normal way to go about it is to advertise and get someone local in. Or pay someone to travel…" Her voice trailed off as he shifted impatiently.

"Would you have come if I had paid you? I doubt it Ms Johnson and it does not matter. It is better your family think you are dead. You will not leave here for a long time and you will be a very different person when you do. Your life here will depend on you, whatever you choose to do with it. It could be pleasant and if you wish to clean... well there would be plenty to do." He flashed an even set of white teeth.

Tina stared, what was he talking about, her life would depend on her - was that a threat? He shifted again and a waft of dusty herbs drifted towards her. She gave a start as she recognised it, the pungent scent of rosemary, the dream she'd had before waking that morning - she hadn't dreamt it.

She said softly, "You were the one, you kidnapped me. I had a flat tyre, I remember now. When I got out to look, you grabbed me." Tina shivered at the cold hands. Quieter, she asked "What did you do to me? Knock me out? Drug me? Why me? Why not another woman closer to here? I can tell we're not near my home. Why go to all this trouble?"

A sense of danger crept over her, the predatory edge she'd felt in the other room and she tensed without knowing exactly why. She hadn't seen anyone else in the castle apart from the useless Wolfie. She took in his size fully for the first time and twitched away from him. The dim light in the room and the silence didn't help her thought processes, she couldn't concentrate.

"We have watched you for many years Ms Johnson and have waited for you to reach certain milestones in your life. If it had not been myself, then it would have been another. There is no doubt of that." Satisfaction coloured his voice. "Few will challenge me, fewer still will attempt to winkle you out of my territory. You will be safe here."

Safe, with him? Tina smothered an incredulous snort and snapped back, "Who is this 'we'? What organisation are you talking about?" She had to keep him talking, while he talked he wouldn't try doing anything else. His composure frightened her as though all of this were normal. She didn't think she could deal with any more shocks. She wanted to go home and be in bed, not be talking to a madman living in a fantasy world.

"We are not an organisation. We do not… organise easily. I will not explain further for the moment. You are special, there are not many like you Ms Johnson. I wanted you and I have you. That is all you need to know for the moment but you will want to know why I want you. Yes?" He leant forwards, "The answer is simple and is best dealt with now. I have brought you here to feed from you. I wish to drink your blood."

Tina woke with a jump at Wolfie shaking her. It was fully dark outside, the hall light making her blink. That admission from a vampire, so calm, so reasonable, how could she refuse? The knowledge of what had been done to her, without her permission... The warm human hand gave her shoulder another shake, Tina muttered something rude and tried to roll over, still half immersed.

Wolfie yawned, "Get up. He wants to see you."

"Fuck off." Her response was half hearted, childishly wanting to hide. He refused to indulge her, stripping off the covers until she gave up clinging to them. After that she had to get fully dressed, rubbing her eyes and resenting his calmness. She promised herself everything if she could keep her composure, knowing that it wouldn't make a difference if he tried to bite again.

Wolfie held her hand down the stairs and pushed her towards the library. Tina stayed in the doorway, as far from the Count as she could. Wolfie was behind her, his presence stopping her from sliding away. The monster politely enquired after her health, she replied. Not expecting further conversation, she turned to leave.

The Count stopped her by saying, "There are some magazines on the table, you may wish to look at them." At her confused look, he gestured. Not feeling as though she had a choice, Tina gave him a wide berth and gazed at the table he'd indicated. Her nerves and half asleep state gave the room an unreal feel. She leafed through them, her fingers shaking. She noticed Wolfie had gone from the doorway in one of her glances around the room.

"Do any interest you?"

Her attention jerked back, "Yes?" She whispered it, unsure what he wanted from her.

"Good, then you may sit. When you find an article you think will interest me also, you may read it aloud and we will discuss it."

Did he expect her to be entertainment as well as dinner? She closed her eyes and tried, "But it's the middle of the night. I'm tired."

His voice was quiet as he put his glasses back on, "A pity, I had believed that you were human, capable of intelligent conversation. I do not keep animals unless they are tied up in the stables where they belong." She hesitated, not sure if he was making some kind of joke. Finding his place in the book he continued, "I believe we also have rats in the stables, Wolf has commented on their size."

She suppressed the impulse to glower in his direction, grabbed a New Scientist and thumped herself into a chair as hard as she dared. Several hours passed while he enquired about her reading, insisted on her opinions and questioned them until her head span.

Tina stumbled through reading articles she was positive no one had ever read aloud. She'd not had any in-depth discussion like this since university and then it had been fuelled by drink at the student bars. Twenty years later and she was out of practise, fighting fatigue as well as her numbing fear of him. When Wolfie reappeared looking dishevelled, she was allowed to escape back to her room.

The next night was worse. Half expecting the disturbance this time, she stumbled down yawning. The usual greeting and then, "Please open your collar." Tina looked at him disbelieving, an icy fear waking her completely. She began to back away, her legs trembling. Irritation showed on his face. "I merely wish to ascertain that you have healed. Nothing more. You can allow me to do so or I will check anyway."

He had crossed the room to stand in front of her and Tina tried to slide away. He caught her easily, wrapped a long arm around her to stop her struggling, twisted her backwards against his chest and pulled her collar out of the way. She froze in his arms panicking at the cold hands. Kalmár sighed when she kept her chin down protectively over her neck. Putting his hand under her chin, he forced it up so he could see. Having checked, he let go and pushed her towards the table with the magazines on it.

"Now, read."

She rubbed the feel of him off her arms and sat glowering. She flicked through the papers, finding it difficult to separate them with her fingers shaking. One caught her eye, it was a newspaper local to her town. Tina had often joked with her friends about how little news it contained but still bought it religiously, all the locals did.

It had a picture of a burnt out car on the front page and a large headline saying a woman had died in a blaze. She read the article, her stomach becoming queasy as she realised it was about her supposed death. The police refused to speculate about the cause of the engine fire. Her funeral was to be next week at the local church. She looked at the Count who ignored her, reading his own paper. Her indignation built up and over-ruled her fear of him. "Did you do this?"

He raised an eyebrow at her demand, "Do what?"

"Get this paper. Why? To torment me?"

"You need to know your old life is finished and that there is no going back." His calmness about her reported death chilled her. Tina gazed at the picture not knowing what to say. Her head swam with thoughts she couldn't put into words. He watched her patiently, his own paper on his lap.

Eventually she asked, having to know, "How did you get me here?"

"You had a puncture, a nail in your tyre. You got out to check on it, do you remember?" She nodded, the memories slowly coming back as he reminded her. It had started to rain after a long hot spell, her swearing in the dark as she'd realised her predicament. That smell in the air, cold rain on hot tarmac, a coolness in the night after the stuffiness of the day.

"You almost turned in time to see me behind you. I fed and you fainted, a normal reaction for the first time. I took you to the airfield several miles away and injected you with a drug to keep you asleep."

"I remember you carrying me," Tina whispered. "Through the trees and lanes. I could see the moon between the clouds." She looked sharply at him, "You drugged me to make me docile."

Not in the slightest bothered by her tone, the Count shrugged, "A necessary evil." He continued,

"I own a plane with a pilot. I have permits to fly through various airspaces." He waved his hand as though the details weren't important. "We landed and brought you here by car."

"Where is here?" Tina didn't expect him to answer and he stared at her, making her shift in her seat, uncomfortable until she tried a different question. "But it must have been daylight when you arrived."

"Yes," he agreed. "I can not be outside during the day as you must realise. I have a large container I sleep in. It is locked from the inside. I kept you with me."

Tina gazed at him, her mouth worked and nothing came out. She remembered those dreams from waking the first morning. They'd been superseded by the nightmare she'd been living in since. The dream of driving and walking along dark tree covered lanes. The cold hands holding her, the smells, the sounds. She'd slept with him in a coffin, unable to get out with him holding her close. She felt sick.

"Are there any further questions you wish to ask?"

She shook her head and he went back to his own paper. She must have slept for longer than she'd thought. Wolfie would have been unable to get her out until the Count had woken. Tina sat shaking, a hand over her mouth. Trapped, held in the dark. Helpless and drugged by a monster that fed off her. She'd been awake enough to be aware of what had happened. The terror rose, she had to get out of here, away from him, be anywhere but in here with him. She pretended to read while she desperately tried to think of a way out.

After a while she shifted in her seat. "I need to go to the loo," she said, feeling like a child asking permission.

"Do not make me come looking for you." Taking this for a yes, she slid out of the chair and walked quickly to the bathroom near the kitchen. Tina did some deep breathing away from him and tried to calm herself down. It didn't work, she couldn't stop shaking.

Peeping in at the empty kitchen afterwards, she saw the knife block on the side, her eyes fixed on it. Dare she? Holding her breath, she crept in and wrapping her fingers around the biggest knife, gazed at the long sharp point. Her stomach knotted, terrified, not sure she knew what she might do with it or if she could.

No longer thinking sensibly, she crept past the door to the library and on to the main entrance. Vague ideas of escape slid through a mind unable to grasp them. The front door was locked. Hitting it in frustration, Tina felt the warning twinge of a sixth sense and turned to find the Count behind her. She shrieked and swiped out with the knife, missing. He knocked the knife out of her hand and on the reverse swing hit her hard around the face. She stumbled backwards and landed against the door, her mouth filling with her blood. She heard him hiss. He grabbed her and this time he did bite.

Afterwards, through the haze of blood loss and pain, she heard him say as he carried her back to the library, "You should not try to go outside Ms Johnson, many unpleasant things walk about during the night."

Chapter 4

The atmosphere had been tense at breakfast, her face had another bruise down it and Wolfie had been upset when he'd noticed. She'd been so angry that she'd flaunted it at him, making the point that he wouldn't help her get away and so he was partly responsible. She'd talked about Jo and wanting to go back, deliberately adding to his misery.

Tina looked at the window, it would be a squeeze to get through. Despite her appetite, she'd lost a few pounds since coming here but her backside wasn't as svelte as it could have been. Tina hauled herself onto the deep stone sill, scuffing the thick dust as she wriggled through feet first. Dizzy with height she stood with her back to the wall and concentrated on not looking down.

Having spent the time looking from below, she'd decided to climb out of an upstairs window, across the top of the sheltered walkway and into one of the towers. She'd checked all parts of the castle she could get into, there were no other doors to the outside apart from the gatehouse but there must be some other way out. At the very least she might be able to see it from high up. She had to try something after last night, she couldn't believe Kalmár had bought her local newspaper just to show evidence of her own death.

Tina crabbed sideways along the flat piece of stone anchored to the side of the castle. The merlons on the corridor side to the courtyard were shoulder height on her. She scrabbled up and almost wet herself - she was three stories high. The corridor below her was two stories, including the roof and the rest was a false wall to match the other three sides of the large courtyard.

Trying to control her spinning head, Tina looked around. A square tower she could climb into was another shoulder height higher. It was worth trying and she squeezed herself up and through. The view from the tower was tremendous, she peeped over the edge, attempting not to scare herself and rubbed at her scraped hands. It was another beautiful day, warm with a light chilly wind, the trees rustling below and mountains beyond.

The other courtyard below, aligned itself as a diamond to the bigger one. It had rooms coming off at an angle from the separating corridor to complete the shape and was tiny in comparison. This side of the castle seemed older, the stones were a different size, rougher and the three towers were round, not square. It had been patched in places with newer stonework. There was a small chapel-like building below her with a steep red roof and tall thin windows.

Tina sighed, Jo would have loved this, she'd had a mad time a few years ago learning all about castles and asking to see different ones every weekend. Jo had delighted in running round them, exploring all the corners, finding out where everything went and all the names for the different parts. Well, this was one castle Jo wouldn't come to see, no matter how much she begged.

To her surprise, the door in the tower opened when she tried it. She waved her hands in front of her and wished for her spider stick as she felt her way down the steep curving steps. Past the first turn, she could see nothing and the walls of the tower were disgusting. There was no handrail and she had to place her feet with care on the worn edges of the steps.

She nearly banged her face on the door at the bottom and it opened reluctantly, leading to the forbidden corridor. Tina could see the door opposite that the Count had gone through the other night and the windows to the large courtyard. She stifled a squeal as she shook a large spider from her leg and shuddered - she had cobwebs all over her. Not wanting to leave footprints in the dust, she tried to keep in the clean parts of the floor as she walked along.

The door closest to her opened onto a small room with a table and some chairs in it, nothing else. She tried the other door, furthest from the kitchen. Dimly lit from sunlight, she could see several computers and desks with papers on. This must be the study, Tina crept in and left the door ajar. She swore quietly, no phones had been left out and the desk drawers were locked. She ran her fingers down the map on the wall of Central Europe, wondering if the castle was on there and sighed when she couldn't find any indication of it.

She flicked through the papers on the desks. They were in a different language, she couldn't even make a guess which one, she contained the frustrated impulse to kick something. Rattling the drawers in the filing cabinets, she found they were locked too. After a hesitation, she switched a computer on. The screen lit up, the writing was unreadable but the meaning was clear – password please.

Tina slumped in a chair, her face in her hands. There was nothing in here that could help her. Failing to think of anything else she could do, she switched off the computer and left, hoping there wouldn't be any indication that she'd fiddled with it. The last door at the end of the corridor looked like it would lead into the other tower. It was locked.

She walked back into the first room and stared

through the window at the small paved courtyard, trying to see a way out. Part of the window opened but it was too small for her to get through. The leaded panes flexed under her fingers, fragile and delicate. Tina turned to look at a chair wondering if she could smash the window with it. She could see several doors in the courtyard, would they lead to the outside?

Tina grabbed the chair and her insides screwed up with indecision. What if there wasn't a way out, what would he do? Her hand left the chair and touched her bruises. He terrified her, he was inhuman and she had to have a way of escaping she was sure of. She wavered between breaking the window and not, swaying as she tried to think through all possibilities.

At last she stopped, the risks of not getting out were too high and with the smashed window he'd have evidence of her attempted escape. Tears ran down her cheeks as she left the room, not seeing the smears she'd left on the window and chair back. Without thinking clearly, Tina negotiated her way round the high walls and scrambled back in through the window, bruising herself without care. Numbly she cleaned herself off so Wolfie wouldn't guess what she'd been doing.

Later she lay on her bed, staring at the old-fashioned wallpaper, calling herself a coward for not acting decisively and tried not to think about the horrendous intimacy of a monster who fed from her, sucking her blood to survive. She brooded over the locked doors and being hundreds of miles away from her friends and family. No way to contact them - she sank into a pit of despair.

Kalmár's eyes watched her, like a cat stalking a mouse, waiting for her to move. It was too much and she moaned in her sleep, not wanting to remember the culmination of that day. For a moment Tina returned the look and picked out every detail, seeing the huge black pupils in the dim light, the pale skin and the sharp crease of the folded collar against his neck.

The fire snapped a log in the grate and instinct took over. Her bare toes dug into the carpet and she launched herself towards the door. Quick as she was, he reacted faster, reaching out with a long arm to catch her. His fingers closed around her elbow, swinging Tina painfully round. She swiped at him with her other hand and gaped in stupidity - she'd missed.

He slapped her, open handed across the face and released her to stumble backwards. She hit her head against a bookcase and saw lights from the impact. Stunned that he'd hit her, she stood, dazed and unable to run. He stepped forwards, took both her wrists in one large hand and pinned her there. His face was shadowed, his fingers cool and dry as he began to undo the neck of her shirt.

"No," Tina whispered. As he ignored it, she tried louder, "No." She attempted to struggle, to wriggle away and found she couldn't shift him. She pretended to faint, rolling up her eyes and went limp in the hope he'd loosen his grip and she could twist away. It didn't work. She couldn't think, didn't know what to do, her mind blank with panic.

She cried out as he adjusted his grip, forcing her to stand straight. Kalmár undid her buttons and pulled the shirt collar out of the way. Twisting her arms around to her back, he dragged Tina up to his height with her feet dangling off the floor and held her against the bookcase with his body. His free hand grasped her hair and pulled back her head, exposing her neck.

Cool flesh pressed against hers and she felt his fangs slice in. She whimpered softly, desperately wishing for the dream to take her back so she could wake from this nightmare. The horror blossomed at the long slow sucking, a monstrous baby feeding. The lights dimmed, haloed, the flickering of the fire beyond him. The dust settled, swirling in patterns. She could feel her heart thumping, working against his feeding and refusing to give in.

Tina went limp with shock and his arms changed from holding her down to cradling her, keeping her upright against him. After what felt like an age he stopped, his tongue nuzzled at the wounds, licking them. He drew his head back, inspected, and licked again. He picked Tina up easily, carried her over to a reading couch and lay her there. She stared at the ceiling unable to move, she could smell his scent everywhere, cloying with its intensity. Kalmár sat next to her and wiped his mouth with a clean white handkerchief. He reminded Tina of a cat, licking cream off its whiskers. Blood, thought Tina muzzily, my blood. She had no energy left to be anything other than faintly outraged at the sight.

The monster reached over, tilted her head to inspect her neck and grunted in satisfaction, leaving her to ring the bell. He was sitting in his chair and reading the abandoned newspaper when Wolfie appeared.

He peered over his glasses, "Ms Johnson will need food and water shortly."

"How is she?" Wolfie sounded hesitant.

"Much as expected." Kalmár went back to his paper, once more the picture of elegance and decaying wealth. Wolfie glanced her way and walked out, returning with a tray. Placing it on the table, he bent towards Tina and exclaimed at the bruising on her face.

"You didn't need to do that." He directed this at Kalmár who ignored him. Wolfie left again and came back with a bowl of water and a cloth. He wiped her face and hands and held it against the bruises. The water was cold and felt good. Tina watched him humming and tutting as he worked, she recognised the same lethargy as earlier in the day, too tired to do anything other than glower her outrage.

"Can you sit?" He didn't wait for a reply and propped her up with enough cushions to his satisfaction, then gave her water and tilted a mug of soup to her lips. "This will help." He refolded the cloth and held it, cool to her face, using her hand. After a while she made it stay.

The light blurred as she lay on the couch. She heard the Count say something to Wolfie in a different language. Wolfie went to him as he replied, standing next to his chair. The papers rustled in the semi-lit darkness. She slid into an exhausted sleep and half woke to vaguely protest when the cold hands picked her up and carried her away.

Tina slowly woke, shivering in the dark, having been taken back to that first assault. The vampire was awake, she could feel it. Despite Wolfie's kindness, she had no one, he wouldn't help her. She could almost feel the chair back under her fingers, could she have escaped this afternoon? Her daughter was waiting for her in the outside world, the memory of her smiles and chatter fading before her eyes. She couldn't cope, she wasn't made for this. His cold hands, the touch of them proving he was something inhuman, why had she been selected for this torture? She muffled her shrieks with the bedclothes, stuffing them into her mouth as she selfishly promised anyone else to this nightmare if she could get away.

She curled up under the bedclothes and refused all Wolfie's entreaties to come down later on, waking again with a horror creeping over her. She couldn't see anything in the dark room and her skin crawled as she tried not to panic. Feigning sleep, she tried to keep her breathing steady as she strained her ears past the blood pounding through them.

A soft rustle of clothing and she caught the smell of rosemary - he was in the room with her. She frantically tried to work out where he might be. She knew she had a lamp on the table next to the bed now and as though shifting in her sleep, Tina rolled towards it. Her hand reached out and she smothered a shriek as her wrist was grasped by the long cool fingers.

"You make this too easy Ms Johnson." Trying to wriggle free, she slapped in his direction. He took that wrist too and pinned her to the bed, pulling her head back by her hair to expose her throat. Tina froze and whimpered, expecting him to bite as his mouth came into contact with her. The Count merely held her down and brushed his lips against her neck.

Point made, he reached over and threw her clothes on top of her. "I expect you downstairs Ms Johnson." This time she heard the click of his heels on the wooden floor as he walked to the door. She lay panting and crying through helplessness. The terror of what he might do next drove her to switch the light on and she found the room empty. Sniffing, Tina pulled her jeans on and wiped her face on her sleeve. She walked slowly to the library, hating herself for giving in but not daring to rebel any further.

The Count greeted her as she entered and gestured to a chair. She curled up, her rebellion limited to glaring at him. He picked up his book and glasses and ignored the look, saying, "You are easier to train than a dog Ms Johnson. You understand consequences."

Past caring, she muttered back at him, "I wouldn't train a dog like this. They end up hating you."

Kalmár refused to look at her as he found his way to his bookmarked page, "I do not require your eternal love or devotion Ms Johnson, merely what is inside your veins."

The baldly spoken reason of why she was here brought tears to her eyes and the magazine blurred. He ignored her sniffs and carried on reading. Wolfie came in later on, he noticed her upset and not knowing the reason, treated her gently. He tried to talk and then left her on her own when she didn't respond. The Count had equal success in getting anything out of her, she dutifully read and spoke when verbally prodded but his increasingly acerbic comments got no response. He dismissed her back to bed with disgust.

The stone walls closed in on her the next day. Tina wandered the castle like a ghost, uncaring of her bare feet and the spider webs clinging to her. The castle felt timeless, she couldn't keep track of the days, one was too much like another. It was as though she would walk the corridors until she disappeared and leave nothing behind her but footprints and melancholy. The gorgeous mountain scenery and brilliant sunshine outside added to her feelings, trapped as she was in the grey and dusty castle.

It was deathly quiet in comparison to her normal life, there were no cars, no sirens, no people. As she wandered the corridors, she started to hear things, see things move out the corner of her eye. When she turned to look at the movement, everything became still. Tina wondered how long she could go on like this, without going completely mad.

Wolfie kept a bubble of noise around himself, the television or radio constantly on the go and often in a language Tina couldn't understand. It didn't help her state of mind. Wolfie's clatter and chatter in the kitchen also irritated her. She avoided talking to him, his cheerfulness too much hard work. He noticed her limping and asked why. She'd banged her knee while climbing round the battlements but she wasn't going to tell him that. He wanted to help and she wouldn't let him. Despite Wolfie's encouragement and her hunger, she ate little.

Unlike the Count that night. He batted away her feeble attempts to fight him off and fed. Tears streaming down her face, she sank further into depression and didn't object when he carried her upstairs and dumped her on the bed, leaving her in the darkness.

When she crept into the kitchen late morning, Wolfie talked at her while he sorted out breakfast. "You've got to snap out of this. It's no good for any of us." Tina just blinked at him miserably and he slammed a plate down in front of her. "It's not going to change anything. You think life's hard now? The Count just needs to feed that's all."

That woke her up. "Feed?" she spluttered. "You make it sound so bloody normal. Let's have half a pint of Tina please. No, don't bother warming her up, I'll just take her as she is."

He looked amused but refused to be side-tracked, "I know you're not happy but let's face it, you could have ended up with Lord Tangent. He chains his pets up in the dark with him during the day while he's training them. He doesn't let them go until he's broken them completely and they're sworn to him. That's why his pets don't tend to survive - he doesn't care.

"You've got it easy in comparison, you can walk around, eat and drink in the sunlight and you've got me to help you. Lord Tangent's guarded you for the last few years. He's been biding his time, boasting about you and the strength of your blood. They can all smell it and want it you know. His Excellency had to call in a few favours to get him distracted so he could get at you."

She didn't care about other vampires and what they might do but the concept she should be grateful prodded her into snapping, "Am I supposed to believe he kidnapped me out of the goodness of his heart?"

"No!" Wolfie snapped back. "He took you because you've got something he wants and he's got one over on Lord Tangent - they don't get on. As a human you are a lot safer here but if you insist on moping round like this, then you'll end up at the bottom of the pile when we meet any other vampires and their pets and at that point I won't be able to protect you."

"Pets." She said the word flatly, why didn't he chain her up and be done with it?

"Yes. Pets. It's what we are to them, at least to begin with. Later on if you're lucky, they come to think of us as companions." He looked at the face she pulled and responded, "Yes maybe like dogs but who cares, there are other compensations and you'll find that out once you've snapped out of this. What I care about at the moment is that you will end up at the bottom of the heap if you carry on and I can't help you if that happens and yes, I do care. Just because we pets," he said this with sarcastic emphasis, "are human, doesn't mean we're all nice. Most are complete bastards and if they think you're weak, you will end up being used, by all of them."

Tina stared at the table feeling herself sinking further, her eyes no longer focussing. There was worse to come, when would all this stop? Wolfie carried on with his rant, pacing and waving his arms, ignoring her shutting down.

"Do you think His Excellency likes you walking round like a wet weekend? For the next God knows how many years? I know I don't. Do you also think he wants a pet who is at the bottom of the heap? He won't interfere but he won't be happy. He'll try to break you, if you keep on like this, sworn to him or no longer alive. He'd prefer that than have you taken by another. Do you want that? Shall I leave the tall tower door open? Nice big drop, get it all finished?"

She felt something give inside at his suggestion of suicide. It was too much and he was telling her it could get worse. She'd dealt with so much in her life, been successful, she'd held down stressful jobs, gone through childbirth, divorce, exams but this, it was so completely out of her experience. She had no support from familiar surroundings where the rules where known. This felt vicious, the fear, the constant nervous tension from not knowing what might happen next. Tears rolled down her cheeks, she missed her daughter, her bungalow, her familiar job where she knew how everything worked.

"Oh fuck..." Wolfie sighed and reached out to grab her hand. She sank her head into her other hand and tried to explain how she felt through her sobs. He interrupted her, "Look, I'm sorry I upset you and I can see it's not easy but it's not easy for me to watch either and yes, he could find ways of making you swear to him if you became difficult. Lord Tangent manages. But you don't want that, do you?"

He paused as she shook her head, staring at his fingers holding hers. "Also, if we meet up with anyone else, I'm going to have to walk away, otherwise they'll use you to get at me. I know I'm being selfish here but you haven't seen both sides of it like I have. I'm not a top dog but I am respected and they don't mess with me. Oh they try occasionally, they all do. All I need you to do is to give the impression you might be dangerous if pushed. Then I can help and be seen to help."

She looked at him, sniffing. "Dangerous, you?" That was one word she wouldn't have labelled him with. She'd barely blinked before a knife appeared, pressed against the soft skin of her left eye and an arm slammed down on hers, pinning her there. His eyes glared and Tina whimpered in shock. After a moment Wolfie let her go, the knife disappearing.

Shakily she said, "Okay, I believe you but I can't do that. You think he'd rather I jumped off the tower than give me up?"

"Yes. They're possessive, especially the older ones." Wolfie thought and said, "Why don't I teach you how to defend yourself? Would it help if I taught you? Might make you feel a bit more in control although it won't help against him. What else do you need to help you function?" He perched on the edge of the table, looking down at her with concern.

"Apart from being with my family and in familiar surroundings you mean?" She waved her hands in frustration, unable to tell him about the struggle she'd had with breaking the window and her need to escape. Tina saw him watching her with sympathy and tried to deflect him by saying, "I'll sort myself out eventually. It overwhelms me when I think of it all. Castles, vampires. Maybe learning that trick with the knife will help."

"It wasn't such a shock to me. I'd been brought up with the Count and the castle. Anyway, don't you think I make a good Igor?" Tina gave a wan smile as he crabbed sideways with one shoulder higher than the other. He laughed, "Yes, I have seen the films. That's better, smiling helps. Shall we start after breakfast? Can't give you a knife to practice with at the moment, not after the other night but I can teach you other things."

Tina thought while they walked to the inner courtyard. No, she didn't want the Count to force her to do anything. She had too much to lose and she intended to escape, to get away from him. Slowly she rebuilt her determination. She had to fit in, pretend she could deal with this and keep looking for a way out. Tina decided to let Wolfie help her where he could. If he started feeling protective of her, it might help at some point.

The 'other things' turned out to be starting to get her fit. Exercise hadn't been a priority for a long while, coming under work, Jo and keeping the house clean, a poor fourth. Wolfie got her running up and down the courtyard doing something he called burpees, which she found hilarious until she discovered what was involved. He joined in, making it all look effortless. Eventually he decided Tina had warmed up enough. She was red in the face and puffing when he started showing her some basic blocks and punches.

She was determined to try, let's face it she was dealing with vampires. She might magically turn into Buffy or maybe not - Buffy was a tiny blonde stick. Tina was short but reckoned she could get a Buffy in each leg of her jeans. Wolfie cheered her on despite her awkwardness. Emulating his flowing movement was harder than it looked. Afterwards she had to admit she felt better. Tired? No, she was exhausted but it felt good. She went to have a bath on spaghetti legs, knowing she would ache tomorrow.

Chapter 5

She woke in the night before Wolfie came up. In keeping with her new resolve, she got dressed and went downstairs. The Count raised an eyebrow before standing to greet her. She read and made an effort to discuss while fighting her nerves.

After an hour or so, when the light and her tired eyes made the walls go dim, he stood. Anticipating him wanting to feed, she grabbed the arms of the chair still unable to deal the reality of his nature. Instead, he merely said, "Come," and walked out of the room without looking to see if she followed.

Curious, Tina followed his straight backed figure as he walked through the corridors. He led her to the locked part of the castle and held open the now unlocked door for her to go through. They walked along the corridor to the study, she looked for any bare footprints in the dust and relaxed when she couldn't see any.

Wolfie sat in the study, hunched over one of the computers. She'd learnt he was a bit of a geek on the quiet, always reading a computer magazine. BBC World service chattered away to itself while he worked. He looked up and grinned as she stopped next to the door. Nothing else had changed since she'd been here, just the lighting. It felt strange to be in an office in a place that had so few other mod-cons.

The Count sat in front of a computer and started typing rapidly, his long fingers dancing over the keyboard. She blinked in surprise, she'd not expected him to be able to do that.

He turned having found the webpage he wanted. "You may order as you wish. When you have finished, I will review your order." He pulled out a chair for her and sat close by, another laptop in front of him and began to type, ignoring her. Tina slipped into the chair, passing close behind him as she did so. The page he looked at was full of numbers and foreign words, she couldn't make head or tail of it. She didn't like being this close to him, was he dead? Or not quite? She shivered, not wanting to think of an animated corpse.

Staring at the screen she thought of all the things she needed and slowly started to order. Tina began in her usual fashion of finding the best bargains until in a nervous rebellion, she deleted that list and found the clothes and items she wanted, refusing to worry about prices. He'd not stated a price limit, that was his problem, not hers.

A phone rang, making Tina jump and Wolfie answered it in a foreign language. It rang a number of times, Wolfie would check the number and change his language accordingly, he appeared to be fluent in several. Once, he answered and gave the phone to the Count, who responded to questions in his deep voice. It all gave the impression of them having worked together for a long time.

She concentrated on her own list. Clothes, toiletries, deodorant – she needed that after today. Tina added a number of different pairs of shoes and tried to think of items that might help her escape in the hope that something might slip through. She kept thinking of things as she ran through the list in her mind she used when she went away. The phone rang again, Wolfie answered this time with obvious pleasure, his gaze resting on Tina while he spoke. She met his eyes, unable to understand what he was saying and listened as he said something in a teasing tone. He flushed at her attention and took the phone and the conversation outside. She shrugged and carried on thinking.

Fuck. She'd forgotten her period. How long had she been here? Surreptitiously she counted on her fingers, she had a week to go. She added a bulk order of tampons and pads to her list and twitched as she heard a grunt from behind her.

"You will wish to stay away from me during that time."

"What do you mean?" she asked, glancing at him and at the huge list in the shopping basket. She hadn't realised he'd been watching and hoped she'd be able to press the order button before he could look through the list properly.

"When you bleed."

"Why?" Stupid with lack of sleep, it came out before she'd thought.

"Because I can smell it." He smiled. "And I am aware you would prefer not to deal with a vampire aroused by the scent of blood." Amorous vampires, Tina shuddered. Talking to him in a well-lit modern setting, she found it difficult to remember he was a vampire. When she looked at Kalmár dispassionately she could appreciate he was good looking and carefully dressed. The only give-aways to his nature were his pale skin and the worn parts to his clothing, there were never any sign of any fangs unless he tried to bite.

"How much is real about vampires, that I've read I mean?" She eyed him as she asked, not knowing if he would reply.

The smile broadened. "Religious symbols?" He reached out to pick up a pen and sketched out a cross and various symbols from other religions. "I do not have any problems with these. Holy water is merely wet. Garlic only affects the changes I will make to you through taking your blood. That is…" he paused, "if you discount halitosis from eating it raw."

"Oh." Tina realised even Buffy would have problems with this vampire. "What about stakes?"

To her surprise he chuckled. "I believe a stake in the heart would cause most people difficulties. There is one effect you may be interested in. Come." He rose and walked out of the room, holding the door for her.

Tina's fingers twitched at wanting to press the order button and found she couldn't with him waiting there. She swore to herself and followed him, passing Wolfie in the corridor, still talking animatedly into his phone. She waited outside the ballroom, jittering at the thought of her order while the Count put the lights on and pulled a curtain back on a wall by the door. He held out his hand and picked hers up when she hesitated. Ignoring her reluctance he pulled her into the room, in front of him and out to the side in a practised dance movement.

She stopped next to him and looked at the mirror, it was less tarnished than the one in the bathroom and large. Tina gazed at her reflection and grimaced. She looked pale and scruffy, her face had the remains of a yellow bruise down one side. Her jeans didn't fit, she must have lost some weight and her shirt was crumpled. The bare feet peeking out from under her jeans looked grubby despite repeated washing. She reached up to touch her hair, the choppy cut was messy and had no style left in it. She winced, thinking how she must measure up to the immaculate Count next to her.

The space in the mirror next to her showed her other hand held out with nothing in it. The ballroom could be clearly seen behind and to the side of her.

No Count. Tina could feel the pressure of his unseen fingertips, cool and dry and fear clenched her stomach as she turned to stare. He stood, one hand holding hers, the other behind his back. His mouth was a straight line, black eyes gazing at her – no - in this light she could see them properly. His eyes were brown, like old coffee grounds left in a cup and they were not happy.

She looked in the mirror again, no sign of him not even his clothes, although that would be spooky enough. Tina stepped forwards to touch the mirror. Her reflection touched her fingers, echoing the fingers holding her other hand, smooth and cold. The Count didn't appear.

"Why?" she asked softly.

"We do not know," he replied, his voice equally quiet.

A thought occurred to her while she stared up at him. "How do you shave without a mirror? Or don't you…" She trailed off embarrassed. One day she'd learn to keep her mouth shut. He blinked, surprised by the question.

"Yes, I shave." He ran his free hand over his chin as though checking "Although not as often as when I was human. It is merely practice, like touching your nose with your eyes shut." Kalmár folded his fingers around hers, touched Tina's nose with her own fingertip. He held it for a moment, gazing down at her, then pulled himself together and let go.

"I will review your order next Ms Johnson. The majority of it will not be a problem." He left her to stare, swearing quietly at the mirror as he walked away down the dark corridor.

After her talk with the Count in the ballroom, Tina decided to wait with any plans for escaping until her period came. Wolfie slept late during the mornings and if she got a full night's sleep, she could wake early and have plenty of time to get away. She was also clinging on to the vague hope of something useful being delivered.

Tina had discovered the view from the top of the tallest tower at the front of the castle, she'd spent her time up there working out her next moves and had realised part of her problem with the days running into each other was that she had no structure. Her life had been all about working to earn money and looking after Jo. For years like most adults with children, she'd had little time to develop hobbies, any spare time she'd had would be taken up meeting with friends or family. She now spent part of the afternoons doing martial arts with Wolfie. Or in reality she spent a lot of time getting out of breath, running around the courtyard and then practising kicks and punches.

Wolfie on discovering her delight with the tower had pointed out with macabre humour if she wanted to jump then at least he wouldn't have to clean up any mess - the tower was right next to the drop. She'd thumped him with pleasure, pleased to see his mock wince.

With her ideas slowly forming for escape, she relaxed and allowed herself to enjoy the time while she waited, deciding to make it look as though she was resigned to her captivity. Asking for some paper and pencils, Tina had started to draw again. She'd gone through the library, looked for books with pictures to copy. She spent a lot of time there, picking up books randomly. Some were old, the spines cracking when she opened them to leaf through. Most were in foreign languages. So many books on all sorts of subjects, the breadth fascinated her despite not being able to understand the different languages.

One morning shortly after she'd placed her order, she found a large envelope on the table in the kitchen. It had her name on, nothing else. She opened it and some photos of Jo fell out. Tina sat and gazed at them, they were of her daughter, both in her school uniform and at the local park. There was a shadow in her small face that hadn't been there before, a graveness in her large eyes. Tina took the photos upstairs to her room and allowed herself to cry, then wiped her face and reminded herself – she would get out.

Wolfie collected her order from somewhere while the Count was awake. He dumped it all on the table in the dining room and bellowed for her. Kalmár dismissed her with a wave to unpack. It was like Christmas, large and small packages everywhere. Wolfie sprawled in one of the chairs near Tina and joined in by making comments on her choices. He refused to tell her where he'd got the parcels from, it was obviously not a postal delivery to the castle. The shirts were fabulous, soft and far more expensive than she'd realised. The jeans were going to be too large for her soon, she was slimming her thighs and stomach with the exercise. Fortunately she'd also ordered a belt. Underwear, toiletries, tampons – thank goodness, she shuddered at the thought of starting her period without them. No shoes of any sort and nothing she could use to escape, he had checked through the order. Damn.

The Count fed several times during the week. Tina had learned to notice the difference between his normal attentive look when he was in conversation and the intense gaze he had when his thoughts changed to hunger. The pupils of his eyes would expand into his irises, turning his brown eyes black. Her parent's kitten had a similar look when he chased feathers. With Kalmár it felt like being stalked by a tiger, a large predator flexing its muscles. Her whole body would go taut in response, instinct shouting for her to run. He captured her easily every time and once caught she would struggle but wouldn't allow herself to be hurt more than she could help. She couldn't maintain her state of terror around him, it was too exhausting. She settled into a wariness, doing what she had to but no more.

Aside from that, the week felt civilised, she'd made her plans and now waited for her chance to bolt. One night just before she was anticipating going back to bed, the Count said, "I will not expect you here tomorrow night. You may come down if you wish but you will be bleeding."

"Oh. You can tell?"

"Yes. You will find as the months pass, they will become lighter and in time they will stop." He returned to his paper. She said her good nights as Wolfie came yawning from his nap and left, her stomach tight with anticipation.

The next day started similar to previous days, Tina read for much of the afternoon on the front tower, listening to the trees whispering in the wind. Her period began as promised and she looked forward to a good night's sleep without any interruptions although she was beginning to get into the forced routine of waking at midnight to go and talk to him. The change in the castle's atmosphere would also disturb her when Kalmár woke in the early evening and the same at dawn, just before the birds began to sing.

Instead Tina woke at dusk and despite expecting to fall asleep again, she was kept awake by an irritation, a nagging sense of itchiness under the skin, of not feeling right. She tossed and turned, unable to drop off and nothing she tried shifted the mood. The long night was made longer by having no watch, she had no awareness of the time passing. She finally fell asleep at dawn, exhausted.

At lunchtime she woke, sandy-eyed and irritable and Wolfie came into the kitchen looking equally harassed. Apparently the Count had been in a foul temper, Wolfie hadn't seen him like that for years. All night he'd paced restlessly through the castle, pausing to look up the stairs in the direction of her room and making acerbic comments. Wolfie had been kept up and refused any chance to sleep or get away. He couldn't work out why and Tina didn't feel like saying what Kalmár had said about her period. She was however tiredly amused to see Wolfie's vows didn't stop him from swearing at the Count's actions – total happy obedience wasn't required then. She promised herself she would escape tomorrow, at the moment she could barely focus on the floor.

The following night she paced her own room in the same irritable, itchy mood. Walking from one wall to the next, she slapped her hands against the panelling as she turned, and imagined the Count mirroring her actions below. When she became too tired to walk, she lay on her bed trying to find a comfortable position and failing. She considered going downstairs and decided she couldn't cope with being so close to the Count, this felt bad enough at a distance. Again, she had no chance to no sleep again until dawn.

They were both in a vile mood that day, Tina slumped at the table with Wolfie, picking at her meal. At a twitch from her nether regions, she rushed to change herself in the toilet and started yelling swear words having stubbed a toe on the way there.

Wolfie swore as she came back, "What the

hell's the matter with you? I know you're tired but…"

"It's my period." Tina snapped at him, flushing at having to explain.

"Oh fuck," Comprehension dawned on Wolfie, "That's why he's so antsy at the moment – you're bleeding." He slapped his own head in embarrassment, "They can smell blood, and he wants it, I should have guessed. Sorry."

"Is that why I can't sleep?"

"Probably, you are sensitive to his moods, comes with the territory."

She had to get out of here, the thought of the Count lusting after her was revolting. It was unsettling enough to realise someone could influence her mind enough to prevent her sleeping. The knowledge didn't help much, just gave a time limit as to how long it would last. Could he make her swear herself to him like Wolfie? Panicking, she asked, "What if I get drunk – would that block him from stopping me sleeping? What about other drugs?"

"No, you don't want that. Seriously, it won't help. Besides," he smiled. "We don't have much in the way of alcohol here."

Tina put her head in her hands, near to tears. She couldn't escape today, she was too tired. She'd have to wait, again.

For the fourth night she walked her room as she had previously, peering out the window to watch the clouds pass over the stars in a haze of twitchy exhaustion. Her period had slowed to a dribble and she hoped it wouldn't be long before she could sleep properly again, she wasn't made to be this nocturnal. Eventually her body won out over her mind and she fell asleep halfway through the night, sprawled over her bed. She had strange erotic dreams, half waking at times to stare unseeing into the dark room.

The next morning she woke early, tucked up under the covers and grateful to have fallen asleep. She rubbed her face feeling tired but more alert than she had been. There was a knock on the door and Wolfie bounded in with a very large bunch of flowers in his arms.

"For you!" he exclaimed and sprawled over the bottom of her bed, looking immensely pleased with himself.

Tina pulled the bedclothes around herself, picked up the flowers and smelt them. "They're lovely. Why?"

"Because I went out last night for the first time in ages. He let me go out. I saw the lovely lady I've pursued for months and haven't seen for weeks. She'd missed me." He smirked wickedly, "And she decided to prove exactly how much." He stretched cat-like along the bottom of her bed. "We made love all night. I was fabulous of course..." He yawned, "God I feel good... and knackered..."

Tina laughed, they'd got on far better since he'd started teaching her how to fight. She almost forgot at times that he was in league with the Count in keeping her captive. He was dreadful this morning, full of that male smugness and so pleased with himself.

Wolfie leaned forwards on one elbow and inspected her. "You're looking happy considering..."

"Considering what? I don't mind about your lady, so long as she's happy."

"Oh, she's happy all right." Another smirk made Tina throw a pillow at him. He grabbed it and tucked it under his arm, chuckling. "What I mean is, you aren't usually this happy after the Count's bitten you."

"He didn't." Her hand crept up to her throat, "I didn't see him last night. I was so exhausted I managed to fall asleep during the night."

"Aha! Have any interesting dreams?" He cocked his head grinning. Tina thought then flushed, there had been some erotic dreams. She was vague on the detail but she also remembered a shadowy figure standing next to her bed. Shit and now she was noticing a tender part to her neck.

Watching her face, Wolfie started to laugh, "He got you and you didn't even realise!" He looked intently at her. "Was it good?"

"Shut up." Tina glowered at him, furious.

Wolfie howled with laughter at her expression and calmed down enough to explain. "How do you think His Excellency feeds on normal people? While they're sleeping, he can influence their dreams, then he can feed without waking them up. They wake up later, a bit lethargic and with a stiff neck. They've had a good time and he gets fed. That's why there's this thing about teenage girls being preyed on by vampires, their dreams are vivid and easy to slide into. Although he's not picky, male or female."

She started to wind herself up. "Why hasn't he done this to me before?"

"Because we're both sensitive to his presence. Normally if he came anywhere near you when you're asleep, you'd wake up. Like you do at dawn and dusk, haven't you noticed? Last night you were so tired, he could slide in and feed without you noticing. He can only do that if you are very deeply asleep or relaxed and allow it. He's very good." He grinned, "I have to change my trousers every time he bites."

She flushed, ignoring the last bit of information and concentrated on what was important to her. "So, you have to surrender your will."

"Yes." As she relaxed, he wriggled round to the side of her bed. "So, need anything more physical to finish you off?" He looked at her from under his eyelashes, levelling a roguish charm her way. She gaped, he'd told her about his girlfriend and now he was making her an offer? He laughed at her face and rolled off the bed gracefully. "See you later then." He smiled and stretched as he sauntered out.

Tina curled up in bed smelling her flowers and chuckled at Wolfie's outrageous comments. As she fell asleep, memories of erotica twined its way through chilling visions of the Count next to her bedside. She woke with the sunlight streaming in and the lazy, remembered sexual warmth flooding through her limbs. She wondered what would have happened if she'd taken Wolfie up on his half joking offer. Damn his new girlfriend, despite everything happening here, it had been too long. With one eye on the door she slid her hand down and finished off what the dreams had started.

Chapter 6

In the kitchen, Wolfie greeted her with a one-armed hug and a peck on the cheek. He sang and hummed his way through the music on the radio station. His good humour was infectious, she'd slept until lunchtime and felt remarkably good. She decided to attempt her escape this afternoon, after martial arts torture – practice she meant. Tina divided her flowers up in various jugs and glasses. There was a definite shortage of flower vases in the castle. She put some in her room and the rest in the kitchen. The sight of the flowers lifted her spirits no end in the gloomy castle and increased her determination to get away.

In the late afternoon, Tina took her book and paper and made as if to draw on the front tower as usual. Instead, she wriggled out of the upstairs window and crabbed across to the back tower she'd been in last time. She wanted to see if she could get into the small courtyard, there might be an exit somewhere - a postern gate or whatever it was called and she was determined to break a window this time if she needed to.

She rattled the door and discovered it was locked. Uneasy at the thought of someone having noticed, she looked across at the other back tower, she had to get into the locked part of the castle and there was no other way apart from through that corridor that she knew of. She scrambled back through the window and walked round the courtyard, clambering back out and up to the other tower on the other side. When she tried the handle, she found it was locked as well. Swearing, she gazed at the three older towers surrounding the small courtyard. They looked lower than the one she was in. Surely she could get across the roof and into one of those. There must be a way down somewhere.

The back tower she'd climbed first had the chapel-like building attached, it had a steep roof with nothing to stop her falling off. This tower had proper buildings attached with merlons sticking up where the pitched roof joined the walls. She tried to tell herself that it was something between her and the drop, her stomach twisted at the height and she sternly told herself that she'd got used to clambering on the walls and keeping her fear under control - the roof couldn't be much worse.

Looking at it, she decided the roof was wide and shallow and not too far underneath the tower battlements. Carefully she climbed over and let herself down, holding on while she turned on the roof ridge. She watched her progress through narrowed eyes, biting her lip in concentration and stubbornly refused to allow herself to see anything other than where she was going. Her bare feet helped her grip the slippery tiles. The wind blew and her hair whipped in her eyes and made them water. It was only a gentle breeze but more than enough to unnerve her. Leaning against the tower, she walked her feet down so she could straddle the ridge. She lurched forwards as they slipped and caught herself, banging the inside of her thigh as she grabbed for the ridge with her hands.

Proud she'd achieved the first part of her goal, she stopped with her eyes shut and waited for her heart to stop pounding. Well, Wolfie had told her to be brave but Tina didn't think he would approve of this sort of bravery. She'd done more adventurous things in the last week than she'd done in ten years.

Tina tended to delegate any high octane activities to other people when Jo wanted to do them. What Jo would say if she saw her mother doing this? She grinned shakily, Jo would be jumping up and down telling the world her mum was frightened.

She took a deep breath and looked around, down the cliff side. There was very little between her and the drop and she tried to swallow the sick feeling bubbling up. It was a long way down and it was very different from the walls she'd become used to. The trees looked tiny and the air so clear it felt as if she could reach out and pluck them from the ground. Swearing, she swayed as she straddled the roof and decided to keep her eyes straight in front of her and tuck her doubts back where they belonged.

Tina inched her way across, feeling exposed and not sure what she would do if Wolfie spotted her - wave back at him? She smothered a terrified giggle. Her jeans became soaked from the damp moss she scuffed through and several times she had to carefully wipe her hands clean. The wind grew harder as she edged out, it tugged and played with her. Tina shut her eyes and reminded herself to breathe before she moved again.

While her eyes were shut, her hand slipped on a mossy tile and skidded downwards. Tina shrieked as she grabbed at the roof tiles, the ridge, anything to stop her whole body sliding. She clung on with one hand, unable to get a grip with the other. Her knee was hooked over the ridge but she couldn't swing herself up. Her sweaty hand began to slip.

Sliding head first with another scream, she landed on her ribs against a merlon, her legs dangling into space. Tina clutched at it, winded, and through terror, kicked herself up with a strength she'd not realised she had. Sweating, she curled up behind the stonework, trying to control her panic, reduced to expressing herself in single syllable swear words.

She was on the outside of the castle building, the side with the drop. Tina peered around the stone merlon, vertigo hit her and she froze. After long moments she managed to pull back, certain she would throw up. By closing her eyes and holding on to her thoughts tightly, she managed to control herself. She wiped her streaming nose on her shirt sleeve and coughed back stomach acid.

Concentrating on her breathing she looked at the roof and realised she couldn't get back up, the ridge was too tall. She wouldn't be able to reach the top of the tower either. She'd have to crawl along this side and hope to find a way down, otherwise she'd be stuck until someone found her and that could be a long time. Tina looked up at the sky. It had been late afternoon when she'd started. The sun was coming down slowly but it would still take several hours to darken into early evening. Wolfie would be looking for her at some point, not that he'd find her here.

She sat in a narrow gutter behind the battlements and steeling herself, she looked down and along. This time, through a controlled glaze of panic, she saw what looked like a stone balcony close below her. It was a storey lower than the roof, although still a good height. She might be able to lower herself partly and drop the rest. Bracing herself against the roof, she inched her way along on all fours through the muck and got to her goal. Looking both forwards and twisting back, she realised the balcony was her only option. Both towers were too high for her to get back into and the drop from the walls would break her legs if she fell.

Square above the balcony, Tina lowered herself over the edge. It was horrible doing this deliberately, it looked tiny when compared with the space around and below it. Legs kicking into the emptiness and arms shaking with both nerves and the strain of holding herself, she managed a controlled fall.

She sat where she'd dropped for a while, happy with the solid wall between her and the view beyond. Her jeans were damp, coated in dusty mud and green with moss. She wiped her hands off the best she could. Tina wondered if Jo would believe her when she told her about all these adventures. She shook her head, she had to get out and back home first.

There were two large doors behind her, partly glazed and locked. They were newer than she expected and looked like they had been replaced not too long ago as the glass in the doors was modern. Tina peered in through the glazed panels, all the glass she'd seen so far had been old and delicate, distorting the views. She touched it and found it solid, she had no chance of breaking it without hurting herself. The windows on this side of the castle were bigger, not needed for defence unlike at the front of the castle. The sun lit up the large room, shadows of furniture were all covered in thick swaths of dust and cobwebs. Not one of the used areas, a shame, the view was amazing.

Bracing herself, Tina peeped over the edge of the balcony to see how far down the ground was. It was still too far, she'd break a leg. She'd need to plan further for the next time she tried to escape. Walking her fingers down her side, she checked her ribs. She didn't think any were broken, although she would have some good bruises tomorrow. More bruises, she sighed, now the adrenalin had stopped pumping, she could feel her muscles protesting. Her hands and feet were also scraped from sliding down the tiles. She twisted, trying to stretch herself out and stopped as she discovered more places that hurt.

The sky had shaded into dark dusk when Tina felt the Count awake. Bats streamed out of holes in the rocks below the castle. As they flitted, Tina worried about the Count and how he'd react to her being here. The last time she'd defied him, he'd hit her and now he had proof of her trying to escape. She waited in the darkness, wondering how long it would take for him to find her. Unsure how well he could sense her, she was staring out at the black shapes of the mountains when the doors clicked open and she felt his presence.

Tina decided to brazen it out. "Evening," she said brightly. "I got stuck. Couldn't get back through the doors. They were locked." She managed to get a note of disgust in on the last point. With relief she heard a huff of possible amusement come from the Count's direction.

"How did you get here?" His voice was neutral.

"Through a window and over the rooftops. No locked doors."

She heard him take a deep breath, "You are like a little mouse. Running around, finding all the holes in my castle. Do you know, I found some mouse prints in the dust near my study and in the tower a number of nights ago. One of the computers had been switched on and off. You would not have found much on it Ms Johnson, I use that one for financial records only."

He'd known. Damn and he'd not said anything, just watched to see what she would do next. To cover her dismay, she said the first thing that came into her head. "The sunset was lovely tonight."

"I have not seen any sunsets from this castle or

sunrises either." Tina winced and looked at him in the darkness. What was it like to live on the margins of society, in the shadows and to never see daylight, living in a monochrome world? She'd come to realise he was fiercely intelligent. His questioning of her opinions, finding out the reasons behind the way she thought, were his way of working out how life was lived today. He was constantly curious as his library showed and not above adapting to modern life when it suited him. Tina was struck by the thought that he was trapped as much as herself. It disturbed her to think in that way about him as a person rather than as a monster that fed off her.

To distract herself from these unsettling thoughts, she babbled on about the sunset. The stunning views, how the mountains had blushed pink and orange with the light of the sun. How the shadows had stretched and crept across the forests in fingers, the light reflected in the few clouds and the deepening blues and purples of the dusk before he'd woken. She spluttered to a halt and there was silence. Tina was kicking herself for being an idiot when to her surprise he said quietly.

"Thank you, for allowing me to see through your eyes." She heard the rustle of his clothing as he came to stand next to her, looking into the night. "Shall I take you back?"

With little other choice and relieved he wasn't going to punish her, Tina nodded, "Please."

"There are no lights in this part of the castle and you will not find the floor pleasant to your feet. I will carry you." This was a statement not a question, for he picked her up as he spoke, ignoring her squeak and walked inside. She didn't know what to do with her hands, no way would she put them around his neck. She settled for tucking them round his shoulders, trying not to hold on or touch him too much. Being occupied with this almost made her miss the doors closing behind them. Tina caught a flash of starlight off the glass as they moved and realised he'd not touched them.

"How did you do that?"

The Count didn't answer and kept walking. Tina cringed at the expected feel of cobwebs and felt nothing. She heard the click of the next door and felt air movement over her face. It clicked shut behind them. She shivered, he could open doors without using his hands. Every time she got a grip in this place, something else happened to make her twitchy. As they moved out of the room and into an unlit corridor, Tina could no longer even see the shadows. Kalmár however didn't hesitate.

"Can you see in the dark?"

He adjusted his grip of her body. "Yes. You will need to tuck your head in, we are going down a narrow staircase." She did as she was told, curling up in his arms. Tina's insides twisted into a knot, she didn't like being dependant on him, felt uncomfortable about being this close to him.

They emerged into the small courtyard. The moon hadn't risen over the battlements yet, the stars shone in the dark night, the courtyard was a shadow and the Count a darker presence. A gleam of light showed from a downstairs window, she presumed it was the study.

The Count put her down, one arm around her waist and a step below her. Tina's hands were flat against his chest, trying to keep some distance from him. Her toes curled around the edge of the stonework. She could see nothing, vulnerable in the night as he held her.

"You will allow me to feed." Again, a statement. Already she could feel him begin to grip her tighter, waiting for her to twist away. Her hands braced herself against him, elbows locked. She couldn't get away from him, he held her too close and her mind raced as she tried to think of a way to distract him.

"Wait." To her surprise, he paused. "Can't you ask me, my permission I mean, instead of assuming?" He said nothing, she could imagine his look of amusement at the thought. She rambled on, "What I mean is, give me the chance to refuse you. I might be more amenable the next time you ask. I could be tired or something. It's basic politeness." She heard him chuckle this time, could feel it rumbling through his chest.

"And if I disagree?" It was her turn to say nothing. The silence stretched, they both knew he could take what he wanted. He ran the fingers of his free hand down the side of her neck and with exaggerated courtesy asked, "May I?"

Tina's heart thumped, she'd wrung one small concession out of him even if he found it amusing to ask. She would have to allow him to bite her. Mute and stiff with fear in his arms, she tilted her head up in his fingers and he took that as a yes.

Kalmár took his time and pulled her closer to him. He wrapped his arm around her tighter, his other hand rested on her neck, his thumb under her chin and tipped her head into the right position. His mouth moved down her neck, his breath like a soft breeze tickling. His lips were cool and the bite sudden, his mouth hot with her blood. It still hurt. Her hands flat against his chest, her elbows tucked in and she could feel his chest moving as he drank. She watched over his shoulder as the first glimmers of moonlight peeped over the battlements, lining them with silver.

He stopped sooner than she expected, he licked the bite and nuzzled at her throat, holding her close in an unwanted lover's intimacy.

"Why do you do that?" she asked as he licked her. "Can't I use a handkerchief?"

Kalmár shifted, cradling her in one arm, his hand light on the back of her neck. His voice was unfocussed as he replied, "My saliva will help you to heal and prevent scarring. It will also allow your body to adapt itself to my needs." He returned his attention to her neck and straightened to pull his handkerchief out, movements she was already familiar with. He wiped his mouth, holding her close. She could smell his scent of herbs and the iron tang of her blood on his breath.

"Are you dead?" The question surprised them both. She'd had thoughts about walking corpses for a while and didn't like the idea of being cuddled by one.

He considered her question, "I do not know." The moonlight crept down the walls, forming pools of silver. "I breathe and my heart beats, albeit slower than it used to. I walk and talk, reason as a man does but my skin is cold, yours is hot in comparison. I must rest in darkness during the day among other things. It does not suggest dead to me, merely different. How would you define dead?"

She shrugged, it was a harder definition than the books generally described. In books it was easy, recite the Lord's Prayer, bang in the stake and kill the vampire. "How long have you been like this, a vampire I mean?"

"In human terms I am old. I came to this castle as a vampire and re-built its crumbling walls. There is an inscription in the chapel that was added after I came, for the former owner I believe."

Tina looked up into his shadowed face, distracted, "You killed the previous occupant? Why?"

"Yes. You are shocked? I wanted the castle."

The simple brutality made her feel uncomfortable. Taking this place because he wanted it, killing the people who had what he wanted. This part of his nature as with others, she found difficult to deal with. He'd taken her because he'd wanted her, no other reason. Tina shifted in his arms, looking for more space between them and failing miserably asked, "You took his lands?"

"Such as they were at the time and the peasants who worked it. Before you ask, I was no better or worse a master. Or were you expecting me to be the master of fat pink-cheeked farmers, toasting my health whilst shovelling roast meats into their faces?"

No, she hadn't expected that of him, times in the past had always been worse for those at the bottom of the heap. "What about compassion?" she countered.

"Compassion? You seek to tame the vile monster I am within?" She could hear his amusement. "We do not become any better or worse due to living longer. We merely have the time to become more ourselves. Nothing else."

"And how did you become a vampire?" She'd realised it wasn't through the one bite like in the books or several for that matter.

A pause and the Count removed his arm from around her. "We will go back inside. Can you walk, or do you need to be carried?" His standard way of not answering, to change the subject or walk away. He'd talked more than she'd expected, Tina didn't dare to press him further. He shifted to give her the chance to stand on her own. She tried to walk and stumbled. Without further comment he picked her up and carried her to the door leading out of the courtyard.

He took her into the study, tucked her into an armchair and went to sit behind his desk. Wolfie had been tapping distractedly at a keyboard and his face had filled with relief when he saw her come in, changing to curiosity when he saw how. He immediately stood to get her a drink and food and stopped when he saw the state of her clothing.

"What have you been doing?"

Now embarrassed, she muttered, "Climbing along the roofs."

"I found Ms Johnson on the balcony."

Wolfie's jaw dropped and he stared. He picked up one of her dirty hands and ran a finger down it. "These will need cleaning." As he turned to leave, he let loose a volley of words at the Count in a different language, waving his arms to emphasise his point. Kalmár merely grunted, now absorbed in his laptop. Wolfie shook his head as he left and came back with food and a damp cloth to clean her hands.

Despite having been less than two weeks, it felt like such a long time since she'd lived what she would term a normal life, everything before she came here now seemed like a dream. It didn't help with the tiredness from sleeping odd hours and the blood-taking. Wolfie's kindness didn't help either, it was difficult to hate him for keeping her away from her family. Even the Count, she had to admit that a thread of fascination ran through her about him. Did her running trigger an instinctive response to catch a victim? His feeding had been less hurried this time. There was always the threat of violence if she didn't co-operate and yet talking to him tonight… What was that syndrome called when you began to sympathize with your captors? Stockholm syndrome? The old Beauty and the Beast thing? The thoughts chased one another around her exhausted brain and she held on to the paper thin determination that she would escape.

The room was bright in comparison to the rest of the castle, the radio played softly in the background. Wolfie hummed along with it and Kalmár sat at his desk, every so often raising his dark eyes to watch her. The phone rang at various points. The room blurred as she sank into sleep and only stirred when he picked her up like a child and carried her upstairs to her bedroom.

Chapter 7

The next day Tina tackled Wolfie on the subject of the Count and vampires. He refused to tell her the how, saying he couldn't but that she'd find out at some point.

Tina snorted, "Yeah when it happens to me, I suppose."

"Not quite." His voice was distracted as he flicked through his magazine.

She looked at him properly for the first time, the Count appeared to be in his fifties and from what he'd said he must be centuries older. Wolfie looked her own age but… "Wolfie, how old are you?"

He grinned, face lighting up. "I was wondering when you'd ask me. How old do you think I am? Guess." His eyes laughed at her as she looked. Red hair, slim, compact body, no extra weight - obviously a mature man. Old enough to be confident in himself, young enough for the boyish grin to be endearing.

She hesitated, "Forties?"

"Nope, try again."

"Higher or lower?" Desperation wormed its way through her, he couldn't be much older, could he? This couldn't be another cornerstone gone in her muddled life?

He had a mischief in his eye, "Higher."

"How much higher? Wolfie, I can't guess. Please don't tease me."

Wolfie caught her worry and sobered a bit. "I don't know precisely, I don't have a record of the year I was born. The Count did find me like I told you. It was in Scotland, I remember being thrown off our lands. I was starving in the streets of a large town when he found me." His face turned inwards, "I knew my family would feel only relief at me disappearing, one less mouth to feed. As far as I can reckon, it must be about a hundred years ago."

Wolfie stopped, waiting for her reaction. Tina stared, at least a hundred years old, no wonder he had that relaxed confidence. She remembered the Count's words about becoming more of yourself, would this happen to her? One hundred years, she couldn't stop the words running through her mind, he looked the same age as her. The things he would have seen, so many changes. Cars, aeroplanes, phones, computers, life in the last century alone would have been fascinating.

"Will this happen to me if I stay here with the Count?"

"Yes, it's already happening to you. Haven't you noticed you're losing weight despite eating constantly?" Tina nodded, despite being pleased by the effect she hadn't been able to work it out. She'd tried not eating as much and it had led to shaking hands and a desperate craving for food.

Wolfie continued, "When the Count feeds on normal humans it doesn't do anything to them. You and I are different and the vampires can smell it, they can't resist us. When they feed, their saliva gets into our system and it changes something, infecting us. You're losing weight due to your body adapting to His Excellency feeding from you, in theory you're eating for two. That's partly why the Count adopted me so long ago, if I'd been a normal street child he would have ignored me and I would have starved to death."

"So he fed from you when you were only a child?" Tina was horrified by the thought.

He shook his head, "They do have rules. They

aren't allowed start the process on a child or a childless adult at least not until the adult has hit a certain age. If the adult has children to care for, then the youngest child must be over ten." Tina thought of Jo, her tenth birthday had been a short while ago.

Wolfie carried on, "Vampires don't tolerate any rule breaking that threatens them, the punishments are severe. In return they get to take those they want. Like yourself, with no repercussions from the human authorities."

"How do the vampires know these things?"

"Believe me, they keep a very good eye on people like us. We're too rare for them not too, there aren't many that get away."

"But why do they insist on children? You've not had any."

"Yes, actually I have but most of them have grown old and died. The few left are grandmothers now. This castle was occupied in the last war and I was sent to Switzerland for my safety while the Count stayed here. There used to be a village down below about ten miles away. I had some children there - amongst others. The population was mostly Jewish, when I came back the village was empty." Wolfie stopped, gazing at the wall, remembering.

The subject of children and missing them was close to her heart, she was curious. "Didn't you stay in contact with any of your children or their mothers?"

"No, why should I? I wanted to have the relationships and any children that happened were sent a form of maintenance but no. Why should I stay in contact and watch them grow old? Don't you think they wouldn't notice my staying the same? And before you say it, yes, I was encouraged to have the relationships and the children. There aren't many like us Tina and we don't breed true."

She shuddered at the thought of breeding programmes. "What if I hadn't met him? Will you grow old? Will I?"

"No, not now you're here with his Excellency. If you hadn't been taken by a vampire, then you'd age like a normal human. You'll live a long life if that's what you choose. You'll out-live Jo and everyone else you know."

Tina didn't notice Wolfie go quiet while she readjusted her view of him. He'd had children and a past for over twice the amount of time she'd been alive. He felt a stranger in a familiar skin, she didn't know him as well as she'd thought. She'd had the idea he stayed in the castle, serving his master, she felt the walls close in around her and wondered how he dealt with it.

"Do you ever leave here?"

He seemed distracted, "Yes. I normally travel a bit during the year to sort out the Count's finances, to go on courses and learn things. This year will be a bit different with you here. Nice to have someone to talk to but quieter in some ways. The Count travels too, not so easy for him obviously but he does enjoy it."

Tina nodded, another chunk of information to digest, more chains wrapped around her and preventing her from escaping. Tough, she would try again. She went to walk around the covered walkway in the large courtyard. It was raining in the real world, so her favourite place for thought on top of the front tower wasn't an option.

Breeding programmes, she shivered and not just from the cool rain. What about her daughter and the possibilities of meeting a grandchild in the future that had inherited the same attraction of vampires as her? Did the Count expect Tina to become pregnant? At some point in the future would she be encouraged to do this with Wolfie? She imagined herself pregnant with dread, the morning sickness had been horrendous the last time. Then she remembered the Count saying her periods would stop and she sighed with relief. If her periods came to an end, she couldn't become pregnant. Wolfie had talked about his remaining children being grandmothers and he'd spoken about having a sexual relationship with this unseen girlfriend, so he could be sterile. She clung to the possibility in desperation.

What about out-living everyone else? She hated the idea of her body being changed or infected without her consent, a creepy side effect of the Count's appetites. It was bad enough that he took her blood in the way he did, but she couldn't deny the thread of greed running through her. Time and technology moved so fast these days, what would she see in one hundred years? To remain the same while you witnessed history happening, a heady thought. No growing old, no worries about needing anything, wanting for anything. All she had to do was to give up everything she cared about and live with a man who fed from her. As for the idea of him travelling, she couldn't stop images of coffins and hearses surfacing. She paced around the walkway deep in thought with the rain pattering above her.

Come the evening, she was curled up in the library flicking through a book. Wolfie bounded up from his chair when the Count came in, anticipating getting on the computer forbidden to him during the day.

"Good evening." Kalmár gave his usual greeting and nodded to her, "Little Mouse," he began.

"Mousie!" Wolfie hooted.

Tina shot upright and glowered at Wolfie. The

Count might have found a nickname for her but there were limits. She snapped, "You call me Mousie and the first frog I find goes in your bed!" Wolfie left the room, shaking his head and laughing.

The Count looked amused and tried again, "Little Mouse I am hungry." He sat close to her, his arm resting along the back of the couch.

Still needled and not caring, Tina responded, "You fed last night and the night before. This isn't hunger, you'll get fat."

He reached out and ran a finger along her jawline, making her look at him. "But do you not find the same, when you have something you enjoy? A sweet, maybe? Do you not find it difficult to stop? And you are very sweet."

His tone was light but his eyes challenged her to refuse him. Visions of cakes and biscuits rose in her mind and her insides twisted at the thought of someone savouring her. She wasn't brave enough yet to say no, not with him this close. Little Mouse indeed. It was a ridiculous name, but she did feel small and insignificant when he sat near her like this. He raised his eyebrows in query and she nodded, miserable about giving in.

Again, he took his time. Despite her best efforts she rested her head on his shoulder while he fed. The red velvet jacket was soft under her cheek, lining the hard muscle underneath. She closed her eyes, pushing her thoughts away from him and tolerated his feeding. An edge of irritation as she realised he'd pulled her legs over his lap and wrapped his arms round her. He was enjoying this far too much, she couldn't get out of his embrace until he allowed it.

Kalmár was nuzzling her neck as she opened her eyes. He drew back and touched her face when she shifted. "I could make this far more pleasant for you. You would not feel any pain but you would have to allow me to do so."

"Surrender my will you mean? Like Wolfie has?" She wanted to make sure she'd understood it correctly.

"Yes. Would that be so dreadful?" The Count held her in position with one arm while he got his handkerchief out to wipe his mouth.

Tina stared, he asked so calmly as though swearing your soul to a vampire was an everyday occurrence. A new sense of horror rose in her, he'd raised the stakes, it was no longer just about him feeding and keeping her here. As she'd found out, he already changed her body without her permission, he now asked to gain complete control over her. This close to him, she could feel the force of his personality, the pressure to say yes. Unable to look his way Tina panicked, trying to think of a way out.

Kalmár took a breath to continue and was interrupted by Wolfie running in from the corridor. "Excellency, it's Consort, he wants you." The Count dumped Tina on the couch as he stood and grabbed the phone Wolfie held out.

"Yes?" He spoke in English, his tone terse. The voice on the other end did the talking. "Indeed, I will be there." He switched the phone off and gave it to Wolfie. "Get the car ready." He looked down at Tina. "Get up." Dizzy from his feeding and his offer, she gazed at him not responding.

He reached down and took hold of her upper arm and repeated, "Get up. You will need to stay in your room." As he spoke, he marched her out of the library and Tina could barely keep pace with his long legs. "It will not be for long. I am needed elsewhere. Wolf will be back shortly." He stopped and turned to look at her. "If I find you have escaped while I am away, then I will chain you up with me when I sleep.

Understood?" He shook her slightly and Tina nodded. He shoved her into her room without ceremony and locked the door behind her. She leant on the door and listened to his footsteps walk away on the wooden floor, relieved the decision had been postponed.

The castle felt empty without the Count in residence. Despite her questions Wolfie had refused to talk about where or why Kalmár had gone. After she'd badgered him one too many times, he'd waved his hands in frustration and said he couldn't.

Out of routine, Tina woke at odd times during the night, expecting to have to talk to the Count. On the second night she did get up and found Wolfie mooching around the library, not knowing what to do with himself either. They talked for a while and Tina became aware of not feeling well. Her stomach had been queasy all day, she concentrated, she didn't want to lose the little she'd eaten. She shivered as a light sweat ran over her skin.

"Tina, are you all right? What's up?" She belched, ran for the toilet and reached it just in time. She washed her mouth out and opened the door feeling shivery. Concerned, Wolfie was waiting for her outside.

"I don't feel too good, I'm going back to bed." He walked her there, sorting out a drink and a bucket in case.

Tina wrapped herself up in the bedclothes, shaking. She was terribly thirsty, her head was pounding and her bones ached. Flu, she thought – brilliant. A million miles away from anyone and I get flu. Her flesh felt puffy, like during a hot day when the blood pools in the fingers. She drifted off unaware of Wolfie checking on her during the night.

She slid in and out of consciousness over

several days. Wolfie gave her water when she couldn't keep anything else down and finally even that became too much for her stomach. She went hot and cold, kicked her covers off, then shivered. Crying in between because everything hurt, she whimpered when she no longer had the strength to weep. She fell into a pit of blackness, her head whirling round, her arms spread, helpless against the pain.

Tina felt cold fingers on her hot body and cried in relief at the coolness on her swollen limbs. She regained enough awareness to notice the Count's inspection of her and to protest weakly when he bit her. It was unfair of him to expect to feed while she was ill. She felt him cradle her in his arms as she lost consciousness again, the cool hands holding her as she fell into the darkness.

Her eyes were gummy as she woke, her mouth felt as though something had died in it. Tina became aware of a nasty smell and realised it belonged to her. She couldn't move her arms and her vision was blurred.

A shape moved close by. "Tina?" Wolfie spoke, sounding wary.

She heard the door open and a taller blur appeared. The bed creaked as the Count sat and he inspected her, sniffing her wrists and touching the side of her neck. He grunted, pleased with what he found. "She is safe, you may deal with her now."

Wolfie did something to her arms and she could move them. He told Tina to be careful of a drip in her left arm and wiped her face with a damp flannel. Her eyesight started to clear with the water. Wolfie covered her with another sheet and gave her a wash down all over with the flannel. Too worn out to be embarrassed, she let him without protesting. It stung but she felt better when he'd finished. The Count picked her up, swathed in the sheet and Wolfie changed the bed.

Licking her lips, she tried to get some moisture into her mouth. "Thirsty," she croaked. Kalmár nodded and Wolfie let her sip some water. The Count changed the drip, she could see it now, hanging from a nail high up on the four poster. She curled up and dozed off, exhausted.

Tina woke up at various points during the night. She became more alert, drank more water and kept it down. Her skin felt swollen, her bones ached but felt more rested every time. As dawn approached the Count took the drip out of her arm.

"Keep giving her water," he instructed Wolfie. "And a small amount of the soup later in the day."

She took more water during the day and the soup too. Tina began to look around and pay attention to her surroundings. There were chairs and a table that hadn't been in her room before with a pile of books on them. Dirty cups and plates from Wolfie eating were scattered everywhere and some blankets and a pillow on the floor. They all had the look of having been around for a few days.

Wolfie was asleep in the blankets. He looked knackered. He hadn't shaved for several days and his clothes were crumpled although that was normal for him. Tina wriggled, her skin itched. She stuck one arm out of the sheet to look and found short cuts everywhere plus the marks from the drip, it looked as though someone had run a piece of glass up and down her arm. No wonder the bath had hurt. Slowly she fumbled the other one out - it was the same.

Wolfie roused as she made a small noise of dismay and muttered sleepily, "Oh shit. I had hoped you wouldn't see that for a bit."

"What happened." She didn't have the energy

to make it a question. She dragged the sheet down and looked at her shoulders. The same marks, nothing deep but everywhere.

"Where do I start? You were ill a few days after the Count left. Do you remember? I didn't think anything of it to begin with. I'm rarely sick these days but I know normal humans do get ill quite often. Well it was only after you were unable to keep water down that I got worried. The Count wasn't back and I couldn't get hold of him, he was out of mobile range. I've not seen it first hand before, so it took me a while to figure out it wasn't a normal illness. It was your body fighting off his influence, the changes he's been making to you."

"Not a bad thing surely?" She was wearily confused.

"Yes, it is a bad thing, for you. I got a drip sorted, actually several, to get fluid into you but the one thing I couldn't do was to help the infection."

"Help it? Why would you want to?"

"It's your body fighting what the Count puts into you. You need your body to adapt to him, you've been with him too long. If your immune system had won something else happens, your body rots around you but you don't die. I've seen the results before, seen this thing chained up. They had to destroy it…" He trailed off with a shudder.

"I had to tie you up not that it would have held you. Thankfully the Count came back in time. The only thing he could do was to introduce more of his saliva into you, that's what all those marks are from. That's why he had to check you last night before I went near you. You were that close to turning." He held up thumb and forefinger an inch apart.

Tina gazed at him exhausted, Kalmár had won, her body hadn't. She wasn't sure if it was a good thing or not. Wolfie got up, offered a drink and tucked her back in. Nodding her thanks she drifted off.

She woke at dusk, the room half lit by the moon. Wolfie lay on his back, awake, his eyes gleaming in the light. He turned his head smiling as she shifted, "Evening," he said quietly.

"Hi," she returned.

The Count entered, he went to stand next to Wolfie who hurriedly stood, shedding his blankets. Wolfie ran his hands through his hair and stopped, looking at the Count's face. Neither of them spoke. There were a few inches between them, Wolfie was more compactly built in contrast to the Count's loose-limbed height. Kalmár stepped closer and ran his own hands through Wolfie's hair, bringing them down to caress his face. Wolfie, gazing into the Count's eyes, dropped his hands to undo his shirt collar, breathing heavily. Tina wanted to avert her own gaze but couldn't, she felt like a voyeur as transfixed as Wolfie. He slid his arms around Kalmár's shoulders, drawing the silver head to his bared neck. He buried his own face into the Count's shoulder as Kalmár's arms went around his waist and pulled him tight.

It was sexual, the complete surrender of Wolfie as he shivered in the Count's grip. Possession. In the moonlight it felt like a dream, the two men standing, holding each other. As Kalmár finished, Tina could see Wolfie's entire body tense and shiver, his fingers clutching. The Count cradled him protectively, his eyes hooded and looking into the distance as he dipped his head to lick the wounds closed. How many years? Tina felt a chill run down her spine, how many years had he been bitten like this? Kalmár helped Wolfie to lie on his blankets and touched his face gently. He turned to look at her. The spell broken, Tina started to breathe again.

"Little Mouse," he greeted her. He pulled up her arm to inspect it, brushed at the scratches and some of the scabs flaked off. "Good. You heal quickly. I should have realised you would have problems. Your blood is strong, it fights me. A lesser vampire would have lost you." He said this with great satisfaction, Tina wasn't so sure it was a good thing.

"Where did you go?" she asked, wanting to know what Wolfie hadn't been able to tell her.

He sat in the chair next to her bed. "One of the old ones woke. They do not always remember to conceal themselves so we have our people watching them. We sometimes have to cover their tracks after they have finished. Most simply wish to feed and go back to sleep, they do not care about the politics of staying hidden. I was called in case of problems."

"Where there any?"

"No. She woke, fed on what we had and slept again."

"She?" Tina had the vague image of an actress in a revealing nightdress and fangs but guessed she was wrong. Her mind shied away from the idea of them feeding her victims. The Count looked amused.

Sounding drunk, Wolfie spoke. "There are women. Not as many but just as dangerous, sometimes more. Who do you think Consort is attached too?"

"Our current leader if you can call her that, is female. You will meet her at some point no doubt. You will call her Madame and treat her with great respect."

Tina nodded, her mind whirling at the thought of a woman more frightening than the Count. The image she now considered had nightwear nowhere near it.

Chapter 8

Tina sat in her favourite place on top of the tall tower. She'd recovered, though she had the occasional bout of weakness. With the Count back the castle returned to its usual feel, its purpose restored.

Wolfie almost had to carry her the first time up she'd wanted to sit up here. He'd teased her, making mock complaints that she expected him to carry her around like the Count did and wanted to know why she couldn't have a favourite spot somewhere a bit more accessible. He'd had to bring everything she needed, including a pot to wee in so she didn't have to come down quickly. He'd also brought cushions and blankets and rigged up some shade near the door. Despite her fear of heights, peeping over the edge at the views made her feel good.

Late summer was passing in the mountains. She was losing track of time, one day ran into the next and she reckoned she must have been here almost a month. Some of the trees far down below had changed colour. They looked like beech trees, bright and vibrant reminding her of Wolfie's hair in the sunlight. Tina smiled, relaxed and peaceful. The wind tugged at her own hair, she pulled it forwards to look ruefully. It needed cutting, a reminder of the time passing. Another was that she'd got into her first pair of size twelve jeans yesterday, she'd lost weight despite eating constantly. Her skin was no longer grey and baggy from the illness, the thin red scabs had healed very fast.

The Count hadn't tried to bite her until last

night. He'd sat next to her, wrapping an arm around her waist and pulled her close. His fingers had traced a line along her chin to make her look into his dark eyes.

"May I Little Mouse?" he'd asked. Thinking about it sent shivers down her spine, if she were honest, she no longer knew what the shivers meant. She'd gritted her teeth and replied she was still tired. To her surprise, he'd nodded and let her go, acknowledging her refusal. Well tonight he would ask again and she would have to let him.

Was this Stockholm syndrome, this becoming accustomed to the strangest things? Or was it survival or were they one and the same in this situation? Life here felt normal, the outside world a dream. A twist of guilt. She thought of Jo constantly, fighting to keep the memories alive but every day took her further away and disconnected her further from what she considered real life.

A couple of days later when Tina woke earlier than usual, the door to her room was locked. Wolfie left it unlocked these days unless he was out or busy. She kicked at it without thinking, then realised this might be her chance. She listened, nothing as usual broke the silence.

Checking out of the window, she tried to get an idea of the time. It looked as though it was coming up to midday. Wolfie was normally awake and moving around by this point, she had to assume he was out. That was another thing she missed – watches. There was a clock in the kitchen, nowhere else in the parts she had access to. In her room she had to guess the time by looking at the sun and the direction of shadows.

Hidden up in the canopy of her four poster bed was a large brooch, the pin long and sturdy. Tina had found it guarded by an enormous spider under a piece of furniture during her explorations. Thankful that no one had noticed during her illness, she unpinned it, stuck it into the lock and wriggled it around. This must work, the lock was a simple one, she'd seen the key at various points when Wolfie unlocked the door. It just should be a question of shifting something around inside. She'd seen so many people do it in the movies, it must be easy. Several times she almost managed, feeling the tumblers move and losing them again. Tina scuffed her knuckles and pinched her fingers, swore as she tried to pull the pin around. All of a sudden the lock clicked and the door opened.

Tina stood for a moment in the doorway, not quite believing she'd done it. For a wild second she wondered if she could lock herself in again, wait for a more concrete chance and shook her head. She had to be careful and take what she'd been given. She snuck down the corridor, placing her feet carefully in the quiet dustiness. She checked the front door and decided that there was no way her pin would undo that lock without breaking.

Wolfie wasn't in the kitchen and not in his bedroom which was a mess as usual. The castle was quiet and empty, sighing in relief she presumed he must have taken the car somewhere. She checked the time and found it was after eleven thirty. Tina picked up a pair of scissors, some food and water and put them in a bag. She ran lightly back to her room, pulled several sheets off the bed and slinging them over her shoulder, ran up the tall front tower.

At the top, she cut the sheets up into thick strips, folded them double and tied them into a long chain, trying to keep an eye on the road at the same time. She coiled them and carried them bandoleer fashion over her head and shoulder. Now for the difficult bit, the doors and gates were locked, all the windows on this side were too small for her to get through, the only way out was off one of the towers. Tina looked over the wall, she could see the old battlements underneath and below was freedom. Sick with anticipation, she took the first of her improvised ropes and tied it to one of the merlons, tugging to make sure it was secure. She took a deep breath trying to control her shaking hands and swung herself over the edge.

Tina hung, swaying on the rope and with the ever present breeze blowing, shut her eyes tight, squeaking in terror. She swung until she'd realised that the expected fall hadn't happened and no ripping tear had heralded a short lived flight to the ground. There was no way she could go up again, she had to go down. Gradually she collected herself and wiggled her foot into the next 'link' in the rope.

"There." She talked herself down as she went, it was better than scolding herself that she was like the mouse the Count had named her for - it didn't help her fear. "Right leg. Move it." The rope swung her against the stone, scuffing her bare knuckles and toes. "Arms next. And again. Next one. Move it. Finally…"

She crouched and sucked her scrapes while she balanced on the small ledge where the battlements joined onto the tower, clutching at the merlon. She allowed herself time to calm down, reminding herself why she did this and tied on the longer rope and discovered it didn't reach the ground. No matter, she could jump from the end.

Tina swung herself over the edge, not finding it as bad this time although she must still be at least two stories up. Close to the bottom she could felt the fabric rope stretch and start to rip. She tried to climb down quicker and succeeded in only hearing it rip faster. She landed awkwardly, squeaking in shock but with nothing broken, having dropped four foot when it gave way. There wasn't much of an end left dangling from the battlements, she threw the broken rope over the edge of the cliff with relish.

Dizzy with the space, she couldn't believe she was outside the castle at last and straightened her clothes in determination. She hopped through the long grass, not enjoying the scratchiness under her feet and set off quickly down the road. Her bare feet slapped against the hard surface. All this time and she'd never persuaded the Count to buy her shoes. Still her feet were tough from the floors in the castle and she had some of the sheet left in her bag for wrapping round them later on. First she wanted to get into the trees. It was exposed up here, the castle stood on rocky grassland and there was no cover if Wolfie came back.

She hurried with the sun hot on her head, once she'd got to those trees she'd be in the shade. Tina kept her ears open listening for the sound of a car engine. Her breath came in short bursts and she realised she was almost running. She deliberately slowed, making herself walk. No point in wearing herself out this early in the day, if she was caught then it would happen, there was nowhere to hide up here. She tried to relax, listened to the birds singing and stopped to wrap her feet against the hard road. Looking back, she noticed she couldn't see the rope. If she could avoid Wolfie on the road, he'd take a while to realise she wasn't in the castle and he'd have to spend time looking for her escape route first.

It took ages to leave the castle behind and reach the first trees. They were beeches, she loved beech woods. Tall slim trunks, always beautiful. The dappled shade felt lovely after the heat of the sun. The wind was loud in the trees, the rustle of the leaves like the sea, she couldn't hear much above it.

Tina moved off the road into a dip out of sight and settled down to eat in the brown leaves. She closed her eyes and relaxed with the smell of plants and earth. A faint sound in the distance above the leaves, she listened without registering for a moment, then her brain recognised it. A car engine - she flattened herself to the ground and peered through brambles at the road, the earth damp beneath her. A large old fashioned silver car swung around the bend. It had been closer than she'd thought, the powerful engine little more than a purr. Wolfie was at the wheel, his arm on the open window, relaxed in the sunshine.

Her insides screwed up as the guilt hit her, knowing he'd be worried when he discovered her gone. That was half the problem, Wolfie was nice, she liked him and it wasn't his fault. She shook her head, tough, she had to get home. She waited until the car had passed several bends and moved back onto the road eating her lunch as she went, no longer relaxed.

Tina worried about Wolfie catching her on the road now but didn't dare walk away from it. She had no way of knowing the quickest way through the woods. She climbed over a set of gates with a small car park on the other side. The gates had a padlock as well as a notice on them, she couldn't read it. Must be 'Private. Keep out' she thought grumpily.

Mid-afternoon, footsore and tired she looked down a small road with what appeared to be houses further back. She walked down it hoping to find someone and swore in frustration when she saw the roofs sagging and the windows empty. This must be the village Wolfie had mentioned. She trudged back to the main road and kept going, always on the lookout for a hiding place, walking to the side of the road. Trying to listen out for the sound of an engine over the trees kept her on edge, sure Wolfie would look for her when he'd searched the castle.

Tina limped now. Her feet were tough from walking barefoot in the castle but this was different, it was rougher than she was used to despite the tarmac. The pieces of sheet she'd wrapped around her feet wore into holes and the soles of her feet got scuffed. She kept herself going by thinking of Jo and how every step brought them closer.

There was a river below one side of the road fed by various streams. Several times she stopped to go and look at the water run and leap over the rocks. The extra noise made it difficult to hear anything. By chance she saw a flash of reflected light in the distance. The car - she couldn't hear it above the river, she flattened herself against the bank. It rounded the corner and she saw Wolfie looking out above her, no longer relaxed, he was alert and swinging his head from side to side, his face tense.

She stayed where she was as the car swept by, decided to have a rest and wait until he came back, hoping he would look along the road and not down at the river. Twenty minutes later he returned, slower this time. Tina flattened herself again, burying her head down to make sure he had no chance to see her. She waited a while longer and decided he wasn't coming back. Wet and stiff from the ground she carried on.

Tina passed woodland walks, signposted from the road, with spaces to park for walkers. One had a car in it. She tried the doors, locked. One of the few times she wished for a mis-spent youth - she had no idea of how to steal and hot-wire a car. The river fed into several lakes at the bottom of the valley and the trees thinned out as the valley widened.

The afternoon drew steadily on, turning into

early evening. Tina drank the last of her water, her food she'd finished hours ago. Determined, she plodded, her feet on fire, bruised and sore and her legs were like jelly. The sun dropped in the sky and in her tiredness, it raced her to the horizon turning the sky orange.

She came to the top of a small rise and in the distance she saw another road. Cars with lights on flashed by. She stared numbly, it had to be at least three miles - an hour of brisk walking. It could have been the moon it was so far away. Dusk started to fall, she wouldn't be able to see the road or anything else shortly.

Hope drained out of her, she couldn't walk along a winding road in darkness, there was too little to indicate the edge of the road, she'd be stumbling into the wilderness. Her bladder was full and out of habit she moved off the road into some trees. It was dark in there and as she finished, she heard a sound, an engine. It wasn't the purr of the silver car, it was louder, it must be that car she'd seen parked up, it was coming past. Tina dragged her trousers up and tried to run to the road shouting and waving as she did. She saw the lights from the headlamps sweep over the brow of the hill, full beams on. She stumbled over tree roots, scraped herself on brambles, blinded. Music blared through closed windows and it went past without seeing her.

Alone in the middle of the road, she watched the red tail lights weave along the lane, blink in and out of the trees and hedges to join the rest of humanity in the distance. She did up her belt and plonked herself on the side of the road. She'd scratched herself all over, stubbed her toes and she abruptly hated the world for not knowing she was trying to escape and not caring.

Tears leaked out and she brushed them away

angrily. Looking out into the dusk she knew she'd blown her chance, they'd watch her to make sure she didn't escape now. Frustrated and exhausted Tina put her elbows on her crossed knees, her chin in her hands and forced herself to calm down. She had nowhere else to run to, no one to call. She'd noticed how the Count could always tell where she was, she was sure he would be able to tell she wasn't in the castle and would find her. She wondered how long it would take and if he would be angry.

The sun set and the landscape faded into complete darkness. There was no light apart from the occasional beam of a car miles away. The faint hum of an engine in the distance and small noises. There was a vast loneliness in the night as she listened to the unsettling country noises, rustling, the leaves on trees and a chill from the breeze. The moon hadn't risen, she had a sneaking suspicion it might be a new moon tonight.

She heard the rumble of an engine behind her, it stopped a distance away. Tina felt a tingle of something watching her and a quiet footfall behind. She jumped despite her exhaustion.

"Good evening Little Mouse." A darker shape in the blackness, she turned and greeted his voice, standing awkwardly as her cold muscles protested. "You have run a long way this time. Why did you stop?"

"There wasn't any point." She shrugged, fed up. "I got here too late." Her reply was as quiet as his question, in her exhausted state she was simply relieved he wasn't angry.

"Come." He took hold of her upper arm and walked her along the road, Tina stumbled with him, unable to see and with her feet protesting. He didn't slow.

The silver car was in a dip, tucked into a parking space and close up she recognised the Spirit of Ecstasy on the bonnet. The Count opened the passenger door for her. Tina curled up and watched him drive. He was impatient at the wheel, his eyes sweeping the road noticed everything. The car responded, engine purring. He said nothing during the journey back.

Chapter 9

It was heart-breaking how little time it took to return, the sweeping turns in the dark merged into one another before her tired eyes. He left the car in the middle of the courtyard, walked around and opened the passenger door for her. The stable entrance was open, showing another car inside. Wincing at her legs, Tina clambered out. The Count huffed with impatience at her slowness and picked her up. He carried her into the library, dumped her on the couch and left without saying a word.

Gingerly she stretched, everything hurt and she knew it would be worse later. She stopped when Wolfie came in, anger radiating off him. The Count followed behind, carrying a small box. He placed it on the table beside his chair, picked up his glasses and proceeded to read as though nothing had happened. Wolfie glanced his way and sullenly came to look at her feet. He muttered something at the state of them and stalked off. He came back with a bowl and a flannel and started picking at the knots holding the sheet footwear together. Tina pulled her legs away and unpicked the first layer, taking the flannel from him. He squatted next to the couch and watched her. Eventually he couldn't stay quiet.

"I thought you were dead. I saw the rope you made halfway down the cliff, I thought you'd fallen. I spent the afternoon imagining you stuck in a crevice injured and not able to shout for help. It wasn't until His Excellency told me you were miles away that I knew you were all right. I drove up and down the road this afternoon to see if I could spot you. I didn't believe you were there though, didn't you see me? Can you imagine what I've been through? I checked all the cliff I could safely get to. Don't you think I fucking care?" He stopped unable to continue.

"I'm sorry," Tina whispered. Despite everything, she was sorry for him. The throwing of the rope hadn't been conscious, if she'd left it on the ground next to the wall, he would have realised she'd landed okay. He was decent and despite everything he tried but she couldn't help not wanting to be here. He threw her a hurt look, obviously deciding she could deal with her own feet and stalked off.

Tina stripped off the pieces of sheet footwear. It was dirty and matted together from the walk, wetting the fabric helped. There were plenty of blisters, her feet were bruised and they would be worse in the morning. She washed them and left them to dry. She rubbed her eyes, exhausted from the day.

"How did you get out?" The Count spoke in his normal quiet tone. Tina told him about the brooch and picking the locks. She'd learnt not to lie around him, he'd told her that he could hear her heart beating faster when that happened. One threat of being hit had put an end to it and despite her fears, she'd discovered that telling the truth seldom brought more than a snort from him.

The Count sat next to her, shifting her hips along to make room with the box on his lap. He took hold of her hand and clasped something round her wrist, he did the other as quickly and returned to his chair. She stared, he'd put a slim close fitting bracelet on each wrist. They were a dull silver colour with a trace of a vine pattern around the edges, elegant, even beautiful in its way. Tina tugged at one, the seams didn't open. How had he shut them? She couldn't see a catch, no hole for a lock, she looked at him panicking.

"You will not be able to open them. I took a cast of your wrists on the night I brought you here and had them designed to fit you. They are made of titanium and there is no key, the lock is within the manacle itself. The only way to open them is if I release it. If you attempt to climb down my walls again, I will have you chained in your room and in the unlikely event you should escape me, you will wear them for the rest of your life." He paused to allow this to sink in. "Do you remember when I suggested that if you escaped, you would spend the day underground with me? I believe I will make good that threat." He picked up his paper, "You will learn to behave."

Tina put her head in her hands, she'd been collared and had no chance to remove it. The manacles fitted around her wrists with very little gap, there wasn't any rubbing or rough edges and they didn't feel heavy just wrong. Everything had gone right this morning, if she'd reached the road earlier would she have escaped? Nothing seemed so certain now. Could he really sense her from so far away or had he guessed? Were there other vampires around or would they stay away from him? Were they territorial? There was so much she didn't know.

Wolfie came in with some bandages, his eyes flicked to the bracelets but he didn't comment. He dried the rest of her feet and bandaged them, his anger burnt out for the moment. She let him, exhausted. He spoke to the Count while he worked, "Tina will need something on her feet if she's to spend the day with you."

"I will carry her. It will be dark."

Wolfie shrugged. He looked up at Tina, "You'd like some food?"

"Please." She moved to get up.

"No, I'll bring it." She gazed pleadingly at him and he relented, "Well if that's what you want," and walked beside her as she limped out.

"I'm sorry," she repeated as they reached the kitchen. "I didn't think how much you'd worry. Well, I did a bit but…" She faltered, "I had to get away."

"Is your life so bad here? Am I so bad you don't want to stay?"

He didn't seem to understand and she tried to explain. "No, no you're fine. I want to go home, see my family and cuddle my daughter. Wake up in my own bed and not have someone sucking my blood." Tina added the last bitterly.

Wolfie sighed, "When will you realise? This is your life now. The life you had before has gone and everyone you knew, think you're dead. I know it sounds harsh but that's why the fire was arranged. They've had closure, they will grieve for you but they're not wondering where you are." He shook his head while he took food out of the fridge and put it on the table. "How long can you bang your head against this brick wall? What will it take for you to accept this?"

"I'm supposed to believe the car fire was arranged to help?" Incredulous she paused as she was about to sit.

"Yes. At least they know you're not coming back." He nodded at her look. "Yes, they could be at home worrying about you, or going through a murder investigation if the police had got hold of it in the wrong way. Look I can see this isn't going anywhere. If it happens again, I'll try not to take it personally." He put the kettle on and started to make the meal. She swallowed her frustration at his lack of understanding and bit off her argument that he'd chosen to be here and she hadn't. Everything had been taken away from her and even if she'd been asked, she'd have still said no.

She sighed, she didn't want to alienate Wolfie by more arguments, he was the only good thing she had here. Tina thought about her day, she hadn't managed to escape but at least she had an idea of what she needed for the next time. She changed the subject, "I saw a map on the way down in the car park."

"We get a lot of walkers around here, it's better to give them paths and a clear idea of where to go. Most of the estate is run as part of the national park."

"Doesn't anyone climb over the gate and come up here?"

He laughed, "Sometimes I have to discourage the occasional long distance walker."

"Discourage?" The gleam in his eye suggested something else.

"Okay, I shout at them to bugger off normally." She giggled at the thought and he joined in, launching into a long story about a particular group of obstinate walkers a few years ago.

As they talked through the night, they regained their former easiness. Wolfie was too relaxed to stay upset for long. She decided it was why he found his vows to the Count so easy, he naturally followed the path of least resistance through life. At times one or both of them would drift off to sleep and carry on the conversation at a later point. Tina couldn't be bothered to move, she was too warm next to the stove.

Kalmár came for her before dawn. To her relief, Wolfie had told her the Count had several areas underground where he liked to sleep, it wasn't a case of sleeping in a coffin with him.

"Just remember," Wolfie had said, "Even if

something scares you there, nothing can actually hurt you. He won't allow it." It didn't help much. Tina winced at her stiff muscles and sore feet, drunk with lack of sleep. She'd only napped in the chair, not slept properly. Her feet hurt so much she didn't protest when the Count picked her up and carried her through the castle.

He carried her through the corridor into a chapel, Tina remembered seeing it from above. She became fascinated at how the doors opened for the Count and she watched over his shoulder as they shut behind them. The dim light of pre-dawn lit the tall windows, there was an eerie calm but she didn't find it spooky. There was a door at the back behind the altar and he bent to go through, Tina scrunching up in his arms so not to knock herself against the frame.

The darkness was complete inside and there were many steps, all going down. The Count continued to walk without hesitation, his long legs covering the ground. Dis-orientated, she knew she would never be able to find her way back without him even if she had a light. He made various turns while carrying her easily, only shifting her in his arms when negotiating tight corners. Eventually she heard a door open, the Count put her down and Tina stayed where he'd put her.

A light. He lit a candle, no, a lantern and placed it on a table. With her eyes adjusting in the dimness, she blinked, she hadn't heard a match struck and his hands were empty. The circle of light showed the table and a few chairs. The shapes of covered bowls and a flask were on the table and a pile of bedding was on the floor close by. The rest of the room was austere with bare stone walls and she shuddered as she saw a large stone box on a platform in the darkness.

She heard a clink, he'd picked up a slender chain attached to the wall. He looped a c shape into it, took her wrist and pressed it into some covered holes she'd not noticed in her bracelet. The chain would allow her to reach the table and bedding but no further, certainly not to the coffin.

"There is food here and drink." The Count waved at the table. "There is a chamber pot." He pointed to a covered pot on the floor underneath. "Nothing will harm you while you are here. The chain is for your own protection. I am a danger if you should come too close while I sleep."

"But I slept with you when you brought me here."

"Yes, you were asleep and still. While I rest, I am primed for any movement that may be a danger to me." He picked up the lantern and as he moved away, it went out. Tina squeaked at the sudden return to darkness. Her mouth worked unable to speak and she heard him walk towards his coffin. "I am conscious of you even if I can not reply. Good night Little Mouse." This was said wearily as she heard him settle and then he switched off.

It was the only way she could describe it, his presence that she could feel as a normal part of the castle at night stopped. Tina stood in the darkness on her own underground, she covered her mouth with her hands and tried not to panic. She shut her eyes, opened them as wide as she could, it made no difference. Time, place, nothing had any meaning here. She sank into a crouch, ignoring her protesting muscles and rocked gently in the darkness. Not crying just comforting herself with her own presence, the reality of being here.

Tina's leg muscles soon burnt from crouching, she had to stretch them. She had to deal with one fear at a time, and she decided that she was not going to sleep on the floor. By touch she found the table and chairs. Carefully walking her fingers across the table, she found the dishes and flask and put them on the chairs. It felt strange hearing the chain clink in the dark while she ate and drank. The chamber pot she found and used, putting the lid on afterwards.

She spread the blankets and pillow out on the table and curled up in them, more comfortable off the floor. Although the room had looked clean in comparison to other parts of the castle, she didn't like the idea of the floor. Things ran around on floors and she giggled at her exhausted fastidiousness.

Tina stretched out in the pitch black and tried to look through to where the Count lay, no breath or movement came from his direction. She might as well lie in the same room as a corpse. Panic started to rise as the walls pressed down on her. How far down was she? What if an earthquake happened? What if the Count didn't wake up?

With difficulty she controlled her breathing again, tiredness overwhelming her. She imagined walking through the beech woods below the castle, the river running next to her. The sun shining and the birds singing, the sounds of the wind in the leaves and she drifted off.

She dreamt of roads, of plodding along them and never getting anywhere. Unsure of her direction, she only knew she had to keep moving despite her feet aching. It was always dark in her dreams, the trees rustling overhead. There was some unseen figure behind her, no menace coming from it, just a presence. It made her keep walking with no chance to stop. She saw Jo with her hands reaching out towards her, no sound coming from her mouth. Tina held her own hands out, unable to touch Jo's no matter how hard she stretched.

Tears streamed down her face and she woke

with a desperate longing to see her daughter. Her arms had a dreadful emptiness, with a gap that could only be filled by Jo. She wiped her eyes and gazed into the blackness, the silence and darkness were complete. She now could understand why Lord Tangent chained up his pets to break them, a few days of this and she would also do anything to get out. Would this happen to her - would the Count not let her out without swearing herself to him? Fear chilled her skin. If he chose to force her, she could say goodbye to her hopes of ever seeing Jo again.

Eventually she slept again, disturbing at several unknown points in the day. Each time she strained her eyes into the blackness, unsure of where she was. She finally woke as Kalmár opened his eyes, his presence like a light switching on.

"Good evening Little Mouse."

"Hello." She could hear him moving, the soft rustle of fabric shouting in the dark. Tina struggled with the blankets to get up and stood stiffly, her muscles aching, her feet on fire from yesterday's walk. Anxiety curdled through her, would he keep her down here?

Straining her eyes and ears, she flinched when he spoke close to her, "I will carry you." He undid the chain and let it fall. Resigned despite being relieved to leave, she put her arms around his neck and let him pick her up.

The way back to the surface seemed quicker. He put Tina down in the chapel and touched the bracelets. "When you have bathed, come to me and I will take these off so you may dry underneath." He left her. She sniffed herself and winced, the smell from yesterday's sweat and the fear at being underground was noticeable.

The door they had come through was locked again and she wandered through the chapel. It was plain, the sweeping lines of the arched roof were simple and she touched various inscriptions on the walls as the last of the dusk faded from the windows. It had a peaceful feeling, she liked it.

The relief of release put her in a good temper. She had her bath, relaxing her tired muscles and admired her figure in the tarnished mirror. Tina grinned, she enjoyed being able to eat what she wanted and still lose weight. Blisters she had plenty of but none had broken, she patted her feet dry gently. She tried to dry underneath the bracelets and sighed. The Count was right, they fitted too well, he'd have to remove them first.

As she left the bathroom to hang her towel up, she noticed a strange feeling. It was similar to the one she'd had the first evening here. Tina twitched her shoulders, she'd got used to the Count, she knew roughly how close or far away he was but this felt different. Another vampire? Wolfie had said she'd know and this time she was more curious than frightened. She hung up her towel to dry and went downstairs.

Tina peeped in at the library, the Count was in his usual chair and a stranger sat close by, talking quietly. She slipped in, limping on her bare feet. Kalmár rose as she approached.

"Little Mouse, this is Vinceti." The stranger stood and nodded. She studied him out of curiosity, he was a few inches taller than her and dressed normally with nothing to suggest his nature. Neat clothes – jeans, shirt and a jumper knotted over his shoulders. His straight black hair was pulled into a tail at the back of his head. She didn't like him.

"Good evening Little Mouse. I have heard so much about you." His dark eyes watched her intently, his manner was pleasant and yet her hackles rose. Why did he make her twitch?

"Good," she said tartly. "If you've heard so much then I don't need to say anything." She turned away and held her wrists out to the Count. "Please Excellency, would you mind undoing these?" The Count ignored her rudeness to his guest, he rested a finger on each bracelet in turn and they clicked open. He caught them and placed them on the table next to him.

She noticed Vinceti watching her avidly as she wiped her wrists on her shirt. He stepped towards her, holding his hand out and she moved back instinctively, they were too close for her liking. The Count reached up and caught her by the wrist. His hand encircled it much as the bracelet had and with as much hope of removing it, she stayed next to him.

Vinceti smiled and asked, "Frightened Little Mouse? It is a good name for you, small and timid as you are. I only wished to greet you."

That irritated her even more. Small and timid maybe but as far as she was concerned mice still had teeth. Tina lifted her chin and lied, "I'm not frightened. His Excellency is just stopping me from punching you into the middle of next week, where you belong." She saw the Count raise an eyebrow, he'd be able to tell she lied. To her surprise he looked more amused than offended.

Vinceti chuckled as if he also found her amusing and took her free hand. She narrowed her eyes and glowered at him, refusing to struggle. His hand was cool like the Count's, he lifted hers as if to kiss it and turned it over to expose her wrist. Tina saw the glint of fangs when he bent his head. She tried unsuccessfully to pull away when another long fingered hand curled around her wrist, blocking him. Vinceti looked up in surprise.

The Count was standing. "You seek to challenge me? In my own territory?" His voice was mild.

Vinceti's face went from surprise to chagrin. He let go of her hand to her relief. "Of course not Excellency. I was merely hungry and she smells so sweet." Heart beating fast, Tina thought grumpily, *shouldn't have had that bath. Wonder what he would have made of me then?*

The Count had kept hold of her hands, he lifted her wrist to his own lips and bent to kiss her lightly on the inside. "Yes, she does." He smiled and inclined his head, "Leave us."

Tina snatched both her hands away from him and stalked off, rubbing the feeling off her wrists. Her back tingled and she paused, looking through the doors. Vinceti was watching her from his seat, she shuddered and walked out of sight.

Wolfie was slamming around the kitchen when she came in. "What's up?" she asked. "Did you see our guest? He gives me the creeps."

"You have good taste in vampires. Vinceti is an arsewipe," he said succinctly.

"I think he tried to bite my wrist. Himself stopped him."

Wolfie paused to work out Tina's phrasing and agreed with her. "Sounds about right for Vinceti, he'll try anything. He's one of Lord Tangent's successes. One of the few nasty enough that is, his pets don't tend to survive."

"Why is he here?"

"Who knows?" Wolfie shrugged. "It's probably information. He can get privileges for information and lots of people want to know about you." He gave her a deep meaningful stare and Tina shrugged off the teasing as something else she didn't want to hear.

"How come he's here? Does the Count allow it?" She cut the bread for more toast.

Wolfie nodded. "The younger ones can travel how they like through an older vampire's territory, otherwise they'd all end up fighting for space like in the old days. They're allowed to feed within those territories providing they obey certain rules. It means messages can be passed on and information gathered about what everyone's doing. Vampires don't mix well with those of their own kind, they tend to be solitary and suspicious of each other."

"What about when the Count kidnapped me?" Tina asked as she pinched his butter knife, "Wasn't he on someone else's territory? Lord Tangent's?"

He swiped at her trying to get his knife back, "Yes but he was allegedly passing through. He planned it very carefully and now you're in his castle no one can come in without his permission so you're safe." They both laughed as he grabbed for her arm and pulled her close, stretching for the knife she held out of his reach.

The bell rang. Wolfie rolled his eyes, left the knife and went to answer the Count's summons. Tina thought about what Wolfie had said. She wasn't sure the word safe applied to her situation but strangely she hadn't been worried about Vinceti. Irritated yes but not frightened, was it to do with being under the Count's protection? He had stopped Vinceti from biting her.

A short while later Wolfie came back and said he'd shown Vinceti out. Tina grabbed her plate and went to find the Count.

"What did he want?" she asked, her mouth full.

The Count looked at her over the rim of his glasses. "He came to see if the rumours were true and that I had you here. I believe you may have impressed him." He went back to his reading with a smirk as Tina snorted.

Chapter 10

The weather grew colder. There was a chill to the mornings when Tina got up, the breeze that hung around the castle had a distinct edge to it and the beech trees far below turned a glorious red and gold.

The inevitable was happening between Tina and Wolfie. Stuck together in each other's company, they formed a teasing relationship. It created a spark between the two of them, a pull they both enjoyed. Wolfie was a problem Tina mused, he had a very tactile personality which caused her difficulties, she liked him far too much but she didn't want to get involved emotionally with him, she wanted to get back to her family. He also had his girlfriend, she heard him talking on the phone during the evenings. She didn't know what excuses he made for not phoning during the day but Tina recognised the playful tones, he spoke to her in the same way. Even if she couldn't understand the words, she could still feel jealous of the other woman, especially when he came back to the castle in such a good mood after having been with her. Some women could have an affair without thought, she wasn't one of them.

Her period came and went, the Count was as vile as he'd been previously. Wolfie escaped to his girlfriend during the nights, Tina had to endure the constant irritation and tiredness. She felt desperate, she needed the car. Once it had snowed there would be no way out until spring and she knew she couldn't hold out against him for the duration of the winter months. Racking her brains she could think of nothing, both the car and keys were locked away - Kalmár was determined to take no chances.

Wolfie was now in the middle of ordering everything he needed for the winter and Tina learned not to protest when she discovered her door locked. One morning, she found a huge quantity of wood had been delivered and stacked inside the castle walls, he grinned and told her most of this would be used by spring. Bulk orders of frozen and tinned goods arrived from somewhere, she helped him store them and listened to his stories of previous winters. He made suggestions to Tina about ordering warm clothes and nagged Kalmár about footwear. The Count refused to discuss the possibility of shoes and her grumbles about the cold floors were also ignored.

One evening she was stood on the tall tower. Tina watched the sun go down wrapped up with a sweater and scarf, a thick pair of socks on her feet and gazed as the stars came out, putting off stumbling down the awkward steps. She hated walking around in socks and no shoes. It was strange, bare feet she was happy to get dirty and wash them but socks - yuck, they collected the dirt.

She wriggled one of the bracelets on her wrist, they irritated her at times and swore quietly. Kalmár would take them off when she asked to dry underneath them, she gritted her teeth and refused to struggle when they went on again. He'd not used them to chain her up since the day she'd spent underground with him. On her telling him that they were pointless he'd said they were a reminder that she was not free, wherever she was.

Tina gritted her teeth and stopped twisting them, she'd only make her wrists ache. She jumped as the Count came to stand next to her in the lanternlight. She'd felt him wake as usual but hadn't heard him come through the tower door. When she turned to check, it was still shut. He gave his usual greeting and sat on the edge unconcerned about the drop behind him. Tina shivered, she could hold onto the wall to look at the view but climbing down had taken all the courage she'd had. Watching him sit there so casually made her stomach go funny.

"How was the sunset this evening?"

"Beautiful." She wondered if he'd heard her muttering to herself.

"May I show you something? Do you trust me?" Kalmár stood and held out a hand, challenging her to take it. Tina stretched out her own with reluctance, not entirely trusting him. He took it, placing one foot on the stone wall. He tugged Tina close, wrapped his arms around her to stop her pulling away and lifted her onto the top of the wall with him. She squeezed her eyes tight shut and clutched at his jacket not daring to move in case they toppled. The wind whistled, making them sway and her legs trembled like jelly. Only his arms held her up otherwise she would have collapsed into a puddle.

"It is a good view, yes?" She felt him look around untroubled by the drop. "But not as good as the one elsewhere." He picked her up and to her shame, she buried her head in his shoulder. Tina could feel him chuckle to himself as he carried her. The wind blew around them, she couldn't work out where they were. He stopped, turned and joggled his shoulder at her. "Look Little Mouse."

She uncurled a bit, expecting to be on the tower, instead she saw the castle some way off. Tina's breath caught as her eyes travelled downwards and stuck, there was nothing underneath them but air. Her fingers unthinkingly crawled up his jacket and locked themselves around his neck. She planted her face firmly back in his shoulder and this time he laughed out loud. He whirled her around a few times and only succeeded in making her squeak

132

and curl up tighter.

After what seemed like an age, he shook his arms and told her to get down. Tina peeped out and saw they stood in a cave high up on a mountainside. Glowering at him, she put her feet on the floor and let go. Her legs collapsed and she sat where she'd fallen, not wanting to move. The cold floor felt reassuringly solid underneath her. She didn't know how he'd managed to get them here, she presumed it must be an extension of his ability to open doors.

The moon showed bright outside the cave mouth, the shadows sharp and black. Kalmár busied himself in pulling some branches from a pile of wood into the middle of the cave, snapping them into smaller sections. The remains of an old fire were to the side of her. He took some tinder from a pocket, Tina leaned forwards curious about what he did. She saw a sudden spark, the tinder in between his fingers flared and he dropped it onto a pile of moss and twigs that caught quickly. Tina shivered with cold and tucked her feet close into the warmth of the flames, they felt icy with no shoes on.

He went to stand in the mouth of the cave next to the edge. "What do you think of my view?" Tina stretched her head up as far as she could from her sitting position and tried to make an appreciative noise, she'd realised she was dependant on the Count taking her back.

"Come and look, I will not let you fall." He snapped his fingers. She sighed and crawled over on hands and knees, yep it was high all right. Kalmár reached down, pulled her upright and she grabbed at him, holding onto his jacket, eyes squeezed shut.

He shook her, "Open your eyes Little Mouse."

Tina pried one eye open, the view was magnificent. The cave was inaccessible, a sheer drop fell below them, the castle could be seen in the distance. Trees and mountains shone in the silvery moonlight. "It's lovely," she managed.

He chuckled and led her back to the safety of the fire. "I could make you swear yourself to me just by threatening to drop you." Kalmár said it casually waiting for a reaction.

Tina didn't disappoint him, she sat near the fire, shivering as the stone floor sucked the warmth out of her. "You've proved I'm too valuable to you. You wouldn't do it."

He sat nearby, stretching his long legs out and leant against the cave wall, ignoring the dirt clinging to his clothes. "Shall we try? You would not be frightened?" The firelight gleamed in his eyes, he was enjoying himself.

"Yes, I would be frightened." She didn't care about admitting it. Frightened? She'd be fucking terrified, he knew it too but she refused to give him the pleasure. "I'm not going to do it. I don't want to be like Wolfie. He's given up his own free will."

"He has more freedom than you do. You could go out of the castle, meet people, do many things if you swore yourself to me. You are not free, none of us are."

"He can't say certain things, do certain things. How is that free?" She tried to make him understand. "Even if I did swear an oath to you it doesn't make me free. I can't go back and see my family. I can't go home."

"You can never go back Little Mouse." His voice became gentle, "Your family is dead to you, your home is now here. When you lived with your family you were not free either, you had responsibilities. Society makes you conform to a way of behaving otherwise there are punishments." His voice was soft and persuasive as he carried on, "There are a different set of rules here, other

134

penalties for not obeying. I will not make you swear to me but you will not have the freedom I can offer until you do. You are shivering. Come here, the floor is cold and I am warmer. Are you going to be stubborn?"

His last comment riled but she was freezing her backside off here. Tina got up and put some more wood on the fire before sitting on his lap, primly attempting to sit upright. Kalmár immediately shifted her to curl up in his arms and she resigned herself to staying where he wanted her. He was cool but still warmer than the cave floor. She stretched her legs out on top of his, warming them in the flames as though it didn't matter where she sat.

"If I'd known we were coming here I'd have brought a blanket. You don't have much freedom. You have to hide yourself, you can't tell people who or what you are."

"The majority of humans would fear what I am. It is not pleasant to have a mob of peasants shouting at your door Little Mouse. What would that mob be like today? We choose to live quietly on the edges. The leaders of your countries do not trouble us while we do so. We keep out of politics and conflicts, we do not interfere. When you have lived for many centuries, life's repetitions become familiar. The arguments between countries and people do not change or the excuses for the disagreements."

His disregard for millions of lives lost in wars and famine upset her, "But you must have seen so much suffering, how can you ignore it? If you have the money, power and influence, you could choose to do so much. You have the long view, you could help to see a way through."

"Yes I can ignore it. I have taken you out of your life, given you the chance of a new one. What happens? You rebel against me and try to escape. What would happen if we tried to make a better world? The same thing. Humans will run around like rats, creating their own problems. You do not like interference."

"Of course I rebel, it's not a better life than the one I had, I was happy."

"What if I had told you that your life would be better in five years, ten years? That it would be better within your child's lifetime? Would you feel the same?"

"You didn't ask, you just took me. You've been making changes to me without my knowledge, infected me without my permission." It was difficult being indignant while curled up on someone's lap. She crossed her arms, she knew he wouldn't let her off without a struggle and refused to indulge him. She got the feeling Kalmár was enjoying having her at a physical disadvantage.

"You would have refused to see that your life could change, you would not have come, even if I had asked. Humans would not accept that we ruled over them for their own good. There could be no half measures, once they realised we were in control they would believe we were using them for farming purposes. Do you agree?"

He leaned around to look at Tina and she had to nod. She'd felt like that on more than one occasion. She gazed into the fire, the smoke rising to lose itself further back in the cave. She disliked restrictions and she was only one person, what about whole countries? What about after they had that control, would they give it up? Unlikely.

He shifted, resting his chin against her head as he spoke. "There are too few of us to take control these days, too many of you. In centuries past we might have done. But are we better than humans? I can assure you that a number of us are not, living more years does not make you a superior person. Would you like to be ruled over by let us say, Vinceti?" Kalmár paused, amused as Tina shuddered.

"Imagine what would happen if we were known about. Your scientists would not leave us alone. They would want to know the secret to our longevity amongst other things. Can you conceive the idea of them trying to contain me, to study me in a laboratory?" He smiled and waved a hand in disdain. "But they might hold a younger vampire and this we will not tolerate."

"Why would that be wrong? They might find a cure, find out why it happens. Don't you want to know why? Don't you want to walk in the sunshine? Don't you miss it?"

Kalmár nodded, "A number of us have spoken over the years, of finding the reasons for our differences. We made the decision that the knowledge would be too dangerous. Any experiments that had been started amongst ourselves have been halted. There is no certain way of keeping any knowledge separate once it has been discovered, we can not risk it."

"Have you never regretted what you are?" With his unexpectedly open consideration, Tina gave into her curiosity. How must he feel after having lived so long, especially as the restrictions he had were so absolute.

"You have a daughter, have you ever considered what your life might be like without her? Can you honestly tell me you have never had times when you wished she were not there?" Tina watched the flames, silent. She loved Jo. Her daughter was part of her but yes, there had been those times.

He continued, "I have not walked in the

sunlight for many centuries and there have been times when I have craved the concept but the risk is too great. I would not wish to find the cure would also be my demise. It is better to live in the shadows and because of this your leaders allow us to live in peace. They accept we will not interfere that we take certain people like yourself. Of course they also know if anything should happen to one of us…" He left the threat hanging.

"Was that why you had to go and be there when the older vampire woke up?" she asked.

"Yes, the old ones do not care much for the world. They wish only to feed and sleep. We make sure their feeding impacts as little as possible, hiding the results if we can not get there in time."

Tina shivered, thinking of some ancient body covered in dust emerging to feed. The fire settled into a pile of embers and ash, the expiration of something warm and living. Kalmár ran his fingers down her neck and brushed them under the edge of her scarf, they were like icicles in the cold night. She waited for him to ask, she had no option to refuse him here, there wasn't any way back to the castle without him. It must have shown on her face for he smiled and stopped.

"Come Little Mouse, we will go home. The past has gone and there are some choices you can not fight against. Your efforts to rebel are like drops of water against a stone, you will surrender yourself to me at some point." He pulled her up with him and wrapped his arms around her ready to pick her up. Tina bristled at his easy arrogance, no way would she let him get away with those remarks.

"Actually," she pointed out as she tapped his chest with a finger, "waves erode cliffs, they crumble them constantly. So maybe you should be the one who thinks about surrendering."

She made him laugh. Kalmár took her hand, turning it to kiss the inside of her wrist. "You are welcome to try and make me Little Mouse."

He picked her up and she buried her face back in his shoulder, she didn't want to see the point where he walked off the precipice. She would have to trust he wouldn't drop her.

Chapter 11

The next evening she found her door locked when she woke from her nap. She turned and kicked it hard. It echoed satisfyingly in the corridor, expressing her disgust. The nights had started to draw in, Kalmár woke earlier and demanded more attention from them both. She took naps day and night to compensate. Wolfie simply slept in most mornings. Tina was sprawled across her bed reading when the lock clicked.

The Count stood in the doorway, as usual he was dressed beautifully. "Tonight you have two choices. You may either stay here in your room or you may come downstairs. I have some musicians visiting that I have an interest in. They will play and we will listen. If you care to come then I expect no indication that you are not here of your own free will." She stared and nodded.

"They do not speak English well, that is not the point." Kalmár pointed at the candle lantern on her chest, she still used it on occasions. "Do not imagine I can not stop people from talking. Do you understand?" The wick spluttered, catching light as Tina went cold.

He smiled, "Humans travel in such combustible vehicles without thinking of the dangers." Yeah thought Tina, dangers like your local vampire taking offence at you. Remembering her own 'death' she didn't need much imagination to think of the musician's car running off the road and catching light. "Would you care to come?" Muted by the demonstration Tina nodded again.

He opened the door for her and escorted her one of the rooms they rarely used. It was smaller than the library, chairs and a long table at one end and the musicians setting up at the other. People - she hadn't seen anyone else apart from Kalmár and Wolfie for a number of months. Tina stared greedily at them, noticed the Count watching and tried to stop. What would he do if she tried to talk with them, what could he do? He had a ruthless streak and they looked nice, she didn't want anything to happen.

She squeezed her eyes shut and sat in the chair the Count had indicated. Wolfie bustled around the musicians, sorting out drinks and speaking to them in their own language. They were all at ease with each other, Tina bit her lip in envy. She noticed them sneaking looks at her and the Count and wondered what they made of them. She twisted her legs underneath her to hide her bare feet and keep them warm.

Wolfie bounded up, they were ready. He sat, waiting with relish. The violinist said a few words and they began. Tina was transported to another world, she listened with her hands over her mouth in delight, the music was sublime. She recognised it vaguely as Eastern European but no more. The Count applauded and made comments, Wolfie was enthusiastic. When they looked towards her for approval, she smiled and clapped. She watched the violinist, she'd played viola for years before she'd gone to university. Seeing him play made her miss the instrument under her fingers. She'd stopped lessons during her exams and not gone back to it except for a few brief moments. It must be at her parents' house, homesickness rolled over her.

The musicians played for several hours. Tina could tell Kalmár was pleased, he was charming, playing the gracious host both to her and the musicians. He quietly translated some of the comments made during the introduction to each song. He noticed her staring at the violinist and asked why. She reluctantly told him and he called the violinist over. The musician nodded at her nervously and listened to the Count. He went back to his bags and brought out another case, opened it on the table.

He offered a viola to her, "Please," he said.

Tina thought about refusing, it wasn't her instrument and then fingers itching, she couldn't resist. She sat up, tucked it under her chin and shyly tried a few notes. They fell under her fingers as though she'd never stopped playing. The violinist nodded again, encouraging her. Memories of playing a simple klezmer piece rose into her mind, she tried the notes in her head first then quietly started to play. It didn't come out as well as she remembered but they came out correctly. She stopped unable to remember any more.

The musician laughed and said something incomprehensible. Picking up his violin he leant against the table and played the tune back to her once and then slower with her. They played through several times and he improvised carefully around her. When they came to the end, everyone clapped as she gave the viola back flushing. Glancing at the Count she saw him look on with approval.

The evening ended far too quickly, the musicians were waved out with much joking and laughter from Wolfie. When he came back, he told her that she should have said she played an instrument. He played the piano in the dining room, she should join in with him. He mostly played in the winter when there wasn't anything else to do.

The castle felt empty when the musicians had left, she felt torn. She thought about Kalmár's offer, the chance to go out, to see people and socialise. She hadn't realised how much she missed it. All she had to do was swear herself, nothing much – only body and soul. She'd seen what it had cost Wolfie, was it worth it? All this could be hers. The Count could afford a lot and he would most likely pay for anything she'd ask for. A very long life of luxury, doing anything she wanted. Knowledge, protection, power, money, a powerful cocktail. It was becoming difficult to hold out against him especially since he'd started to be charming, a fascinating side to his personality. She saw Jo's face on the other side of this, it was getting fainter. She wanted Jo desperately, the feel of her small body hugging her hard, her voice asking questions constantly. She didn't notice Kalmár watching her and correctly guessing the reasons for her quietness.

She went to have her nap feeing miserable and nothing apart from the usual change in atmosphere, disturbed her until morning. Tina wandered over to check her door to see if it was locked. It wasn't, she yawned as she walked down the corridor to the kitchen. No Wolfie and not in his bedroom either.

Curiosity sparked as she tried some more doors, Wolfie wasn't normally this careless. The front door opened to her surprise and the door to the stables had been left ajar. There was no sign of the Rolls Royce, the other car was inside, a sleek blue BMW. Tina walked round to the gatehouse and pulled at the big door. She stared at the wide view as it opened and her brain stumbled to think through the unexpected.

She almost ran down the road and had to stop herself, for some reason the prison had been opened, she had to plan past getting out this time. Checking the time in the kitchen she found it was past eleven, there was no point in walking she'd be in the same position as last time. The door was open to the corridor that led to the study. She began to smell a very large rat - no way Wolfie would do this without the Count's permission and her stomach tightened as the study door opened. The computers were switched off as usual and when she checked, most of the drawers were locked. One drawer did slide open, she was almost unsurprised to find it contained money and the keys to the BMW.

Under the keys she saw a small dark red booklet, the shape familiar. It was a Romanian passport, she opened it and felt a chill down her back. Her face was inside and her name. No, not her name, she peered at the tiny writing and found it said Christiana Johansen. Under the passport she found a driving license, again a photo of her and a scrawl that looked like her signature. Where had Kalmár got these and when? She remembered him saying he knew the right people to get things done. Under both of these, were several letters addressed to the name on the passport. They'd been opened and one contained a bank card, the other a pin number. She didn't recognise the name of the bank.

Tina turned and ran her fingers across the map on the wall and found Romania. The castle must be somewhere in the mountain region. No chance of finding it, there were too many mountains and the map wasn't detailed enough. No doubt both Wolfie and Kalmár knew where they were. She sat in the chair for a while, her head spinning as she tried to think. Her stomach growled and she swept the documents up, she'd think about it over lunch.

She sat and ate on the front steps, gazing at the view while she considered what to do. Should she take this opportunity? It had obviously been arranged but why? Autumn had come and winter would arrive shortly. She knew she couldn't last the winter here without giving in. Kalmár had increased the charm and he could be immensely charming when he chose to be. A moment's irritation, it had been easier to hold out against him when he'd been unpleasant despite the element of fear. Tina hissed at herself in frustration, it was ridiculous that when freedom was offered, she sat and debated with herself. Had she become so caged? She decided to take the car and documents, escape and work out the rest as she went.

Her decision made, she brushed the crumbs from her lap. The car felt enormous. The steering wheel and gear lever were on the wrong side for her, she'd have to get used to it. As she adjusted the seat as far forwards as it would go, Tina muttered rude things about tall men with long legs. She smothered a grin as she thought about the saying that men who drove big cars compensated for other deficiencies. She knew what Wolfie's response would be – he'd offer to prove her wrong. She wondered what the Count would have to say and her eyes grew bigger at the puerile thought of asking and sniggered again.

Tina took a deep breath and started the engine. Slowly she drove out of the courtyard, it was tight getting through the gatehouse. The road felt narrow and she reminded herself that she had to drive on the right hand side. It was a powerful engine, smooth and quiet, a joy to drive, very different from the tiny car she'd owned before. She had to drive slowly both for the road and for herself, it was no fun driving in bare feet.

The gates at the car park were locked. She found another key on the keyring. Fumbling at the padlock, she felt exposed out of the car and wary at the space around her. Tina recognised all the corners she'd walked the first time, the lakes at the bottom and the road to the abandoned village. She reached the main road in no time, sighing with relief at not bumping into Wolfie.

Tina watched the traffic for a while as it buzzed past, dizzy even with that small number of cars and then allowed herself to be swept into the long line of humanity. There was no sat-nav, she regretted not taking note of the names on the map in the study, but it hadn't been very detailed. Never mind she'd guess and she might recognise a name if she was lucky. She put the radio on and hummed along to it, delighted to be driving.

There were no names she recognised that afternoon and she couldn't read the road signs. The countryside was rural, the mountains hulked behind the foothills and the scents of autumn wafted in through the open windows. She found herself driving slower, dawdling as she gazed at the fields full of golden stubble, the houses whitewashed and red roofed. It was beautiful in the autumn sunshine. Her eye was caught by a field of cabbages, the huge purple tipped leaves and she slowed again, then jumped as a car over-took. She had to concentrate, she could fall in love with this place if she wasn't careful.

Keeping an eye on the mileage, she filled the car up with petrol and shopped at the petrol station, swallowing her panic at being away from the familiar enclosed surroundings. She bought snacks and a local map and was surprised and embarrassed at how well the girl serving spoke English. She managed to play the daft tourist and despite the strange looks discovered she'd gone the wrong way for the larger towns. If she went back in the other direction, she wouldn't be very far away by nightfall. She decided to keep going in the same direction to cover more distance and told herself off for dawdling.

Tina found a shop in a village selling shoes.

Again she had peculiar looks as she bought a pair of trainers, having arrived with no shoes and driving an expensive car. She shrugged the looks off with a vague smile, everything happening so fast in comparison to the slow life she'd become used to. Her feet felt constricted wearing shoes after the months barefoot. She considered going to the police and discarded the idea. After finding the passport and driving license, she wasn't sure how much influence the Count had and this close to where he lived, they might just hand her back. She decided to drive as far as possible, over the border if she could. They might listen to her further away, she might be able to contact an embassy and get help.

At five she decided to stop. Tina wanted to be in a safe place before night fell, somewhere with lots of people around her and food. She'd seen basic hotels on the road. Stopping at a small town, she saw a place that looked reasonable and decided to stay, a café close by served food.

Tina asked for a room and an older woman in her fifties showed her to it. She felt embarrassed and shy at her inability to say please or thank you in the woman's own language. She paid in the Count's cash and signed in under the false name.

In the café she looked at the menu and found to her relief most items had a description underneath in English. Thankfully they appeared well set up for tourists so her appearance wasn't commented on. Eating slowly, she watched the people around her with equal enjoyment. She had a sense of disconnection to the real world. So much to see and watch, the TV chattering in the background, various people arriving and leaving. The lights were bright, the colours sharp and clean, everything loud in comparison to the castle. Through the window she could see the car drawing a lot of attention, thank goodness she hadn't taken the Rolls. Finishing her meal, she walked back to the hotel. A young man in his late teens sat at the reception desk. He grunted and waved her in with a brief look, immersed in his book.

It grew dusky outside as Tina gazed through the window. Alone and out of the castle, away from the vampires that lusted after her. She shut the curtains and excitedly looked at the map, working out how far she had to drive tomorrow to reach to the border, how far to the next city. She rehearsed her story, aware the truth would sound fantastical to most people. She decided to keep it simple and not mention vampires or blood sucking and say she'd been kidnapped and not seen their faces.

Tina was desperate to ring home and talk to her family. She'd have to wait - they wouldn't believe she was alive until they saw her in the flesh. She imagined going home, seeing her family, their reactions and normality. Out of habit and the long day driving she curled up on the bed and fell asleep dreaming of tomorrow.

Chapter 12

Through the gap in the curtains, the sky was completely dark and the clock showed after midnight. Tina strained all her senses, she must be imagining things as a familiar uneasiness crept over her. It couldn't be the Count not this soon, it would take hours for him to reach here. She lay on the bed trying to work out what had woken her as she watched the luminous numbers change in the dark room.

The feeling grew stronger. She heard a faint tinkle downstairs, it sounded like a glass being dropped and she started to sweat. Surely the saying about a vampire not being able to come in without an invitation was true, wasn't it? Kalmár had never mentioned it.

Sliding off the bed, she wriggled her trainers on, padded across the floor and slipped the chain onto the locked door. She tucked her documents into a pocket, she hadn't undressed earlier, so at least she didn't have to find her clothes in the dark. Tina quietly walked over to the window and peeped out through the gap in the curtains to the car park. Everything was still in the orange lighting, the BMW in its space below. It felt dreamlike, so quiet and peaceful. Still aware of the uneasiness she rubbed her arms and tried to work out where they were. Her room was on the first floor, she could open the window and let herself down if she was careful. She had the keys in her pocket, she might be able to sneak out.

A flicker caught her eye as Tina decided to move the curtains. There was a movement in the shadows, someone was watching her window. She remembered Kalmár's words. They'd been watching her, they'd known where she was. Sweat trickled down her back. How the hell could she get out and what could she do even if she did manage to get to her car? She could only drive so far before she'd need to stop and rest. If they had a car, they'd keep up with her, it would be like a game for them. She began to realise that getting out of the castle and away from the Count would be the start of her problems, not the end.

The knock on her door made her jump, stopping her deliberations. She froze and stared at it. The knock came again louder this time. Her breath came faster close to panicking.

A voice came from behind the door. "Come out, come out Little Mouse or my new friend here will suffer the consequences." She thought she recognised the voice, Vinceti. He was the only person who knew of her nickname from Kalmár. She heard a slight scuffle and a whimper. Tina remembered the youth from behind the reception desk and feeling sick moved towards the door. She unlocked it and looked through the gap left by the chain.

In front of Vinceti was the young man, his arm twisted behind his back and a gun held under his chin. Vinceti grinned, all his teeth showing. She stared, the Count kept his fangs covered when they were extended. Vinceti's fangs looked huge.

"Come and play Little Mouse. You don't want our friend to get hurt, do you?" Tina hesitated, she knew it was a ploy to get her to come quietly. If Vinceti used the gun, people would hear it and come running. On the other hand, if he used the gun then the youth in front of her would die. Vinceti twisted the arm further and wiggled the gun. "Come out.

Now." His voice became sharper.

The youth stared at her terrified. She couldn't do this, couldn't leave him to die in front of her. Tina made her decision knowing it would make no difference to his fate, they would both die and him faster than her. With shaking hands she undid the chain and as though in a dream she stepped out of the room. She followed Vinceti's instructions to the car park. The figure from the shadows joined them, another vampire. A truck waited for them, someone in the driver's seat. Vinceti held the gun pointed in Tina's direction as they got in. The young man whimpered in the corner, his face white with fear and Tina remembered the horrible feeling of the cold hands. He wouldn't respond to any form of soothing from her so she settled for sitting between him and Vinceti. She glowered at Vinceti, refusing to show her own fear.

All the vampires kept turning and staring at her. She shivered with the itchy feel of their hunger. She licked her lips trying to get some moisture into her mouth, "His Excellency won't be very happy with you Vinceti."

He snorted. "His Excellency isn't here," he mimicked back. "He can't come into where we're going, not without an invitation. It's ours and besides his Excellency wouldn't have let you out on your own. I can tell you're not sworn to him, you're fair game for anyone."

So she had been right about the need to be invited. "How did you get into the hotel then?" She put as much uppityness into her voice as she could, trying to hide the fact that Vinceti was right about her being here without permission.

One of the other vampires laughed and said in accented English, "Vinceti has a passport."

Vinceti waved the gun at her. "It's amazing

the invitations you get when you have the right passport." Tina fell silent. The reception desk had been opposite the front door, it would have been easy to point the gun and demand to be invited in.

They drove for several hours along the main road then turned off and up a rutted track. Trees were picked out by the headlights and they reached a solitary farmhouse. They stopped and got out. The young man with terror clear in his face, ran the minute the door opened. Vinceti had kept hold of her, she was the one he really wanted.

Tina thought for a moment the lad might make it when she saw Vinceti raise his arm. The gun went off with a sharp crack, loud in the night and the lad fell to the ground with a cry. She saw his face white in the light of the car headlamps, his face twisting in disbelief and pain. Unable to move, she stood in shock. One of the vampires snatched at his arm as he clutched it. He was picked up and thrown against the wall of the house. The other vampire moved in and they fed.

She retched at the sight, held up by Vinceti who watched intently. Tina could hear him breathing harshly in her ear. They finished and the lad was carried away, his neck wilting like a flower under the weight of his head.

Vinceti twisted Tina's arm. "Come on, inside."

She struggled trying to get free - he wouldn't use the gun on her. Even one-handed Vinceti, was stronger than she was, it didn't stop her attempting to make it difficult for him. Vinceti tucked the gun into the back of his trousers and the other vampire helped pick her up. They took her into the farmhouse kitchen and tied her arms one to each leg of a table, the bulges in its legs preventing the ropes from sliding. The second vampire came in and leant against the kitchen wall, watching in fascination.

Tina shook, angry at herself for getting into this situation and frightened at what was to come. Vinceti straddled her legs stopping her from kicking out at him.

"Now," he said softly and she froze as he stroked her face. "We are going to have some fun together. I've been looking forward to this, do you remember how I said you smelt so sweet? Maybe in a few days I will let Tangent know I have you but for the moment this will be your home. Now you are going to give me some of that sweetness."

He grabbed her chin, forced her head up to expose her neck, ripped her shirt out of the way and bit down hard. She started to whimper and swallowed it, forcing herself to stay quiet. Through the pain she felt something touch her arms, her sleeves were being pulled back. In horror she realised that the others intended to feed too. A few days of this and she wouldn't be in a fit state for anyone. Stabs of pain came from elsewhere and she slumped, allowing her mind to drift away from reality.

They left her at dawn, tied to the table and half fainting from blood loss. She stared at the light coming in through the open windows, at the checked curtains flapping in the breeze, and at the other items of normality sitting on the worktops. The light gave a halo around everything. No point in yelling for help, they'd chosen the place well, it was off the beaten track and away from the main road. She wondered who had owned it and what had happened to them. It didn't look as though it had been abandoned for long.

Tina was thirsty. They'd given her some water but not enough. Paradoxically she also needed a wee.

Eventually she gave up holding her bladder as one less thing to think about. Her nose wrinkled at the smell and hoped it would put them off, though she doubted it. She'd had no food since the previous evening and her stomach felt as though it was starting to meet her backbone.

Her head swung, she had nowhere to rest it, the edge of the table was too high. She could rock the table but had no chance of moving it, her arms felt like spaghetti. The ropes were tied behind her bracelets and she couldn't slide them off. Tina tried to jack her knees up attempting to rest her head on them, but she couldn't crunch up enough and they kept sliding on the floor. She slumped her head onto her chest and breathed in her rank smell.

She dozed off and woke with thirst burning in her throat. They didn't have the experience to deal with her. Didn't they care that she wouldn't last like this or had they forgotten what it felt like? Tina could smell the cool dampness, tormenting her from the woods outside. She had half her buttons missing from Vinceti ripping her shirt and the breeze coming through the open window chilled her, goose bumps covering her exposed skin.

Her hands and wrists were in agony, puffy from the blood pooling and they ached from holding her up while she'd slept. She moved her fingers trying to get the blood flowing and pins and needles added to her discomfort. Tina wriggled round, stretching as she tried to take the kink out of her back, her jeans chaffing from the urine. She dozed intermittently through the day. The sun swung around to shine through the window during the afternoon, torturing her further. Squinting through it, she had no way to move away, no way to shield her eyes.

She was thankful when the sun dipped below

the trees and the coolness of the evening came through. As the sun disappeared the vampires came back. One of them noticing the state she was in, held a cup of water to her lips. She drank, trying not to gulp, slopping some of it down her. The vampire untied the ropes and Vinceti snarled at him to stop. He replied in a language Tina didn't understand and continued. She thumped onto the floor unable to move, her arms aching from being held up for so long. To her surprise he began to massage her wrists and muttered at the pain. Any vague thoughts she'd entertained of escape disappeared, she was too weak and stiff to run.

Vinceti dragged her out from under the table by her ankles and straddled her, cuffing away the other vampire. He pulled her up by her shirt and sank his fangs in. Her arms and legs felt leaden, the water had helped moisten her mouth and tongue but not enough for her body. A low call from the other vampire and Tina whimpered as Vinceti let go, dropping her back onto the floor. She saw him snarl as he shifted off her legs. His canines showing, her blood trickling down his chin and beyond a familiar figure stood in the open doorway.

"You can't come in," Vinceti's voice was loud in the stillness, "You don't have permission." The figure said nothing. The others drew away, her wounds slowed to a trickle and stopped. She watched everything with the passive fascination of a drunkard.

The silhouette put his hands up, fingers splayed as though feeling for some unseen barrier. Slowly as though walking through treacle, he stepped in over the threshold. Tina squinted as he came into the light and it reflected off the angles of his face. She noticed a thin line of black appear from his left eye and ooze down, it was joined by another on the other side. Kalmár took another step and something began to seep from his nose. Vinceti watched with horror with his mouth open, clearly he'd not anticipated this. He fumbled for his gun. It galvanised her into action, Tina kicked out, hitting him in the small of the back. Her kick didn't have the strength needed to hurt but it spoilt his hand reaching. At the same time she whispered, "Come in... welcome," to the Count and hoped it would work.

As though shifting into a different gear, Kalmár slammed a fist into Vinceti's stomach faster than she could follow. The gun skittered onto the floor and Vinceti curled up choking. The other vampires gave no resistance, immediately giving in. The one who had untied her sank to his knees, offering his throat in surrender. They were ignored as unworthy of attention as the Count kicked the gun out the way. He gave Tina more water and checked her wounds, his cool fingers gentle.

He said nothing as he carried her to the car, put her on the back seat and returned to the house. She drifted off no longer caring what happened to her. Kalmár had come, she would be safe. The bump of the car along the track and the sound of the engine lulled her into proper sleep.

At some point she came back into consciousness. The Count drove fast, overtaking any traffic, his fingers tapping impatiently on the steering wheel. The car suited him she thought drunkenly, big, powerful, smooth... He spoke into his phone while he drove, she didn't understand any of the words, they all ran into one another. One of the shoulders of his jacket had been torn and she watched it in weary fascination, the white shirt showing in the gap underneath. A movement caught her eye. Vinceti sat in the front seat, hunched up and cowed. The threat of Vinceti was unimportant with the Count around, she slept and the miles sped by.

It came close to dawn when she woke again, the car drove up the final curves to the castle. She could see it as a blacker silhouette against the lightening sky. The Count stopped outside the gatehouse. Wolfie had been waiting for them, he pulled the door open and got Tina out, wincing at the state of her. He wrapped his arms around her, supporting a good chunk of her weight. The Count opened the passenger door where Vinceti sat. He grabbed Vinceti and dragged him towards the gatehouse.

"What shall it be?" the Count asked, with no threat or malice apparent, his voice almost conversational. "Shall I take you inside and throw you off the tower roof?" Vinceti gaped at him in terror and was grabbed by the throat. "Or perhaps you prefer to be invited in before I do so? Hmm?" With a dispassionate stare Kalmár shifted him backwards into the shadow of the gatehouse.

Wolfie and Tina watched in a horrified fascination as the younger vampire flattened against an unseen barrier, his feet kicking against nothing and pinned there by the Count's hand. Kalmár pushed gently and Vinceti began to whimper, his arms and legs trembling. A further push and blood ran down from his nose, trickling out of his eyes and ears. He clutched at the Count's arm and couldn't move it, held in the iron pincer grip. He began to panic, the breath whistling out of him as he was pushed further in. He managed to stammer words, apologies, pleading and his eyes rolled up to show the whites.

The Count leant towards him and said clearly, "You may come in and welcome." Vinceti flopped, boneless in the Count's grip, the barrier gone. He was dragged through the gatehouse and up the steps like a rag doll.

Wolfie turned to Tina, "Come on, we don't want to be around here when he's dropped." He helped her through the outer courtyard. "Do you want food first or a bath?"

"Bath, drink and then food," Tina said. She was starving, shaking with hunger but wanted to wash away the feeling of the last few nights more, to scrub away everything that had happened. Wolfie helped her up the stairs to the bathroom.

"I'll get you to tell me everything that happened tomorrow but why did you go? Didn't you think you'd get caught?" Tina shook her head not wanting to talk. "Tell me tomorrow," Wolfie repeated. "I'll need to get the car in. Think you can sort yourself out?" She nodded and he gave her a last squeeze before heading back down the hall.

Tina drank pints of water from the tap first and washed herself thoroughly. Wolfie had left clean clothes in the bathroom and her head was reeling by the time she'd finished dressing. She leaned on the door frame as she came out and heard the Count speak to Wolfie further down the corridor.

"...bounced a few times and stopped. He crawled off afterwards. If he is fortunate, he will find a soft patch of earth to dig into before dawn, if not..." He shrugged, his torn jacket gaping.

The Count turned and came to pick Tina up. He'd not wiped his face and the flaking blood streaks gave him the look of a malevolent Pierrot. "Those bites will need attending to," Kalmár told her shortly. He put her on the bed and sat next to her, "This may hurt a little."

She felt him gently bite at the wounds in her neck and then licking, pushing his saliva into them.

It didn't hurt much through her haze of exhaustion. It was strange, despite the macabre element of him reopening the wounds, it made Tina feel cared for. He checked her arms and legs, giving the bites he found the same treatment. Wolfie in the meantime had brought food and drink and was intent in getting as much down her as he could. The Count said his goodnight as tersely as the rest of his conversation had been and left as dawn approached.

All the attention had exhausted her and when Wolfie tucked her up and made to leave, she held onto his hand, not wanting to be left alone. When Tina asked him to stay, Wolfie smiled and lay on top of the covers next to her.

He tapped her nose. "Sleep now, I'm here."

Chapter 13

She woke with a heavy weight across her waist and something pressing against the back of her neck. Wolfie had tucked himself around her during the night. His breath was warm and gently stirred her hair, his arm wrapped tight around her waist. She lay for a while, enjoying the sensation and finally with reluctance, had to shift and disturb him. He rubbed his nose against her collar, rolled over onto his back and sneezed.

Tina wriggled over smiling. Wolfie smiled back, reached out and tucked a strand of hair behind her ear then pulled her close, kissing her. "I'm pleased you're safe. I worried about you." His arms felt good, she cuddled up in them safe in the daylight. She winced as the muscles in her back and arms protested. "What's up?"

"I ache, Vinceti tied me up and left me all day." With prompting, she talked Wolfie through the last twenty four hours. "I think the worst thing is that he died and was left somewhere alone as though he was rubbish. It was my fault, wasn't anything to do with him." Tears came as she remembered the lad lying against the wall.

"That lad'll be fine." She frowned, confused at the unexpected heartlessness. "He'd just fainted. His Excellency told me they'd dumped him in a back room. One of them had even bandaged him up." Tina realised he would have heard her if she'd shouted, they might have helped each other. She'd assumed no one else had been around.

Wolfie continued, "Anyway I contacted the authorities and they will have told the police. He'll

160

be in hospital by now. They'll have thought of an excuse for him being there, he won't remember much."

Tina was relieved, she'd felt responsible for him being picked up. "What about the other vampires?"

"They've been told to leave the area, they won't want any more attention paid to them at the moment." He shifted, "I wanted to come last night you know. He wouldn't let me, he said he didn't want two to protect. I spent most of my time here, hanging around waiting for news."

"Where were you yesterday morning?" She lay on her back with his arm around her.

Wolfie grinned, "In the trees by the village. I watched the road for most of the morning, daren't move away in case I missed you go past." His face turned wistful, "You looked happy."

"Whose idea was it to leave the castle open?"

"Not mine. Although I knew you don't want to be here."

She pressed him, "Did you suggest it? Did you know what might happen?"

"You know me, just following orders." Wolfie looked uncomfortable, "I don't have much choice in certain things. But yes, I did know what might happen and I hoped it wouldn't. I wanted you to be able to get home and be happy for a while. He followed you at night you know, that's why he got to you so quickly."

"You mean if I had managed to get home, he would have left me?"

He shrugged, "I don't know. I don't try to second guess him, I've learnt that much over the years."

"What about Vinceti? I remember something about him being thrown off the tower? That wouldn't

161

do anything would it? He'd levitate like the Count, wouldn't he?"

Wolfie chuckled, "Vinceti's not strong enough to hold himself in the air. His Excellency was pretty fed up with him and was looking forward to teaching him a lesson. It could have been off the tower roof plus a few hundred feet. I didn't ask."

Tina rested and took it easy for most of the day. When she got up, she found the bracelets on her bedside table. She'd not remembered him taking them off, they'd been locked shut the join barely showing.

She came into the kitchen for company and Wolfie kept her topped up with food and drink. It felt strange walking around the castle with shoes on for the first time. She noticed a number of doors had been left open, the study was locked when she checked.

By late afternoon she felt surprisingly good, the scabs on her arms and neck itching and flaking. Wolfie came to find her. "The BMW's at the top car park, near the gates," he told her. "The truck can't get any further, it can't turn around up here. Do you think you can come and help me pick it up?"

"Aren't you worried I'll drive off?"

Wolfie stared at her in disbelief. "After last night, you want to do that again?" Tina shrugged, he did have a point.

Wolfie drove them down to the car park in the big silver car. He rolled his eyes when she asked him about it, saying the Count refused to get rid of it, that he liked driving it. He told her it had been built in 1955 and the back seat had been designed to allow for a compartment underneath so the Count could rest inside during the day while Wolfie drove. It had to be taken to a specialist garage, miles away to be serviced. They had the BMW as back up and as a more discrete car, people tended to notice when they went past otherwise.

"It's fabulous to drive though. Fancy taking her for a spin yourself sometime?" Tina nodded enthusiastically.

He pointed out various landmarks and chatted whilst he drove. Wolfie stopped the car while he pointed out the view, leant over and kissed her with a grin. He teased her about spending the night with him, promising her more than a lazy day in bed the next time it happened. She laughed, he couldn't possibly be that good. He refused to answer, simply looked smug as he started driving again.

The truck had unloaded the BMW by the time they'd arrived and the men waited to be paid. Tina stood in the autumn sunshine and gazed at the beech trees in their reds and golds, the carpet of leaves underneath, feeling lighter and more content than she had done for months. The last few nights felt a million miles away, she daren't think about the reason why they'd happened.

"Bloody hell." The truck drove off and Wolfie, rubbing his hands through his hair, looked at the open driver side door of the BMW. He pointed to the seat pushed as far forward as it would go. "Has a midget been driving this or what?" Tina snorted and shoved him aside, the set of keys still in her pocket. She followed him up the road and parked inside the castle.

When dusk came, she went downstairs feeling nervous. The Count sat in the library, he greeted her and she curled up on the couch.

"Thank you for last night," she tried. He grunted and carried on with his reading. An edge of irritation ran through her, he wasn't going to make this easy. "All of the doors are open," she said quietly.

"Yes." He put his book to one side and leaned towards Tina, his glasses dangling from one hand. "The doors are open. I decided you would not stop attempting to escape until you realised it is futile so I am giving you choices. I require one promise that is non-negotiable, that you will not tell anyone about us. If you escape and start to talk then those you care about will suffer, the people you have told will suffer and so will you. Do you understand?"

His voice was mild in his threat and Tina nodded, she had no doubt he would do as he'd said. Unsure of what he might demand next, she asked, "You say I have choices?"

"Yes. Within these castle walls, you are under my protection. No-one may enter or threaten you here and you may carry on as you have previously. You may not leave these walls without my permission and if you do, I will not help you. You will have to deal with any consequences yourself." Fair enough, he didn't want to chase around the countryside after her and if she was honest with herself, last night had given her enough of a taste of what her life could be like.

"Should you wish to swear body and soul to me as Wolf has, you will have the same freedom and privileges as Wolf. You will be able to leave the castle. As one who is sworn to me, few will dare to threaten you."

Kalmár waited patiently while she thought. Wolfie went out a lot, seeing his girlfriend and coming back with a smile on his face. He was bouncing around, planning things and enjoying himself. She had to admit her jealousy but she'd also seen Wolfie not be able to say or do certain things or have to do things he didn't want to. He coped with the strictures but she wasn't so relaxed. She struggled between wanting her freedom and needing to get out of the castle and see other people. Tina finally shook her head, she couldn't give someone so much power over her.

The Count continued, "If you wish to go to another vampire?" He raised his eyebrows and looked amused as Tina shuddered, shaking her head violently. That was unthinkable, no way would she go to another vampire after Vinceti. The thought made her blood run cold, he'd treated her as dinner. She didn't want another vampire to bite her, the one she had was bad enough. At least the Count was partly house trained, she smothered a snort - she'd got him to ask nicely before he fed.

"The last option I have is that you may go back to your family." Tina stared at him, after all this time? "I will take you back and deal with the authorities. What you choose to say to your family is your business so long as you do not disclose my presence." He leaned back in his chair. "There will be difficulties, you will not be under my protection. You will be vulnerable to others but if you would wish this?"

Tina's head whirled. To go back to her family, to be with the people she loved and who loved her in return, back to her old life, it beckoned seductively. She saw the Count watching her assessing her reactions and asked, "But I might be taken again, by someone else?"

"Yes. It would most likely be Lord Tangent. You live on his territory."

She rubbed her face thinking hard. No protection from other vampires. She could be home for a day, a week or a month and get snatched again. Her family would be devastated and she might end up in a worse situation and what if her family were used as bait? Tina couldn't cope with the thought of Jo being threatened. She'd be on edge every night, waking at every sound. Could she put her family through that? Being unable to talk to them properly about why she couldn't go out at night. Wolfie had refused to talk much about Lord Tangent, she'd come to her own conclusions based on Vinceti. Kalmár could be ruthless enough when he wanted to be, she didn't want to find out about anyone worse.

"There is one other difficulty you need to be aware of." Tina looked up warily. "Your body is now attuned to ours. It needs us as much as we desire it. The infection you have will alter if you avoid contact from us. You have felt the first stages of the illness, the end result is terminal." She looked away, unable to cope and unsure if she could see sympathy in his eyes.

"How long?" she whispered.

"I can not say. It depends on the individual. Judging by how your body has reacted to the infection so far, I would suggest you would have less time than most. Maybe six months."

Her hopes collapsed. If she went home, she'd die and painfully if it happened in a similar way to the last illness. Tina accused herself of every form of cowardice as she began to let go of seeing her family again. It hurt. She wasn't brave enough to go back and die. She'd had dreams about them, seeing their faces excited at her return, now she saw them gathered around her while she lay on her bed dying. She couldn't do it.

"You do not need to make a decision now, you may have as much time as you require." His voice was soft.

Tina shook her head, rubbing her eyes, "I can't go home and I can't swear myself to you."

"Then you may stay here, under my

166

protection." She nodded and he left her staring into the fire.

Chapter 14

The next day she wandered the castle listlessly and found her way through to the small courtyard. Tiny in comparison to the other one, it had a large wooden door in one side opening onto a tunnel running through the castle and to the outside. She found an iron gate on the far side, the postern she'd been looking for. A key hung on a nail, Tina opened the gate and went through. The drop looked horrendous by the side of the castle and the square towers blocked the way to the road. Tina didn't try to look over the edge, she was no longer desperate to escape. As she went back through, she saw small holes in the sides and ceiling of the tunnel – murder holes.

With a candle lantern she explored the rooms surrounding the courtyard, a few rooms she found locked, others were stacked high with boxes and books. Rooms with microscopes, scientific and astronomical equipment, other things she couldn't even put a name to. All dusty and untouched in years.

Wolfie jumped as she found him in the study fiddling with one of the computers, he'd not indulged himself during the day like this for months. She asked him about all the equipment she'd found. He told her they were from various projects of the Count's over the years, they'd been boxed up and left after he'd lost interest.

"What's his current project?"

Wolfie gave an evil grin. "Not managed to guess yet?" Tina folded her arms and glowered at him. He laughed, waved a finger in her direction and said, "It's you." She rolled her eyes and still laughing, he pointed her in the direction of a large pile of boxes in another room. Tina had to chuckle when she opened them and found all the things she'd ordered over the previous months and assumed Kalmár hadn't sent for. She counted at least ten pairs of shoes and boots.

Tina put some walking boots on and went outside, the stiff leather feeling strange to her tough soles. Wrapped against the cool winds coming off the mountains she sat outside the gatehouse in the sun, to make the point to herself that she could. Her brain turned itself inside out, Kalmár had let her go, to find out what it was like for herself. Despite what Wolfie had said about other vampires, she hadn't believed him. Tina had thought once she'd got away from the castle, she'd be free and able to go back to her old life.

She didn't like the idea of the Count feeding from her but at least he treated her as a person these days. She knew Kalmár had his own reasons for wanting her and they were nothing to do with what she wanted. Tina wouldn't have blamed him for making her swear herself after the last escape, there were plenty of ways he could make her if he chose to. For reasons of his own he was content to leave her a free agent, he appeared to want her to swear herself of her own free will.

There was now nothing to hold her here apart from herself, it was no longer the Count keeping her prisoner, the ownership of the chains had changed but they were still chains. Tina sighed and rubbed her face, stretching stiffly. She couldn't make a decision. It was all too big at the moment, too raw with the realisation she couldn't do what she wanted. She'd have to think further.

Tina spent several days wandering the castle, no longer sure what to do with herself. She made a determined effort not to allow herself to become depressed again but there was a part of her missing. She took her frustration out on Wolfie during their martial arts sessions, until he cried surrender, laughing at her ferocity.

One late afternoon Wolfie told her to get ready to go out for the evening. Tina blinked in confusion, she wasn't allowed to go outside. He threw a parcel of clothes at her and on inspection they were more refined than the ones she usually slopped around in and she'd not ordered them either. When the Count appeared looking smarter than his usual elegant self, she peered at him. No frayed cuffs or worn elbows this time, he was wearing a newer suit, fitting as perfectly as they always did.

Wolfie jumped in the BMW and drove off to spend the night elsewhere, no doubt with his girlfriend. The Count walked Tina to the Rolls and opened the door for her.

"Where are we going?" she asked.

"Out. You will be safe with me." He refused to say any more as he drove to a larger town she'd managed to miss on her last escape.

They parked in the large square and he took her into the town. He tucked her hand into his elbow and she noticed people looking their way. Tina felt nervous being out at night after her last experience, she had to take a deep breath to steady her nerves and tried to look relaxed.

Kalmár took her into a theatre, where they sat in a box and watched an orchestra play a late night performance. So many people, so much noise, she peered over the edge and drank in the atmosphere like a child at a party. The Count sat back and watched her delight, his own evident as he bought her drinks, chocolates and a rose from the rose seller. The dimmer light hid his pale skin and he looked relaxed and elegant. The lights, colours and noises overwhelmed her having spent so much time in the quiet castle. When Tina's eyes sparkled as she pointed out something to him, he reached over and ran two fingers gently up the side of her neck. She raised her chin, nervous at what he might want. He smiled and took his fingers away in a tacit understanding.

They returned late with Tina's head spinning, so much had happened in comparison to the last few months. The next night was the same. She'd mentioned her hair needed cutting and he took her to a flat where she was treated to a haircut. Kalmár had told her that he would wait in the car a short distance away, there were too many exposing mirrors in the flat.

Delighted at her new look, she stepped out into the night on her own. People walked past her talking and laughing. She watched them and wondered. What would happen if she walked in the other direction, away from the car and towards the train station she'd seen? A shiver went down her spine. She felt a brief moment of dislocation and the faces of the people drained of colour in the street lights. Any one of them could be a vampire, they could snatch her at a moment's notice. Abruptly she no longer felt safe in the night, the panic rising. Someone stopped and asked her a question, they must have seen the look on her face. Shaking her head, she only understood the concerned tone, she tried to smile at them and walked quickly down the street to where she knew the Count waited.

With relief she saw him get out of the car as she approached. He touched her face, tucked her hand into his elbow and walked her to a smoky jazz club. The night relaxed back to normality. Kalmár spared no expense in anything she wanted. For himself, he had a glass of sparkling water in front of him, at times he would raise it to his lips. When he caught Tina's puzzled glance, he admitted he could stomach a tiny amount of water, he liked the bubbles, no more.

He took her out in a similar way the following nights. Tina realised he was courting her and decided she didn't care. It was doing her so much good to be out of the castle and to be around people. The Count delighted in her enjoyment, was old fashioned in his charm and biting in his observations of the people around him. It worked, he'd had hundreds of years to perfect it. The slight edge of fang to his smiles added to his good looks, twisting something inside her, making her flush and look away.

They walked back to the car from the jazz club one evening, talking about the last number they'd heard when Tina became aware of the vampire. She slowed to look around, trying to spot him. As they reached the car, a figure detached itself from some shadows. She shrank back.

Kalmár placed his hand in the small of her back and held her next to him. "You are safe."

Tina looked at the new vampire with fascination, even if she'd seen him, she wouldn't have realised his nature until he came close. He was short, stocky and dressed casually in jeans. His swarthy skin was pale, receding hair clipped short. She dropped her eyes when she noticed him look at her in a similar way and remembered Vinceti saying that he could tell she wasn't sworn. She caught a slight smile on the Count's face, unsworn and outside, nothing to hold her with him. Tina hesitated and deliberately took a step in towards Kalmár and his smile deepened as he wrapped a possessive arm around her waist.

The new vampire's eyes widened and he ducked his head before he began to speak. Not understanding the language Tina only heard the name Vinceti mentioned a few times. The other vampire half-bowed to the Count again and walked off swiftly.

"What was that about?" she asked as they got into the car.

"That was Samsa. I had instructed him to watch Vinceti. He survived his punishment and removed himself from the larger part of my territory last night. Samsa believes he had help. No doubt from Lord Tangent, his patron."

Arriving in the courtyard Kalmár stopped her before they got out of the car. He leaned over and turned her face towards him and asked, "May I?" He hadn't fed from her since before her escape. Memories of Vinceti rose in her mind and she sat on them - his fingers touched her gently.

She nodded and he slid over onto her seat, pulling her into his lap. Tired from the long stimulating night, she put her head on his shoulder and closed her eyes, pushing her thoughts elsewhere. He undid her collar and buried his face in her neck, nuzzling into the right place. Tina whimpered as he bit and relaxed, his scent of dusty rosemary now familiar as Jo's little girl smell. He finished and stayed, licking at the bite marks and stroked the back of her neck softly. Tina realised she had her arms around his neck, one hand idly playing with his hair and she stopped hurriedly.

"You realise if you surrender yourself, it would be far more pleasant for you," he said as he took his handkerchief out.

Tina pulled herself together enough to speak,

"I can't." He shrugged, opened the car door and carried her upstairs.

Chapter 15

The castle was being cleaned, a team of workers had moved in during the day and Tina felt like she was being chased from one room to the next. She'd not seen the castle like this before, curtains were being hoovered, ceilings lost their cobwebs and spiders ran for cover while the floors were swept and washed properly. She discovered that certain rooms like the chapel and study were left as they were and much to her disgust, Wolfie had insisted his own rooms were left in their usual mess.. The castle smelt of the wax used to polish the wood and the bustle almost made her long for the quiet. Tina had arrived too late and found her own room being blitzed, she slid out of the way feeling shy of the loud conversation flowing between the staff.

She was helping Wolfie to make a few rooms habitable in the same corridor as her bedroom, the cleaners had left a few days ago. The accountants were coming Wolfie told her. This happened yearly and triggered the clean although it was normally a smaller portion of the castle. The accountants would come for a few days, sort out any problems and disappear again. It was an old firm dealing with the Count's money, very respectable Wolfie told her. They'd been looking after Kalmár's accounts for as long as Wolfie had been around.

They changed the beds and warmed the mattresses so they wouldn't be cold from storage. Unnerved by having had people around in the previously quiet castle, she asked, "So, they know about him?"

"There's a special branch of the firm, only

those in the branch have any idea of who the Count actually is. I think they deal with others like him as well."

"How does he hide in plain sight? Things like dates of birth and so on, doesn't anyone notice he hasn't died?"

"His records are changed constantly to stay up to date which prevents most people from finding out the truth. You'd be amazed at how little people notice or can persuade themselves that they're seeing a mistake. Those that are of aware him know there are consequences but also that they will be rewarded for good service. They are discreet, they also deal with any extra documentation or paperwork he needs."

"Did they sort out the passport for me and the bank account?"

Wolfie nodded with a grin and continued, "We're going to have fun this year, Mr Silverman his regular accountant is retiring shortly so there's a new man coming with him. He's not come here before. The Count met and approved of him in London a while back - that was his excuse for being in England when he kidnapped you." The reminder of her unforeseen arrival stung and she muttered something rude. Wolfie grinned and threw a pillow at her. "We're going to have to deal with any problems the new accountant might have. It's always hard when they realise what His Excellency is and times have changed fast over the last few years."

Tina agreed absently plumping the pillow and her mood turned wistful as she wondered what Jo would be doing now.

She saw the taxi arriving from the airport in the late afternoon. She felt nervous at meeting them, she'd spent so little time with people over the last year and the Count's new decision to trust her didn't sit easily. Tina felt even more flustered when Wolfie introduced her as Mouse, the Count's nickname not quite feeling right being used by those from the real world. Her newfound shyness at having people in the castle made her ultra-aware of them, they didn't seem to notice. The large American getting out of the taxi first took her hand immediately and introduced himself as Bob Silverman. He was balding and in his sixties. Madame de Berg made Tina feel small and under dressed, being a tall and elegant woman. She radiated intelligence but gave a warm welcome, she dealt with the branch as a whole and had come to keep an eye on procedures she said. Tina wondered if this was anything to do with the third member of the group. Mr Durrant was around Tina's age and she could see him trying to conceal his curiosity as he shook her hand.

The guests freshened up in their rooms and joined them in the dining room where they talked for several hours over dinner and drinks. Wolfie knew the two older visitors well from previous visits, they were curious about Tina but didn't pry into her past. She wondered if they dealt with many people in her situation and what they thought of it. Mr Durrant was easier to read, he kept hesitating when there were gaps in the conversation and then stopping as if reminding himself there were things he'd been told not to speak about. He glanced at his watch frequently as the light faded, obviously expecting the Count to appear. Tina cleared in rotation with Wolfie and she heard Mr Silverman speak quietly to his younger colleague, saying the Count wouldn't be long. He sat up in his chair as he saw Kalmár walk in and stood with the others.

The Count was in a good mood, Tina noticed he had on one of his newer suits with no wear on the elbows or cuffs. He looked elegant, his brown eyes interested and almost flirting with Madame de Berg and she responded in kind. Tina had an unexpected twinge at his behaviour and felt a justified satisfaction as she deliberately adjusted the roll-necked top she was wearing. Kalmár noticed the loathed item of clothing with barely a flicker and publicly ignored it.

Both of the older visitors were at ease with him. Mr Silverman flattered by the old world charm, talked and laughed, the conversation of shared experiences. Mr Durrant was less relaxed, he listened more than talked. Tina watched Kalmár, his grave interest in Mr Durrant as he found out about him and his family slowly warming the younger man to him. They talked until early in the morning, their three guests politely trying to conceal their yawns. The Count offered his elbow to Tina, said his good nights and left with her. Wolfie stayed with their visitors in case they needed anything.

Kalmár took her into the large courtyard. It was a beautiful starlight night with the moon shining full, everything lit up like the day. She leant against a pillar while he stood on the step below.

"You know how I dislike these." He fiddled with her collar, his long fingers brushing her hair.

"Not my problem," she countered. "You bit me last night, I've got to hide the marks somehow, there's been far too many people around recently."

His face twitched in frustration and he casually reached round to the back, ripped the seam open and neatly folded the collar flat. "Much better. Find another way to conceal them." He bent to kiss her neck, his breath cool.

She pushed at his chest laughing. "You were flirting with Madame."

"Jealous?" Amused, his eyes were dark in the

moonlight. They caught hers, and for a moment she felt a frisson between them – was she jealous? She'd never felt that way before. Alone in this castle with her kidnappers she'd been so busy trying to escape that she'd not considered him a man. The last few weeks of his courtship had changed the balance between them and she shook her head.

"Nothing to do with me," she said primly and smothered a yawn, she'd foregone her usual naps in waiting for the visitors. "I'm tired, I'm not used to having all this company."

"The company is good for you and the night is beautiful Little Mouse."

Tina looked up at the stars above them in the clear sky. It felt unreal in her tired state and speaking to new people in the previously quiet castle had been a strange piece of normality. She wondered if the visit had been planned and if she'd have been kept out of the way if she'd not had the consequences of her attempted escape. Her eyes started to close and she felt herself begin to drift off in the moonlit courtyard with him holding her. His whispered question was a part of the night and she nodded sleepily, barely jumping at the sharp pain.

Late next morning she met up with their guests in the dining room. Madame de Berg came down first, she came up to Tina saying, "I hope you do not mind. I bought you a little present." Tina opened a small bag to find a gorgeous silk square and exclaimed in delight as she shook it out. Madame de Burg helped her to roll and wrap it around her shirt collar.

"Count Kalmár, he is so elegant. When I was younger, I wished he would sweep me up and take me away with him." She sighed with mock sorrow and laughed with Tina. "It was not to be. He told us

179

all about you, about how beautiful you are and he was right."

Tina's mouth dropped, she'd never considered herself more than average, she scrubbed up fairly well when she intended to go out but here in jeans and with her hair scruffed back in a pony tail she felt far from that. Despite the warmth from another woman catching her out, she tried to deflect the compliment, "He talked about me?"

"Of course! We asked…" She was interrupted by the other two coming in and smiled, adjusting the scarf. Tina found her manners and invited them to eat, picking at her own breakfast. Mr Silverman talked cheerfully enough for all of them while he ate. Mr Durrant was quieter, he had his phone on the table, he kept picking it up and fiddling with a frown on his face. He gave Tina a deep searching look after he'd finished and wandered off afterwards, phone in hand.

They retired to the smaller room to deal with paperwork, Wolfie had come in yawning and tousled. Mr Durrant checked the computer with a distracted air, "There's no signal, no Wi-Fi."

Tina glanced at Wolfie, not sure how to reply and noticed a shadow of a smile on Mr Silverman's face. She shut her mouth as Wolfie cut in smoothly, "We're in a dead spot here, some peculiarity of the mountains. It's fine ten miles down the road."

Mr Durrant didn't quite snort but he started taking out the files and papers they'd brought, shuffling them and sorting them into order. He was tensely involved with the other two until Tina brought coffee round. He'd been making her nervous with the way he'd been looking at her and she'd noticed the others watching him.

Finally unable to contain himself, he burst out, "How could you let him do that to you? I saw you in the courtyard last night, he had blood on his face, there was blood on your neck." Mr Durrant shook with indignation. "He ripped your top."

Tina swore to herself, nothing like a quick introduction to the Count's nature. She'd not even thought about there being other people around last night, despite knowing Kalmár was well aware of everyone's presence in the castle. He would have known Mr Durrant was watching and must have bitten her deliberately, leaving them to deal with the consequences.

How would she have looked on this before she'd known about vampires? She remembered the first time she'd seen Kalmár bite Wolfie, she'd been transfixed and the darker memory of her first few weeks rose behind it. Tina took a deep breath, hiding her irritation at Kalmár for putting her in this position and said, "Mr Durrant, I am a consenting adult. I believe my private life is my own business. I'm not going to enquire what happens in yours." She daren't look at Wolfie, she could imagine his snort if they'd been talking privately. She took a gulp of her coffee.

Mr Durrant looked shocked, "You mean you don't mind him doing that to you?"

She nearly spat the coffee out. Was he aware of her past? How much did he know about her? Could she actually tell him that she'd been kidnapped against her will? She thought she'd started to accept her place over the last few weeks, knowing that she couldn't be without a vampire re-infecting her and she remembered Kalmár telling her what the consequences of her actions would be if she said anything. Tina forced her voice to work, "Did I look as though I minded? Seeing as you were watching…?" She allowed her voice to trail off.

"Marcus, I offered you this promotion because

I thought you could deal with it," Mr Silverman had watched his younger colleague during the last hour's work and the good natured smile had slowly faded. "The accounts side is easy but we need people who are flexible enough to cope with the Count's nature and that it can be disturbing sometimes. You met his Excellency in London and you were fine with him."

"Yes, I know I met him but that was different, he was charming. I don't think I believed it until now." Tina could well believe him, having seen Kalmár when he wanted something. Frustrated, he asked, "Is he the only vampire? Are there any more?"

"The company deal with a number of similar accounts, in similar circumstances."

"More vampires?" Marcus was aghast as his superior inclined his head. "What's next? Werewolves? Banshees?" Tina could see how Wolfie's eyes had widened at the man's tone, if it wasn't so serious she was sure he'd be sniggering.

Mr Silverman remained calm, "None I'm aware of, when we get back to the office, I can give you the names of those in the company dealing with our other clients. We are a very select group." He continued, "Marcus, the relevant people know about Count Kalmár. We are to be discrete as I told you when you first accepted this post. Remember? There are rewards if you do this job well. It's no different from a high up government posting, there's plenty you can't speak about with those positions either."

"Please remember there are penalties as well. You can choose not to deal with His Excellency's accounts however you are under threat if you speak about us." Wolfie had recovered himself and his voice was serious, "Mr Durrant you need to understand this."

"What do you mean 'under threat?' What are

you threatening me with?" He sat upright, pugnacious and ready to fight.

Wolfie tried to explain further, "Can you understand the problems it would cause if word got out to the general public? His Excellency wishes to live quietly. It's not a big thing. Treat the Count as any other confidential client you can't mention. If you have any queries or concerns you are welcome to speak to anyone in this room but no one else, not even your wife."

They sipped their coffee in silence. Tina worried, he wasn't buying their argument and threatening him wasn't working. She hated herself for being put in the position of defending the person who'd taken her away from her family despite now knowing that the alternative may have been worse. She could see Marcus had a deep rooted fear of an intelligent predator, which unfortunately was precisely what the Count was.

She asked, "Mr Durrant, who are you going to tell?" He spluttered a bit, suddenly unsure of himself. The dilemma she'd faced more than once – vampires didn't exist for most people, especially the authorities. "Can you imagine the media attention if this gets out? It would be chaos."

She allowed him time to think. There would be crowds of people everywhere, no peace. Newspapers, television crews, people attempting to get in and succeeding. Tina knew the Count would be forced to react and it wouldn't be pretty. How much would scientists pay for a lock of his hair, a drop of his blood? What would happen if he were disturbed while sleeping? She shuddered, she had to try and get this across to Mr Durrant in a way he could understand. He only thought of himself, of the fear he felt, he didn't know he was the one in danger. Kalmár would deal with him otherwise. She knew the Count had influence, would it be an accident? How would the other accountants take it?

She had to keep his mind on why he was here, "Mr Durrant you are here to deal with his Excellency's accounts so he can pay his taxes. If he'd wanted the attention, he would have sought it. We are concerned for you."

Madame de Burg nodded, "I have heard of many people ruined purely because they crossed the wrong powerful man." The tall lady had been carefully assessing the other man's reactions to their arguments. She had a surprisingly cool look in her eye and Tina got the impression that if Mr Durrant didn't match up to her expectations then he would be dealt with. He blinked, starting to follow an idea he could understand, those incredibly wealthy, human people who lived another world away from normality, who thought nothing of destroying someone's life and didn't care. Tina started to breathe a little easier as Mr Silverman reinforced it.

"I've dealt with His Excellency's accounts for the last twenty years. There have never been any problems. He is far less trouble than many of our other clients and far more rewarding to work for."

She looked away as they gave him the time he needed. He opened his mouth, hesitated and gave what felt like a last protest. "But Bob he's a vampire, what happens if he..."

"Mr Durrant, he's not going to bite you," Tina stifled a retort that a vampire would have zero interest in anyone else with both her and Wolfie to feed from, knowing as with most heterosexual men, he had problems with the idea of being bitten by another man.

"He's never bitten me in all the years I've worked with him Marcus." Mr Silverman was warmth itself.

"Nor I." This was said with a sigh from Madame and the mood split into hysteria. Tina started and realised that Madame had done it deliberately. The working relationship between the three was winning, it needed very little else to convince him now. She caught the look on the other woman's face as she went to sip from her cup and realised that she'd only been half joking. Madame de Burg was a romantic, for all her intelligence given half a chance she'd be out on the balcony in a skimpy negligee.

The laughter died down and Tina sobered a bit as she said, "Let's face it Mr Durrant, you can work with both of us ladies without any problems, can't you? You're not going to ravish us because you're a man?" He nodded slowly at Tina's reasoning. "And if you see a cow, you're not going to rush to rip out its throat, are you? It's the same thing, his Excellency is an intelligent man. He only needs you to deal with his accounts nothing else. He doesn't want to bite you, he can separate work and pleasure." Or dinner she thought to herself, noticing Mr Durrant shudder.

"So Marcus, we've established that the Count's private life is his own. He pays his taxes, his accounts are legal and above board and he's known about by those that need to. What other problems can there be?" Mr Silverman wanted to wrap up the argument and move back to business.

Mr Durrant shuffled his papers, looking to distract himself, "Maybe I was wrong. It's different being told something and seeing actually it happen." He shrugged, "It's something totally out of my experience." Worn out by the argument, he needed time to think. Tina sympathized, being confronted by a real vampire was not a comfortable experience. She was unsure how she felt herself about the whole business, her only plus was that Mr Durrant appeared to be safe for the moment. She saw Madame and Mr Silverman exchanged glances with Wolfie and she saw him smile as he said that he would begin preparing lunch shortly.

Going back to the accounts settled Marcus back into the boring normality of everyday life. Later that afternoon, in the middle of various figures and forms he asked Mr Silverman, "How do you deal with the threat of him? He is a predator after all."

The other man was enthusiastic in his response. "It's something you're always aware of but there are compensations and I have never felt deliberately threatened in that way. He's a fascinating individual, I've had some amazing conversations over the last twenty years, been to places that I would never have gone to. You can never forget what he is but it has been worth it. That's why we select our people carefully, to make sure they can deal with him." Mr Durrant looked dubious at the honour but seemed to accept it.

Tina did however catch him sneaking glances at her neck. She decided to appease his curiosity by letting her collar gape and show the bite marks, they healed quickly these days and the bruising didn't look so bad. Eventually he edged up to her and asked if they hurt. She turned it around and asked him if she should ask his wife the same question. He backed down quickly, his cheeks pink and she glared at Wolfie's stifled snigger.

Mr Durrant froze in his chair when Kalmár appeared that evening. Gradually he relaxed in the Count's presence and twitched only when Kalmár made a sharp movement. The Count choose to ignore it, speaking to all as graciously as usual. Tina sat next to Kalmár, absently he raised her wrist and kissed it while he listened to the conversation. She gritted her teeth internally thinking of all the rude comments she'd make when their guests had left.

The accountants dealt with the last details that evening and said their goodbyes. Unusually Kalmár wrapped his long fingers around Mr Silverman's and shook his hand. He was sincere in his thanks for dealing with his business for so many years and wished him well in his retirement. Mr Silverman went pink with pleasure and managed not to jump at the touch of the cool hand. The Count nodded to both Madame de Burg and Mr Durrant and left them.

"Well Marcus, do you think you can cope?" Mr Silverman asked.

He took a deep breath and said, "Yes I think I can." He added in an undertone, "Just so long as I don't see the fangs."

Madame de Burg glanced at Tina and rolled her eyes, "I would love to see the fangs." Tina giggled and set everyone off again.

Chapter 16

Tina was in the hallway when the bell went one evening, she hesitated, unsure if she should answer it. Wolfie appeared and indicated she should come with him. "Not likely to be walkers at this time of night," he explained.

Outside the gatehouse waiting patiently was a vampire she'd met before, she dragged his name out of the depths – Samsa. A motorbike was parked up in the shadows. Wolfie nodded and invited him in. Samsa looked intently at Tina as he passed, she edged around him and followed them. Wolfie showed him into the library and pointed out afterwards to Tina that she didn't need to fear anything in the castle. Despite inviting Samsa or any other vampire in for that matter, the castle was the Count's personal territory and no one could hurt her without risking his anger. Samsa brought Kalmár information, kept an eye on certain things.

A short while later the bell rang, Wolfie went to answer it and showed Samsa out. Relieved that he'd gone, Tina asked why he'd come in person to give information, surely he could give it over the phone.

Wolfie shook his head. "It's payment, in blood or money. Money means he can afford things in the human world to fit in. Blood means power. If the Count gives him some of his own blood, Samsa becomes that little bit stronger. It's why Vinceti is always after information."

She leant out the window several days later

and gasped in delight, she couldn't believe it had actually started to snow. Tina wrapped up warm to dance outside in the whirling flakes. Wolfie came out his hands in pockets and a sour expression on his face.

"What's up? This is wonderful!" She pulled him around with her, waving her hands excitedly.

"That's it. No more trips to town unless we're sure it's not going to snow for a few hours." She looked at him, not sure what to say, snow was something to celebrate where she came from. "We can drive using snow chains but going up the mountain roads can get tricky. We don't want to end up in a snow drift. You'll have had enough of this stuff by the time spring comes."

That's why he was so grumpy, Tina grinned as she realised what she thought the real reason was – no more girlfriend. It would also mean an end to her outings with the Count, she shrugged and tried making a snowball and failed, there wasn't enough to throw yet. The ground was being covered rapidly and she made plans to stuff a load down Wolfie's neck as soon as she could.

The snow distracted her all day, bringing out the child in her. She had twinges thinking about Jo and how she would love to be here. The wind blew the snow in flurries, making it impossible to see below the castle. Tina ran around in the courtyard getting cold then went inside and warmed up in the kitchen. Despite himself, Wolfie became infected with her mood, he pulled her close and kissed her, their warm breath melting the flakes.

Tina sat with Wolfie in the kitchen during the late afternoon, curled up in a chair. He was bad tempered again, his girlfriend had dumped him over the phone. She'd complained he was never around and had realised he wouldn't be seeing her now it was snowing. Tina could only listen with amused sympathy.

As the snow grew deeper, her nights became long and cold. The Count insisted on her wrapping up so he could take her out and show her the beauty. A frozen waterfall, deep trackless snow, the mountains and the moon on a clear night were spectacular, everything clear and sharp edged. She couldn't get used to him taking her to high up places, Kalmár found her reactions highly amusing. He teased her by making her look at various points and suggesting he might drop her, all the time while holding her securely. On other occasions when he took Wolfie out, Tina wandered the icy corridors or sat next to the warm fires, uneasy at the empty castle.

The castle grew colder over the weeks and the fires had to be kept going permanently. The Count didn't need them but he preferred the warmth. The snow changed the light coming into the castle. When the sky was clear, it lit up the inside with a bright intensity. When it fell out of the sky, the castle grew as dark as dusk and the windows froze over making it darker still. Tina had no fire in her bedroom. She had hot bricks for her bed and the curtains around it had been replaced. Once drawn the tiny space heated up from her body. There were a few small oasis' of warmth in the icy castle, the kitchen, the study and the library.

Her days were kept busy. Tina had become competent at kicking and blocking Wolfie's punches, moving fast to get within his guard. She'd started to fight with real knives and he'd given her a set. Knowing she was nervous about them, he made her carry them constantly and showed her how to attach the sheaths to her forearm or leg. Her favourite place was tucked under her jumper in the waistband of her jeans, out of sight.

She had her new viola to practice, another present from the Count. Kalmár had made suggestions he would like to hear her play, maybe later on she would. Wolfie played the piano in the dining room at times to accompany her until the cold drove them back to the fire in the kitchen.

Tina had also started to learn Romanian, she'd insisted after not having been able to speak the basics during her time outside the castle. Much to her disgust she found it difficult, so much so that for nearly a week both the Count and Wolfie had refused to speak to her in English. They'd found her reaction predictably amusing. She began to find it easier as the weeks went by. Her favourite phrase was still along the lines of, "Excuse me I don't understand, do you speak English?"

Wolfie and Tina found themselves forced further into each other's company. She leant against his back while he made tea one afternoon and wrapped her arms around him, he turned and kissed her. She thought for two seconds, she couldn't leave the castle, why bother to fight the attraction? She kissed him back, took his hand and led him to his bedroom. Wolfie was as attentive to her needs as he'd suggested he would be, his soft whispers belying the outrageous queries that made her gasp with laughter.

They lay afterwards, warm under the covers in the cold room. Tina traced designs on his chest while he held her close. "Will he mind?" There was no question of who 'he' was.

"So long as I don't make any claim on you, then no, I don't think he will. They don't tend to worry about what happens during the day with their pets."

"You could blame it all on me. Say I seduced you."

Wolfie blinked and thought with a serious expression, "Well," he said at last with a smile, "I'm not objecting if you want to practise…" She laughed, rolled on top of him, pinned his hands to the bed and kissed him.

Spending their days close together, Tina and Wolfie found it difficult to control their responses to each other during the long nights while the Count was around. They excluded him without thought, involved in the new side to their relationship. Wolfie was naturally tactile, he wasn't used to restraining himself and Kalmár noticed everything that happened between them, commenting sharply.

One night Wolfie forgot himself and began teasing her. Eyes lighting up, Tina responded by touching his face and laughing. The Count wasn't amused, it had been one reaction out of many that evening. Irritation showed as he looked at Wolfie, "Remove yourself."

Wolfie shut his eyes and left, rebellion showing in every part of his body. Tina stared at Kalmár, she'd picked up undertones to the command, she'd felt them tug. Wolfie'd no choice about leaving.

"You can't do that," Tina brindled. "He wasn't doing anything wrong."

"You are mine. I brought you here. He has no claim on you." Kalmár stood, his hands clenched against the back of a chair. His face was tight, dark eyes shadowed in the dim room.

Needled by having to justify their relationship, she snapped back, "Wolfie doesn't own me and neither do you. You can't put two adults alone together for long periods and expect nothing to happen. What we do is our…"

She stopped short as the wood cracked under his fingers. Tina stared, the damaged wood was thicker than her wrist. A touch of fear ran down her back, she'd got used to his differences. He'd been charming for so long she'd forgotten or no longer thought about the other side of his nature.

He let go to pace around the room, his gestures sharply contained as he spoke, radiating his disapproval, "What you do during the day is nothing to me. During the night you are mine, both of you."

"I'm not yours." Tina sat on her fear and refused to be intimidated. He'd walk all over her if she allowed him to. "I'm here because you kidnapped me and it's the best choice I had out of a lot of bad ones. If I were yours in the same way as I'm Wolfie's, then you still wouldn't own me. Just as I wouldn't own you."

"You would have no choice if I made you swear yourself."

"You could make me but you'd have to collar me up with you day and night, never let me out of your sight. I won't live like that, I can't live like that, not on a chain." Fear mixed in with the anger, he could make her swear. She had no power here, only what he gave her. He could easily take Wolfie away, all he had to do was give the order, neither of them had the choice. The fear boiled into anger, she wouldn't let him do this and threw the challenge back at him, "Try it."

He hissed in frustration. "I will not have you attempting to incite Wolf into rebellion. He is sworn to me even if you are not."

"You're jealous. Wolfie has a part of me. You can't have it and you don't like it that I've given it to him. Besides, I remember you telling me that you only need what's inside me. What's wrong with me giving the rest to someone else?"

She felt his anger filling the room, his presence grew. The candles wavered and became dim as though cowering. Equally furious and refusing to give in, she tried to leave and he stopped her by grabbing her arm. Kalmár towered over her raising his hand to strike, his lips were pulled back and Tina could see his fangs turning the elegantly dressed man into a predator. She put her chin up and stared him down, despite her shaking. He snarled in frustration, pulled her close and fed with no attempt at gentleness.

Seeing the bruises the next day, Wolfie became upset. "I can't protect you. Not against him. What sort of man does that make me? I never had a problem with the vows I swore to him, not before you came." Tina put his arms around him or tried to. He didn't want her comfort, he was angry, with himself and at the situation. "I've never found them like they are now, a leash. I can't do anything." She let him go, realising she'd have to deal with this on her own.

Tina felt caught between the two men. She had no respite during the day due to Wolfie being angry and frustrated. For nights afterwards the Count guarded Tina, insisting she stayed with him and refusing to let Wolfie near her. His temper was vile, he fed at every opportunity proving she had no choice. She allowed him to have his way, preventing herself from being hurt was her priority but she found it exhausting.

Wolfie spent his time glaring at the fire in the kitchen, blaming her for the breakdown in his relationship with the Count. Tina realised he'd always had a free rein with any woman he'd liked up to this point, he'd never been in competition with the Count. Unlike Tina he'd never had to deal with the consequences of any relationship, including pregnancy.

She controlled her reactions, disgusted by both of them. She told Wolfie he'd made his decision a long time ago and the consequences were nothing to do with her. Kalmár, she confronted again. Despite his possessive mood terrifying her, she refused to back down, telling him that he was being ridiculous and unreasonable in his jealousy. She had to bite her tongue several times to stop herself from calling him names, she couldn't call him anything to infuriate him further. He refused to comment on his actions and walked out, leaving her alone for the first time since it had started.

Tina sat with her head in her hands, too exhausted to cry and tried to think. Kalmár had to have some form of victory, his pride wouldn't allow him anything else, he would be impossible otherwise. She sat for a while and then picked up the magazine she'd been trying to read and found both men in the study. The atmosphere was terrible, the Count's vile temper beating through her in waves. Wolfie pretended to work, fiddling with things on the desk. Kalmár stared at his laptop, ignoring both of them when she came in.

She sat near him, took a deep breath and put the magazine on her lap. "I've found an article that may interest you. Would you like me to read it?"

Kalmár jerked his head at Wolfie and he left them, glancing miserably at Tina as he passed. The Count took his glasses off, closed the laptop and listened. He made few comments, allowing her to make the conversation. She stumbled through the night, far past the time when she would normally go for her nap. Eventually she fell asleep in the chair, woke to find a blanket tucked over her and the Count close by, staring into the fire.

The next evening Tina lay in her own bed, aware that Kalmár was moving around. She sat up as he walked in and pulled the covers around herself. He ran his fingers up her neck and across her jaw. They weren't gentle, he just stopped short of bruising. He leant over, swamping her with his presence.

"Surrender to me. Swear yourself." Tina shook her head against his hand, refusing to look as his eyes bored into her. After a long pause he breathed out heavily, his face tight, "May I?" There was no conciliatory note in his voice, he forced it out grudgingly.

She took this as it was offered and undid her collar, exposing her neck for him. He wrapped his arms around her, running his hands down her arms, possessing her, his cool fingers pulling yet more cold through her thick pyjamas. She shivered as he licked the bite marks with more gentleness than he had in previous nights. Kalmár left her curled up, having pulled the bedclothes around her to keep her warm. She wondered what more she could do, she couldn't swear herself, not at the moment.

Tina's nights slowly improved. With more attention from her Kalmár's jealousy calmed, although there were still times when he stopped to look sharply at them or make comments. Wolfie recovered his easy going nature despite being wary of showing his affection for her around the Count.

Their days relaxed back into routines and laughter. Wolfie dragged an old sledge out. "There's no problem with you coming out while we're snowed in," Wolfie said in response to Tina's reluctance. "No one can get this far in during the day. Come on, enjoy it." They played like children, skidding down the road together, laughing as they fell off in the snow.

She refused to learn to ski even the basics. She hated the thought of long sticks attached to her feet and not being able to take them off., she'd listened to far too many stories of accidents. Wolfie grumbled and called her a control freak. She made good on her promise and stuffed snow down his neck, doubling over with laughter at his yells as it melted. He walked in circles swearing, attempting to shake it out and finally gave up. Chasing her around, he threatened to wash her face with snow and ended up kissing her instead.

With both days and nights filled, she had to nap at strange times to keep on top of her sleep. Her period came and she refused to stay away this time, it was far too cold upstairs. The Count spent those nights watching her with intent, he was irritable with both of them and the atmosphere in the castle was horrendous with his frustration. Wolfie stayed out of the way, not wanting a repeat of the last upset. Tina got fed up on the second night. She'd been trying to read and Kalmár had been absorbed in staring at her for what had seemed like an age, tapping his fingers against the arm of his chair.

She threw down her book, undid her collar and said, "Look, if you want it. Here it is, have it." She flapped the open collar at him. Kalmár moved faster than she expected, pulled her into him and buried his face in her neck. He held her, breathing hard into her throat, running his hands over her then abruptly put her down and stalked off. She felt offended and laughed at herself. It hadn't been so long since she'd been fighting him off. She sobered, wondering what she became.

Chapter 17

It had been a long afternoon and the sky looked dark with the promise of yet more snow. Tina felt restless, with her hands and feet twitching, she couldn't settle at anything, Wolfie had suggested a martial arts session but she couldn't concentrate. He gave up having dumped her on the ground and 'killed' her too many times and she'd outright refused the other suggestions he'd made.

The Count woke while she was curled up on the couch in the library, her head had been aching and she'd eaten nothing all afternoon. As he walked in and stared at her, she shivered, abruptly feeling cold. Frowning he came over and sat next to her, touched her forehead, picked up her arm and pulled her sleeve up to her elbow, smelling the inside. Wolfie appeared in the doorway his eyes questioning.

"I'm fine." Tina tried to bat Kalmár away, his cool fingers were making her chilly.

"No you are not," he said shortly. "You are still fighting me." Tina frowned, she'd not crossed him in ages. "Your body is fighting the infection I give you. Your immunity has built up," he explained. "This time, as I am here at the beginning, it should not be so severe. I will need to cut you in a similar way." He glanced at Wolfie. "Start a fire in her room, she should be kept warm." He picked her up and carried her upstairs.

Tina protested as much as she could when he stripped and wrapped her in her bedclothes but she was already drifting off into the pain of her joints and body aching. She whimpered as he drew his fangs down her neck in a series of short shallow cuts and worked his tongue over them, pressing his saliva deep. By the time he'd covered her arms, she'd heated up and become feverish.

She woke the following evening exhausted and aching but better, much to her relief. The Count checked her over when he came in and grunted his satisfaction. Tina snuggled under the covers and watched him read next to her. She dozed and recovered her strength, feeling safe in his presence. Wolfie wandered in and out, bringing food and drinks. The two men talked quietly over the bed while she rested, Wolfie teasing her when she surfaced enough to comment on their conversation.

The long winter drew on. Wolfie had been right in a way, Tina longed to see colours other than the blacks, whites and greys. The only colour seemed to be when the sky became clear, blue and intense. She craved the soft greens and browns of summer. Despite this she found herself humming one afternoon, anticipating some activity later on. Tina stopped for a moment and realised she was happy. She had plenty to occupy her mind, exercise and companionship. Guilt hit her - she'd not thought of Jo for days, only as an ache like a healing bruise. She knew she still couldn't give herself up to the Count but there might be a compromise.

Wolfie was in the study that evening, his nose buried in something technical. She sat in the library with the Count. Unsure at how to broach the subject, she began, "I can't swear everything to you." He stopped reading and took off his glasses.

"What do you wish?" he asked quietly.

"I can't go home, I know that and I don't want to go to another vampire." He raised his eyebrows waiting. Tina rushed on, not wanting to think too hard about what she was saying. "You can have my body, I'll swear that to you. You've got that anyway but my soul isn't mine to swear."

"You swear your body to me so you may be safe outside my personal territory," Kalmár explained. "No vampire would touch you without risking my anger. Your soul is sworn so you may not speak of certain matters or act in a way that would endanger us."

"I can't do it. It feels like making a pact with the devil. I can give my soul but I can't swear it. There is a difference to me." Struggling to express herself, she waved her arms as if it helped her explanation. "Besides, I made a promise to keep your secrets. I wouldn't go against that."

"You speak of making a pact with the devil. That idea started in times when the priesthood were jealous of any they did not understand. Our long lives enabled us to look beyond their mumblings and attempts to control the ignorant population. Lecturing of rewards in heaven and punishment in hell after death." He snorted his distain, "There are very few ways in which I can die and it is my understanding that people are more likely to create their own hell on earth. But is that still how you feel about me? That I am some devil or demon?"

She was honest. "At first yes but not now. I simply can't swear what you ask. Maybe in times to come I can give my soul but that's different to me."

Kalmár considered her words and nodded. "I will be patient and accept what you will give. Come and swear your body and our safety to me." He held out his hand and pulled her onto his lap. Tina curled into his arms and he shifted so her head rested on his shoulder. He had an intense hunger radiating from him, a greed that made her shiver.

He stroked her face claiming ownership, ran

his fingers down to her neck and tilted her chin towards him. She wanted to ask what difference it would make – he'd fed from her so many times before. Then her eyes became caught up in his and his mind pulled her towards him. She had a moment of terror, unsure if she'd made the right decision and felt silvery chains wrapping around her. They shifted and anchored themselves, the delicate links stretching between them. He bound her to him as he fed, his arms holding her as tightly as his mind.

Tina felt dis-orientated for a moment, her vision blurred and doubled. She became aware of his body, a slow heartbeat and cool blood, it cleared and she could see again. He let her go, a satisfied look in his eyes. Conscious of him like an empty hole where a tooth should be, she waggled an imaginary tongue in that direction.

He picked up his book and hesitated, raising his eyebrows, "Yes?"

Tina stopped waggling. "Nothing." This was going to be very different to what she'd expected.

The snow receded further, leaving behind wet mud and battered grasslands. As Wolfie had promised, the woodpiles were almost finished and the cupboards and freezers were emptying rapidly. Everything dripped and ran with water. The trees were bare and would be for a while and the nights were cold but the sun began to shine hotter with the promise of warmer days to come. When the road cleared of snow, Wolfie took Tina to check for any damage. It was heady escaping from the confines of the castle, they laughed and giggled about silliness.

While checking an area near the river, he pulled her close and kissed her. His arms and mouth warmed her in the chilly breeze, the river rushed full and white below them, grinding rocks along its bed.

She responded with enthusiasm until his hands became more intimate, attempting to find a way through the layers she wore, while he whispered ideas in her ear. Tina laughed at his frustration as she refused any further advances from him, it would be just her luck to have the only walker in fifty miles to happen upon them. With reluctance he got back to the job in hand, apart from a few floods the road looked fine. Wolfie showed her the barn in the village, the only building intact and set back from the road. He had a code and a key, he could pick up parcels and post from here at any time and it meant delivery lorries had space to turn, unlike at the castle.

The Count called Tina into the ballroom that evening, she watched while he put some music on. "I wish to teach you how to dance."

With reluctance she stepped closer and took the hand he offered. The nearest she'd come to dancing had been in nightclubs. She winced at the memories, she didn't think that sort of dancing was what Kalmár had in mind.

Kalmár kept her with him for several hours, walking through a simple waltz again and again. Typically he refused to tell her the reason why, only that she would need it at some point. She'd learnt a certain amount of co-ordination from her martial arts with Wolfie but the Count was a lot taller than her, his stride longer and she wouldn't let him lead. Patiently he adjusted his stride to hers, he wasn't so tolerant about her attempts to lead him. Tina kept looking to see where they were going, peering round his shoulder, tripping over his feet and getting cross. She didn't have the same patience, she got angry and he refused to let her walk out. Tina was in a vile temper when he finally let her go, kicking things and swearing in both the languages she knew.

He insisted she keep trying over several nights. The promenade dances she could learn, with minimal grace but she felt they were pointless. He got stubborn, he'd decided it was important. It was definitely the partner dances she had problems with. At the end of his tether he matched her up with Wolfie, she danced better but not much. She was sure the only reason was that Wolfie would let her lead.

At last exasperated one evening, he let her go from the ballroom into the library to warm up. Tina glowered at him and rubbed her hands. His hands, always cool, hadn't helped in the cold ballroom.

"Why will you not allow me to lead?" Kalmár demanded as he sat in his chair and watched her stand near the fire.

She shrugged, staring at the flames and feeling rebellious, muttered, "Don't like being pushed around."

"I am not pushing you around, I am guiding you. That is the point. You should move effortlessly, be graceful in my arms, a delight to behold. Instead you move like a wooden marionette. You do not move like this when you fight, I know you are capable of it. Why can you not relax and allow me to take control? Do you not trust me?"

His face changed and he murmured to himself under his breath. He moved a few chairs aside to make a larger space in the middle of the floor and switched off the lamps scattered around the room. Tina watched, fascinated as he made a pinching motion with his fingers and the candles on the table furthest from him went out obediently one by one. The only light left was from the fire flickering. He stood in the middle of the room, waiting.

"Are your hands warm Little Mouse? Come here." His voice had become deep and inviting. She eyed him, suspicious at his changed mood and walked over. Kalmár wrapped a long arm around her and pulled her in close against him. He curled her arm around his shoulder and put her other hand on his chest.

"Close your eyes," he instructed her and shook her gently until she did. His arm had pulled her up onto her toes, she closed her eyes and leant into him, her head resting on his shoulder.

Kalmár wore her favourite jacket - the red velvet one. It was soft against her cheek. She could hear the crackle of the fire, the warmth and the light of it against her eyelids. His free hand came up and stroked her cheek, the coolness contrasting with the heat. He ran it through her hair and dipped his chin to rest it on the top of her head as she shivered. His fingers came down to touch lightly on the pulse under her jaw.

She felt his chest expand with one of his long slow breaths and he shifted forwards. Tina compensated by moving backwards with her eyes still shut. Kalmár stepped again and once more she had to move or lose her balance. Being this close to him, she could feel the tendrils of his mind brush hers, blurring her thoughts. It made her muzzy and relaxed. He continued to move, stepping around obstacles in the room, faster to a tune she couldn't hear. She moved with him, his body shifting against hers and she responded without thought. He swung her round and blocked the warmth of the fire with his body.

Tina woke, realised what they were doing and stumbled, over-compensating. He caught her and came to a stop, allowing her to pull away. She shook her head, clearing the cobwebs out of her mind.

"So Little Mouse you can choose to surrender to me when you wish." He said this with great amusement. Tina glowered and spluttered several rude words in return.

Chapter 18

Spring was on its way, the beech trees under the castle wore the vibrant green of new leaves and the birds sang in the mornings. All three of them went out together while the early evenings were still dark.

Tina was in the position of having two men courting her, both good looking and charming in their own ways. It was a new and heady sensation for her. She'd sorted out her body and no, it wasn't the body she'd had at twenty but hell, she looked good. She had a waist again, she could move without tripping over her own feet and she could run. Her skin glowed and her eyes sparkled with pleasure.

The nights were full of good humour and conversation, Kalmár seemed to have forgotten his jealousy. She watched others noticing them - the Count with his aristocratic features and immaculate dress and Wolfie, a few inches shorter and more casual but handsome with his bright hair and ready smile.

Having come back from a night out, the Count took her around the small courtyard to the older part of the castle a few hours before dawn. They walked into the room with the balcony that she'd tried to escape from months ago. The doors had been locked since and she could still see the footprints from the Count deep in the dust.

"This room plus the rooms on either side are yours," he said. "Inform me if you need anything for them." With that he left her. The entire room looked disgusting, the other two were as bad. A lantern in hand, she moved to the balcony, unlatched the shutters and opened the doors. The wind blew lightly. She shivered and peered into the blackness. She resolved to return when the sun had come up.

The sunlight didn't do much, the rooms faced west and were in deep shade. Tina had brought her spider stick and tied her hair up. Buckets, brooms and rags started the job of cleaning. She swore to herself through much of the morning. Spiders ran for cover and she shrieked more than once much to Wolfie's amusement. He'd stuck his head around the door and removed it quickly when he'd realised there was work to be done.

By lunchtime she'd cleared the main room of dust and cobwebs. Tina was hot and sweaty, she'd taken down the curtains and dumped them in a corner, she'd also shoved the furniture to one side. Plaster came off the walls in places as she cleaned, the wallpaper peeling. A lot of the grime wasn't going to come out with hot water and soap. Fed up at the state the rooms were in and the amount of work it would take to make them reasonable, she made a list.

By evening she'd got the other two rooms into the same condition. She bathed and found the Count in his study. Wolfie hunched over when he saw her, certain she'd ask for his help with cleaning.

"These rooms you gave me," she began. The Count looked up and put his laptop and glasses to one side. "I need a professional to deal with them." Behind her Wolfie gave a loud sigh of relief. Tina ignored him and carried on. "I can't get them clean. They've been left for too long." Kalmár nodded. "There's no electricity. I want lights, proper lights and sockets. The curtains are disgusting, they need to be thrown but they can wait until I've decided on colour schemes. The walls need to be stripped and re-plastered in places. I'm happy to paint but there's no point with them in that state."

"Anything else?" Kalmár sounded amused as Wolfie sniggered in the corner.

"Yes. I'm going to scrub the furniture but the wood panelling on the walls and the floor needs to be stripped and re-stained." She folded her list and waited.

"Very well, you may organise tradesmen to do the work and I will pay. If you need help ask Wolf." He went back to his computer. Surprised at how easily he'd agreed, Tina went to Wolfie to start enquires.

It was fun organising a project like this. The Count hadn't specified a cash limit and when Tina had talked to Wolfie about it, he'd said to enjoy herself. The workmen came, electricians, plasterers and carpenters. She tried out her new language on them, spoke a mixture of the two and laughed when she got things wrong. Tina had the third room divided into a bathroom and a small workroom. She scrubbed the furniture. It turned out to be delicate and ornate, it must have been a lady's apartment at one time.

When the workmen had moved out, she badgered Wolfie into dismantling her four poster bed and they brought it piece by piece into her new rooms. Tina began on the room that would be her bedroom first. She called in a local curtain maker and had a fun afternoon going through fabrics. She'd decided on green and gold, rich thick fabrics, the curtains around her bed and at the windows would be the same. She remembered how she'd craved colour during the winter. This room would be like the beech woods in spring.

Wolfie teased her about her enjoyment and backed away with mock horror when she asked him for help. Gradually the rooms took shape and colour. She had a small wood burning stove installed in the middle room, the curtains would be deep red, the walls cream. Tina stole furniture from elsewhere in the castle and had chairs re-covered to match, she wanted it warm, to invite people into.

Tina sprawled across her bed in her new bedroom. The smell of paint had faded, unlike her delight of having somewhere of her own to retreat to. Her old bedroom had never had this feeling of being hers. She dozed, aware of the Count moving somewhere close by. Dusk had come and she was sleepily thinking of excuses for not getting up when she heard a click.

She sat up and looked round. The door leading to her living area was shut, the other door to the next room wasn't. She'd tried this door many times, it had always been locked. She'd asked Kalmár about it and he'd said it led to his dressing room and changed the subject. Now it was not only unlocked but ajar.

Tina got dressed and slid her shoes on. She pulled the door towards her and slipped through and was immediately glad she'd put them on. The dust was piled high and with no footprints she could see. In front of her was a large four poster bed covered in thick cobwebs. Tina wasn't sure if the curtains around it would stand up to being hoovered, it looked as though they were being held up by the cobwebs. The covers were grey with dust and her fingers itched to clean them. The room was lit by a few fat candles, heavy dark furniture dominated the room and the curtains at the windows were drawn.

The Count sat on a long stool at a table drying his chin, having finished shaving. Tina had to look twice to realise that the mirror was missing. He was dressed less formally than she'd seen him before, no jacket, only a waistcoat over his shirt. She went and sat next to him on the stool, facing the other way.

"Letting a woman into your dressing room is bad news. Especially if you aren't properly dressed yet," she teased him. "Are you thinking about surrendering?"

Kalmár smiled, shook his head, undid her collar and brushed his lips into her neck. As Tina felt him nuzzle, she leant against him. She didn't think he'd bite, it was his equivalent of a lover's caress, exploring possibilities and the warmth of her body. His body felt as though it had been starved. His shoulders were wide but ropey, suggesting he used to have more muscle on him at some point. The dancing had done them both good. She'd learnt to relax around him, although there were still times when she had to count to ten first. He had also relaxed, responding more to her teasing.

"Are we going out tonight?"

He sighed and pulled himself away. His face was inches from hers, his eyes were dark and the pupils huge. "No, we have a visitor." He enunciated his words carefully, she'd noticed speaking wasn't so easy when his fangs were extended and had teased him about it.

"Really?" Tina brushed her fingers across his cheek.

Kalmár stood and took a tie out of drawer and knotted it swiftly. "Yes. His name is Master Hiro. He will make you a new dress."

She swizzled on the stool to watch him, tucked her feet up and wrapped her arms around her knees. "I've got plenty of dresses. You bought them. Not that I'm complaining," she added hastily. He shook a jacket off its hanger and put it on, dark grey, a thin red pinstripe through it.

210

He adjusted his cuffs and put items in pockets as he spoke. "Master Hiro is a craftsman." High praise from Kalmár, he respected those who devoted themselves to a skill and excelled in it. "He will make you a ball gown. He has made many of my clothes. I believe you will enjoy the experience." He buttoned the jacket and offered his elbow. She jumped up and took it.

When they entered the library, Wolfie was already there talking to a small Asian man. She saw a lady waiting close by.

"Master Hiro," the Count made a half bow. "May I introduce Little Mouse?" Master Hiro bowed and Tina bobbed awkwardly in return. They exchanged pleasantries and Master Hiro suggested they retire somewhere to measure up. Tina realised with delight she could show off her rooms to someone new. Wolfie didn't count, he'd been in and out all through the process. Apart from paying the invoices Kalmár hadn't mentioned the rooms at all.

Master Hiro was short and stocky, his eyes bright under neatly combed hair. He had a great deal of energy, his enthusiasm for his work barely contained. Shinko his assistant was lovely, she helped Tina into a silk dressing gown through which Master Hiro measured her. His touch was professional and quick, he made a few quiet suggestions to Shinko and left the room.

Shinko helped her into a corset and petticoats for the gown. It caused a lot of giggling between them. Shinko showed her how to pull the laces so Tina wouldn't need anyone to help, the corset did wonders for her figure, her slim waist pulled in further into an hourglass.

She waved at the top of her corset, it appeared to be barely holding her in. "I feel like I'm going to fall out."

Shinko laughed and shook her head. "You won't, but don't bend down to pick anything up, that's for the men to do for you." She mimed standing, waiting, arms folded while tapping her foot imperiously. Tina laughed with her, touching herself nervously.

Master Hiro knocked again and measured her through the dressing gown with the corset on. He moved her body round. She had to stand straight with the corset on but he tweaked her shoulders back, turned her wrists round and lifted her chin.

"Remember you are a beautiful woman. Not a bashful child. Use it." She blinked and flushed a bit from the compliments.

She changed back into her normal clothes. Master Hiro had made notes on her and sketched out ideas refusing to let her see when she tried to peek. They looked at fabrics, rough silks, colours fresh and vibrant catching her eye. Tina chose a soft spring green like the beech trees outside and a dark blue. Master Hiro chose a dusky pink over-ruling her, much to her disgust. She didn't want to look like a little girl she protested, women of her age didn't wear pink dresses. He was adamant she wouldn't look like a little girl, he insisted the colour complimented her skin. In the end she gave way, the green and the blue were lovely, she didn't have to wear the pink.

To Tina's delight, Shinko returned at points during the following week to help her with makeup tips. She cut her hair and suggested ways to style it. Tina nagged Wolfie into making some of his fancy cakes and nibbles for them, not that he needed many excuses. Tina's style ran to fairy cakes eaten several at a time but she wanted something special for this.

The days were like a balm for Tina. It had

been a long time without female company, they chatted about everything and nothing. Tina avoided all mention of the past and Shinko didn't press her. She had a plain dress to practice in, she learnt how to walk in it and how to make her skirts move. It was harder than it looked to make everything appear graceful. Shinko laughed at Tina worrying about men stepping on her dress while dancing, it was almost a disappointment when Master Hiro said he had her first dress ready.

Master Hiro's face showed bright with anticipation when he arrived in the evening. The dress was draped over his arm, concealed by its cover. Shinko had refused to say anything about the dresses despite Tina's questions. Tina got herself ready with Shinko's help, underwear, her face painted and hair swept up. It was just long enough to look elegant on top of her head. In her dressing gown, she waited as Master Hiro came in and undid the cover.

Tina's heart plummeted and she shook her head firmly, "I'm not wearing it."

"Please say if you do not like my creation," Master Hiro said with dignity. "But trust my judgement first and try it on." Tina bit her lip and stood up. He shook the dress out and Shinko helped her into it, showing her how to do up the buttons at the back with the long button hook.

It wasn't the same pink all the way through Tina realised, the dusky pink shaded through to a darker colour depending on the light. The skirt finished on the diagonal showing a midnight blue underskirt and a riot of embroidery in the same shade twined its way up the bodice. Shinko adjusted her corset to fit both her and the dress.

When she'd finished Master Hiro came up

behind and fiddled with the back of her skirts where they came out from her corset. "I was asked to make a change," he said. "Can you feel this?" He took her hand and put it round to her back. She found a small slit, he guided her hand in and she wrapped her fingers around the handle of a knife. She pulled it out and looked at it. Smaller than the ones she normally practised with but still big enough to cause damage.

She smiled and nodded, "It's good."

They put her in front of the mirror, Tina barely recognised herself. The pink accented the colour in her cheeks and she didn't look like a little girl, not with what the dress showed. The wide straps of the bodice skimmed the sides of her shoulders, everything held up by the corset. Her waist looked tiny and the skirt flared out from her hips, she turned to make it swirl around and lift up. Master Hiro beamed with pleasure at her reaction and he corrected her posture again.

She turned and thanked him. "You were right, it does suit me."

Master Hiro looked sly and said that was why he'd made this one first. "You would not have worn it otherwise." He wagged his finger at her knowingly and she grinned in reply. "Now it is time to present you to His Excellency." He held out his hand to lead her out of the room. Shinko had packed everything and was waiting. For a moment Tina panicked, she had to show people? Butterflies ran around her stomach. She was used to dressing up to go out, but wearing this gown changed everything.

Master Hiro kept his hand held out. "I would like to show everyone how beautiful you look in my dress." He smiled and she took his hand feeling nervous. "Remember," he continued, "you must act how you look even if you do not feel like it inside." In Wolfie's words 'buck up' thought Tina. She stuck her chin up, squared her shoulders and walked to the door.

"No, no. Not like that. As you have practised." He mimed picking up skirts and sashaying to the door. Tina laughed and had to remember she couldn't breathe deeply in her corset.

They walked the length of the corridor, Master Hiro turned and walked her back to give her time to gather her confidence. Tina picked up a small amount of skirt to enable her to walk down the stairs without tripping and he nodded encouragingly.

As they came down the last section of staircase, Wolfie came through one of the doors. He stopped dead in his tracks and gazed at her. His eyes lost themselves down her cleavage and with a visible effort he dragged them back up. To Master Hiro's widening smile, Tina winked at Wolfie, put her chin up and carried on. She tried not to chuckle as she noted Wolfie's face turning thoughtful and knew he was considering some naughtiness later on.

Kalmár met them at the library, leaning elegantly against the door frame. Master Hiro bowed to him and held her hand out. "Your Excellency may I present your lady?"

The Count took her hand from him. "Little Mouse," he greeted Tina. Her stomach still tight with nerves, she remembered to put her shoulders back and nodded.

He returned Master Hiro's bow, "Master Hiro as usual you have surpassed all expectations." Master Hiro beamed with pleasure. Wolfie showed them out helping with the bags and glancing her way when he thought no one was looking.

"Shall we see if you remember how to dance?" Kalmár led her into the ballroom. He lit a few candles, leaving most of the room in darkness and put some music on. Tina took a deep breath and tried to relax as he took her in his arms.

It was a slow dance and her practise had paid off, the dress felt different to dance in but not impossible. Despite her worries, her hem wasn't trodden on by the Count, he was adept at sliding his feet underneath it. He pulled her closer till she could feel the length of his body against hers. She rested her cheek against his shoulder, closed her eyes and moved with him. Every so often she shifted with the music to pull him in a different direction. Teasing him as she forced him to move with her. He did and then gracefully swung her in to dance with him again.

Tina relaxed as they danced and started to feel the tendrils of his mind wrapping themselves around hers. The hypnotic effect pulled her into a space where she felt only a serene calm. He let go of her hand, tucking it into his chest as he used his free hand to stroke her jawline and neck, brushing lightly along her bare shoulder. She shivered, pushed away and undid his jacket buttons to slide her hand underneath, over the satin of his waistcoat. His back was cool, the muscles moving beneath her fingers.

They danced as though they were the only people in the universe. She didn't need to look to know his eyes would be black, his fangs extending. His fingers rested on the pulse on her neck. Tina tilted her face up to him inviting, her mind began to expand and she no longer cared if it was surrender. She felt the muscles in his back gather as he bent to pick her up. His face moved towards her neck and she shifted to help him.

Chapter 19

Tina jumped as the lights came on and blinked in the brightness. Kalmár had pulled her behind him, tucking her under his arm and protecting her from something. Fear ran down her spine as in between her eyes watering, she saw his face snarl, fangs bared. She blinked again and he'd composed himself, his black eyes glaring towards the door. She looked for the intruder and felt him. It was a vampire, how did he get in? She peered around the Count, dis-orientated. A group of people stood in the doorway and Wolfie hovered apologetically. The man - no - the vampire in front smirked, his pleasure evident in the interruption. Tina could feel the Count's chest rumbling through her hand although no noise could be heard. He controlled himself and raised an eyebrow.

The other vampire had a way of holding himself that gave the impression he expected any orders to be followed even if they were suggestions. He waited not quite long enough to be insulting and said, "Your Excellency."

The Count replied in a tightly controlled voice. "Tangent. I gave you permission to enter. Not to disturb me." So this was Lord Tangent, Tina was intrigued.

"My apologies. I did not realise you were busy." Lord Tangent smirked no apology in his voice. "I was merely impatient to see the pet you had liberated from me." His gaze fell on Tina and his eyes were cold as they perused her, making her feel unclean. "Playing with your pets Kalmár? They get ideas if you give them too many allowances."

Tina straightened under the Count's arm, her fingers hidden under his jacket twisting the satin back of his waistcoat while she tried to appear calm. While she was sure the Count would protect her, this new vampire was unnerving enough for her not to want to upset him and she'd end up saying something rude if she stayed - she'd been insulted enough. Kalmár turned to look as she moved out from under his arm.

She gave him the sweeping curtsey taught by Shinko and said, "With your permission your Excellency?"

He took her hand, turned it and kissed her wrist. "Of course Little Mouse," he replied and bent his head in return.

Gathering herself, she raised her skirts and swept down the room past Lord Tangent, nodding to him in passing. She paused at the door to allow the others to move aside. Wolfie looked tense and unhappy, the man next to him frankly leered at her.

He bowed and introduced himself, "Ivan, Consort's pet." Tina was confused, Lord Tangent wasn't Consort but she refused to let it show.

"Mouse," she snapped back with her best Duchess impression. It felt strange using the Count's nickname for her but she didn't want this person knowing her real name. His grin grew wider as he moved out of her way.

Tina made to sweep past him when she noticed another man who stood in Ivan's shadow. Shorter but wider than Ivan, he avoided her gaze by looking everywhere but at her. He had a beaten neglected look about him despite his girth and neat dress. Catching Wolfie's warning glance, she turned to see the two vampires watching and she slipped out the room, away from their gaze.

Once in the corridors she paused, allowing

herself to catch her breath and let her heart slow down, it wasn't easy trying to breathe with her ribs restricted. She walked at a slower pace to her rooms, so that was Lord Tangent. He seemed familiar - why? She'd never seen him before, or had she?

Tina cast her mind back frantically trying to place him. A memory began to surface from many years ago, of coming out of a nightclub, giggling with friends and the door being held open by a man. The uneasy feeling that had sobered her despite her friends continuing to laugh. He'd been pleasant for the few seconds they'd made eye contact but she'd hurried on and gone home early, not wanting to stay out.

Now she'd remembered, other memories came swimming up through the depths. The same feeling as she walked home at night, someone passing her and nodding. Another man turning to look at her in the lamplight as she got into her car. She shivered, none were recent. Wolfie had been right, she'd been watched for a long time. She counted herself lucky despite the despair she'd felt when she'd first come here, she was content and happy at times. She got the distinct feeling things would have gone very differently if she'd been picked up by Lord Tangent.

Having reached her bedroom, she started the frustrating task of unbuttoning herself. Millions of tiny buttons to be undone with the long button hook. She had to twist and look at her back using the mirror. She swore her way down the row in the midst of thinking about their visitors. If Ivan was a companion or pet like her and Wolfie, who was the third man? He gave her the impression he was like she'd been after she'd arrived. What had Wolfie said? If you don't fight then you end up at the bottom of the pack? He didn't strike her as a top dog. She undid the last button and hauled the dress off over her head and started on the corset and petticoats. Thank goodness Shinko had tied the laces at her waist instead of at the top or bottom, she unlaced herself with a sense of relief.

As Tina got dressed in jeans and a shirt she wondered about Ivan, no doubts there that he had the cockiness needed to dominate. She tucked her knife into the back of her trousers as a precaution, she wasn't sure how far she could go with using it but it might act as a deterrent. If Ivan was Consort's pet, that might explain why he was so assertive but Lord Tangent wasn't Madame's consort as far as Tina knew. They had been mentioned to her in the past as separate people, had she changed partners? Tina shrugged at herself as she washed most of the makeup off and bundled her hair into a clip out of the way.

She made her way to the kitchen and found Ivan and Wolfie talking at the table, the other man hunched in his seat, eating. Ivan grinned gape mouthed as she helped herself to a mug of tea kept warm near the stove.

"Well well, here's the princess come to dine with us." Ivan turned to Wolfie and continued casually, "Have you fucked Cinders yet?" Tina stared, her mouth open, not sure what to say.

Wolfie rolled his eyes and started to say something but was beaten to it by Ivan who turned back to her and said, "I bet you'd wriggle if I fucked you." He lazily appraised her. "I do like a good wriggle. Dear old Ludy doesn't wriggle much anymore." He sighed with mock sadness, the other man ignored him, concentrating on his plate. Tina noticed Wolfie hiding a grin behind his hand and glared, it wasn't funny.

Ivan sauntered over to her and took hold of her wrist. Shocked from his words Tina let him, the tea slopping over the rim of her cup. He was tall and his warm hand completely encircled her wrist. "So, do you fancy one?"

He smiled, his other arm leant against the worktop blocking her in, she had nowhere to go. Tina could see he expected her to struggle, she gritted her teeth and controlled her instinctive reaction. She moved closer until she all but leaned against him, dragged her knife out from where it was hidden and scraped it gently up the inside seam of his jeans.

"Shall we see if vampires are happy at having a castrati as a pet?" she asked, viciously mastering her voice to stop it squeaking. "Or how quickly they can smell a major artery having been severed?" His grin didn't even flicker as he peered down to look at the knife close to his crotch.

"Very nice," he said admiringly. He released her and went to sprawl back in his chair, "Of course, if you change your mind do let me know," His voice dropped, becoming intimate, "I wouldn't like to keep you waiting." He sipped his tea and smiled while he watched to see what she would do next. She tossed her head, refusing to answer and sat next to Wolfie, trying to conceal her shaking hands.

Wolfie was obviously struggling between amusement and relief and no help to her. Tina tried to change the subject and bring it onto more normal lines, she gazed at the other man stuffing himself. "Your name is Ludy?" she asked. To her surprise he ducked his head, refusing to meet her eyes or answer.

"Ludovic." Wolfie answered for him, "He is Lord Tangent's." Tina felt a growing sense of horror, so this would have been her fate if the Count hadn't taken her, she realised the narrowness of her escape. She remembered Wolfie saying Lord Tangent broke his pets until they swore to him and that he didn't care if they survived or not and felt a wave of sympathy for the silent man.

"So you said you were Consort's pet." She braced herself to look at Ivan.

He grinned back. "Yes, I am here to lend weight to Lord Tangent's words with your Count." She looked confused at him. Ivan glanced at Wolfie. "You didn't tell her? Poor Mouse. Lord Tangent has come to tell your Count when the next ball will be."

Wolfie stared fixedly at his mug, moving it around in circles on the table, he wasn't going to help her on this. Much as she disliked Ivan patronising her, she had to ask, "What ball? Why is it so important?" Wolfie looked tense, Ivan rolled his eyes.

"The ball. Where most of the major vampires will be and where the new vampires will be inducted." At her blank look he sighed, "You haven't been told anything have you?"

Wolfie broke in at this point, agitated. "Mouse hasn't been here long enough to be told much."

Ivan waved his hand dismissively at this and continued, "It's simple, all the various pets that are ready, are drained and blooded for the last time. Then they turn but the catch is, only one is allowed to remain."

Tina's own blood ran cold. "How are they chosen?" she asked.

"They aren't," Ivan said with glee. "The newly made vampires fight, to the death of course and the one left standing at the end gets to live."

She stared at him and turned to look at Wolfie. He avoided her gaze. "You're one of them aren't you."

He continued to stare at his mug and reluctantly muttered, "Yes."

"And so am I." This was said gleefully from Ivan. He was completely potty thought Tina.

They were interrupted by the bell from the library, Wolfie pushed back his chair and frankly ran to answer it. She didn't blame him. While he could be tough when needed, he wasn't a killer. Ivan looked as though he could kill without thought - so long as he could fuck them afterwards, she thought sourly. The kitchen was quiet after Wolfie had left. Ivan stared at Tina, trying to unsettle her, Tina stared at the fire crackling in the grate. Ludovic kept eating, ignoring both of them and intent on clearing the large plate in front of him.

When Wolfie came back he said, "He wants you."

Tina walked quickly to the library where the Count waited for her. The animosity between the two vampires had changed to a coolness.

"Please excuse us. Wolf will show you to your rooms later. Ring the bell if you require anything." The Count spoke with icy courtesy. Lord Tangent nodded, ignoring Tina. Kalmár took her hand and led her out, she had to walk quickly to keep up with his long stride. To her surprise he stopped outside the door to her rooms.

"You have not yet shown me." he said. He waited as she opened the door and he remained there after she'd gone through, hands clasped behind his back.

"Do you need to be invited?" she teased and Kalmár inclined his head gravely. "Come in!"

He came inside and stalked through the rooms. It was like introducing a cat to a new territory she decided or in his case, a large tiger. He inspected everything, touched things, commented and approved, he opened the balcony doors and looked out into the night. Finally they came to the bedroom.

He stopped and looked at the soft green walls, touched the hangings and the re-waxed wood panelling, gazed at the photos she'd taken of the spring woods.

"It is beautiful," he said as he indicated the room as a whole.

Tina had sat on the bed while he looked. "Thank you, the colours remind me of what the woods are like in the spring. It'll be good when I'm fed up with the snow and ice in the winter." He nodded and Tina remembered he hadn't seen the beech woods in the sunlight for many years.

Kalmár sat beside her and she noticed a line on his wrist, where the cuff had been pushed up. Tina hadn't looked this closely before, his pale skin concealed it from a casual glance. The atmosphere had turned strangely intimate in a way she'd not felt before. It encouraged her to touch his wrist and then move his cuff back in curiosity. The deep scar wound towards the inside of his wrist and was joined by others.

She winced, and glanced up at him. Kalmár had an odd look on his face at her compassion and he undid his cuff link to allow her to pull back the open cuff. More scars criss-crossed each other in a network, deeper ones overlaying others. He took his jacket off when she asked and tolerating her pulling his sleeve up to his elbow. Tina held his arm and ran her fingers along the maze of scar tissue running up the inside of his arm. His skin felt cool under her fingers, the hair on the other side prickled softly. She took his other arm and pulled up his sleeve to look at it and found the same.

"Who did this? The vampire who made you?" He nodded, still bemused. "All over?"

"Yes."

"Let me see." She reached up to undo his tie,

fumbling a bit. He took her hands away and undid it himself, raising his chin to unbutton his collar. Below the edge of his collar, the scars started again. They puckered the skin of his neck, there was very little smooth skin left. She ran a finger down his neck, following one and felt him shiver.

"Did he hurt you?" He removed her hand and held it.

"Yes," he repeated. "She did." Tina looked at him, startled. He gazed back calmly. "She was a tiny thing and yet she mastered me."

"When was that? Who were you? Why?"

He smiled wryly, "When? I do not know. A long time ago, many centuries, I have chosen to forget how many. Why? For the same reason I took you, because I wanted you and I could have you. As for who…"

Kalmár was quiet for a moment remembering. "I was a craftsman. Good at my work, a master. I had apprentices, workshops, I travelled. My need for glasses dates back to this period, looking at fine detail in dim rooms ruined my eyesight. Long distance and quick movement I can see clearly, no longer small print. You can imagine my delight when glasses became commonplace." He paused and continued, "I was important in my own small world."

"Many of us hope we are important in our own small worlds," she pointed out.

He smiled, "I was called upon to represent my town, to travel, I met many other important men. I was discrete, trusted by many for business."

Tina imagined him during the day, seeing him relaxed and talking, laughing with other men, tanned by the sun. In times gone by when many could be disfigured by disease or birth defects, his features would have been arresting. Kalmár flashed a charming smile, following her thoughts.

"I never needed or wanted to marry, why should I? I could have any woman in the parish and more from further afield. There were many children who would call another man father.

"My downfall if you wish to call it that, was when I spotted a woman watching me one evening. In the shadows, lit by fires at a festival I caught glimpses of her face, nobody else saw her or knew of her when I asked. In the nights following I saw her, here and there, but never for more than a second. The glimpses were more than enough for me, she looked exotic, different from any other woman I had seen.

"I could not believe she would not allow me to approach her. Never had a woman refused me before, not allowed herself to be charmed by me. She planned it well.

"After a week I was desperate, I discounted the feelings of danger or unease I felt as excitement. I was a strong man, a woman that small could not hurt me. My apprentices thought I was going mad, speaking of a person no one else had seen.

"One evening she appeared at my window, small and delicate – shy I thought. I coaxed, pleaded and eventually invited her in. She gave me what I thought was a night of pleasure and I woke the next morning exhausted. The following night the same happened and the next. Others began to worry about me. After several nights I was finding it difficult to get up and they decided I was being haunted by a demon. They were to call in the local priest to exorcize it the next day.

"That evening she took me. I believe she waited until I was too weak to resist her. Strong as she was, if I had been well, she would have had difficulties. She tied me up in a cart and drove me away like many of the goods I had taken myself. She did not concern herself with feeding me much and I ended up on the edge of starvation. Weak, I was little problem to her. If I escaped, she found me quickly and tied me up again.

"We travelled far away from the places I knew. I no longer understood the language or the customs of the people we lived close to. They sent tributes to her, to stop her taking their people. I survived off these. I was no hunter or trapper, I had made or traded for the essentials I needed all my life. Everything I learned during that time I had to learn by trial and error."

"What was her name?" Tina asked.

"I never knew. She did not give me one. She did not speak my language well. If I refused to do as she wished, she would lash out or starve me depending on her mood. I came to realise she had little intelligence, merely the cunning to get what she wanted. Eventually the time came when I changed. I escaped and preyed on the tribe's people. She had not realised that I could become stronger than her, she tried attacking me one night and she died trying." The muscles in his forearms had become knotted, his hands hardened while he spoke though he kept his clasp around hers light.

Tina was silent for a while. "Didn't you try to get back home?"

He relaxed his hands, "I had been with her for many years Little Mouse. I had no idea where I was. By the time I had wandered back to where I partly recognised the language, it had been decades and more. There had been war and disease. When you have lived for a long time, everything becomes familiar. The shape of a river echoes one in your memory but the landscape is different. A pair of eyes can recall someone and be destroyed by them speaking. No Little Mouse, I never found my home again."

Tina reached up to touch his neck, pulled his collar back to look. "And these are all from her?" He nodded. She stretched and kissed them at the base of his neck, feeling him shiver at her warm breath. "Is that why you try not to leave me with any?"

"I prefer you without," he agreed.

His eyes showed black in the lamplight and she was reminded of their dance earlier in the evening, something hanging in the balance and waiting for a decision. She touched his lips. "How sharp are they? How do you manage not to cut yourself?" He smiled and pulled back his lips and opened his mouth for her curious fingers. This close they looked enormous, she touched one lightly and drew a sharp breath. A knife cut and the blood welled out. The Count folded his fingers around her hand and gently sucked at her finger, touching the tip of it with his tongue. Tina found it surprisingly erotic. She leant against him, her head on his shoulder. Closing her eyes, she breathed in his scent and wrapped her other arm around his waist.

A mischievous thought occurred to her. Her finger was being inspected, he held it up, squinting in the dim room. It had finished bleeding. Tina took it away from him, pulled his head down and with one hand behind his neck, kissed him. His mouth was cool over hers, she slipped her tongue in and flicked it against a canine. It flooded with her blood and his mouth turned hungry.

Her next coherent thought took time as he pulled her close and held her tight. Lying on her bed, wrapped round each other like lovers, she became absorbed in the feeling of his body next to hers and his refusal to allow her to dominate him. Her tongue stopped bleeding quickly due to the saliva in his mouth but he continued to kiss her, lazily taking everything he could find.

When Kalmár let her up for breath, he said, "Do you trust me Little Mouse?" His face was centimetres away from hers, his black eyes pulling her in.

"You've asked me that one before," she muttered.

"Do you?" Insistence from him as his long fingers undid her shirt collar and the itchy feeling of his hunger skittered over her skin.

The decision had been made without her realising it and she didn't care what the consequences might be. Tangent being in the castle, what Wolfie might think or even never seeing her daughter again, none of it mattered in comparison to him lying next to her, his hands shifting her to suit himself. Tina could feel a fierce desire rising, she wanted him to kiss her again and she reached up to touch his face. "Yes."

"Do as you did before."

He pulled her to him and as she cut her tongue, she tasted his blood. Colder and denser, it coiled around her tongue in the same way his mind did. She swallowed without thought, sighed and let go of any resistance. His mind wrapped itself around hers, swamping her with his emotions.

The chains he'd placed round her mind months ago loosened, changing into tendrils that curled and knotted through hers, like bindweed running up a plant. She had the same double vision as before, of being in two bodies, she could feel his excitement mounting at the touch of her warm skin, her fragility and his desire for the hot blood that lay beneath. Her body responded to his lust in the only way it knew. Tina shivered in his arms and twined herself around him as warmth prickled down her body.

He took his mouth away and moved down her

neck. Closing her eyes, she stretched against him, aware only of his cravings and her reactions to it, her insides pulling into an insistent throbbing knot that matched the blood pounding in her throat. He sliced in shallow cuts, taking tiny amounts, kept his mouth on them to heal then shifted, moving to where the blood pulsed closer to the surface. His arousal grew, the hunger becoming more intense as he came closer to biting her fully. Wrapped in the warmth of his mind, she whimpered and caught her breath at the instant where time stretched her awareness into a single point, waiting for release. As he finally sank his fangs in to feed, she arched against him, muffling her cries into his shoulder, her mind running through his, curling into tendrils, twisting and spiralling into ever smaller threads.

Tina lay like water in his arms and slowly became aware of him brushing her neck open mouthed, licking the wounds and holding her close. His presence enveloped her, a fierce watchful counterpoint to the tender way in which he cradled her. A lashing side, ready to defend her against any opponents. Smiling she settled herself further into his embrace, undid a few more of his shirt buttons and slipped her hand inside the open neck. She was hot and sweaty, he felt cool against her curious fingers.

"So, this is me surrendering." She didn't care, it wasn't important any more. Her body was utterly relaxed against his, her cheek resting against the crisp cotton of his shirt. She breathed in the herbal scent and sighed, closing her eyes.

He smiled lazily and shook his head, "Bonded." Whatever, thought Tina.

She slept in his arms and woke to feel a weariness coming from him, a pull that made him want to settle in dark places. Over his shoulder she saw the sky begin to lighten in the pre-dawn. He untangled himself from her and started to do up his collar and cuffs with an absent look on his face. Tina lay watching, lazy and relaxed.

"You have a key for your doors?" She nodded. "Good, I will lock them when I leave. Do not leave them unlocked whilst others are here."

He recovered his jacket from the floor and shook the creases out before he put it on. Kalmár touched her cheek as he left her. She could feel him as he walked through her living room and into the corridor as though he carried her with him. Would this dull? Like the feeling of her first awareness of him? She hoped so, it could get distracting. He was deep in the bowels under the castle, his tiredness infecting her. Tina curled up on her bed and felt herself dragged down with him as he slept.

Chapter 20

It was lunchtime when Tina opened her eyes, the sun shone bright outside and she was hungry and thirsty. Her muscles protested as she stretched and she grinned, that had been good last night. She had no sense of Kalmár, he'd completely switched off.

Her clothes stuck to her in various places, she wrinkled her nose and padded into the bathroom. Tina inspected her neck, looking at the red scratches all now healing nicely. Having bathed, she flushed as she twisted to look at her back in the mirror. She had bruises from his fingers, she'd been too wrapped up in other sensations to notice them happening. She could almost see how his hands had held her, how they'd changed position moving down her back. Embarrassed, she dressed quickly, tucked her hair up and a knife into her jeans.

She wandered in the direction of the kitchen, humming to herself. Tina heard a noise in one of the rooms off the corridor and remembered their two human guests. Peering around the door, a hand on her knife she saw Ludovic with his arms around Ivan's shoulders, his head resting there. Leaning against the wall, Ivan had one arm curled around Ludovic's waist and his other hand was busy as he looked directly at her. Tina's eyes dropped and saw it moving in the other man's trousers. They were undone and she could see the red tip of Ludovic's penis bobbing in and out of Ivan's hand. She snatched her eyes away, feeling herself go red and meaning to walk out quietly.

"It's not all one way you know."

Tina jumped. "Sorry? I didn't mean to

interrupt," she stammered trying to leave.

"I said, it's not all one way." Ludovic grunted into Ivan's shoulder and Tina saw a dark stain appear on his shirt. Ivan grinned at Tina as he wiped his hand on Ludovic. "Because it's my turn now." Shameless he undid his belt and dropped his trousers and pants. Tina averted her eyes. "Come on Ludy." Ivan urged him while he watched Tina.

Ludovic knelt in front of him and wrapped his arms around Ivan's waist. Ivan smiled at her as he touched Ludovic's head bringing him closer. "Do stay, I appreciate an interested audience. Unless of course you'd like to participate, I could think of a lot of…" He paused, clearly enjoying her discomfort, "…stimulating ways for you to join in." His invitation broke the spell and Tina fled to his laughter.

She found Wolfie in the kitchen and told him what she'd seen. He chuckled. "You will see a lot of that at the ball during the day. It does take a bit of getting used to, most people are very open about it although Ivan will cheerfully fuck anything that moves. There was this horse last time." He shook his head with mock sadness, "It'll never be the same again. Spent the rest of its time there with its bum to the wall." He laughed, daring her to believe him. Flushed with embarrassment she joined in, know him well enough that this was one of his tall stories.

"Do you join in on any of this?" Tina asked curious.

It was Wolfie's turn to look embarrassed. "On occasions, I prefer to be with just the one person though. Anyway enough about me," he grinned, "How was last night?"

"Last night? What do you mean?"

Wolfie gave her a significant look, "Last night. Was it good? Knicker changing?" He leaned over and leered in imitation of Ivan and she shoved him away, giggling. He joined in and said, "We all felt it. What does it feel like to join the rest of us and be sworn in?"

"You felt it?" she asked mortified. Wolfie nodded laughing at her reaction as she groaned. The equivalent of noisy sex in a tent - brilliant. When they'd sobered, she said, "I asked him and he said I wasn't sworn, I was bonded. Is there a difference?"

Wolfie looked startled. "Whatever you do, don't mention it at the moment. Act as I do. Pretend you're sworn if they ask." Tina frowned and stopped talking when Ivan and Ludovic came in, despite wanting to know more. Ivan was swaggering as he went to reach for the bread and jam. Wolfie nearly fell off his chair laughing as Tina snapped at Ivan to wash his hands.

Lord Tangent left that evening taking Ivan and Ludovic with him. Tangent had come up to Tina and looked her over with cold eyes. "You took your time," he said to Kalmár who leant close by. "I'd have sorted her out months ago."

The Count smiled aware Tina disliked being ignored, despite her fear. "I find the wait makes them sweeter." Tangent snorted and snapped his fingers at Ludovic who jumped to open the door for him.

Ludovic had surprised her by raising his eyes to meet hers when she'd said goodbye and nodding. Constantly aware she could have been in the same position, she'd spent a good chunk of the afternoon fussing over him, making sure he was happy. He'd not spoken to her, Wolfie said he could, but seldom did.

Ivan had shown his disgust over Tina giving Ludovic her time and energy. Ivan had been a constant irritant, trying to get Tina's attention both verbally and physically, ending up with her having to threaten him with her knife again. He'd retreated grinning with good grace having got his reaction. As he left, Ivan blew her a kiss goodbye and laughed when she ignored it.

Tina found she could pin point Kalmár's exact whereabouts at any time, could feel him wrapped delicately around her, a thread attached between them, tugging. It wasn't as strong as it had been the first night and he refused to speak to her about being bonded when she asked. He informed both of them that he would be going away for a short while and left early the following night.

Tina felt let down, she thought they'd shared something. Feeling like a stroppy teenager, despite the knowledge he was unlikely to change, she swore and kicked out at the punch bag hanging in her workroom after he'd gone. Wolfie wasn't much help either, all he knew was that very few vampires bonded and he didn't know reasons why. The only vampires he knew of were Madame and her Consort and that was partly what made her so dangerous – there were two of them ready to back each other up. Other vampires tended not to, being solitary creatures. Tina assumed not much had changed between her and Kalmár and Wolfie agreed shrugging.

Embarrassed, Tina asked about Ivan. "Don't they mind? Him doing what he does?"

Wolfie laughed. "No, so long as it doesn't interfere with what they want. By the way, you should have seen your face when Ivan was teasing you the first night, it was a picture."

"Would he have done anything?"

Wolfie shrugged, "Never sure. Think he likes you though, he doesn't tend to move so fast normally. Saying that, some of the men he's said similar to, he's nearly got hit at times." Tina laughed with him and went quiet. "What is it?" Wolfie asked.

"Just thinking." He raised an eyebrow and Tina rushed on. "How do you feel about the Count and me."

"I don't know. There's not much I can do," he shrugged. "I have enough to think about at the moment."

"The ball?"

Wolfie nodded, slumped in his chair, he leant his elbow on the edge of the table, resting his fist against his cheek. "I have no idea if I will survive or not. I have no idea what will happen if I do survive. I will have to kill people I have known for years. Ivan can be a pain in the backside but when you've known someone that length of time…" He shrugged unable to continue.

"Ivan didn't seem worried."

"He just deals with it differently, we all worry when it gets close to our time."

She pressed him. "Surely they can't make you fight."

"They won't need to. I won't have any choice, I've seen it happen too many times. Vampires don't deal well with those of a similar strength to themselves, it's instinctive for them to attack. That's why the new vampires end up fighting until there's one left and if I survive, I'll get thrown out to cope on my own."

Wolfie stared out the window not seeing the view, his fingers tapping at the table. "I've been with the Count for a century. A century, think about it Mouse. He won't have me back once I've changed, not with you here. I'll be competition as far as he's concerned and they get protective of their pets. I'll be one like the rest of them, to be put in my place. If

I survive, I can come to the next ball and I'll be welcomed in at the bottom ranks." He rubbed his face and admitted, "I'm frightened. Everything is changing."

Tina took his hand. "I was frightened when I came here. You were good to me." Feeling lost, she waved her spare hand. "I've got to sort this place out when you're gone. How will I manage without you here?" Tears prickled behind her eyelids.

His hand was warm, so different from the one she'd held last night. Warm and human, she kissed it. Without saying anything he pulled her onto his lap and kissed her back. This was why Ivan was like he was she realised, being around creatures that were cold as the vampires no matter how charming, human affection was needed. She sat astride him and he pulled her shirt up, undoing her bra to play with her breasts. Tina didn't care any more about the Count, he wasn't here, had left her to go elsewhere.

Kissing Wolfie, she undid his belt and tugged his trousers down. She pulled her own jeans off one leg and sat half naked against him, fondling him until he was hard enough for her. She wanted him, Tina shifted and pushed him into her. He muttered something into her shoulder and pulled her close while they moved. In a short time it was over. Tenderness was for afterwards, this was reminding each other that they were alive and human.

The days that followed were good. They didn't speak of bonding or the approaching ball. Tina felt the thread between her and the Count twitch on occasions during the night. She mentally prodded it and was disappointed when nothing happened. She and Wolfie spent their days working through the castle, she learnt how he did things, where everything was kept. Her other two dresses arrived and some clothes for Wolfie. At his insistence, she tried the new dresses on while he watched and had fun helping her take them off again. They spent their nights in bed, not thinking about the future.

Tina found herself almost obsessively checking her reports of Jo during the day. They were sent on a regular basis and stayed in a file on her computer. She didn't look at them all the time, just when she needed to feel close to her daughter's life. She flicked through the photos and imagined what she would have been doing in her life if she hadn't been here. Her ordinary life was so far away, another lifetime at least. At least she no longer had to worry about Jo's sleeping, she'd been told that Jo had been picking up on Tina's awareness of the vampires around her and reacting to it. As an adult Tina would have told herself there was nothing to worry about even while she'd been aware of them.

She remembered wondering why she couldn't have Jo here to begin with. Could she have coped with Jo growing old while she stayed the same? How would Jo feel, would it have caused jealousy between them? She tried to imagine in thirty years' time with them both appearing the same age and shook her head. Tina slowly came to the conclusion that this was the best she could do for her daughter, at least Jo had her ex-husband and her grandparents around. She'd grow up in a normal situation, lead a normal life. This wasn't a place for children, even Wolfie had been given the chance to grow up in a family.

Tina had been aware of the Count for some time before he entered the castle. It was early in the morning, a few hours before dawn. Anticipation warred with nervousness as she stood on the tower watching for the car lights and saw him drive into the yard. She wandered downstairs affecting a casualness she didn't feel and stopped when she saw him waiting for her. Without speaking he walked over and picked her up.

Turning, he said over his shoulder to Wolfie, "Remember, she is mine," and carried her up to her rooms. Tina had been resigned to him picking her up, she'd stopped fighting him on that point – this declaration of ownership was different. She tried to sit upright in his arms and failed miserably.

Steaming, she waited until they'd arrived. "Excuse me?" Ignoring her, he plonked Tina on the bed and started to undo the neck of her shirt. She smacked at his hands. "No!"

He stopped to her surprise and looked at her. "I presumed you would prefer to be here, not downstairs." She glowered, furious at him treating her like a commodity. "In the meantime, I am tired and hungry Little Mouse." Kalmár resumed his attention to her collar. She concentrated and slapped at the thread between them. He sighed, "You learn quickly. Let me show you something else."

Kalmár touched her neck and she turned her head away. Closed her eyes, not wanting to look at him. Sensations rippled down the thread between them she couldn't ignore, spilling over into her mind. She was swamped by his hunger, she could sense how he felt her warmth, the delicate thinness of her skin, the blood pulsing under it and the jolt of his wanting her. The need to master her, to make her submit to him and his fight to allow her to remain as she was. She could feel her body start to respond to him, warmth ran down her limbs, her anger replaced by a different desire. Tina opened her eyes, he was inches away, eyes bottomless. Shaking, she tilted her head to give him space and let him take her.

The next day when she went downstairs, Wolfie came and wrapped his arms around her, both of them feeling lost.

Wolfie admitted, "I'm jealous, you get to stay with him in safety here. He can't bite me anymore, I'm too close to turning." He touched her neck gently. "The next time he bites me, we'll be in the grand hall being watched by everyone. I've seen it before, he'll bite me and slash a wrist and I'll drink. The last new vampire standing gets to live. It'll be a bloodbath. You see them come up afterwards coated in it, to swear fealty and then they're gone. Running out of the room, out of the building. Sometimes you see them again, sometimes not, but they're different regardless, never the same." He sounded hysterical. Tina kissed and held him tight, she couldn't think of anything else to do.

The date she learned was midsummer, the longest day or shortest night depending on your viewpoint. Only a few months away. She struggled through the days and nights supporting Wolfie emotionally as much as possible. It was dreadful having the knowledge that he might not survive past midsummer.

Tina realised he'd never had to look after himself before and the concept frightened him. Everything he'd done during his life had been supported by the Count, even if he hadn't been living at the castle. He admitted he was terrified of going back to the poverty he'd experienced as a child. He was pulled between the two scenarios unable to decide whether survival or dying was worse.

When she finally felt she could do no more, she threw his own words back at him. "Buck up," she said. "You're not dead yet. You've lived a damn sight longer than most ever dream of."

Wolfie glared at her and stomped off

muttering. She rubbed her face, exhausted from his moods and grumpily thought that at least him getting angry was better than him getting hysterical.

Her relationship with Kalmár was also demanding, Tina doubted she would ever understand what went through his mind. There were the days when she thought he genuinely cared for her and others when she felt like a cow waiting to be milked. She could be swamped by his emotions when he was near and then there were times when she became exasperated by his being a thick headed man. How did you deal with a man used to living by himself for centuries? Tina had heard confirmed bachelors were bad enough but he was used to getting his own way on everything. She chose her battles carefully, surrendered when she had to, and teased him at every opportunity.

This proved entertaining during her period, these had been growing shorter and less regular as he'd promised. She drifted around the castle, knowing Kalmár could smell her and wanted her. When he appeared at a doorway lusting, she smiled and wandered off to find him following. Tina had discovered she could make him wait and used it mercilessly. That was worth every second of the frustration she had from him, battering her senses. He took his revenge in seduction, a delicate stalking through the tendrils that bound them. To pinpoint the places he could brush within her mind then swamping her with his own lust, until gasping at the molten desire she couldn't deny his feeding any longer. She came to realise that if he was in the right frame of mind then he enjoyed being teased, the thread between them at these points pulled with a steady tension, balanced.

Chapter 21

The journey to the ball took many of the short summer nights and for reasons of his own, Kalmár refused to take a plane flight. While they all took it in turns to drive at night, Kalmár did most of it. His eyesight and reactions were superior in the dark and he drove in his usual style, fast and impatient with other traffic. Tina's driving was more cautious, Wolfie teased her about it. She'd ignored him and kept going, refusing to give in until the night tired her and she curled up to fall asleep with her head in someone's lap.

Tina remembered the conversation she'd had with Kalmár several days before, he rarely told her anything unless it was convenient and pressing him for information never worked. She'd not been able to stop turning the latest snippet he'd let drop through her mind since.

The memory of having the accountants in the castle had been nagging at her and Tina had wandered into the study early in the morning to find Kalmár gazing at a laptop. He'd stood as she came in and removed his glasses, holding out a hand. She'd casually sat in his lap putting her arms around his neck.

"Yes?" He raised an eyebrow and drew her close, "You would like something Little Mouse?"

It encouraged her to ask, "That first night when the accountants were here, you knew Mr Durrant was watching us, didn't you."

"Of course, was there a problem?"

She sighed in exasperation and poked his chest as she counted off her grievances, "Only having to defend your kidnapping of me, the fact that you were biting me at a point when I wasn't happy about it and that it would be detrimental to his career and possibly his life chances if he talked about you. So no, not much." Tina carried on over his intake of breath, determined to finish her list, "And… it would also have helped if I'd been told me about the mobile jammer you have here. I nearly wet myself when he was walking round looking for a signal."

"Did you ask about it?" He looked amused at her indignation. "We normally switch it on when we have visitors."

"I never had to – I don't have a phone and I hadn't been allowed anywhere near the internet at that point!"

"You may have a point. Would you like a phone?" One win, she'd thought she'd never be offered. Refusing to be side-tracked, despite being irritated and amused in equal amounts, Tina returned his smile and kissed hm lightly as she remembered, "Madame said you told them I was beautiful."

He ran a finger along her jawline, "And?" he enquired back.

She glared at him, no longer so amused. "Why haven't you told me?" He shrugged elegantly allowing his fingers to trail down to the buttons of her shirt, she could see him becoming more distracted. She caught his hand, determined to capitalise on his rare, open mood and changed the subject. "Are you going to tell me what you mean by us being bonded?"

Kalmár sighed and allowed her to play with his fingers. "It does not happen often. It involves both sides being willing to give up a part of themselves. For the human it is easier, however for the vampire…" he trailed off and she waited. He stared at the wall and started again, "Our nature is such that we wish to control, to possess. To make the other surrender. To allow the other a measure of control is difficult, it is to be fought against every second you are with them." He took his fingers away from her and returned to undoing her buttons.

Tina thought for a moment and laughed in delight, "So what you're saying is that you've surrendered to me."

Kalmár returned her look calmly, "No more than you have." She ran her fingers through his hair and pulled his face down, kissed him and let him bury his face in her neck.

Bonded, more than a pet, less than a vampire. The thought had disturbed her in a way she couldn't pinpoint. Sitting in the back as Kalmár drove through the night, Tina stretched to lean over the seat, tugging at Wolfie's bright hair and stroked the Count's shoulder. To distract herself, she mentioned the joke about men and large cars.

Wolfie turned around in mock disbelief. "You think I'm small?" he asked, waving his hands in the direction of his crotch. "What was your ex - a donkey?"

Kalmár said nothing until she looked at him. Straight faced and watching the road he said, "If you would like a tiny car similar to the one you used to own, I will buy you one but do not expect me to fold myself into it."

She laughed, she'd driven this car, it was fabulous. The mood was subdued at times during the journey, whatever happened there would only be two of them returning. They made the best of it, Wolfie controlled his terror, finding pleasure in small things. During the day, the Count curled up under the seat in the back of the car. They would find somewhere off road and sleep as well, wrapped around each other on the seat above him.

They were deep in Russia now and came to a summer palace behind tall gates and shaded by birch woods. The tall towers were coated in ivy hiding the beautiful brickwork and shading the enormous windows. It had a similar look of neglect to the Count's castle, it would have been beautiful in its heyday. Ivan greeted them at the gates, he shifted from one foot to another unable to stand still for a second. He formally welcomed them in, bowed to Kalmár, hugged Wolfie and swept Tina off her feet, kissing her soundly.

She gazed around as they entered taking in the artwork and paintings. A sense of spaciousness filled the building, it was light and airy even in the night. A few people milled around in the corridors some human, others not. Tina watched them as she walked, tried to pick out which were which. The humans looked back, equally curious. She could feel many vampires, the few that she saw were on edge, wary of each other and her head ached with the tense atmosphere. She saw many bow or incline their heads to the Count. He ignored them all and walked swiftly through.

They had a suite of rooms, one for the Count, another for Wolfie and Tina, the last for entertaining. Kalmár barred himself into his room as dawn came and they were left on their own to unpack. Wolfie made sure Tina had her knives, warning her not to go anywhere without them. They fell asleep on the bed together, exhausted from the long journey.

It was lunchtime when Tina awoke, she poked Wolfie. "Where do we find food? I'm starving."

Wolfie muttered and turned over, his eyes tightly shut. She tickled and kissed him until he showed more interest in her than sleeping.

Afterwards, he resigned himself to being awake and took her out to show her the palace. They found food in the kitchen piled in the cupboards, Wolfie pulled out various items to eat and made tea.

"Not many people awake yet." Tina commented as they sat at a long table and watched others wander in and out.

Wolfie shook his head, "There aren't huge numbers of us, only the older vampires tend to have pets as there aren't enough to go around with the right blood. That's why they set an age limit and insist on children. We're dying out."

"Not necessarily a bad thing," observed Tina.

He shrugged, "Anyway, there are five ready this year including myself and Ivan."

He spoke Ivan's name as he walked in, his arm wrapped around a tall blonde woman. He waved a hello at Wolfie and leered out of habit at Tina. Tina rolled her eyes at Wolfie as Ivan ate and watched him fondle the woman absently who smacked back at his hands with relaxed swipes. Wolfie introduced her as Sasha. She blew a kiss at Wolfie and he ducked his head smiling. Having seeing Ivan's outlook on life, Tina decided not to ask why, she'd interrogate Wolfie later when they could both enjoy it.

Wolfie showed her round the rest of the palace, the huge stunning rooms and enormous windows looking out onto the countryside. She met more people during their exploration, some were wary, others more friendly. Wolfie introduced her to them and afterwards gave her a potted history of each one, letting her know who not to trust and why. They went back to bed and woke in time for dusk.

Tina came back into the main room, having had a bath. Her hair was wet but thankfully she was properly dressed when she saw they had visitors. She put her towel down, bowed to them and came to stand close to the Count.

"Madame, Consort, this is Little Mouse." She stared, remembered herself and bowed lower. At a motion from the Count, she curled up on the end of the sofa and studied their guests. Madame was tiny, her face fresh as if she were twenty and wrapped in an embroidered silk Chinese dress. Her eyes were dark with age and sparked malice as she gazed at Tina. Power radiated off her, it made Tina anxious in a way she hadn't felt for a long time. The Count ignored Tina and talked to Consort, they mentioned places and names she'd never heard of. Consort looked older but had a nicer face, more open. His eyes laughed at things, at her when he caught her peeking at him. She reminded herself that he was also dangerous although it was far harder.

Wolfie sat in a chair further away, his face tense while he watched and listened. The presentation would be tomorrow night, afterwards there would be dancing and the following night would be his last. They rose to leave after what felt like ages talking.

As they left, Consort came over to Tina, a cool finger under her chin raised her face to look at him. "You are a cute one," he said and walked out with Madame. Tina looked at Kalmár confused.

"Do not allow his manner to deceive you. Remember you are mine." He added, "I would not like to have to challenge him, although I would." Tina thought about having to stay with Madame and shuddered. No fear, Madame terrified her. She snorted and both men looked enquiring at her.

"Just remembered I thought you were terrifying when I first met you."

Tina fussed over her clothes for ages the next

night. Wolfie had dressed in a mossy green jacket and dark trousers. She didn't want to look like a matched pair so she'd decided to wear the pink again. Sprawled over the bed he watched, laughing while she swore over fitting the corset to her dress. Eventually he got up and helped despite teasing her about taking it off again. The Count appeared later in formal black.

There weren't enough people to fill the great hall and they were all dressed differently. They wore individual versions of finery, some more shabby than others. She found the presentation fascinating, each one would come to the front, bow to the others and say his or her name.

Amongst the sea of heads and shoulders Tina could see glimpses of the few she knew. Lord Tangent, with Ludovic behind him, trying not to attract any attention. A scarred vampire whispered into Lord Tangent's ear. Tina froze and pointed Vinceti out to Kalmár who shrugged and ignored her concern. Vinceti's face looked a mess, his shoulder didn't look right and he moved with a limp when it was his turn to go up. The crowd murmured when he did, clearly some hadn't expected the injuries. She saw Madame and Consort in a gap. Consort spotted her at the same moment, looked her up and down and winked approvingly. Tina looked away, finding his friendliness unsettling.

The vampires seemed to have a system for the presentation, Tina couldn't work it out. It appeared as though it was some reminder of rankings. Wolfie had told her a while ago that titles didn't count, some had them, some didn't, it had no impact on where they were ranked. Physical age she could dismiss, she'd realised that depended on what age you were when the infection took hold. In fact she noticed most of the older looking vampires had presented themselves early, neither Madame nor her Consort looked old and there was one across the hall that couldn't have been more than eighteen when he'd been made, his face was cherubic.

She shifted around, taking the weight off one foot then the other, wondering when Kalmár would go up. There couldn't be many left to present themselves, that meant Kalmár must be high ranking. The cherub went up, looking bored. She caught a glimpse of his eyes as he walked past, no he wasn't young, those eyes had seen too much. He also had a human walking next to him, Sasha, the tall blonde Ivan had been fondling. It was the older ones that had companions with them, none had two.

Lord Tangent swept up next. He made his bow, commanding the room and announced himself and Ludovic. Tina breathed a sigh of relief, Ludovic wasn't in tomorrow and shifted again to relieve her aching feet. Her hand was taken and the Count started to move. After her initial surprise she remembered to put shoulders back, chin up and make her skirts swirl as they walked. People moved out of their way, inclining their heads and making quiet comments. The Count stopped and turned at the front of the room.

"Kalmár." He bowed shortly, "My companion Wolf, who will participate tomorrow night." Wolfie bowed low looking rakish in his smart clothes, for once his bright hair neatly cut and combed. His face was pale and composed. "And bound companion, Little Mouse." The eyes focused on Tina as she remembered to curtsey. It was terrifying having the attention all on her. The muttering grew louder and she remembered what Kalmár had said, binding rarely happened. The Count stood for a short moment, it felt like an age to Tina and walked back to their place.

Madame and her Consort walked up next, Consort in the middle with Ivan on the other side. They introduced themselves and Ivan announced as entering tomorrow night. Madame clapped her hands, "Let us dance!"

Vampires and humans alike swirled away to talk, to find partners or instruments. Wolfie disappeared to find the piano but promised them both a dance later. The presentation had taken a good half night. Tina looked forward to taking the weight off her feet when the Count pulled her into a promenade dance. She matched his elegance the best she could, this dance had the partners changing throughout and she had to think to stay in time with the music. She swapped through having to dance with Lord Tangent, he ignored her while he whirled her round and she mentally blew a raspberry in his direction when they'd finished. The cherub was graceful in his dancing and equally graceful in his attentions.

So many cold hands touching, shivers of hunger running over her skin as the eyes watched her, lusting. Tina was passed from one to another like an expensive toy at Christmas. When she got back to the Count, she laughed in relieved delight and he smiled back. It seemed to go on for ages and she was flagging by the time she was allowed to stop.

Tina spotted refreshments on a small table near the back of the room. She slipped over and found a glass and a drink, too aware of the vampires turning to watch her go past. Un-nerved with all the attention she put her head down and tried not to notice. She bumped into someone and jumped as she recognised Vinceti. He glowered and stalked off - his face was even worse close up. Shaking she went to find the Count. The musicians played a waltz and she stepped in time to the music, beginning to hum. She stopped as someone moved into her path, looking up she found Consort in front of her.

"May I have this dance?" he asked. Tina stared, not sure if she could refuse. He plucked the glass from her hand and held it out without looking, someone took it. He took her hand and pulled her into the dance. She looked around wildly for Kalmár and couldn't see him

Consort was a good dancer, he was not as tall as the Count and moved gracefully to the music. He chattered to her, charming as he told her about the various people around them, none of which she knew. She wasn't sure if she should laugh when he made rude comments about some of the dancers. He had an appeal similar to Wolfie's, although every so often she had a flash of power off him. The combination frightened her close up as much as Madame had at a distance. She could tell he wanted something but couldn't work out what.

When the music stopped, he released her with a smile. She didn't like to admit she fled to the Count's side, promising herself not to leave it again. Kalmár wrapped a long arm around her waist, took her wrist and kissed the inside, his eyes looking across the room while he did.

She whispered, "I didn't think I could say no."

He nodded stiffly, his eyes hooded. Wolfie came and claimed both of them for a threesome. A slow waltz came after, Kalmár drew her close and the room ceased to exist for Tina. She put her head on his shoulder and relaxed into him as he moved her around the dance floor. Her eyes closed, she ignored everything except his fingers stroking her neck and his mind wrapping itself around hers. When they came to a halt, she smiled up at him. She found him looking across to one side, she followed his gaze and saw Consort flicking irritably at something on his jacket. Hiding her smile Tina tucked herself under Kalmár's arm as they walked off the dance floor.

The dancing continued almost until dawn. Tina felt exhausted, the other humans looked equally tired. Ivan persuaded her to dance with him, he had the ability to dance and have his hands everywhere at once. He reacted with delight when she slapped his hands away. Tina's threats about her knife didn't work, she immediately had her hands full trying to stop him undressing her to find it. He made suggestive comments all the way through until she laughed so much, she had to stop and wipe her mascara. She wondered if Ludovic would ask, but he stayed behind his master when Tangent wasn't dancing and next to the wall when he was.

Most terrifying of all was when Madame partnered her. She had asked Kalmár's permission and when he'd agreed, Tina had gone reluctantly. Madame wore something filmy, it concealed everything while appearing to show much. Tina didn't want to hold her hands and was frightened of touching her dress in case she ripped it. Madame was unconcerned by such trivialities. The cold eyes assessed her and Tina couldn't begin to imagine what went on in the mind beyond. She seemed completely inhuman, far away from what she had started life as. Her cold hands competently took Tina through the moves and steps. She felt very aware if she became a problem then Madame would squash her like a bug rather than move an inch from her course. At the end of the dance she stopped and held Tina with her.

"You are bonded to Kalmár." Her thin voice grated.

"Yes," Tina whispered, bobbing her head.

Madame took her chin in hard slender fingers and looked into her eyes, "Do not allow yourself any ideas above your station. Consort is mine."

She shook her head, stammering that she had no intention of having anything to do with Consort. Tina was relieved when she was released and she walked back to the Count shaking. On reflection she thought as she wrapped his arm around her, you needed an iron will to get this lot to do anything together. From what she'd seen, they were all highly individualistic and very obstinate.

The Count told her they would leave and collected Wolfie on his way out. Tina had noticed very few women around and fewer female vampires, she asked why. The Count replied that the genetic component appeared to be mostly connected to the male side, not so many women were born with it.

Wolfie chimed in, "Also women don't tend to survive the process. They either die through injuries or kill themselves due to not coping in the early years. If you do meet any female vampires be wary of them. They've had to be both mentally and physically tough to get so far." No fear Tina thought, having met Madame, she felt primed to be very wary.

Tina collapsed on the bed when they got back and groaned when she realised she had to get out of her dress. The Count said his good nights and left them. Wolfie grinned and asked if she needed a hand. He sat behind her undoing buttons as he whispered his suggestions for aching feet. She giggled - they had nothing to do with her feet at all.

Chapter 22

It must have been close to lunchtime when she stirred and decided to go and find some food. Wolfie was sprawled naked and face down, snoring gently. Tina gazed at him, enjoying the sight as she pulled on her clothes. She found her way to the kitchen and stopped in the doorway to see Sasha sat on Ivan's lap kissing Ludovic, who was responding with enthusiasm.

"Um, morning," she tried as she walked past. Ivan's hands were up Sasha's shirt, no surprises there then. Sasha untangled herself from the men and came towards her.

"Congratulations on your first presentation Mouse," she said her arms outstretched. Without thinking Tina responded to the hug as she would for any girlfriend. Sasha kissed her lightly on the lips, then drew back and asked, "Would you like to join us?" Tina hesitated not sure what was being offered.

Ivan called out from the table, "I tried asking Cinders to join in a while ago, she got shy."

Tina glared at him and he grinned back, enjoying being unhelpful. One of Sasha's hands slid under her untucked shirt and along the side of her rib cage, the other held her close. Tina nearly spluttered something rude when she realised Wolfie wouldn't be here next year and she'd need allies.

Taking a deep breath she kissed Sasha back. "Not this time thanks. I've got to get Wolfie some food." Sasha's nails tickled as she ran them across her back and flicked her bra undone. Tina swallowed nervously, women weren't her thing.

"Are you sure?" Sasha asked. "You could

bring him." The hand caressed her back rubbing at the marks left by her bra. Out of the corner of her eye she could see Ivan sprawled across the table, leaning over to watch. Ludovic was flicking his eyes between them and the table, trying not to show his interest.

"He's asleep at the moment, needs his rest." Tina winked, trying to imply she'd worn Wolfie out. "Maybe next time," she repeated smiling. Sasha lazily smiled back, removed her hand and tucked her shirt into her jeans. Tina saw Ludovic smile as Ivan slumped on the table, fed up that nothing more exciting had happened.

"Right boys," Sasha said as she turned back to them, "Where were we?" Ivan immediately perked up. Tina felt sorry for the men, she got the idea Sasha was going to wear them out. Grabbing a tray and some food, she got out before anything more embarrassing happened.

Wolfie laughed when Tina told him about Sasha's offer, she'd decided not to try doing up her bra with a tray in her hand. Sasha was all right he told her. She was Ansell's pet, the cherub Tina had noticed last night.

"Have you joined any of their threesomes?" Tina asked teasing.

"Might have," he answered, refusing to be drawn. He pulled her close and teased her on what might have been should she have taken up their offer. The detail he added confirmed her suspicions that he'd spent quite a time with all three of them and not necessarily one at a time either. To her surprise she found a shy curiosity creeping in, and began to whisper her responses back with an increasing enthusiasm to both their delights. Too aware that this was the last day they had, they spent it in bed together. She held him while he slept and they talked while touching each other, neither wanting to let go.

At dusk they got ready, they had plenty of time as nothing happened until midnight. Tina wore trousers, it had been suggested it might be a good idea. She helped Wolfie get dressed for the last time, his hands were shaking too much to deal with his buttons. She strapped his knives in place, kissed him and tucked her own into the back of her trousers.

"I'm not sure how much I'm going to remember of all this. I spoke with the Count. He can only remember certain things about his human life and those are like snapshots or short films. He doesn't know if it's to do with the long life he's lived or becoming a vampire. I hope I remember you Mouse."

"I'm Tina. Why don't you call me by name any more?"

"Because you aren't Tina any more. You left her behind a long time ago, you just didn't realise it."

Tears rose in her eyes, "Nobody else calls me Tina. I'm going to miss you." He tucked a strand of hair behind her ear and held her close.

Kalmár entered, his usual quietness overlaid by the sombre mood. He looked at Wolfie and ran his fingers through the red hair, touching his face. Tina watched them, thinking about all those years they'd been together. They waited patiently, the time dragged and then sped up to only drag again. There was nothing left to say, the attempts at conversation fell flat and they stopped trying.

"Come," the Count eventually broke the silence and turned towards the door.

They walked to the main hall, most people stood near the edges of the room, away from the centre. Tina noticed a large circle pattern in the tiles, the grouting between was stained black, nicks and chips showing. She held Wolfie's hand, not wanting to let go before she had to. Midnight approached. Wolfie gave Tina a kiss and a firm hug He'd calmed since arriving, the inevitable was going to happen.

"Bye bye Mousie," he said and tweaked her nose. Tina bit her lip as he walked off with the Count and left her forever, she wrapped her arms around herself feeling terribly alone. There was a noise close by and looked round through blurred eyes. It was Sasha with Ansell close behind. Tina noticed Sasha was inches taller than Ansell. Sasha held out her hand and she took it gratefully, desperate for any sympathy.

Madame sat in a chair on a low platform, leaning on one elbow, her dark eyes unreadable. The five candidates were presented again. Two women, one dark and stocky, the other smaller and fairer, the other man was shorter but wider than either Wolfie or Ivan. All five looked nervous. They arranged themselves around the inside of the circle and at a nod from Madame it began. Tina could see the Count's face, his eyes hooded as he pulled Wolfie close and fed. One by one they slumped into their vampire's arms.

Tina had been told it was a race, whoever finished feeding first got a head start. The Count pulled his collar away from his neck and broke the skin, he placed Wolfie's limp mouth against it. The other vampires had slit their wrists. Wolfie's form jerked and he wrapped his arms around the Count, his face set into a mask. The room silent, everyone was intent watching the ten in the circle. Consort next to the Count, his own face in a grimace as Ivan sucked at his wrist.

The Count jerked and threw Wolfie into the centre of the circle, Consort reacted, attempting to do the same. Wolfie whirled round his knife in hand and buried it into Ivan's spine. He shrieked and collapsed onto the floor in front of Consort. Tina's hand clutched Sasha's, the other over her mouth as she tried not to be sick. Wolfie's face snarled, she'd never seen him like that before. Consort stared at Ivan in shock. Blood oozed down his wrist as Wolfie pulled the knife out and wrenched the head of the stocky woman back, away from her vampire to slit her throat.

The remaining two had disengaged. The smaller woman feinted and stabbed the other man, wounding him, Wolfie finished him off from behind and they faced each other over his corpse.

The crowd murmured avidly, the silence broken as the fight began. Tina's eyes fixed themselves to Wolfie's figure, not wanting to miss anything. Her only wish was she wanted him to survive, he had to. The five vampires moved back, the Count taking hold of Consort's sleeve and pulling him away.

Tina watched the two left in the middle, their eyes black, the pupils huge as they focussed on each other with blood around their mouths. Wolfie was coated in blood from the others. Ivan shifted impotently on the edge, white and silent in shock, both ignored him, he was no longer a threat.

The fair haired woman was fast, she slashed with precision, her eyes narrow in concentration. Wolfie fell back with several shallow wounds, he had the reach but she moved faster. She would get in close where his extra length could do no good, block his arms, slash and twist away before he could react. Tina could feel the mood in the room, her head tight with it. The vampires aroused by the scent of blood leaned in, watching avidly. Sasha held her hand hard, their knuckles were white.

Both had wounds, Wolfie had one to his face that dripped, distracting him. She had one on her knife arm, he'd got that close before she'd forced him back, she wouldn't give up. They came closer to Ivan, he'd stopped moving, exhausted. The woman slashed and retreated. Slashed and retreated, Wolfie was hit again. Moving slower, his leg dragged, a long gash weeping through his trousers.

Tina could see how her eyes gleamed, certain she could win, she would wear him down by degrees, even if it meant cutting him to pieces. She took a step to the side to avoid Wolfie's knife and Ivan shifted, grabbing her ankle. He shrieked as she pulled him across the floor. She dropped her knife and sat down, shock on her face.

Wolfie took his chance and jumped on her, finally able to use his greater strength to push her onto her back. He pinned her arms down and knelt on them. She kicked and struggled and weakened by the knife wounds, she nearly threw him off. He shifted and jammed his knife up to the hilt between her ribs. Tina jumped again as she screamed. The knife was twisted and dragged out. She stopped kicking.

Wearily he turned to Ivan, who gazed at him, still holding her ankle. Absently, without emotion he pulled Ivan's chin up and Tina looked away. When she turned back, Wolfie stood on his own in the circle with his arms dangling. It was quiet. Tina realised it hadn't taken more than ten minutes for the entire process. Wolfie's gaze passed over Tina and she shivered, he wasn't the Wolfie she knew. The eyes were blank and with no understanding of what had happened. He was covered in blood, dripping down his knife hand.

She desperately wished she could help, Sasha's hand held her tight, preventing her from going to him. Before Tina could move, Madame beckoned, Wolfie went and knelt in front of her. She whispered a few words, he nodded and took her wrist. She broke the skin and allowed him to drink, whispered something else. He stood dazed and then stumbled down the steps and out of the room.

Sasha pulled her into the circle with the rest of the companions and Tina was horrified when she discovered that she was meant to help clear up. She looked around for Kalmár and saw his back as he spoke with Consort across the room. The iron stench of blood and opened bowels smelt horrendous, she had no choice but to walk through the sticky blood, making tracks through it.

Tina helped Sasha load Ivan onto a stretcher and hauled him outside, retching through her tears. He was floppy and heavy and no one else offered to help them. Others dealt with the three remaining bodies, soaked the blood off the floor and cleaned the circle. The vampires ignored them, talked amongst themselves or left the hall.

Sasha led the way around to the side of the building, to various holes that had been dug earlier. They bundled Ivan into one and Tina stared numbly at Sasha over his cramped body. There wasn't even enough space to lie him down decently. The tall blonde rubbed her hands together, pulling her fingers through each other.

She looked at Tina and said, "He was bonkers, good fun. In some ways a gentleman." Tina's face twisted, the one word she wouldn't have used for describing Ivan. Sasha giggled, slightly hysterical in her grief, "He'd always make sure you came first…like I said…" Tina joined in hiccupping, that was a better description. Sasha continued, "He was the first person I met when I came here…" her voice trailed off. Tina saw tears welling, she walked over and wrapped her arms around the taller woman.

They stood a while looking at Ivan and then Sasha said, "Come on, let's tuck him up." A spade waited for them on top of the heap next to the hole and they took it in turns to cover him. When they'd finished, they walked around the corner and saw Kalmár and Ansell who were talking quietly.

On seeing them, Ansell offered his arm to Sasha and the Count picked Tina up. She noticed he still had blood on his shirt from earlier, she held her dirty hands out of his way while he carried her to their rooms. Tina scrubbed her hands and fell asleep on the bed exhausted.

She woke several times during the morning, lost and disorientated without Wolfie next to her. Despite her stomach growling, she didn't want to get up, exhausted emotionally from the previous night. Sometime after lunch, Tina heard a knock at the door and reaching for a knife went to answer it. Seeing Sasha with a tray in her hands through the gap, she let her in and they wrapped their arms tight around each other.

Tina cried for a long time, surprisingly, she found she also grieved for Ivan. Remembering how he'd danced with her the other night, wishing she could have known him better, if only to take him up on some of his more outrageous suggestions. Sasha held her and allowed her to grieve. When Tina couldn't cry any more, Sasha fetched a flannel and wiped her face. They ate, arms around each other and talked quietly.

Sasha said she'd known Wolfie for many years. Ansell had told her everyone had been surprised when Kalmár had appeared with him one year, he'd always been on his own before. Tina asked if she'd known Wolfie's real name, it seemed more important than ever but Sasha shook her head, he'd always been Wolfie. She said he'd refused to get involved in the jostling for position like most of the human pets did. It made him dependable to be on the outside although he could be nasty enough when provoked.

Sasha told her that Ansell had been the pivoting factor in the vampires organising themselves many years ago. The Count, Madame and Consort had started it and when Ansell had joined them any resistance had collapsed. They'd seen how the human world had started to expand and develop and realised they could no longer stay as they were, assuming their superiority over a peasant population. They would have to adapt to the new world. They'd been vicious in their views, no one allowed to stand in their way. Madame now ruled, with the three male vampires backing her up.

The balls had been started with a view to keeping the numbers of newer vampires down, they had to swear to Madame and survive on their own. Sasha thought they would have to reconsider the circle soon, there were less and less new candidates coming through every year. Ansell agreed with her views although he also thought she hoped not to have to fight. Tina nodded, the idea of having to fight like last night frightened her.

Tina gave Sasha a last hug before evening fell. Sasha kissed her as she opened the door and said teasingly, "Remember, you owe me one."

Tina laughed, tears coming back into her eyes as she recalled Wolfie whispering into her ear that morning. "And Ludovic."

Sasha rolled her eyes. "Oh yes. Ludovic. He doesn't talk much but hey, he doesn't need to. Just you wait." Tina grinned and nodded as she closed the door.

Kalmár came in shortly after dusk, he insisted on leaving, refused to stay. He ignored her distress and wouldn't talk to her about Wolfie. He fed, holding her as though she might break and carried her to the car. She was aware of meeting Consort on the way out, Kalmár spoke to him curtly, keeping the conversation to a minimum. She could feel his eyes on her and she stayed curled up in Kalmár's arms, her head in his shoulder with the feeling of him protecting her. Tina didn't want to think about anything, let alone deal with Consort.

The Count drove for most of the night to put distance between them and the other vampires. It felt strange, lying during the long days on the back seat of the car on her own and with nothing but her own thoughts to distract her. He refused to let her drive, he was right, she wasn't with it.

The castle felt empty. Wolfie had always been busy, a bubble of noise around him and she fell into his habit of having the radio on for company in the silent castle, at least she could now understand the language. She had notes everywhere from him, how to do things, lists to help her. It was upsetting how everything reminded her of him but it was good to be back in familiar surroundings. Tina found herself stopping every so often, wondering what Wolfie was doing, where he was and whether she would see him again.

After a week of putting it off, she went into his room and broke down. It was a mess as it always had been. Clothes and magazines everywhere, the bed rumpled from when they'd left it. She sprawled there, gazing at the walls, wondered how she could go on without him. Tears leaked out and she buried her face in his pillow and howled for a while.

Then she heard his voice in her head telling

her to buck up. Tina smiled wanly, sniffing and got up. She'd sort the room out at another point. It wasn't important, she had plenty of time. At least she'd had someone when she'd first come here. He'd been right, she was a different person now, tougher in many ways. She was determined she would survive and become one of those to be wary of.

As she walked out, she snagged one of his dirty shirts from the floor. She'd take it to bed with her and smell him as she fell asleep.

Wolf

Chapter 1

Wolfie staggered down the steps, everything hurt, the pain pulsed across his wounds, beating in time with his heart. His head span, aching from the heightened sensations of the other vampires in the hall, the hunger, the lust for the fight, for his blood – for anyone's blood. He rubbed his face, his eyes didn't work properly, they pushed through the darkness and changed its colour from black into purple and then switched back again. It made him feel ill and he struggled to keep his stomach under control. All that blood he'd drunk, Kalmár's throat under his mouth, his hands holding him upright...

Someone grabbed him from behind and twisted his arm tight behind his back. Wolfie's reaction was instinctive, he twisted sideways, trying to slide out of their hands. The cold grip clamped around his wrist, refusing to budge and a deep fear rose of being contained - he mustn't be caught. The person swore as Wolfie struggled and he was smacked around the head for his troubles. His feet slid along the path as he was dragged away into the shadows by the front gates. The person released him and shoved him into the wall. Glaring, Wolfie turned and spluttering swear words, raised his fists, only to have a rucksack thrown at him. It bounced off his chest, catching several knife wounds and he winced as the breath was knocked out of him.

A familiar voice, "Right, are you going to help yourself or do I have to knock you out and tie you up?" Wolfie swore again and Samsa moved out of the shadows. "Look, it's up to you. I don't care, I get paid however this happens, so are you coming the easy way or not?"

The oddity of his statement stopped Wolfie's tirade of abuse. "Why?"

Samsa waved behind him and Wolfie turned to look. A few vampires had spilled out of the entrance, scanning the night. Instinctively he moved out of their line of sight behind the gatepost and noticed Samsa had positioned himself out of their eyeline as well.

"You've got Kalmár's blood in you, and Madame's. It's diluted but anything's better than nothing to some. So, are you coming?"

Samsa held out a helmet and waited, an insolent look on his face. A motorbike was tucked in the shadows. Wolfie took one more glance at the hunting vampires and swung the rucksack over his shoulder, he'd be lucky to survive if that lot caught him. Samsa put his own helmet on, started the bike and waited while he gingerly got on. Sounding amused at his change of mind, Samsa said, "Let me know if you're going to faint, I'd rather not have to stop and scrape you up."

Shouts rang out as the bike pulled away, Samsa rode with the lights off, not giving anyone the chance to follow them. Wolfie could only hope he could see in the dark as well as Kalmár had been able to. The ride didn't help his stomach and once Samsa switched his headlight on, the shadowed landscape shifting past made him queasy again. The flash of trees, purples twisting into darker blacks. His wounds begin to throb and sting from the air. He didn't think Samsa would appreciate him throwing up. Shutting his eyes, he concentrated on staying conscious and held on tight.

When they stopped, Wolfie was stiff from sitting and chilled despite the warm night. Silence rang in his ears after the constant rumble of the engine. He staggered off, barely able to swing his leg over the saddle. Holding his helmet, Wolfie looked around, he couldn't see any sign of civilisation and it wasn't dawn, he couldn't work out why they'd stopped. Samsa in comparison was relaxed and alert, a danger radiating from him. Wolfie tensed, he didn't care what had been said at the Summer Palace, there was no way he was letting Samsa attack him. He knew Kalmár would want him away from Tina – how far? Permanently disposed of? Did his service of years mean nothing? Despite swaying through exhaustion he shifted position, ready to defend himself.

"Stop panicking." Samsa waved a hand. "Get changed. You don't think I can take you anywhere looking like that do you?" Wolfie looked at himself in the light of the bike's headlamp while Samsa rolled his eyes at his slowness. Dried blood coated him, his fingernails were dark crescents, and his clothes slashed from knife cuts.

"Change your clothes," he repeated, "Try looking in the bag." Samsa leant against a tree, half talking to himself while staring at Wolfie insolently, "Just imagine, I could be hanging round the ballroom, dreaming of sticking my fangs into that neat little package Kalmár's got but no, I'm here. Babysitting." He pulled a face and wandered off, muttering and kicking at the dirt.

Wolfie pulled out clothes from the rucksack. Slowly he changed, wincing at his wounds and tried to control his temper. Samsa was no longer subservient around him, he was truculent and found him tiresome. Wolfie could feel the difference between the two of them. Samsa was strong and had an edge to him Wolfie hadn't known before. His face went hot, all of a sudden he was a little fish thrown into a big pond and it wasn't pleasant. He stuffed his old clothes back in the bag.

Samsa handed him a water bottle. "Wash your hands and face." When Wolfie had finished cleaning up, he nodded him back onto the bike. A short while later they arrived at a small town. Samsa took him up to a motel and booked him into a room. When Samsa walked back to his bike, Wolfie followed him.

"Right, this is where I leave you. Good luck and don't come near me again if you want both legs working." The other vampire sounded almost cheerful at the thought.

"Hang on. What happens next?" Wasn't he a vampire? Shouldn't he hide from the daylight? He knew so little, Kalmár hadn't told him much what happened next and he'd never asked. All his thoughts had been on the circle, not what happened afterwards. Samsa was all he had and he was being abandoned.

Samsa shifted impatiently. "Look, have you got fangs yet?" Wolfie hesitated, then raised his fingers to his mouth and stopped, feeling stupid when Samsa smirked. "It doesn't all happen at once. Get some rest and get out of here as soon as you can. There are safe houses in the places where the old ones sleep. Otherwise you're on your own. Get used to it baby." He put his helmet on, muttering to himself.

Wolfie watched him ride away, anger growing at the sting in his words. Now Samsa was the stronger, he was deeply unpleasant. He looked at the empty road for a while, then let the anger go and shrugged, anything was better than being back at the Summer Palace with all those other vampires. He shuddered at the thought of the power rippling through the room. As Kalmár's pet he'd never noticed how weak he was, he'd been important in his own right as a human with the blood they'd all desired. Now he was nothing. Everything ached as he found his room and dumped his rucksack on the floor next to the bed. Without taking his shoes off, he flopped across it and fell deeply asleep.

Sunlight streamed in through the open curtains. Wolfie raised his head and blinked, trying to remember where he was. His eyes weren't right, they focused on too much detail and the light hurt. Squinting, he made them behave.

He remembered last night, he'd survived and killed – several times. Wolfie put his face in his hands, shaking. Ivan was dead. Pain in the arse, fuck anything Ivan. He wasn't sure what he should feel, his emotions were all mixed up. His memories of Ivan were as a fellow human, the laughter and friendship over decades, the competing over women and their seduction. But he had another disjointed side to him, one that gleefully murmured he'd killed a competitor and he'd won. He felt sick as his fingers twitched and a thrill ran through him. Numbly he rubbed his face and winced as something stung.

He limped to the bathroom and looked in the mirror. No problems with his reflection, he looked pale but otherwise normal. A thin scab crossed the top of his temple. He remembered her doing it, the look in her eyes and how he'd felt. Rival, the other part of him whispered, you beat her and survived. An anger coiled at the thought of her cutting him. He noticed dried freckles of blood were splattered over one cheek and the anger turned to a physical lust. He fought it down and stared, trying to see the Wolfie he knew.

Abruptly he couldn't stand looking at himself and stripped, he turned the shower on hot and scrubbed everything he could. He checked himself over, he had several knife wounds but none were too deep and all were healing, at least that hadn't changed. He was hungry as well - what did he eat? He squinted into the mirror again, checking his teeth. Nothing had changed there. He thought of normal human food and his stomach growled.

Wolfie went back into the bedroom to go through the rucksack. The clothes from last night were coated in dried blood and he fought the temptation to handle them more than he had to. He'd find a way to wash them later. There were more clean clothes underneath. A jacket was in the bottom, something crackled in the pocket, he pulled out an envelope and opened it to find his tickets to surviving in the human world. Money, a bank card and documents, the name on the documents, Owain Glas. He recognised the bank and the name on the documents, he'd used it before but wasn't sure if it had been his originally. He remembered Owain being right, but the surname?

The memory rose of standing in a dark cobbled alley, the damp mist kissing his face and the sharp pain of hunger in his stomach. A darker figure in the shadows, an amused, accented voice telling him that he was showing his teeth like a wolf cub and his own voice piping back - "Yeah, Wolfie, that's who I am."

He shook his head, feeling troubled that it didn't feel important. Wolfie was the name for the boy he'd been and the man he no longer was. A cub no more, he'd be a Wolf from now on. He'd grow strong and hunt others. Dressed, he walked out into the day, bought some dark glasses and hitched a lift with the first truck heading out.

Chapter 2

Wolf drifted. He'd spent decades in the Count's employment and now had no reason for being anywhere. Rudderless, he wandered for several weeks, going wherever he could get a lift, nowhere specific in mind. Memories of life before the ball faded, he could remember them if he tried but they had no urgency to them. Gaps appeared, stretching unnoticed until triggered by random events. A smell, a glance, a flash of colour and he would be left scrabbling for why it felt familiar. Feeling disconnected to his previous life, Wolf obsessed over Samsa's last comment, maybe he could find a place in a safe house, whatever that was.

He'd noticed the changes happening to him, it was as if the events at the ball had been a tipping point with the infection. It became harder to walk in the strong sunlight, his eyes hurt him despite wearing the dark glasses. He cherished what he had left, trying to appreciate and remember everything he could - flowers, the light on the trees, the brilliance of the sky. Wolf got headaches if he stayed out for too long and his skin itched, going red. At the point when he had problems even on dull days, he made the decision to stop, adding to his loss. He regretted no longer going out while it was light but realised he felt more comfortable in the dark. He tended to lie up during the day, not always sleeping but dozing. A definite drowsiness came over him when dawn arrived, a pull to find somewhere safe and an alertness with the coming night.

Wolf stopped near a town for a few days. On

the outskirts, these rural areas had plenty of barns, ruined cottages and forgotten caves he could sleep in. Failing that, if he became desperate, he paid for a room, giving strict instructions not to be disturbed and wrapping himself in a quilt to hide further. He had plenty of money in his bank account, although he realised it wouldn't last forever.

Walking into town one evening, Wolf felt other vampires for the first time since the ball. He could feel them circling, out of sight. He was being hunted. Four or five of them and in a strange way he could tell none of them were old or strong. A pang hit him, he'd not spoken to anyone for weeks apart from the humans driving the trucks he'd hitched lifts with. He sifted through his scant knowledge of younger vampires – they tended to stay in small groups with a ring leader who was stronger, pooling their resources. As they grew in strength, they'd naturally split, killing off the weaker ones. He felt his lip curl and the thought rose that he wouldn't let himself be killed - he'd be the leader or nothing. Anticipation making him nervous, he checked for his knife, the other side of him coiled and waiting. He squared his shoulders and walked out to meet them.

One stepped out of the gloom and leant against a tree. "Evening." Wolf nodded and stayed silent. "You're new here, you've not been around long." Wolf nodded warily again, waiting for the rest of them to show themselves. "You know, you won't survive on your own, don't you, why don't you join us? We'll look after you." The vampire waved his hand and one by one they appeared.

Wolf narrowed his eyes in contempt. They'd pass in human society but only just, they looked a mess. Worn, dirty clothes, they made him look positively immaculate even after weeks of travelling. He'd spent far too long in the Count's company, he had standards even if he tended towards the casual.

"Thanks but I think I'll pass this time." This dross wasn't even worth leading. Wolf edged away, hoping to get out without having to fight and slapped down the whispering side of him that made his hands twitch.

"Come on, you've not got your fangs, have you?" The talker's voice was persuasive. "There's safety in numbers. Heading in the direction you are, there's lots of older ones. They'll kill you if they find you." Wolf shook his head, he'd take his chance, they wanted someone weaker, someone to push around. He wasn't going to accept that. The talker smiled and showed his wrist, "Here - a token of my goodwill." He slit it and the blood dripped, pooling into the palm of his hand.

Wolf paused, unable to take his eyes off, his mouth flooding with saliva. He could smell it even from where he stood, the iron tang that promised everything. He hadn't eaten much for the last few days. Out of habit he'd bought large quantities and found some food he could no longer tolerate – the thought of eating vegetables made him retch. He'd ended up buying raw meat from the butchers and chewing on it, half gagging from the sensation. He suspected he was at a halfway stage, his teeth hadn't come down yet and were still blunt. He'd started to starve, losing weight rapidly while his body adapted.

He grunted as someone barrelled into him from behind while he was distracted. They fumbled and missed grabbing for his arm. Wolf twisted and to his surprise he realised he was the stronger, he threw the other vampire easily. Furious, he let himself go and his other side sparked with the sheer joy of fighting. He kicked the downed vampire, leaping over him to draw his knife, determined to make them pay for this insult.

Identifying the talker as the strongest, he took the advantage and went for him. He slashed with his knife, allowing the other part of him to take over and snarled, showing his non-existent fangs. He noticed the other vampires moving away to watch. Not enough loyalty to their leader to rush him all at once – good. The wounds from the ball had healed. He was as fast, if not faster than he had been. Part of him coldly calculated and anticipated the moves. Wolf could smell the blood from the vampire's wrist and found himself craving it. His stomach cramped, driving him on.

The other vampire tried to get in close, to pull him into an embrace and strangle him. The other side of Wolf's nature realised with delight that this vampire didn't have as much experience of fighting, no martial arts knowledge and kicked out, smashing a knee. As he dropped, Wolf grabbed him, twisted his arm behind his back and held the knife at his throat, trying to remember through the lust of fighting the questions he wanted to ask. "What's a safe house? Where do I find one?"

The other vampire laughed. "You want a safe house? That's the last thing I'd call them."

Wolf twisted the arm further. "Where?"

He winced. "Listen out for the old ones, the ones sleeping. Ask around. I don't know any more, I stay away." Part of Wolf wanted to slit this vampire's throat, howling for victory. He took a deep breath and tried to stay in control of himself, he couldn't ask any more questions, the scent of blood had sent a red mist across his brain. He was desperate, he couldn't bite, no fangs.

"Give me your wrist, the one you cut." The older vampire twisted away and grunted in pain as Wolf leant on his arm. "Hold it up."

Beaten, he did as he was told. Wolf fastened

his mouth around the offered wrist the best he could and sucked hard. This was what he needed, rich and dark. He could feel it going down, working on something inside him. Awareness of his surroundings shifted outwards, he could feel the night and his senses sharpened, taking in the rustling landscape without seeing it.

The other vampire gasped and sagged against him, the blood flow slowing. Distracted, Wolf relaxed his grip and released the other vampire, he fell, slumping onto the grass. The rest moved towards their former leader as Wolf backed away. Knife in hand and wary of a new ambush, he left the area, wiping the blood from his mouth.

Wolf wandered aimlessly on through the nights, listening hard for anything that might be considered to be an old one sleeping, unsure of what it would sound like. He woke one evening in his rented room to being aware of people around him. They were like bubbles of warmth moving and he froze, not daring to move until he realised they were in different rooms. Animals he felt as smaller, duller bubbles, he noticed how they stayed away from him, dogs cowering and barking when he came too close. He was fascinated, experimenting with how close or far he had to be to sense them. No more vampires around at the moment, at least none he'd noticed.

He could no longer cope with meat from the butchers. It was cold and dead. He felt desperate for the warmth, the tingling aliveness that the blood from the other vampire had woken up in him. He still had no proper fangs yet, he couldn't bite anything. Wolf stopped next to a garden later in the night. Someone had pet rabbits in a cage, he could sense the warm bubbles shifting in the straw. Fingers twitching, he paused, trying to work out if he dared steal one. Desperation forced him forwards. He snuck over the fence, up to the cage and unlatched it, grabbing one as a dog howled nearby. Lights came on, blinding him and he ran, clutching his prize.

He stopped a good distance away, under cover in the nearby woods. The rabbit was stiff with fear in his arms. Wolf sat, holding it, wondering if he could do this. He ran his fingers through its soft fur, feeling the warmth and its heartbeat, how it trembled. He wanted it so much, he felt an exquisite ache as his fangs came down, dull and useless as they were. He was shaking almost as much as the rabbit. Holding it with one hand, he drew his knife with the other. He had to do this at some point he told himself, if he couldn't kill a rabbit, how would he deal with anything bigger?

He had to do this in cold blood to survive, this was so different from being attacked and responding. The part of him he'd designated vampire stayed quiet for once, holding itself still. Looking into the darkness, Wolf centred himself, lifted the rabbit, slit its throat and put his mouth to the wound. Despite the fur sticking to his face, he clutched it to him, sucked hard and pulled out everything he could as the rabbit kicked against him.

He pulled his mouth away and gasped. Dizzy and with a sticky face and rabbit hairs in his beard, sated in more ways than the cold meat had made him. He could do it. Tomorrow night he would hunt a small creature, try again. Wolf laughed in relief and dropped the rabbit - he would survive. He came back to earth with a bump, swearing as he noticed his shirt was ripped from the rabbit's hind legs and the remains covered with blood and filth.

Chapter 3

Tina swore and kicked at the table leg, the computer wouldn't do what she wanted, again. She missed Wolfie and his ease with technology. She could use computers but there were times when she couldn't work out how to get them to do certain things, things that seemed so simple, so logical. She stared at the computer, tapping her fingers in frustration, knowing Kalmár had woken and was moving around close by. When he appeared in the doorway, she looked up, enquiring.

"Would you care to go out?" Tina nodded, eager for anything to distract her. She switched off the computer with a happy sigh and got ready.

Kalmár drove them to the nearest town. As they got out of the car, a group of local youths swaggered past, pushing at each other in the joy of being young. One caught Tina's eye, he felt familiar although she'd never seen him before. The lad laughed at a comment made by friends, his face turning to puzzlement as he glanced at the Count. Kalmár ignored him and stared at the buildings close by, waiting for the group to go by. The lad walked away quickly with his friends, no longer laughing and looking back at them over his shoulder.

His face stayed with Tina and she asked about him while they watched some jazz in a dark corner.

"I have been aware of him for a number of years. He is like yourself. That is why he feels familiar, you recognise the similarities. He does not know what he is or why I make him uncomfortable."

A brief thought occurred to her that he might have been related to Wolfie – did it work that way?

"Will you take him when he's old enough?"

"Would you object?" He smiled, raising his glass of water to wet his lips.

"Might be nice to have some company." She teased him, "Would you mind sharing me again?" It was his turn to shrug as she mischievously thought of all the possibilities having a man in the castle might entail.

"You were having problems this evening." It was the first time he'd acknowledged she might be struggling.

"I'm not as computer literate as Wolfie was. It's not easy."

"You miss him."

Tina was surprised at Kalmár bringing it up, "Yes. Do you?"

"I lived with Wolf for many years. It always takes time to adjust to such changes." He changed the subject, "There is a computer course at the university close by. It lasts for a week at the summer school and is residential. Would you like to go on it?"

"What about you? You'll be on your own."

"I have been on my own before. You however may benefit from being with others from time to time." A smile curved the corner of his mouth, "Especially if you can improve your computer skills."

Tina looked at him, elegant in the dim room and refusing to talk about how he felt. She decided she couldn't drag any further admissions out of him and said, "Yes, I think I will."

That had been several months ago, she'd been busy since with various courses. It was as though once she'd been away the first time, all of a sudden there was plenty she wanted to do. It had been good to get out of the castle, though it felt strange to be on her own and in different surroundings. It was also a challenge for her language skills to keep up with her learning. At times she found herself missing Jo and the feelings would hit her with a sharp ache, crumpling her stomach.

Her reunions with Kalmár were equally intense, he missed her when she wasn't with him, although getting him to admit it was impossible. When she came back from each of her trips away, they would spend nights talking through what she'd learnt. He insisted on knowing every last detail, discussing until he understood everything, finding out about the people she'd met, what they thought and why. Knowing what he wanted drove her to talk more to people than she usually would.

He'd winkled out she'd had several affairs, despite her trying not to mention them. To her relief, he wasn't jealous, he had her to himself within the castle. Tina had enjoyed the human contact, the warmth and sexual companionship between two bodies, different from the deeper bonding she had with Kalmár. She'd surprised both herself and the men involved by initiating and ending them before she came back. Wolfie had brought out another side to her, she'd never been so forward before.

The Count also took time away while she was on her courses, although he never left her alone in the castle. He talked about the places and people, discussing the points of modern living that intrigued him and compared them to other times he'd lived through. This fascinated her as much as modern life did him. Snippets dropped out of his memory into conversation and when she asked him to elaborate, were embroidered into a richer tapestry of a life long gone. Some of his recollections were not pleasant. Despite her disgust, he didn't try to hide them, he simply shrugged and told her that times and attitudes had changed.

The weather changed, from warm summer to cool autumn. The beech trees turned, showing fiery reds and oranges and the wind hinted in the fresh gusts that it was preparing for the deep cold. Tina had started sorting out her lists for winter. This being her first winter of organising, she was nervous of getting it wrong. It felt strange arranging everything in the castle to her own convenience and with no need to consider anyone else. She knew little would be able to get through if she made any mistakes. Kalmár would be fine – she wouldn't be. If she got it wrong, she might end up with only beans to eat for a month and it would be a lot of beans.

In the meantime, there had been visiting musicians and Kalmár had started taking her out now the dark evenings were longer. She worried about being on her own, with the dark days and being shut up in a cold castle. She wondered how Kalmár dealt with it, how he'd dealt with it in the past on his own. Tina ordered anything she could that might stave off the loneliness and boredom, at least she could drive to the town and be amongst people for the time being.

Chapter 4

Another month, another town. Wolf had successfully hunted small animals for a while. They filled him up but a part of him craved more. He worried about this other side of him, it was taking over more and more. He couldn't remember being like this before, it boiled up without warning or whispered to him about what he could do, of what he might do given the chance. It helped with hunting, he'd focus on a small animal and chase it, anticipating its moves. He was fast and could snatch a rabbit with minimal concentration but it wanted larger prey, urging him on as he looked at the humans walking in the night.

He found a drunkard asleep on a park bench and unable to stop himself, crouched close by, fighting his desperation to feed. This was no rabbit, this was a man who lived and talked. Wolf stifled a groan, at some point he was going to have to make this leap to feeding on humans – but how? He crept closer, noticing the rise and fall of the man's chest, the rank smell and unshaven cheeks. His other side rose, it wanted him helpless under him, his mouth on his throat... the hot blood... He licked his lips and gave into his hunger, letting it take over. The vampire glanced around, no one was around this time of night, no one to witness his triumph of feeding. So close. He stretched a hand out to touch his shoulder, to feel the warmth signalling the pulsing blood under the thin barrier of skin.

The man woke, bellowing at the hands on him before he had a chance to try anything. The noise shocked the vampire into hiding and Wolf panicked and ran, not wanting the attention. Frustrated by his desires, Wolf kicked his way along several side streets. His fangs had come down. He touched them and swore as he cut his fingers. Curious about what they looked like, he bent and pulled out a car mirror to look. He couldn't see anything in it. He dug his fingers around the mirror and twisted it out of the housing, breaking the plastic and wires.

Wolf walked over to a street lamp and looked again. It showed the scene behind him, peaceful in the neon glow. He touched the mirror, fascinated despite the vein of panic rising. No fingers showed, the scene remained undisturbed. He tried smearing some of his blood on the mirror – nothing. He wiped it off and dropped it, the glass shattering as it hit the pavement.

Vampire. Determination filled him, he was going to go back and feed. He remembered how Kalmár had wrapped his mind around his and wondered if it would help. The vampire part of him wanted to break the man, snap him, drink his blood and drop him to become someone else's problem. Outraged that prey could make him run away, it tugged at him, whispering he was strong enough. The realistic side of him also knew he couldn't do that. He held his other nature tight, squashing the instincts, he needed to think this through with both sides of him.

Wolf found his man back asleep on the bench, snoring. He hunkered down, trying hard to push his thoughts out to make a connection. He felt the man as a warm bubble, separate. Frustrated, Wolf paced and stared at him intently. He didn't know how to do this, didn't know how to get in. Would he have to feed off animals for a while longer? Was this something he couldn't do yet? Maybe he should go and find a cat, there'd be plenty around here.

The vampire within snarled, he was ready, he just needed the knowledge. He continued to stare, thinking of the blood, a skin's depth away and longing for it. Desperation pushed his thoughts through another channel, it was tight and uncomfortable, like trying to get into a jumper several sizes too small. He wriggled his mind and found a sudden connection as the man sighed and stretched in his sleep, turning towards him. Wolf tensed, expecting him to wake and shout. The connection pulled him closer, his stomach clamping as his expectations rose in excitement.

Creeping up as the man rolled over, Wolf caught him before he fell off the bench. The man wrapped his arms around him and pulled him close. Unsure, Wolf dropped his head, brushed his lips into the unshaven neck and instinct took over as the warm skin intoxicated him, making his hands shake. The vampire inside whispered in exultation. As he bit, he could feel more connections click into place, the intimate closeness of knowing someone's body from the inside, a maze of possibilities forming. His lust flowed through the connection between them and the man's hands flapped, his legs twitching. More blood flowed into his mouth as the heart rate increased. He encouraged the man's own lust to get more and heard the muffled grunts as the man heaved against him. Still clumsy, Wolf managed to feed without losing his grip on his neck.

He finally stopped, overwhelmed by the shock of desire he'd felt and the emotions of the man washing over him. He felt drunk with triumph – he'd managed it. It was so different from animals he'd fed from, so much more. Blood all across his face, he could feel the heat, blood trickled down the neck of the man. He licked at it and cradled the man, a tenderness welling up for what they'd shared.

The bleeding slowed and stopped. The two puncture wounds didn't look too bad., he was pale but still breathing. A vague guilt, maybe next time he shouldn't take so much. Tucking the man back onto the bench, he scrubbed at his own face. He dragged his spare shirt out to wipe the rest off, he'd have to learn to feed neatly, no mirrors to check himself in any more.

Exploring the far side of the town a few nights later, he noticed a gentle breathing at the edge of his hearing. An awareness so subtle he thought he'd imagined it. He couldn't pin point its whereabouts. Wolf thought he'd talk to a couple of other vampires about it and decided not to when they made their annoyance at his interruption clear. Those two were older than him and stronger, unlike the last vampire he'd beaten he'd have no chance against them. With his long legs covering the ground, he easily sprinted away and stopped, puffing in an alley.

He peered around the corner, waiting to see if they followed. One day he wouldn't have run, others would run from him, he'd be strong. A hand grabbed his arm and he jumped. He'd not noticed anyone behind him, having been concentrating on the others. He stopped struggling and swore internally as he took stock, this one was far older and could do him some serious damage if he took offence.

"You're a strong baby, aren't you? Are you reliable?"

Wolf looked at the older vampire, that was not a normal question. Confused, he asked, "Why?"

"I need reliable vampires to watch for me and you look like you need somewhere safe to stay. I'm Yorgias." Still holding on, Yorgias steered him out into the street. The other two appeared and Wolf tensed, ready to slide away and run.

Yorgias yelled, "Bugger off, he's mine." To Wolf's surprise they scowled and walked away. A couple of women laughed further up the street. "Evening ladies." Yorgias leered at them and wrapped his arm further around Wolf in a mock act of lust, the look dropping off his sharp face once they'd passed.

Wolf was walked to a small door in a smelly alley and was told, "I'm letting go. Run and you'll have problems." Wolf stayed. The rational side of him didn't see the point in running, the other part was too intimidated by the older vampire.

Yorgias unlocked the door, invited him in and showed him down the stairs. They led to a large room with a sofa and a few chairs and tables scattered around. Another vampire sprawled in front of a computer. Wolf looked at Yorgias, he didn't have the edge a lot of vampires had, there was no sense of danger radiating from him. He was certainly strong though, his iron grey hair was tightly curled and his face dominated by a large nose.

"I get a feeling for vampires, those who are reliable and those who aren't. Comes with practice. Well, am I right?" Wolf shrugged, staring at the computer remembering the feel of keys under his fingers and the flickering screen. The other vampire hit the keyboard, swearing.

Nodding in the computer's direction Wolf asked, "What's wrong with it?"

Yorgias leaned against the wall and watched, unconcerned at Wolf's lack of response, "Fucking thing's not working."

Wolf walked over and looked. "I could help, used to be good at it." The second vampire shrugged and slid out the way as Yorgias waved a hand. Wolf sat and started tapping at the keyboard, becoming absorbed quickly. Everything came back to his fingertips, it was easier than remembering his life before through the veil.

Close to dawn Wolf became aware of Yorgias sitting next to him, he stretched and yawned. "Nearly finished. You want a decent anti-virus on it, apart from anything. The amount of crap you have on here. Stop people downloading anything and everything and you should be okay. I can go through and delete stuff later if you'd like." He stopped, suddenly aware he wasn't Wolfie anymore and it wasn't Kalmár he was talking to.

Yorgias shrugged, "Computers. They're useful but I've never got the hang of them." He held his wrist out, "Hungry?" Wolf stared at him, not understanding.

"Stick your fangs in. You can have ten heartbeats, for the work you've done and a safe space for the day. Deal?" Wolf became aware of the approaching dawn and his hunger. He nodded and grabbed the wrist offered.

Chapter 5

The clouds hid the stars, it was raining and the weather wouldn't break any time soon. Wolf sat on a stone near the entrance, out the way of most of it. The occasional irritating drip fell on him but there was nowhere else to be comfortable in the cave. He stuck the ear bud back in and fiddled with his MP3 player. It had run out of batteries. He swore and pulled the ear bud out, listening to the long slow breathing below him, deep underground. It never faltered, never changed.

He couldn't stand up straight without ducking out of the cave and then he'd get wet – not that getting wet mattered much anymore. Wolf liked the feeling of drops hitting his skin but getting soaked was different. He shifted restlessly, stretched his long legs out and pulled them back in as they got splattered.

His mind roamed and sought out the living creatures in the vicinity. Most animals were curled up, out of the rain. Some small animals, mice and rats scurried in the undergrowth, keeping well clear of him. Even creatures so small knew instinctively to stay away. Only some domesticated animals were too dense to realise he might be dangerous. Wolf went through his pockets for a spare battery. Dogs barked at him when they saw him, trying to warn their owners, not that the owners took any notice.

He liked small dogs and cats. Big enough for a meal if he couldn't get anything else, small enough to dispose of easily. His fangs extended, tomorrow night he'd be relieved by another vampire and would be able to hunt. No battery, he'd have to get more batteries as well. He peered back into the cave, a human wouldn't be able to see anything here. He saw the darkness in a mix of deep purples, shaded and grading into each other. The darker they became, the further away the cave wall.

Wolf drummed his fingers against his leg. Soon it would be time to find his resting place for the day. The owner of the slow breathing few could hear hadn't thought about resting places for years, centuries maybe. It might wake up shortly or not for another hundred years. Either way he was here to listen and report.

Wolf hadn't experienced an old one waking, he'd not even seen one. It was deemed too dangerous to go down so far, he might disturb the sleep. He'd been told some were so far removed they couldn't communicate any more, just bodies that slept and woke, an embarrassing relative in the attic. They were scattered in different places, always difficult to get to. Sometimes the breathing stopped and when they investigated, all that would be found were piles of dust. Unsettling dust to touch and clinging to fingers as if even after disintegrating, the owner was unwilling to let go of any life. It was swept up and disposed of, he wasn't sure he wanted to know how.

He ducked out of the cave to stretch and rubbed his hands through his red hair. Rain soaked it and ran in drips down his leather jacket. He held his hands out, collected the droplets and sluiced his face. Having got the kinks out of his frame he sat back again, waiting. Jeans sticking to him, Wolf could feel the pull start. A gentle urge - dawn is on its way it said. Come and rest, settle in a safe place away from curious eyes. He ignored it for a bit, waiting for it to grow stronger. The sky wouldn't lighten much before dawn, the clouds obscured any pre-dawn light.

He yawned, fed up and checked his pockets were zipped, he didn't want anything to fall out, nothing to let anyone know he was here. Not that many did. He grinned, the locals knew of the cave, it had a reputation for being haunted and they avoided it.

Crouching, he moved further in. It opened out into an area almost tall enough for him to stand straight and appeared to go no further. Someone had left the remains of a fire in the middle. Wolf pulled himself up, into a narrow high corner and wriggled down, head first, into the concealed tunnel. He didn't like this bit, it was too tight and with no chance to turn back, no way to defend himself if something happened. He didn't enjoy being helpless and without thinking he snarled, his fangs out. His senses roamed in front of him – nothing. It didn't matter, he still didn't like it.

He wriggled his way into a larger cave. This had several blankets rucked up in a corner, enough space to sit and stretch out in safety. He refused to look at the other exit leading into the bowels of the earth. The silent exhaled breath coming from it mocked his fear. Tiredness overwhelmed him. Bone weary now, Wolf kicked the blankets into a comfortable heap and lay down. He looked into the dark purple walls of the cave, then shut his eyes and slept.

The next night he had company when Jon arrived. He was smaller and had dark hair, so he didn't stick out as much as Wolf in this part of the world. People tended to notice Wolf's hair, he'd get another hat when he went back and cover it up. He ran his hand over his chin, he needed a shave too. Wolf paced in front of the cave while he talked, he'd been here for the last month. Jon shrugged off his complaints and listened stoically to Wolf's grumbles about being hungry. He grunted in satisfaction at the regular breathing from the cave and told Wolf to bugger off.

Wolf loped down a track and found the car parked by the side of the road, the keys had been left in the ignition. There was a safe house in the nearest town. Deep cellars to sleep in if you couldn't find or hold on to your own place. Somewhere to relax and find out what had happened in the world while you'd been away.

He abandoned the car in a side street close to the safe house and walked, it was never good to have a routine. As ever, his senses were on alert. Not many people were outside, it was too chilly to linger and too early for throwing out time at the pubs. Wolf made his way to an unremarkable doorway in an alley of warehouses. Rubbish was piled high, scattered bits of paper drifted and there was the sharp smell of urine, not necessarily animal. He unlocked the door using the code and re-locked it on the inside.

There was post on the floor, he picked it up and leafed through as he walked down the stairs - mostly junk apart from some letters for Yorgias, the senior in charge. The room below was austere, they didn't need much. A couple of vampires were talking in the corner, they stopped and stared as he came in. Wolf threw the post on a table and slid through the side door to the deeper cellars without stopping. They were both older than him and stronger. He sighed, everyone was stronger than him.

The sole reason for Wolf being here was Yorgias, the safe house was his. The fact he didn't allow any infighting meant Wolf had a chance to feed and sleep somewhere. Yorgias was in charge of listening for the old one in the hills behind them. He was secure in his position and would be backed up by any older vampire. This made him unusually tolerant, except when it came to his rota for listening. Yorgias didn't like it when his rota was upset. He tended to explain this carefully, normally while beating the shit out of the person who'd messed it up.

Wolf found his room and got changed, thinking over the last few months. His human life was hard to recall. He could remember standing in the great hall, dazed and with the emotions of the other vampires washing over him. The smell of blood, on him, on the floor, everywhere. Alone and vulnerable, then Madame at the front of the hall calling to him and he went to her, needing her protection. Just because he was a vampire didn't mean he was safe with the others. Quite the opposite, an older vampire was likely to kill a younger one simply for being in his way. The promise he'd made not to oppose her in any way still made him uncomfortable, sealed with her blood as it was. No chance to think, death had been the other alternative. He twisted his body, forcing himself back to the present, ignoring the links stretching to her. It was difficult to look through the veil, although images did come through sometimes. Thinking over his human past also made him uncomfortable, it was best to keep in the now, too much introspection could get you killed. He changed his shirt, shaved and went upstairs.

Only one vampire was left in the room, Wolf vaguely recognised him. He nodded without expecting a response and sat at a computer. The vampire stared at him. He was short, his black hair in a tail, with a scarred face and a twisted shoulder, Wolf did recall him now he thought about it but couldn't remember where from – the past – it didn't matter. The vampire came over, his leg dragging as he walked. He was older than Wolf and the vampire side of him whispered he'd be strong but slow, that he'd have lost ranking with the injury and it would make him irritable.

"Don't I know you?" Wolf ignored him, struggling to contain his other side while it gleefully pointed out he'd be able to move faster and finish him off. There wasn't a need to answer, he kept typing. He leant against the table, inches away from Wolf, deliberately provoking him. "Red hair. New. I do know you." Wolf was hungry and irritable and he had to remind himself that he wasn't allowed to fight in here. "You're Wolfie. The Count's pet, you turned last ball."

Wolf sighed. This vampire was asking for a fight, he stopped his typing and stood. Looking down he deliberately exaggerated the difference in height and squared his shoulders. The other vampire bristled. He couldn't back down, even if he lost, this one had got on the wrong side of someone before. Words recalled themselves to him. "Bounced a few times, then crawled off…" The vampire snarled and Wolf realised he'd said them aloud.

"Evening." Yorgias stood in the doorway and stared hard at them. Wolf took the hint and sat, the other snarled again and limped out the room. Yorgias came over and leaned against the table, where the other vampire had been. "Problems?"

"No." It wouldn't have been a problem, he'd have managed.

"If I find you fighting again, you're out. I don't care how reliable you are. That one is attached to Lord Tangent and I can't afford to upset him." Wolf shrugged. He looked at the computer, his hunger starting to shout at him. Yorgias continued, "You need years, you need to find out who you are again. It takes time, I've seen it before. I can give you that, if you stop picking fights with everyone around you. Accept it, you're younger and weaker, bend your neck sometimes."

Unable to contain his hunger any longer, Wolf stood, "I need to feed." Yorgias sighed and watched him walk off.

A fine rain fell, Wolf hunched his shoulders and walked through the quiet streets. He couldn't stop fighting, he wasn't made to be an underdog and the other side of him wouldn't accept it. Wolf could feel his face twisting as he tried not to snarl his frustration. No amount of understanding from Yorgias would change how he felt. He made himself concentrate on his surroundings, working for Yorgias meant nothing if he was caught outside the safe house. The town was mostly asleep, neon lights reflecting on the pavements, a few cars drove through the puddles and a dog barked as he walked by. He headed for the homeless men's hostel and stopped at the door. Peering in through the glass, he knocked and eventually an old man answered.

"Watcha Wolf." Wolf waited silently, leaning on the frame and waited for the invitation. "Come in then."

"How're things going Dennis?" The human showed no fear of him, he was under Yorgias' protection, they had an agreement.

"Fine, fine. Not seen you in a while. Been off again have you?" Wolf nodded, distracted. Unconcerned, Dennis waved his hand. "Go on up then."

Wolf walked swiftly up to the first floor. He leant against the wall and closed his eyes against the harsh light in the corridor. Yorgias had showed him how to do this and after several frustrating attempts, he'd managed. Yorgias had done a lot for him over the last few months and he tried not to think that Yorgias might be right about him fighting.

He let his mind expand, searching and found what he was looking for. It was there, on the next floor and to the right. He took the steps two at a time, touching each door in the corridor as he passed. It was quiet, all the occupants of the rooms were asleep. He found the correct door and stopped. Both hands resting on it, he concentrated, sending his mind through to wrap itself around the person inside. He heard a rustle and a gentle thud. The door opened and a young man stood there. He was naked and asleep, not seeing what was in front of him, although his eyes were open.

Still in dreams, the man whispered an invitation to come in. Wolf touched his face as he backed into the room and lay down again. Wolf felt his fangs extend and with hunger and desire clamouring, he shut the door and sat on the bed. Touching his victim, he ran his fingers down his face and across his shoulders, warm, so warm. His mind was wrapped in Wolf's. Defenceless against him, he drowned, not feeling the cool hands holding him. Lying on the bed, Wolf pulled him close, twined himself around his warmth, brought his mouth down to his neck. His victim's breathing became harsher in his ears as Wolf deliberately teased the man's own arousal through his waking dreams, feeling the shivers run across both their skins and blood pumping harder. His old master, Kalmár had been an expert at this. Wolf hadn't realised what fun it was, to have someone completely at your mercy, desperate for you to bite them. That first time, knowing his master was a vampire, knowing he wanted to bite him and not expecting his own sexual reaction. Lying there, shaking in his arms afterwards, the cold hands stroking his hair and the chains around his soul. The moments pinpointing his life leading up to the now, nothing else was important.

In the present, Wolf was pulled closer and caressed, half asleep words of affection muttered in his ear. He poured his hunger down the connections, knowing it would be interpreted as lust. The primal urges for food and sex, desires that needed no translating. He teased for a few moments longer and then with his own passions spurring him, bit, unable to wait. The young man jerked against him, fingers clutching as Wolf fed, feeling the hot blood course through him.

Enough, too soon it was over. He licked the wounds, they'd close quickly and wouldn't leave much of a mark. Wolf laid him down and covered his nakedness over. His limbs sprawled out, lips parted. Vulnerable in his sleep, he didn't look old enough to be in the hostel.

Wolf closed the door quietly. Coming down the stairs he scrubbed at his mouth and tried to catch any stray drops of blood. He waved at Dennis, ignoring his garrulous enquires and walked out. As he put his hand in his pocket he swore, his jacket was sticky down one side. He pulled out a handkerchief and wiped everything off, making a note to himself to remember to put a sheet over his dinner if it was male and naked.

Wolf sat outside the cave mouth, one ear bud in and humming along. The month had passed fast and it was his turn again, much to his disgust. Yorgias had simply grinned when he'd challenged the rota and offered to throw him out if he wasn't interested. Wolf snorted as his other ear listened to the sounds in the dark, they both knew he had no other choice. It was still and coming close to dawn. The night had been magnificent, starlit, with a huge moon and so chilly there was almost a frost. The breathing below him had been a gentle accompaniment to the peace.

He wriggled through to his personal cave and remembered Jon had been here yesterday - everything was tidy. Muttering, he kicked the blankets into the pile he liked and almost missed the breathing changing. For an instant it had skipped as though someone had turned in their sleep and gone back to its normal steady rhythm. He stopped, unsure if he'd imagined it. He decided to err on the side of caution. Wolf wormed out of the cave again and rang. He got Yorgias' answer phone. Swearing to himself, he left a message, not knowing if what he'd felt was important.

He woke to hear his phone buzzing, he guessed who it probably was and it stopped as he reached for it. Yorgias was an early riser, he tended to be up when the dusk still showed. Muttering, he stretched and rang back, explaining again what had happened.

Yorgias and Jon arrived an hour later and Wolf had noticed another faltering of the rhythm. He was twitchy, not liking the sensation, it shouldn't be doing this. Yorgias quizzed him and Jon sat with a mournful expression on his long face. They sat for several hours listening and talking sporadically, all three on edge waiting. It happened again several hours later.

"Right, that's three times, I'm calling in reinforcements. You two wait here. Anything happens, let me know." Yorgias walked off down the track and pulled out his phone, slapping his hand against his thigh while waiting for an answer.

"What now?" Wolf looked at Jon for information.

"We wait."

"And? What if it wakes?"

"We let Yorgias know, then we distract it." Jon's face looked even longer. Wolf screwed his own up, wanting more information. "It wants to feed, we let it. Simple." The breathing shifted again.

The hair on the back of Wolf's neck stood on end. "When will help get here?"

Jon shrugged. "When it happens." He sat and watched as Wolf paced, eventually getting fed up and telling him to sit down. Wolf had to listen, Jon was stronger than he was and wasn't shy about proving it. He sat bolt upright, drumming his fingers and tried to listen to the breathing, any enjoyment he'd felt in the night gone. Jon's phone rang and Wolf jumped up to pace again while he answered.

Jon switched it off, "Right. That was Yorgias. They're coming, they'll be here by late tomorrow night."

"What…" Wolf stopped pacing, stunned. Tomorrow night. Late. As if to underline his discomfort, the breathing paused. They both froze and listened, subconsciously counting. One…two…three… and restarted into its previous rhythm, their eyes met in shared relief.

"Look, it takes time, they have to deal with transport and things. There has to be two of them as well. This one's always been difficult."

"What do you mean 'difficult'?" Wolf didn't need to be any more wound up than he was.

Jon shrugged, "Sometimes it comes out, sometimes goes back to sleep and doesn't bother. Sometimes it wakes too quick…" His voice trailed off.

Wolf turned his gaze into the night. "Fuck." Jon nodded. "So, have you seen it before?" Jon shook his head. Wolf pressed him further, "Have you seen any of them?"

"Yeah. Once." Jon scuffed his feet in the soil and stared at them. Wolf waited on edge and eventually Jon continued, "Scared the shits out of me."

Nothing more could be said to that. They sat in silence, waiting.

Dawn approached - they'd have to share the small cave. Jon went first, outranking him. Wolf came after, having to trust he wouldn't be swiped at. Jon didn't tend to be vindictive but it never paid to get too sure.

Jon had split the blankets by the time he'd got there, keeping the best ones for himself. He waited for Wolf to complain and smirked when he didn't. Tense at having to share, Wolf lay back and attempted to ignore him. It didn't feel right with the two of them here, there wasn't enough space between them. The breathing had become faster, louder and with more pauses, it made it hard to relax.

Unable to leave the subject alone, Wolf asked, "What happened to the watchers last time this one woke?"

Jon sighed and said, "It woke too quickly. By the time reinforcements arrived, it had gone back to sleep and they had to clear up the mess it'd left. That's why we're here. Happy?"

Wolf stared into the cave. Fear tinged his thoughts, everything since he'd become a vampire had hinged on survival. He was pulled into darkness as the dawn arrived.

Chapter 6

Tina sighed, opening her eyes as Kalmár paused and moved away to reach into his jacket pocket. Muzzy headed, she shifted, trying to work out why he'd stopped. He was normally single-minded, once he'd made the decision to bite, nothing interrupted him. Her mind abruptly cleared from the fog he'd wrapped round her as she saw him pull a mobile out of his pocket. It vibrated again.

"Bloody things, can't you leave it?"

He shook his head and clicked the on button. Mischief sparked through the irritation as she realised he had both hands full. One with the phone, the other held her. Tina stretched and kissed him under his ear, letting her warm breath play over his skin. He shivered and his arm tightened around her. Stroking the side of his neck, she grinned as she saw him close his eyes, having to concentrate while he listened. She trailed her lips down to where his collar covered his neck, enjoying the scent of the wild rosemary he used to stop the moths from eating his clothes.

Nothing showed in his voice as he replied into the phone, "Of course, I will be waiting." He switched it off and put it on the table. Turning to her, he captured her fingers, "I want you in your rooms, take food and anything else you will need for the night."

Not the reaction she'd expected. "Why?"

"Consort is coming and you are bleeding." He touched her face, "I do not wish to open him up to any more temptations than I need to." Gently he licked the marks he'd made on her arm again, pulled her sleeve down and started to do up her buttons. Tina swore as he lingered, kissing her neck, sending tingles across her skin.

"Will I see you later on?"

"Perhaps." He shrugged, "Do not invite anyone into your rooms unless it is myself. I can bar him from entering but it will not hold if you invite him." Muttering rude words, she untangled herself. She collected enough food for several meals and wandered up to her rooms.

She felt Consort arrive and the atmosphere intensified. Two vampires aware she bled and both wanting her because of it. While her periods had become less regular, this was one of those times when the concept of being a man appealed to her. Resigned to not sleeping, she took her frustration out on her punch bag, trying to exhaust herself.

During the day she stayed away from the areas where Kalmár normally put visiting vampires. She felt tired and irritable and not in the mood to do much. Tina didn't think Consort had left the castle and didn't want to know where he was. Not that she could sense him during daylight hours, just as well, she had a sore temptation to expose him to the sunlight after last night.

Her period had trickled to a halt and she couldn't think of a reason to stay separate. Tina waited until she knew Kalmár was around, grabbed some food from the kitchen and joined them in the library. Consort sat opposite Kalmár. His eyes kept meeting hers and wandering over her. He was charming and amusing on the surface, including her in the conversation. She wondered what he wanted, nothing he mentioned appeared important, she didn't know the people they talked about and Consort was making her uncomfortable with his attentions.

She regretted coming down as she perched on

a low stool next to Kalmár but didn't want to be excluded. Kalmár was polite on the surface but bristled underneath, Tina found herself touching his arm for reassurance and stopped herself. In turn, he occasionally picked her hand up to kiss her wrist. Her insides twisted as Consort's eyes followed her hand.

At last Consort took his leave and Tina sighed with relief when Kalmár escorted him out. She sprawled in Kalmár's vacated chair, waiting for him to come back – they had unfinished business. He stopped in the doorway and watched intently as she undid her collar.

Tina grinned as she felt his hunger reaching out, "I think you owe me one and this time you can make sure you switch that thing off." He carefully placed the phone on the table next to them, showing her the blank screen, then swept her up and held her tight while he reminded them both where they'd been interrupted.

They went out the following evening and arrived back late at the castle to find a battered van in front of the gates. Tina felt the unease of another vampire and feeling twitchy, she stayed in the car while the Count got out. She worried it might be Consort coming back until she recognised the voice snarling about people not answering phones and jumped out.

Ansell leant against the van and Sasha was laughing behind him. Sasha kissed and hugged her hard, ignoring Ansell's bolshy mood. They raided the kitchen and curled up on the couch to catch up on gossip. Where Sasha had been, what she'd done in the last few months. Ansell wandered a lot, he didn't tend to stay in one place for long. Sasha detailed the list of people she'd met. Half the things she'd done

Tina wasn't sure she believed.

Despite being friends with Sasha, she didn't know Ansell. In contrast to the elegant Count, he leant on the arm of his chair while he talked, looking like a stroppy teenager in casual clothes. Slight and not very tall, it was difficult to believe his age. Tina felt a jarring edge every so often when his demeanour didn't match his cherubic appearance, especially as Sasha appeared a similar age to herself. Sasha had said there were times when she had to act as a guardian, much to Ansell's amusement. The conversation flowed between the four of them through the night, Tina discovering Ansell had a sly wit that slid under her radar if she didn't concentrate.

Early in the morning when Tina had started yawning and thinking about going for a nap, Kalmár pulled his phone from his pocket to answer it. After a brief conversation, he switched it off.

"An old one is waking," Kalmár said, "Ansell and I will need to leave immediately. We will fly out at dusk tomorrow."

Tina asked, "Do you need to be driven to the airport during the day?"

Kalmár shook his head. "We will drive tonight and stay in the lock up close by."

"How long will you be?" She was on edge, the last time this had happened she'd been ill and she didn't want him to be away for long.

Aware of her unease, he replied, "Not long this time, a few nights at the most, Sasha will be with you."

Sasha dragged her bags out of the van. Ansell's goodbye was brief, he touched Sasha's face and turned away. Tina expected little more, Kalmár saved his affection for private. It felt odd watching them drive off, especially with not being on her own for the duration. She caught the same expression on

Sasha's face and she admitted when asked that she was rarely apart from Ansell. Curious, she asked Sasha what Ansell was like when they were alone, Sasha rolled her eyes and grinned, frustrating was the politest word she used. Tina was delighted, it wasn't just her, Wolfie had been far more accepting. She yawned again and offered to show Sasha to her room.

"I'd far rather see yours," was the reply. A glint was in Sasha's eye. Tina sighed, she had plenty of space in her bed for the two of them although she didn't think sleep was what Sasha had in mind. She gave in and showed off her rooms, responding shyly to Sasha's teasing. They ended up curled up on the bed and Sasha kissed her, grumbling when Tina complained about being too sleepy to return her affections. They fell asleep in each other's arms, the soft breeze blowing through the open windows.

Tina half woke as the sunlight showed dim through the curtains, drowsy as a hand gently ran itself up and down her side, under her shirt. She sighed and stretched with it. She hadn't felt a warm hand do that for a while and sleepily wondered why Wolfie's hand felt different. The hand continued upwards and cupped her breast. Caressing and her nipple hardened as the fingers brushed across. Someone kissed her neck, a body pressing against her back. Tina shivered as the hand explored, moving down over her hip, sliding further under the elastic of her knickers. She shifted her legs to allow it to explore, her breath quickening even as she frowned in her half-awake state - something was wrong with the hand, it was too small and the body curled behind her was soft. She woke completely and turned over, grumbling, "Sasha…"

"Don't deny it, you were enjoying that until your brain got in the way." Sasha smiled

305

unapologetically and her hand stayed where it was, "I can tell you know." Her fingers moved to caress her again and Tina jumped.

She flushed, not wanting to admit Sasha was right, "I thought it was Wolfie."

Sasha chuckled and let her go, "One day you'll realise what you're missing. Don't leave it too late."

"Don't you miss Ivan and Wolfie? Have there been any others you've been close too?"

"Yes, I miss them, and the rest. It doesn't get any easier." She rolled onto her back, "You lose people every year, see them walk into that circle..." Her eyes grew distant, "But it's the same with normal humans too, you can't stay around them for long. They notice that you don't age eventually."

"How do you cope?"

Sasha shrugged and pulled at her knuckles absently. "To be honest I don't always but we haven't much choice. Just imagine, if I hadn't been picked up, I'd be a toothless old hag, if I were still alive. We all go through it, loving and losing." Her face changed and she gave an evil grin, "Of course, the best companions are those like yourself so long as they allow themselves to forget the conventions they were brought up with..." Tina giggled as Sasha wriggled over with a lascivious look in her eye and gave in, returning the kiss she was given.

The day passed slowly, Kalmár was rarely away when she was here. To distract herself, Tina took Sasha walking in the surrounding countryside. They enjoyed each other's company while they talked and laughed for most of the day, picnicking and sleeping in the sunshine.

Chapter 7

Wolf waited as Yorgias walked up the track, two, no, three figures behind him. He heard Jon sigh with relief. Wolf himself felt sick with terror and if Jon felt the same way, then he was better at hiding it. The breathing had got stronger as the old one made its way up. If it had got to the surface before the older vampires arrived, it would have been their job to distract it. No doubt with fatal results as neither of them were strong enough to contain it.

Behind Yorgias walked a slim, young looking vampire, barely a shadow of a beard on his face. To Wolf, he radiated danger, contrasting with the casual jeans and jumper he wore. He supported a man much larger than himself. The man staggered and tripped over his feet, Ansell muttered to him, encouraging him forwards.

The third vampire was a figure Wolf recognised. Dressed impeccably as he always had been, the figure of a gentleman traveller, moving with confidence through the brush. Wolf squinted at Kalmár and found there was something different about him, he'd not seen it before. He had the same power radiating from him as Ansell, Wolf could see it, a haze of red in his peripheral vision but the Count's looked different. Wrapped around him like bindweed running through a bush, were gossamer thin threads of green. They flexed with the haze, curled around him, flickering. The red shone through, constantly threatening to swamp them but never did.

Wolf and Jon both moved out of their way, automatically deferring to the older vampires. Wolf knew he'd been noted despite the Count ignoring them as he passed. He could hear the old one, a strained high mewling sound coming from the last part of the cave. He could feel its uncertainty, how it didn't want to come out and the hunger driving it. Wolf followed behind the older vampires with unthinking curiosity, Jon stayed well back, happy to let others deal with the situation.

As the old one shambled out, it blinked and mewled in the dark night. Wolf looked on in horror, he couldn't tell if it had been male or female, it could have been either. It had no hair left, only a few wisps. The same went for its clothes, rags hung on it, rotten and crusted in dirt, merging with the dust of years engrained into its body. Every bone showed, making it into a walking skeleton while its slotted black eyes searched for food. It appeared barely able to walk yet Wolf knew if it got its hands on him, he'd have problems escaping. He could feel its hunger, felt drawn to it and wanted to offer himself. He strained against the feeling, knowing if he did, he wouldn't survive.

Ansell came closer, supporting the human they'd found. Drugged or drunk he slumped, uncaring of the fate awaiting him. The thing coming out of the cave lurched forwards and Ansell threw the man in its direction. It opened its mouth and showed fangs in a black hole, a couple of teeth made more prominent by the lack of companions. Stick thin arms grabbed the victim and brought it close to suck the life out, not caring about the struggle the suddenly awake man put up, fighting for his worthless existence. It broke the man in two, snapping his bones and his muffled shrieks turned to whimpers.

The old one discarded its meal in a heap of broken bones and looked around. Wolf shuddered and took a step back. The gaze swung and focussed on him, it took a step forward and mewled. Wolf was transfixed, the black eyes bored into his. He couldn't move, panicking inside, fighting to break free. Another step towards him and both sides of him twisted, desperate to run. Another step, his legs were frozen to the ground, staring into the twin black holes. Another step and he shut his eyes, tried to block it out, still seeing the eyes glare into his and was pushed aside, hard against the cave wall. He shook his head, clearing it, tried to think and saw Kalmár stood, no… kneeling in front. His face was in a grimace as the thing was at his throat, drinking.

Yorgias grabbed Wolf and pulled him back, out the way. "You fool. You are too young, it thinks you are still human. Stay out of the way." Wolf staggered against him, knees weak from the shock. That thing had been human once, had friends and laughed…Would he turn out like this one day? He shuddered, unable to contemplate it.

The thing pulled at the Count, tried to move him, to bend him in the same way it had with the man. Kalmár resisted and it let go abruptly. Kalmár stayed where he was, one knee on the ground, his collar torn, holes in his jacket and a hand on the floor supporting his weight. The old one swayed, dark blood running down its chin.

Ansell moved closer, it blinked and seemed uncertain. The mewl took a questioning tone as he reached out and turned it round, talking quietly. It went with him. One hand on its shoulder, Ansell walked it back into the cave, back to its sleeping place. Underground, Wolf could hear its heartbeat slow down already, the tiredness infecting it. He took a deep breath and became aware of the noises in the night. Caught up in the drama he couldn't have said if they'd stopped or if he hadn't noticed them.

Kalmár lurched upright as though drunk. He was dusty and dirty, his clothes torn and no longer immaculate. Blood showed on his shirt. Blood, Wolf's mouth twitched. The Count looked at him and moved swiftly, grabbing Wolf by the throat.

"For that, you will pay."

Wolf daren't move. He'd attracted the old one's attention. Kalmár hadn't had to distract it, he could have left Wolf to be the next victim. He held Wolf pinned easily against the rock face and Wolf pulled his head back in surrender, exposing his throat. Kalmár hesitated and ran his free hand through Wolf's hair, an unexpected gentleness from the long fingers and his mind was thrust into the past.

The same face was above him, framed by the familiar surroundings of the castle and he could almost feel the gun in his shaking hand trying to aim at his target. His voice cracked, "Stay away or I'll shoot."

"I am the same man you have known for years. What has changed?"

Everything had changed with the discovery of him with his victim, her blood on his lips. The brief glimpse of fang warred with the man who had given him ten years of education and privilege in a different country. The man who had taken him out of the gutter was a predatory animal. He steadied his hand. This gun had been given to him by the man in front of him for hunting animals. "What do you want from me? Are you going to kill me too?"

"I want nothing from you. You are too young. Learn and grow, it will be your decision later if you want more." A curve to the mouth and the voice deepened in amusement, "Will you try to kill me? Are you sure?"

They locked eyes and he remembered his

expectations of being preyed on during their first meetings, the detached kindness and fascination he'd received instead. The years of learning and the anticipation for nightfall to show off his new skills. A soft sigh from behind them and the sheets rustled as the body on the bed turned over.

"You have no cause for concern, she is merely sleeping."

He tried to glance across without taking his eyes from his target and failed. Yearning again to have the wicked delight of holding her, the warmth of her skin and the whisper of a giggle in his ears as they made love. His master had drunk her blood, taken her in a different way. His master - his hands began to shake again as the long years won. The muzzle of gun dropped and Kalmár knocked it out of his hand to clatter on the floor. Wolf bent his head and the cool fingers touched his face in benediction.

Past and present merged. Hunger radiating off him, the Count took his blood, replacing what the old one had taken. Wolf slid down the cave wall when dropped, exhausted. Ansell appeared from the cave, picked his way over Wolf's sprawled form and they walked down the track without looking back.

Yorgias pulled him up and shook his head. "The luck you have. Come on." Jon appeared, looking round nervously and listening hard for the breathing. He stared incredulously at Wolf supported by Yorgias and grabbed the spade he'd brought to sort out the remains of the body. Yorgias helped Wolf down the track until he could walk on his own. Kalmár and Ansell talked quietly while they waited by the car.

Parking near the safe house, they walked the rest of the way. Staying behind the others, Wolf saw Kalmár stumble and grab for the wall, his other hand rising to cover his face.

Ansell reacted first, reached out, not quite touching, "What is it?"

Wolf was close enough to hear Kalmár whisper, "No…" He raised his head to look at Ansell and said louder, "I can not find her." At Ansell's confusion his voice cracked in frustration, "She is no longer there."

She? Wolf strained his mind to remember, confused by the memory of his first love, decades ago. In the dimness of the alleyway, Wolf could see Kalmár's aura. The slender vines that curled around him had dried up, turning brittle and lifeless against the red.

"Little Mouse." Barely a breath whispered the name. Kalmár's normally contained face was open and stunned by the loss, not seeing the alleyway in front of him. For Wolf, the name brought an unknown longing for a companion, for laughter and a tangling of limbs in the cold nights. He stood, frozen in his own failure, how could he have forgotten?

Still swaying, Kalmár tried to push himself upright, to turn back towards the car. "I must go to her."

"Wait," Ansell stopped him, "I'll phone Sasha first." His phone out, he waited impatiently for Sasha to answer.

Sasha, another name from the past. A tall blonde woman, open with her affections, instantly appeared in his mind but this Mouse? Wolf listened intently as Ansell talked sharply, cutting across his pet's confusion. Kalmár watched, an anger beginning to smoulder as he regained his strength.

Ansell shook his head and switched the phone off. "Sasha says Mouse went to answer the door about ten or fifteen minutes ago. They'd been in the kitchen, they wouldn't have heard the bell anywhere else. She hadn't realised there was a problem, everything had been quiet. Neither of them had felt any other vampires or they wouldn't have answered the door. She found the front gate open and a small amount of blood on the floor but no Mouse and nothing else." Wolf flinched as he felt the Count's anger ignite, he took a careful step away, trying not to attract attention.

"Consort. He asked us to come here. He has made it plain he wants her. I will kill him for this."

Ansell grabbed his arm this time, "No point in going now. Dawn's approaching, you won't get far." Snarling, Kalmár tried to shake him off and walk away. Wolf had heard the rumours that Ansell was far older than the other three and that he didn't care for the rankings at the balls so refused to comply with them. He now proved it by holding Kalmár easily. It looked strange with the slender youth restraining the taller man with torn clothing. "No. We will wait. I will contact Madame tomorrow to find out if Consort is with her. She will not be awake at the moment."

Kalmár turned his head to glare out over the street, the air crackling around him. "If he is not there?"

"Then I will come with you. She is bound to you."

Kalmár nodded, "And when I find him, I will tear him limb from limb."

Wolf shuddered. No boasting, a simple statement of what would be. He stayed out of the way while Kalmár turned to the safe house and waited for Yorgias to unlock the door, his large hands clenching as though preparing for the kill.

Yorgias watched both older vampires warily and grabbed Wolf as he came past. "Straight to your room. No more calling attention to yourself." Wolf was exhausted and not in any position to argue. He nodded, not wanting Kalmár to take his thwarted anger out on him. He lay on his bed, ignoring the magazines scattered across the room and stared at the ceiling, trying to remember through the veil.

Chapter 8

Wolf wandered into the main room of the cellar the next morning and paused when he saw Ansell and Kalmár talking urgently. The atmosphere was thunderous with the Count's anger. Yorgias looked at him sharply and Wolf sat in front of the computer, trying to look as though he wasn't there, wasn't listening.

"Madame isn't answering." Ansell looked thoroughly fed up.

"Not answering or refusing to?" Unable to reply, Ansell shrugged. Kalmár snarled, "Then we go back to the castle and look."

"Look where? You can't sense her."

"We know Consort's number plate, we can find out if he has been in the area. Humans have cameras on their roads. Make them work for us, they can not disappear completely." Ansell looked dubious as Kalmár carried on, "If Consort has discovered a way of staying unnoticed by any of us, we need to know about it. We can not allow him to do this. What if it had been Sasha?"

"Sasha is sworn to me." Ansell said it mildly in the knowledge that no-one would be daft enough to steal her. No-one would challenge him.

Kalmár ignored him. "We will go back and start from where she disappeared, we will find clues." Ansell gave in, frustrated at having no other ideas to find someone they could no longer sense. They spoke with Yorgias about borrowing the car. The feeling in the room lightened after they'd left and Wolf sighed with relief.

Yorgias leaned over Wolf as he worked on the

computer. "So, he's missing that new pet of his?"

"Mouse," Wolf grunted. He'd spent the rest of the previous night running through his memories. He didn't want to talk about how little he could remember.

"Was that the other pet he had with him at the ball, when you were made?" Wolf glowered. Yorgias didn't take the hint. "She was nice, I took her for a turn in one of the dances."

"They were bonded." That much he did know.

"Yes, I heard that. Neat little thing, wasn't she? Wouldn't say no to having a bite." He leered.

"Have to ask somebody's permission first." Wolf nodded in the direction Kalmár had taken.

Yorgias snorted. "So, you knew her?"

Wolf went on deleting files, ignoring his question. He was aware of the older vampire perched next to him and knew Yorgias was thinking of ways to needle him while he worked, in a strange way he didn't mind. He concentrated on the computer. The amount of crap that had been downloaded and left to clog it up was unbelievable. No wonder they were having problems.

"What's this?" A document marked Rota, he opened it to find it completely blank.

Yorgias leaned over again, "That one's important, leave it alone."

Wolf protested, "There's nothing in it."

Yorgias shushed him, "It's important." Wolf rolled his eyes. Yorgias' legendary rota was non-existent.

It had been several nights since Ansell and Kalmár had left, nothing had been heard about their search. Wolf stretched and rolled his shoulders. It was a beautiful night. He'd been out, fed, walked under the stars and was coming back to indulge in flipping through a magazine he'd bought. A vampire accosted him. He'd seen him before, that one with the limp.

"Hello Wolfie."

"Wolf," he corrected. He immediately stood taller and moved a touch closer. The safe house was a few streets away. Yorgias wouldn't know if he landed a few punches here. He could make up a tale if he was obviously bruised.

The other vampire twitched, not enjoying being stood over. "Not got much protection here, have you baby?"

"Don't need it." Wolf wound himself up, allowing the other side of him to come to the front. He'd be faster. So long as he didn't allow the other vampire get his hands on him, he'd be fine.

"Sleeping at the safe house, are we?" Wolf shrugged. "Surprised you made it this far, Consort wasn't happy with you killing his pet."

Damn, he didn't need a high level vampire upset with him. "So long as I stay out of his way, it shouldn't be a problem."

The other vampire smirked. "You're better off attaching yourself to an older vampire. What's up, Kalmár not having you?"

Wolf started to get angry. There was no way Kalmár would have him near, not with a bonded companion around. A vague whisper of memory floated through his mind. Arms twined around him, teasing. A flood of warm feelings ran through him. The breath whooshed out of him as pain crumpled his stomach. While he'd been distracted, the other vampire had punched him solidly.

He snarled back as the other vampire grinned and swiped several times. Wolf connected a fist solidly and skipped away. The other vampire was surprised, unable to grab him quickly enough. If he'd not been crippled, there was no way Wolf would have thought to continue. A knife appeared in the vampire's hand, it glinted in the street lights and ripped through Wolf's T-shirt, narrowly missing his stomach.

Wolf pulled out his own knife. The other squinted and shifted away. "Speaking of Kalmár, I've heard he's lost his pet again. Very careless of him, almost becoming a habit." Wolf tried to ignore the goading, he'd evened up the stakes. The other vampire couldn't get close, he was too fast, he'd proved that. "So many people looking for her. Who will find her first?"

Still smirking, the other vampire backed away. Unusual. Wolf stopped to watch him limp away, he seemed pleased about something. Frowning, he walked back to the safe house. Yorgias saw him come in and looked at him carefully. Wolf made sure he walked straight, trying not to show any hint of bruises.

Yorgias came over and tugged at his ripped T-shirt, "And?" he enquired.

Wolf shrugged and smiled, "My dinner got excited."

"You've been fighting again."

"Me?" He tried to look innocent.

"I warned you, one more fight and you are out." Yorgias took hold of him, "You're lying."

Wolf gritted his teeth, he didn't want to lose this place. It would be back to fighting to find somewhere to sleep. He tried honesty, "It was that vampire with the limp. He doesn't like me."

"You idiot, that's Vinceti."

"Vinceti?" A memory. "Arsewipe."

"Yes, he is but I told you, I can't afford to upset Lord Tangent. Look, I'm going to have to throw you out. Come back in a few months, no, make that six. He'll have buggered off by then and be sticking his nose in elsewhere." Wolf swore as Yorgias took him outside, he knew better than to struggle against the older vampire. "I'm not going to bar you from here but don't expect to be welcomed if you come back too soon. Understand?" The words were cold comfort as the door was shut behind him.

Chapter 9

Tina woke bereft as she had done for the last week. The room she sat in was empty, with only a few blankets for her to sleep in. Her side was healing quicker than she'd hoped - Consort had thrown a knife as she'd peered out, pinning her against the door. She'd not invited him in, he'd pushed his way through the barrier. She still had nightmares of seeing his hands coming towards her slowly, so slowly, of taking hold and pulling her to the entrance. The blood trickling out of his eyes, black tears weeping in the dim light, she shivered. In surprise and shock she'd not been able to cry out and automatically she'd reached for Kalmár. The bond had twitched under her fingers, then she'd fainted much to her disgust as he'd pulled the knife out. She wondered if Sasha had heard anything and spoken to Ansell.

Tina had woken in the car with her wrists tied and a strange taste in her mouth. Consort had been driving and glancing down at her every so often with satisfaction. She probed the empty spot in her mind, the tendrils linking her to Kalmár had snapped. She hadn't realised how aware of him she'd been until this point. Despair filled her, he'd done something to separate them. Several times she'd tried to get out of the moving car, not caring that she'd hurt herself falling out. Every time he grabbed her, eventually giving her a head ringing thump to make her stay still.

He'd driven for a large part of the night, stopping when dawn approached and had hidden her in a cellar attached to a large empty house. As she'd expected, Consort had fed from her and Tina hadn't fought him. Soft whispers and caresses that she was his had turned her stomach afterwards. She'd tolerated his fingers touching her and his glee at having her and had lain limply until he'd locked the door.

Tina had attempted to break the water bottle he'd left, trying to get a sharp edge. The plastic was soft, the screw top eventually split to give some form of edge and she'd rubbed it uselessly against her ties. Remembering her time with Vinceti, she'd also tried shouting until she was hoarse, desperate to attract any attention, kicking and thumping at the door. Nothing budged and eventually she'd fallen asleep in the corner, exhausted.

The next night, her attack with the water bottle edge had also failed. Consort had twisted it out of her hands and thrown it away. He'd dragged her back to the car and tied her wrists to the door handle. Food and water had been there in quantities and he'd bound up her side. A threat of gagging her and putting her in the boot of the car if she attracted attention while they drove made her behave, she'd rather be free to look around, there might be an opportunity to escape. Constantly trying to reach out for Kalmár, she glowered and ate to keep her strength up. The car doors were locked and he had half an eye on any movement she made. Refusing to speak to him, she curled up in the seat and watched for road signs, trying to work out where they were going.

Night after night the same happened, the neon lights flashing in her eyes, hypnotising her. She kept falling asleep and losing track of where they were. The signs changed languages, preventing her from reading them. Her mind wandered back to how it had been when Kalmár had first kidnapped her and her desperation to get away. This time she wasn't so helpless, Kalmár would be looking for her and she knew her worth in this world.

Last night after they'd stopped, Tina had broken her silence and asked if Madame would be looking for him. He in turn had ordered her to allow him to feed. His frustration had built, she could see that he expected her to curl up with him as she did with Kalmár. Fat chance of that, she would only do what she had to. She'd got so angry that she'd taunted Consort about his refusal to return her.

Tina had stared him down until he'd lost his temper, shouting and lashing out at the walls. He'd hit her then, bruising her face and throwing her against the wall. His anger had an edge to it Kalmár's never had, a desperation. Kalmár's temper, frightening though it could be, had the feeling of being controlled, of iron bands around it, with an awareness of his own strength in comparison to hers. She'd lost consciousness and come round with the same strange taste in her mouth as before. Rubbing her head and shaking, she'd crawled over to find the tin cup of water he'd left her and wash the taste out of her mouth. She wondered when he would start the real game of breaking her will.

Tina sat in despair. She had a claggy sensation over her skin and she couldn't work out why, it had been like that since he'd taken her. She had never been given the opportunity to wash, only just enough water to drink. He wouldn't let her out the room, it wasn't small but the walls were beginning to close in. The lights were harsh on her eyes. She'd not seen natural light since he'd taken her.

She sighed and started to exercise, going through the movements Wolfie had taught her, trying to keep herself fit and supple, while favouring her injured side. She stopped as the door unlocked and Consort entered with food and drink on a tray. Tina refused to look at him, allowing him to close the door unchallenged. She'd tried to push past the first evening and failed, he'd simply held her with one hand while he locked the door with his mind.

He set the tray on the floor and came over. Tina looked away from him, deliberately showing him the bruised side of her face. Taking hold of her chin, he turned her towards him. "I am hungry."

She stared at him and allowed the silence to answer for her. Consort shrugged and pulled her into him, biting hard. She pushed her mind away, much like the old days with Kalmár. It hurt without the bond. Tina refused to flinch, refused to let him in and tried to put up every barrier she could in her mind against him. She was so used to relaxing, allowing Kalmár to wrap himself around her. She ached with wanting the intimacies she knew could happen. He finished and licked her bites to help them heal. A small relief, at least he wouldn't leave her scarred.

She dropped onto her blankets, refusing to lean against Consort and exhausted with shutting him out. He stared down at her, soft brown hair flopping over his face, making him look vulnerable as he asked, "Why do you block me?"

Tina returned his gaze flatly, "Because you aren't the one I'm bonded to."

"You could choose to break the bond."

She pressed him, "Is that what you have done with Madame? Is that why you're here, why you've stolen me?"

He looked uncomfortable and dragged the tray over to her, "Eat."

"You haven't, have you? You've run away. Are you going to blame me for that?"

He walked to the door and said over his

shoulder. "Eat."

"She'll find you. So will Kalmár. He won't stop looking for me you know."

His voice sounded unconvincing as he replied, "I wouldn't stop looking for you either. Why don't you bond with me?"

"What have you done to me? Why can't I feel him?" He refused to look at her as he left, and locked the door. Tina sighed and picked up the food, nothing exciting. He wasn't good at food, it was mostly plastic boxed microwaved stuff, bread or fruit. It filled her stomach, no more. She ate unenthusiastically.

He checked her face when he came in the next night. The skin wasn't broken, just bruised. "I'm sorry I hit you."

Tina shrugged, "Why did you do it then?" She sat on her blankets, not having any other furniture. He sat next to her and she tried not to shift away.

"You made me do it, don't make me angry."

She looked at him, amazed. He'd kidnapped her and she'd made him angry? She looked at him properly and realised she had no awareness of him as a vampire. All the way through the frustration and anger he'd expressed, she should have been able to feel him battering at her senses and she'd felt nothing. If she hadn't known better and despite the pale skin, she would have said a normal man sat next to her, casually dressed, stocky and with a pleasant face. She couldn't work it out, she'd felt him when he'd been with Kalmár a few nights ago, why not here? She cast her mind back to opening the door to him at the castle and realised she hadn't felt a vampire there either. Neither of them had or she wouldn't have answered the door.

She decided to keep him talking, use a different tactic. "Why aren't you with Madame? I thought you were bonded."

"We are."

"I'm Kalmár's. Why did you steal me?" She kept her tone light, trying not to upset him, she didn't want to get hit again.

"I wanted you. I wanted you when I saw you at the ball. You smell good, taste good."

Tina could see him getting excited by this, he began to lean towards her. Shifting away she asked, "Can I have a wash? I'd smell better then, I've not washed in days." Her claggy skin was upsetting her. He shook his head, turning to stare at the wall. He was a strange mix, he'd been charming and witty at the castle, determined on the car journey, now he appeared not to know what to do with her. Maybe reality had set in.

"You want to go back to him." The question was unexpected.

"Yes."

"Why? He stole you. Like I did."

She floundered, "I suppose by the time I realised I couldn't go back to my family, I'd got used to him."

"Do you love him?" He leaned close again, a curious expression on his face.

Tina blinked. She didn't know, it wasn't something she liked to think about. She stepped around the sensitive subject, wanting to keep him talking. "I don't know." She laughed nervously, "Stockholm syndrome has a lot to answer for. Do you love Madame?"

Consort didn't laugh, his face was serious, "I have been with her for centuries. We are part of each other, love doesn't come into it. We are bound together."

"So she knows you're here, with me?"

He looked uncomfortable. "Be quiet." An

edge to his voice, she changed tack.

"What about Ivan? He seemed fun to have around."

A big dreamy smile came onto his face. "Yes. Ivan was wonderful."

"I'm sorry about what happened." His face went cold. Trying to empathize with him, she continued, "It must have been a shock..." She stopped as he turned and slammed the heel of his hand into the wall, a hairsbreadth away from her ear.

"Be quiet." The words were softly articulated as he stared at her, grief stark in his eyes. She froze, not daring to move, plaster trickling onto her shoulder. He leaned on the wall, breathing heavily. Kalmár's breathing had always been slow, difficult to notice unless she touched him. Consort's she could hear, coming fast in comparison. The plaster had cracked around his hand, the dust settling. She watched as he got up, shook his hand out of the plasterwork and walked out. She let her breath out with a sigh of relief.

After he'd left, she spent a long time thinking. He was damaged, she didn't know why but Ivan's death must have hit him hard. She remembered the few times she'd met Ivan. Cocky and assertive, charming when you got to know him, things Consort didn't appear to be. He'd had Ivan sworn to him, on his side. He must have expected Ivan to survive the fight.

She sighed. If Consort had taken her first, she might have grown to like him and become fond of him even. In this strange world of vampires she inhabited, Tina thought he had a vulnerable side to him, one that it would have been interesting to discover. She imagined what he would have been like centuries ago, before he'd met Madame and shook her head. However she tried thinking about it, he still felt unbalanced to her.

Her thoughts wandered on to Kalmár who was perfectly balanced. She snorted to herself, he could be depended on to do exactly what suited him best. She could write lists of his faults so why did she stay with him – apart from the obvious threat of other vampires? Why didn't she drop him and go with Consort? She was only bound, not sworn body and soul.

Tina came to the conclusion she couldn't imagine giving herself up to Consort in the same way and that it wasn't just the desires Kalmár brought when he fed that made her want to stay. From the start she'd been sucked along with him, swept up with his courtship of her and his insistence that she keep up with him intellectually. It wasn't the easy companionship she'd had with Wolfie, this was fiercer and more demanding. Defying him could be terrifying at times but he admired her for it, and his admiration was worth having. Finding ways to tease him was a delight and the only way she could get her own back.

Alone, she felt more than halved. Tina was sure Consort had mistaken her public compliance with the Count to mean she was like that in private. She was simply aware that no matter how much Kalmár wanted her to stand up to him in when they were alone, in public, she was his.

Chapter 10

She lay in the darkness, water dripping in the distance. Hunger twisted her insides and images of her previous life flickered across her vision as she raised her hands to find solid rock above her head. Tina shrieked and woke with a jolt in the cellar room, trapped in her blankets.

Sighing, Tina untangled herself and sat up, trying to clear her head. This dream had been developing over the last few nights and had slowly replaced the one about Consort coming for her. She wasn't sure which was worse. She went to look for her mug, knowing it would be empty.

The door clicked and Consort entered. Still groggy, she watched, not speaking. He paced, twisting as he turned, the room not big enough for him. He didn't say a word either, wringing his hands. Agitated and unable to settle, he picked her up several times, wanting to touch her. He brushed his mouth into her neck, then put her down, not having fed. Moving slowly as though she would with a distressed animal in the room, she went to sit in her blankets, not wanting to startle him. Tina didn't think he would hurt her deliberately but his moods had become more and more erratic. She could feel his frustration only by watching him, the intensity she normally felt wasn't there.

He finally demanded, "What's wrong with me?"

"Nothing. I just shouldn't be here. Neither of us should. Please let me go."

"No!" He bellowed, making her jump. He continued to pace, talking half to himself. "She doesn't want me to have another one."

"Who doesn't? Another what? Another pet?" She spoke carefully, trying not to upset him further.

"Madame."

"Why not, didn't you look after Ivan well? Didn't he like being with you?"

"Yes, I did. She doesn't think I can look after another at the moment." He stopped and leant his forehead against a wall, his hands in pockets, eyes closed.

"I think you've done well enough with me." A white lie for both of them, the basics had been done, little more.

He ignored her, talking to the wall and rocked his head from side to side. "She's jealous. She doesn't want me to have pets. She doesn't like the amount of attention I give them. She wants it, wants it all. She's jealous of you and Kalmár."

Tina clutched her hands together, hiding them in her blankets. The last thing she needed was Madame jealous of her, especially having been warned off Consort at the last ball. Tina was terrified of her. "She doesn't need to be jealous of me. I'm nothing."

He turned to look at her from the other side of the room, desperate, "Bond with me."

"I can't. We are both bonded to others." She rubbed her eyes.

Consort knelt in front of her and touched her face, "We could. They can't find us. Bond with me. Let me in."

She shook her head, near to tears, "They will look for us, they will find us eventually. I can't do it." Tina stole a glance at him. His face was agonised. "Please let me go. You could drop me off somewhere. I could say it was a mistake." His mouth opened, nothing came out. "Please," she whispered.

Something gave and he slumped against the wall next to her, head in his hands. "I'm sorry, I can't do what you want."

His voice muffled, "What will they do?"

"Nothing, if you let me go. I can talk to Kalmár. Please give me the chance."

He turned and looked at her, pulled her onto his lap, "I wanted you." She ran her fingers through his hair, offering comfort in her efforts to persuade him.

"I know. Please, you don't have to take me back, just drop me off somewhere."

His cool cheek rested against hers. "I don't know, don't know what to do." Almost instinctively, his head dropped and he moved his mouth towards her neck. She shifted away the best she could with his arms around her, trying to stop him without upsetting him further. Pulling his head back, his gaze wandered over the walls. It sharpened, "Do you hate me?" There was an edge to his voice.

"No, I don't hate you." She was surprised as she realised she told the truth. "I just don't want to be here. Will you let me go?"

"Tomorrow." His arms tightened, not wanting to her let go.

"Tonight. Please. The sooner I can let Kalmár know I'm okay, the better it will be." Tina held her breath as he nodded and released her. She reached out to him and took his hand as he stood.

Consort unlocked the door and let her out. The cellar led to a deserted farmhouse. She zipped up her fleece against the chilly breeze, rubbed her hands together and tucked them into her pockets. He took her to the car and drove some distance in the night.

He refused to tell her how he'd blocked the bond, Tina presumed he'd blocked Madame in a

330

similar way. Dropping her off in a large town, he gave her directions to a place he called a safe house. They would help her, she wouldn't have any problems he said. She didn't try to get him to drive any closer, the sooner she was away from him the better, she didn't want him changing his mind.

Holding his hand before she got out of the car, she thanked him for letting her go and told him to go back to Madame. Consort nodded. His eyes wandered, looking everywhere except at her. He refused to let her stay longer and drove off. She watched the car disappear, worried for him, despite herself.

Tina walked swiftly, following the directions he'd given her. It was a clear night and the stars were out. A flicker on the edge of her vision, she turned to see the deserted streets behind her. She couldn't sense anything, not Consort who'd left her or any other vampire. Walking the streets at night on her own and with no Kalmár to protect her. Shivering, she wondered if they could sense her. She forced herself to pay attention and to look confident as she counted the roads off.

She turned down a dark street, there were fewer street lamps here and the warehouses blotted out the starlit night. She'd just convinced herself that she could deal with anyone who jumped her, when a figure appeared beside her. She'd not heard him walking up behind and the shadow of his hand blocked her way. He was taller than her and she froze as he took her wrist - his fingers were cold.

Tina squealed and lashed out, hoping to surprise him. The vampire swore and reached out in familiar moves to hold her. She countered in a blind panic, not remembering to scream as she concentrated on fighting. She'd got away from one vampire, she didn't want to be caught again. He used his greater strength to throw her against the wall, snarling as he did. She anticipated the movement and bounced off into one of the few patches of neon in the street. He stopped dead, a dim figure in the darkness.

She turned to run and he grabbed her arm, pulling her around to face him. Both of them came into the pool of light. Tina saw him properly for the first time and stared. The black leather jacket and slim jeans suited him, his hair bright as ever, brighter with his pale skin. The tan he used to have was a distant memory. He needed a haircut. What was new? He'd always needed a haircut.

Wolfie let her go. Tina couldn't think of anything to say. He spoke first, voice low as though he expected someone to be listening, "What are you doing here?" He looked along the street, checking. She couldn't believe it. Wolfie was here, in front of her, a vampire. He'd survived. Tears rose in her eyes and she bit her lip, she'd never expected to see him again, at least not this soon. She opened her mouth to reply and he beat her to it.

"He's looking for you. He was here a few nights ago." He rubbed his hands through his hair in a familiar gesture, "Shit." She wobbled a smile, she'd missed him doing that. "We need to get you somewhere safe." He went to take her arm and stopped in mid reach, beckoned instead and started to walk.

Anxious to prove she wasn't wandering around randomly, she said, "I've got the address of a place called a safe house."

"That's where I'm taking you. You can call him from there, I take it you haven't got a phone." She shook her head, hurrying to keep up with his long strides. This wasn't how she'd imagined meeting with Wolfie, he was curt as though he didn't

332

want her around.

"Wolfie." She stopped as he paused. He held his hand out in front of her and looked round the next corner. Another figure appeared in the lamplight.

"Well well, what do we have here?" The figure limped round Wolfie, trying to get a good look.

"Piss off Vinceti." Wolfie had his knife out. Tina went cold and shrank back, attempting to stay out of view. Vinceti smiled, his mouth open. Tina noticed he stayed away from the knife while he circled.

He craned his neck to see, "Interesting. Who is this non person you have with you?" His eyes became avid as he recognised her. "Little Mouse. You are a popular creature at the moment, all sorts of people have been looking for you." He smirked at Wolfie, "Are you thinking of running away together? You could enjoy her properly now, she's very sweet."

She lifted her chin and tried to stay calm, despite being furious at his words. "You try anything Vinceti and I'll make Kalmár promise to drop you off the highest mountain he can find."

He chuckled at her empty threat and to her surprise limped away, calling, "Have to find him first Little Mouse."

Wolfie breathed out and then looked at her sharply, "Where's your knife?"

"I don't have one." She shrugged, just pleased to see Vinceti leave.

"Bloody hell Tina, why can't you remember? What if I hadn't been here?" He pulled out the sheath, stuck the knife in and passed it over. She felt a shock at the cool fingers brushing hers.

The comment stung and she tried to deflect it,

"I can't remember the last time you called me that."

Wolfie looked embarrassed, "Things slip out. But promise me, you'll keep the knife with you and use it. Don't think first. Use it, then think. Yes?" She nodded and they walked on.

They stopped in a narrow alleyway. Tall buildings hulked over them, the area was seedy and rundown. Strange shapes loomed in the darkness and she was glad to have a familiar face around. She shivered and folded her arms around herself.

Wolfie tapped in the code and unlocked the door, gestured her in first and shut the door after them. Paint peeled on the scruffy stairs and she followed Wolfie down in the harsh light. A large room, a sofa and a few chairs were all she got to see before a figure slammed Wolfie to the wall. The breath driven out of him, he was being held by another vampire, the forearm to his throat slowly strangling him.

"What did I tell you? Don't come back." It was said in a conversational tone, the sort she'd heard Kalmár talk in when he disciplined a younger vampire. Wolfie was unable to answer, choking. His hands pushed ineffectually at the arm.

"Wait. Stop!" She grabbed the shorter vampire. He spun to face her. The first thing she noticed was his large nose, then his shifting eyes, full of curiosity.

He kept his arm on Wolfie's neck, his dark eyes following her as she moved away, "I didn't notice you sweetie. Why not?"

She backed towards the stairs, "Please let him go, he's helping me." The vampire dropped Wolfie and walked towards her. Wolfie slid down the wall, rubbing his throat and coughing. She pulled her knife out as the strange vampire got closer. His hands looked capable and for some reason she felt more of a threat coming off him than she had from Consort. She'd not had much to do with other vampires without Kalmár around, she didn't know if he would consider her knife a threat. He looked amused and stopped to her relief. He leant against the wall, crossing his arms.

"Where have I seen you before?"

"I'm Kalmár's. I need to contact him." She took a risk, hoping he would help.

He straightened, looking alarmed, "Fuck." He aimed a kick in Wolfie's general direction, "What are you doing with Kalmár's little package?"

Wolfie croaked, "Bringing her here of course. Vinceti was sneaking around. Would have got her otherwise."

"Where's your phone?"

Wolfie looked stroppy for some reason, "In my room, with the rest of my stuff." The other vampire hissed through his teeth and pulled a mobile out of his pocket. He tapped at it and she watched as he walked around the room. He shook his head as he left a message.

"No reply, he'll get back. Right, time for introductions. You must be Mouse, Kalmár's pet. I'm Yorgias, I look after the safe house, which is this place. You know Wolf." He aimed another kick in Wolfie's direction and grinned when Wolfie pulled his legs out of the way. They all jumped when Yorgias' phone rang and she took it when he held it out to her.

"Kalmár?" Her voice went high and she winced, knowing she had an audience but it was difficult to think past the emotions choking her. She held her breath and controlled herself, he wouldn't appreciate her going to pieces in public. There was a pause before she heard his familiar deep voice.

"Little Mouse, I know where you are. You

will be safe with Yorgias, stay with him and I will be with you tomorrow night." After a brief goodbye he ended the call. She stared at the silent phone and wished for more.

"Well that was a quick love note wasn't it?" She smiled wanly at Yorgias interrupting her thoughts. He had a sly appeal and despite herself, she was beginning to like this sharp faced vampire. He looked at Wolfie and continued, "Make sure you're out by the time Kalmár gets here. He's not going to want you being this close to his pet. You can come back afterwards."

"Thought I was banned?" Wolfie looked truculent.

"I'll have His Excellency's undying gratitude, won't I? Don't care about the rest." He smirked and turned to Tina, "Right sweetie, let's get you sorted for the day. What do you need?"

She started to relax, unwinding for the first time since she'd been kidnapped. Kalmár would be here tomorrow night and she was being looked after, safety at last. "Food, drink, a wash would be lovely. My skin's been claggy for a while, not been able to do anything about it." She ran fingers through her hair, wincing at the feel.

"No running water here. Don't tend to need it. Wolf can fetch some water for you to wash in and food."

Wolfie shook his head. "I'm staying here."

Yorgias narrowed his eyes. "Don't be ridiculous, I can't leave you two together."

Tina hesitated, this might be her only opportunity to talk to Wolfie on his own. "Please," she begged. "Just give us a chance to talk, nothing more."

"If Kalmár finds out I've left you, he'll skin me…" Yorgias pulled a face and gazed meaningfully at Wolfie, "…and if anything happens between you two, he'll take you apart afterwards, joint by joint."

Wolfie shrugged, "I'm staying." He sat and crossed his arms.

Yorgias looked at both of them and shook his head, "I'll be five minutes and if I find out anything's happened, I'll be the one handing you to Kalmár on a dinner plate." Reluctantly Yorgias left them.

Tina curled up on the sofa. Wolfie sat up straight at the other end, now they were alone together, he looked as though he wanted to be anywhere but here. The silence stretched, they only had five minutes and she had so much to ask. She didn't know where to start, "Wolfie, I didn't get a chance to say hello properly or to thank you."

"It's Wolf." His reply was curt, chin up and refusing her overtures.

She wasn't used to this stranger, they'd always had a warm, teasing relationship. Tina leaned forwards and he shifted away. "I missed you," She reached out to touch him.

He moved further, begging, "Don't. Please, I'm not what you think I am. I want to be with you but not for the reasons you want. Everything's foggy that happened before the ball. There's so much I can't remember. The emotions are different. Yorgias is right, I can't compete with Kalmár. He'd kill me."

He lisped, his green eyes were dark in the harsh light and she'd caught a flash of too long canines when he'd spoken. A vampire, she'd not thought about it up to this point. The man who'd been her lover, this wasn't him. She had to separate the two in her mind, the man before and the vampire after. She had to think of him as Wolf. She rubbed her face, tried not to cry. "This is a mistake."

Tina needed to sleep, so many days of

inactivity, staring at cellar walls and now this. She wanted to find out how he'd ended up here, what he thought of being a vampire and how it had changed him. She couldn't get past the lump in her throat – he wasn't her Wolfie any more.

He looked up from studying his feet and said quietly, "I thought I could talk to you, I thought it would help. I was wrong, it's different now. There's a veil between my two lives. I can't remember much, small things come through but very little."

They sat in silence again, both uncomfortable with the changes. Wolf stood and said, "Yorgias should be back by now. The corner shop isn't far away." He moved towards the stairs. The door at the top banged, Wolf frowned and stopped to concentrate. The word burst out from him. "Shit."

Tina attempted to reach her mind out to sense what he had and failed, when something came down the stairs. She watched, fascinated as it lurched to the bottom and collapsed into a boneless heap. A body, sprawled at an awkward angle. Her hand crept to cover her mouth as she stared. It was Yorgias. His throat had been ripped out.

Chapter 11

Frozen, Tina noticed the body twitch, the fingers fumbled across the floor and an eyelid flickered. He wasn't dead. Injuries like that and he still moved. She felt sick, wondering what she could do for him. Could she do anything for him?

A sound in the stairwell. They both dragged their eyes away to see an elongated shadow appear above the body. Hands and mouth were wiped fastidiously as it came down the stairs. It turned to speak. "Fetch my bag. I will need it. Then you may dispose of the body."

Cold swept through the room as Lord Tangent entered. She stared at him, not believing her eyes as he took off his suit jacket and flung it over Yorgias' head. Tina breathed out in relief and then almost threw up as he pressed his foot down on it. The skull cracked audibly and blood pooled, soaking through the jacket. The fingers stopped moving.

He shifted away, dominating the room easily. "Fascinating." He surveyed her, ignoring Wolf. "You are here as I was told and yet I can not sense you." He was as handsome and repellent as ever. She shrank away, wishing Kalmár was here. Wolf took a deep breath and opened his mouth.

Waving a hand, Tangent said quietly, "You may leave us." Wolf shook his head, shifting into a fighting position, he looked determined to protect her. Tina had been afraid of Kalmár when they'd first met. Tangent terrified her, his reputation preceded him. Consort's anger had frightened her with its desperation, Tangent's moods went beyond that, every action he made was coldly calculated for the effect he wanted. Tangent walked over to Wolf with a cool assurance.

Tina burst out, "Wolfie, please." She couldn't cope with losing him again. Tangent picked Wolf up before he could react and threw him against the opposite wall. A smear of red trailed down the wall as he slid. He grunted and lay still as she stared at the red stain. Tangent turned back, his glacial eyes studying her carefully. Tina flinched as he sat next to her and tried to make herself as small as possible.

"Now, why are you like this? I can not sense your presence or smell your blood. I know how you smell, I have watched you for years." He gripped her chin in cool fingers, making her raise her head. Watched her for years - Tina caught the look and said nothing. Lord Tangent didn't speak to her. His shirt, open at the neck, was whiter than the skin beneath. He touched her skin and hair, bending his head to smell her. He brushed his lips against her skin in a parody of a lover's caress. He smelled expensive, she shut her eyes and tried not to breathe, desperately willing herself not to cry.

"Interesting. Did you know a bonding is voluntary?" His fingers tightened to bruising and she opened her eyes to find him staring into them. She shook her head, the rest of her trembled, it could have meant yes or no. "It is possible to change a bonded partner or to break the bond itself." He smiled. "I look forward to Kalmár's reaction when I come to the next ball with you walking behind me."

Vinceti appeared with Lord Tangent's bag. "It is not long until dawn my lord, we should leave."

Tangent shook his head as he continued to look her over. "Kalmár will not be here until late tomorrow night, I know where they are. We will stay."

Vinceti paused as he gathered up Yorgias'

body, "But my lord…" Tangent stared through her, irritated that someone dared to question him. Vinceti hesitated, struggling to find the correct words. "But we must…"

He turned to glare at Vinceti, "Expose the rubbish in the open somewhere. Do not presume to tell me my business." Tina's eyes met Vinceti's and for an instant saw panic run across his face. It cleared, then Vinceti bowed, head down and carried the body up the stairs. The door banged shut behind him.

Tangent returned his gaze to Tina, his voice soft. "It will be interesting to break you to my will. I have been told you are difficult and stubborn. We shall see." The words chilled her.

Wolf groaned and Tangent turned to look. Terrified Tangent would kill him, Tina reached for her knife and attacked. She heard the crack before she felt it and fell back onto the sofa gasping. The world span and grew black around the edges. He'd broken her arm, moved so fast she'd not seen him. He grasped her by the other arm and pulled her upright.

Dimly she heard him say, "You only need one arm. Attempt that again and it will be all you will have."

He picked up his bag and took her down the next set of stairs. She tried to keep her feet under her, guessing he would drag her otherwise. Swallowing her pain, she supported her arm the best she could as she lurched after him.

There were a row of doors downstairs. Having checked a room, he brought her inside and told her to sit next to the bed. She hunched against the wall, shivering in shock and cradled her arm. He opened the bag, brought out a thin rope and tied her to the bedpost.

He looked down at her, not bothering to conceal his desire, "I wonder if you taste as you should, however I have fed tonight. We shall wait until tomorrow night for that pleasure, shall we?" She looked at the floor, he'd fed on Yorgias, ripped his throat out. He nudged her with his foot. "Reply when I speak to you."

"Yes Lord Tangent," she whispered. He looked pleased enough. He went through his bag and found a thin jumper. Shrugging it on, he walked out and came back with a blanket.

"When you behave you will be rewarded, consider it part of your training." He threw it over her.

"Thank you, Lord Tangent." Despite having to minimize damage to herself, she hated giving in, even this much.

He placed his bag on the bed. "Dawn is coming. I will sleep soon."

Her eyes widened in horror. In here? With her? She dared to ask, "What about Vinceti?"

Tangent stared at her in cool disgust, "You have not been taught to behave. We will start on your education tomorrow." She shivered and tried to curl in her blanket out of sight of his cold eyes. He twitched the sheets on the bed straight and barred the door. Leaving the electric light on, he lay neatly, his arms crossed over his chest.

Tina rested her head on the bed post, exhausted from the night. He'd tied her up at the bottom of the bed, opposite the door, the rope around both her wrists and knotted on the far side of the bed, past his feet. She had just enough slack on the rope to cradle her broken arm against her knees. The pain spread through her, thumping with every beat of her heart. The unshaded light was harsh on her eyelids and she shifted to cover them with a corner of her blanket.

She wondered if Wolfie had recovered enough to escape. What would happen if he were taken into the sunlight? What did vampires do if that happened? Explode? Turn into a pile of dust? She felt numb and sick, she told herself it was shock.

The bed post dug in to her spine and she shifted again. The room wasn't big, all dirty cream paint, breeze blocks and concrete walls. The floor was cold linoleum, grubby from long use. She hoped she could sleep. She needed to sleep in order to have her wits about her tomorrow night. Her thoughts sank. How long would it take for him to break her, how long could she fight him? She would have to live with whatever happened. Even if Ludovic was around, he wouldn't be able to help. He'd be an unwilling accomplice in whatever Tangent had planned.

She raised her head to look at the rope, the knots looked secure. Tina had no idea if Tangent had switched off due to the dawn or not. In a light headed way it was strange, she used to be frightened of the feeling vampires generated, now she felt insecure not feeling them. Holding her arm, she stretched to look. His feet were in the way, polished shoes, black socks. She craned around them, came closer and froze.

His eyes had snapped open and he glared at the ceiling. She stayed where she was, barely breathing. They remained open, glassy and cold. The rest of him was still and corpse-like. Gradually, she moved back, attempting to keep his face in view and the eyes closed. She sank back to her original position, he must be asleep.

Tina looked at the knots again, she couldn't get to the knot on the far bedpost, she'd be too close to him. She would have to untie the end around her wrists. She could use her teeth, he'd not gagged her, there was no point when they were two floors under street level - who would hear her? She inspected the rope and decided which loop to start with. Whimpering at having to move her arm, she put her mouth to the rope. The first tug made her head spin. She wriggled more of the knot into her mouth and began to gnaw slowly, trying not to jar her arm.

The rope became soaked with saliva as her teeth scraped it. It was made of a nylon material, near impossible to chew through. She stopped and carefully dropped her arm to rest it. Licking her lips, Tina tried to bolster her spirits, she had all day to chew through the rope. Once she was free it would be easy. Her eyes were drawn to Tangent, not wanting to think what would happen if she couldn't bite through. Tears threatening, she dropped her head to start again.

A sudden bang and a clatter of feet upstairs made her jump. Somebody was upstairs. She listened and tried to shout, her voice came out in a thin wail nobody would hear. Tangent lay like a cadaver on the bed as she stopped and concentrated on her breathing, she had to get their attention. Tina forced the air past the blockage in her throat and managed to increase the volume. She gasped and kept on, finally getting the air into her lungs to scream properly. Voices talking loudly came her way. She kept screaming and they stopped at her door. Someone tried to open it, thumped and shouted in a foreign language.

Her ears rang from the echoes in the small room, she coughed and her voice wobbled, sounding funny after all the noise, "It's bolted from the inside, I'm tied up." She sank back in despair, they wouldn't be able to open it. The voices talked outside. A loud banging started, something thumped hard. The wooden door frame began to split, unable to cope with the impacts.

Eventually it broke, throwing the door open and bouncing it against the bed. A man rushed inside, she cringed away from his concerned hand, "My arm." She hunched protectively as he put a hand on her shoulder. He blocked her view, she could hear others in the room and she remembered Tangent.

"Don't…" she began when she heard a shout. As the man turned, his hand gripped her shoulder hard, making spots appear in her vision. She moaned as she saw Tangent's arm raised off the bed, his fingers digging into a man's neck. Blood soaked the arm of Tangent's jumper and ran down the chest of his victim as they tightened. The man kicked, unable to scream, pulling at the iron fingers holding him and choked in his own blood.

Another man was in the doorway, the light glinting off his glasses. Tina could see the fascinated look on his face as he watched, he didn't appear bothered by the man dying in front of him. Tangent's eyes were open and his face snarled, showing his fangs. No other part of him moved.

She wondered why she didn't cry, she felt frozen inside. The man stopped kicking and went limp. "Please," Tina whispered, "Don't go near him. He'll kill anything that goes near him." She didn't know if anyone had heard her. Her eyes were dry, she felt empty.

The man in the doorway nodded and barked an order at the man holding her. He had to repeat himself to get a reaction. He slid past the bed, back against the wall and knelt next to her.

"Do you speak English?" He nodded. "Will you help me? My arm is broken." He turned to give orders to the men behind him as they stood transfixed by the sight of their colleague.

"You are being kept here?" he asked in an accented English. He lifted her chin and checked her neck.

Tina whispered, "Please let me go." She had to get away, Kalmar would be here tonight, she had to get to him. A bag was dropped next to them and the man who delivered it stayed against the wall, unable to take his eyes off the dead body Tangent held. Tina could smell the blood puddled on the floor, the stench of opened bowels reminding her of the ball.

"I will stabilise your arm. Show me where you have broken it." She pointed and he took a sling from his bag, tied it round her and cut the rope. Black spot threatened as he moved it but it felt better once it was supported.

"If we move out of the room, then he might drop the body." He nodded and helped her up, they edged out carefully. Tangent's eyes closed and his arm went lax, the body fell with a thump on the floor. It was dragged out feet first. Wolf wasn't in the main room, Tina wondered if he'd got out or if Vinceti had taken him. Her head felt tight, thumping. "You will let me go?"

"You will come with us," he replied. There were various people in the room talking excitedly and gesturing towards the stairs. Someone was taking samples from the bloodstain on the floor where Yorgias had died.

There was no way she was being taken anywhere now she was away from Tangent. Tina had to find a place to hide until the evening until Kalmár could find her. She backed out the way as a stretcher went by for the dead man, secure in the knowledge that Kalmár wasn't far away. Thinking she could slide out in the confusion and get away, she edged towards the stairs that led to the street. The man in charge noticed and pointed. She tried to run and failed, tripping over her feet. Her arm was knocked as someone caught her and she fell into blackness.

Chapter 12

Tina awoke in semi-darkness and groaned. The floor rocked and her head span. A rumbling vibration ran through her and she realised she was in a van. Her good wrist had been handcuffed to the wall. Hazily, she wondered if she would throw up. She cradled her arm to her and protected it from the jolting the best she could.

Her body craved food and her headache expanded. She tried to bang on the side of the van, not having enough energy to shout. Nothing happened, the van kept moving. Exhausted, she fell asleep at various points, with the dream rising to claim her, its hunger clenching her stomach, holding her in its grasp until she woke with a dry mouth and pounding head.

The van stopped and the doors opened. Tina blinked in the sunlight, the first she'd seen in days. They unclipped her and pulled her out, barely able to stand from being crunched up for so long. There was another van close by, its doors opened and abandoned. She had a brief impression of chain link fencing around barren countryside before she was dragged back into the glare of electric lighting. Corridors heading downwards and she despaired at never being allowed the walk in the sunshine. She was pushed into a room and left alone, the door locked behind her.

Tina stared around hopelessly. A bed in the corner, little else. A whine in the corner of the room and she saw a camera moving to watch her. She ignored it, not being in any state to care about her dignity. With nothing else to do, she lay on the bed, waiting for something to happen and dozed with no awareness of time. The thoughts of dripping water flickered over her brain, she licked her lips unconsciously, so thirsty. Hungry too, she bared her teeth. Her limbs were like putty, the sleep keeping her under. She should be in the dark…

Voices outside and the sound of a key in the lock woke her. Tina sat up carefully, finding it difficult to keep her arm supported. She cradled it as two men in uniform came in, the tatters of the dream sliding away.

"May I have some food? Something to drink?"

The taller one shook his head. "Come with us." She hesitated and he came to take her good arm, with little other option she went.

All the corridors looked the same, whitewashed and peeling. Few other people passed them, they averted their eyes from her and hurried on. The guards took her to a medical centre, the person who looked at her arm appeared not to speak any English, any information was passed through the guards who translated. Her arm was x-rayed, set and plastered and she was given pain killers which made her drowsier. Tina gulped down the water to help swallow them. She had her neck checked again and notes taken. The two guards escorted her back to her cell.

Later she woke, light headed and desperately thirsty with her stomach grumbling. Her arm felt far more comfortable having been plastered and set. The two guards entered, this time with food and drink on a tray.

The taller one asked, "Why were you in the cellar?" She shrugged, trying to appear groggier than she felt. He tried again, "What is your name?"

Tina hesitated, "Christiana Johansen." That's what it said on the documents Kalmár had set up for her, although they were all back at the castle. She hoped they wouldn't ask her any more questions. The man nodded and left, mumbling the name she'd given.

She slumped on the bed after they'd shut the door. She didn't know if she'd been right to give that name, would they be able to find out about her if she'd given her real name? Her thoughts turned to her daughter in a way they hadn't for months. What if they could take her home, back to her real home in England? The familiar ache re-surfaced. She knew Jo was fine. As fine as an eleven year old girl who'd lost her mother could be. She also knew intellectually she couldn't go back but the thought of being able to speak with Jo was seductive.

Her stomach growled and she tried to shake the unwanted thoughts out of her head. The food was basic, a spoon to eat it with and a small bottle of water, which she had to grasp between her knees to undo. Not enough to drink, forget washing. She had nowhere else to wash in her room, she was desperate for a shower. She must stink to high heaven, she sniffed herself and could no longer tell.

Not enough food either, she'd start to lose weight shortly. Under normal circumstances she ate constantly to keep up with Kalmár's appetites. Her thoughts changed to Kalmár, wondering if he'd got to the safe house yet or if he was still travelling to find her and what mood he'd be in when he found she'd gone. She wondered if they'd left Tangent, if they'd locked the doors behind them. Tangent would be fine, it was the thought of anyone else stumbling upon him while he slept that worried her.

Nobody disturbed her. Every so often someone would walk by, she could hear the footsteps echoing but nothing else. Tina slept, needing the rest. The lights were left on and she had no idea of time.

Eventually the same men came back and gave her more food. She thanked them and tried to start a conversation. They ignored her overtures and left. So sleepy, why did she keep falling asleep – was it something in the food? Hands pulled her up through the rocks, there was food up there. A desperation filled her, she had to reach it. Creatures squashed beneath her as she crawled, she would survive...

Tina sat upright, flinging her good arm up to protect her head from the hard ceiling and woke up fully to hear footsteps running past her room and agitated voices talking loudly. She listened, trying to work out what had happened. It went quiet then a rhythmic slamming started. It echoed through the corridors, she couldn't work out what was happening.

The voices became louder, more urgent. Abruptly she heard guns. Tina jumped to the door and started to shout, banging on the door, wanting to know what was happening. Nobody came, the guns stopped and everything slid back into silence. Silence, she could almost hear the water dripping. She lay back, covered her eyes with a sheet and slept again.

Tina was woken by the two guards. Food was presented and they stayed while she ate, no conversation came from either of them. Images from her subconscious demanded her attention and her eating slowed. When she'd finally finished, the taller one took her by the arm and walked her through the corridors, past closed doors. They were all similar and with no windows of any kind. The stained white walls and electric lights were starting to get on her nerves. They led her through to a large room with computers. A few people sat at the desks working, they ignored her as she walked in. She didn't know if she should make a fuss. They all appeared nervous, too intensely wrapped up in their work.

An open door at the end of the room caught her eye. No, it wasn't open, it rested against the wall, next to the door frame. The bottom had been badly damaged, it looked as though someone had grabbed hold of it and twisted it out of the frame. She wondered if it had been the source of the noise last night. The pounding, what could do such an amount of damage to an internal door? She went cold, they'd found her in a room with Tangent. They would know about vampires. Her eyes flicked down to find what she expected – two sets of four indentations creasing the metal at the bottom – fingerprints.

She had no time to think further, the guards had brought her to face a man sitting in front of one of the computers. It was the man in charge at the cellar, dressed in a white lab coat. He took his glasses off, briefly reminding her of Kalmár. The rest of him was nondescript, he wouldn't stand out in a crowd, yet his eyes watched her, sparkling and excited about something.

"Good morning Christiana."

Was it morning? Tina took a deep breath, "Morning. Are you going to let me out?" She asked this brightly, making sure the rest of the room could hear. She didn't expect him to say yes.

He chuckled. "No. Where do you come from Christiana?"

"Romania at the moment."

"Why were you tied up in the cellar?"

Trapped in the dark, her arms crossed over her chest. Tina shook the image from behind her eyes away and said, "I'd been caught trying to find some food."

I don't believe you." She shrugged the best she could with her arm in a sling.

"What do you do in Romania?"

She smiled, "Nothing much. I'm a kept woman."

"By whom?"

Tina hesitated, "Look, I don't know who you are or what I'm doing here but if it's a ransom you want, then my boyfriend will pay." She winced internally at calling Kalmár her boyfriend but hoped it was clear to those listening that she didn't want to be here.

"Why are you not with him?"

"We'd had an argument." It sounded weak and she knew it, she couldn't think of anything else at the moment, the parallels of being trapped both here and in her dreams were too much.

He seemed amused, "You had an argument with your boyfriend and you ended up in a different country, rummaging around in a cellar for food. No passport on you, no money, no identification. Interesting. Let me tell you Christiana, I am a scientist. I study many things, things others would not think of. That door is the result of one of them. I think there is a reason for you being in the cellar and it is connected to that door."

She did her best to look confused. "What do you mean?"

"Don't try to lie, you know as well as I do that the door was ripped off by a vampire." He interrupted her before she could reply. "Don't deny to me that you don't know. You were tied up in the same room as a vampire who killed one of my men. I saw your face when you walked into this room. You were surprised to see that door but not shocked. Everyone else in this bunker hasn't been able to take their eyes off it, they have never seen anything like it. You looked once and started thinking. You've seen this before."

Not entirely, but she knew hinges like the ones

on that door would be easy for Kalmár to break. She imagined him ripping through doors to get to her. Her heart sank, he didn't know she was here. "What do you want?"

"Information. While you co-operate, you will be treated well. If you choose not to, I can find other uses for you."

"I do have someone looking for me. He will be angry to find me here."

"Is he the vampire you were tied up with? You seemed to want to get away from him." He shrugged as she shook her head. He waved at the guards and they took her back to her room.

Chapter 13

Wolf opened his eyes, he still didn't know where he was. He could feel a warm bubble in the room with him, an animal. He couldn't sense any other vampires or Mouse close by but he hadn't been able to sense her the other night either.

He'd managed to get through the door last night. He'd twisted the top corner down, popped one set of hinges and wriggled through into the corridor. Wolf looked across, it was still bent across the top. His arms and legs had been shackled to the bed while he slept, he tested them absently, flexing his muscles against them. The camera he'd ripped off had also been re-wired back onto the wall, but the monitoring equipment had disappeared.

He'd smashed his way through into another room, grasping the door from the bottom and pulling and had been forced back by guards shooting at him. He'd had to give way, he was too young, he'd get hurt like any human would. Fighting to suppress the part that wanted to charge them and tear them to pieces for daring to contain him, Wolf had spent the rest of the night pacing and fretting about Mouse. Having had the chance to see her again he didn't want to let her go.

His fangs slid down, he knew what she was and why she was with Kalmár. Her blood would be strong, the rationale behind these powerful vampires wanting her, although he hadn't been able to feel or scent her for some reason. He'd stopped her in the street for that curiosity alone. Yorgias had pointed out a boy with the blood to him once with the strict instructions to leave him alone – too young. The scent on the breeze had made him shake until Yorgias had slapped him around the head.

He fretted about her being with Tangent. He could imagine Kalmár's reaction and didn't want to be around when he found out. Someone would have to tell him. Yorgias he could do nothing for, he was dead, Wolf's own survival was more important.

Wolf lay on the bed and tried to work out what had happened. He'd been in the cellar, Tangent had been there, with Mouse. He'd hit the wall hard enough to black out and had come around before dawn, tried to move and seen Tangent notice him. She'd drawn her knife and attacked a powerful vampire. For a moment he felt absurdly proud of her, a mouse daring to bite her captor and with as much chance of succeeding.

His memory was hazy from the impact and compounded by the dawn talking to him, whispering to find somewhere safe. He'd not been able to move into the cellars below, he'd had to trust that no one would come in but it looked like someone had. Thankfully any damage he'd incurred from Tangent had healed quickly during the last sleep.

He hissed through his teeth and looked around for the animal. He was hungry, the bags of cold dead blood were still on the floor where he'd kicked them last night. A cat was in a cage close by the door. A big ginger tom, it cowered, not even spiked up. It knew he was dangerous and had nowhere to run.

Wolf tested the shackles, they didn't give much, whoever had designed them had done a good job. He shifted his backside down as much as possible and leaned against them. Not a good enough job, the bands strained and twisted his ankles, giving way with a pop. Getting his feet underneath him, he did the same with his wrists. He sat up and looked around, tongue between his teeth. He strolled over, picked up the cage and sat on the bed with it.

"Hello puss." The cat hissed half-heartedly. He reached in and pulled it out, tickling its ears. It wasn't convinced and hunched itself up. He shrugged and tucked it upside down under his armpit, when it fought him, he held it firmly while he bit. Blood, warm and full of life, unlike the stuff in the bags. Once full, he dropped the dead cat on the floor, wiped his mouth and spat the pieces of fluff out.

His mood improved, he peered over the crumpled corner of the door, two guards sat with their guns on their laps watching. Wolf swore to himself, then relaxed his arms on the open part and smiled at them.

"Evening." They ignored him. "Nice breakfast, give my compliments to the owner of the hotel." They glanced at each other, not sure how to respond. "Mind if I come out?" He gave them plenty of time to see him get ready to pull himself over. The guns focussed on him.

"Stay where you are," one of them said.

"Why?" Wolf wanted to get them talking. They hadn't been thinking of him as a sentient being, maybe he could talk his way out. They clammed up. He peered though and saw the door behind them was still missing. "Sorry about the door. I don't like being locked in places. You know how it is." He smiled again, trying for the friendly look.

They shifted uncomfortably, "Stop talking."

"Why?" Wolf repeated. "Could you do something about the smell in here? The cat shat itself. It stinks."

"You've eaten it?" One of them couldn't stop himself from responding.

"Not entirely. What's wrong with that?" They shuffled, glancing at each other, trying to watch him and not look at the same time. He almost found it amusing. In fact it would have been, if he wasn't trapped in here, with them pointing those damned guns at him. He paced the room for a while, stretching his legs, giving them a chance to think.

His own thoughts went back to Mouse. There was something else about her, another pull that he couldn't remember from his human life. The temptation to spirit her away had been there, to find out what it was about her that pulled – the knowledge that he'd be killed for it was a distant threat. She knew what it was and expected him to know. Wolf bared his fangs, nothing had come through the veil apart from a few images of them together, why couldn't he remember? There was nothing in the room, no distractions and it really was starting to smell. The urge to make mischief rose.

"You still there?" He peeked through the gap. "I'm bored. Are you going to sit all night not talking to me?"

"You drink blood." They both stared at him with a horrified fascination.

"Yes. I'm a vampire it's what I do. Don't have to drink yours. Besides, I bet you eat meat, it's practically the same thing." Wolf nearly laughed at the look on the guard's face while he tried to think up a reply.

"That's different. You drink people's blood."

"No, it's not. You have to kill a cow to eat it. I don't kill people."

"But…" The guard was spluttering.

"I only take a little and it doesn't hurt very much. Would you like me to prove it?" He gave an evil grin and the guard stared, unsure what to do next. A footstep in the corridor beyond and the guards sat up straighter, relaxing. It must be someone in charge, he decided to be polite, "Evening."

The man nodded in reply, "Did you enjoy the cat?"

Wolf shrugged, "An appetiser."

"Better than the bags? We will have to see what we can do for you." Wolf nodded, wary of the helpfulness. "Well done for getting out of the shackles, you are stronger than we thought. You surprised us last night by pulling the doors off. That's why we have these gentlemen here, to keep you where you are supposed to be."

"Could you undo these?" Changing the subject, Wolf held up his wrists with the remains of the cuffs on them, while trying to control the fury bubbling up at his words.

The man produced a key from his pocket. Wolf stretched his wrists out, seeing if he would come closer. The man laughed and threw the key. Wolf caught it and undid them, then pocketed it.

"What is your name vampire?" Wolf wasn't going to answer that one. He leant against the wall and stared at the ceiling, thinking of ways to get them to open the door. He'd been brought here for a reason and wanted to know why. After waiting the man said, "You may call me Gunther."

"You aren't German." His accent sounded wrong, a lot felt wrong.

"No. But that is what you may call me." A silence, while Wolf pretended to be bored, not difficult. Gunther continued, "You are fascinating vampire. Did you know that?" Wolf stayed quiet. He didn't want to be fascinating, he wanted to be out of here. The other men were amusing to play with, this man was a threat, he needed his throat ripping out.

"We had problems when we brought you in here, during the day. We couldn't get you through the door. You literally stopped against a barrier. We actually had to invite you in. Do you remember? Can

359

you remember?" Wolf was on edge, didn't want to know what they'd done to him while he was helpless. The other side of him whispered, adding to his agitation.

"Maybe you can't remember, but some part of you still functions, we will have to try different experiments. We tried mirrors as well, so much folklore that is correct. Why do you not show in a mirror?" Gunther paused, waiting for a reply. "Why do you not move when you are threatened vampire? The other vampire killed one of my men. We had to leave him where he slept."

Wolf tensed further, he must be talking about Tangent. Tangent must have killed someone in his sleep. Wolf had been troubled someone could move his own body while he slept and he fought to contain the side of him that wanted to rip this person to shreds for daring to touch him while he was helpless. There must be parts of him still developing. He glowered at the wall, what was he going to bring up next?

Not receiving his reply, Gunther put his hand in his pocket. "Vampire. Can you see this?"

A large crucifix dangled from a chain. In a split second, Wolf took note of it and shrieked, recoiling he disappeared out of sight behind the door. He writhed in agony, hands over his face. Footsteps - he groaned and shook, brain working furiously. Someone peered through the gap as he lay panting. The door was unlocked. It dragged across the floor, hindered by having only one set of hinges. It shoved against his leg and he shifted to give them room to open it.

"No..." he moaned and peeped through his fingers. The crucifix appeared again and he shrieked as loudly as he could. A guard appeared on the end of the chain, started to slide through the gap. Wolf coiled and grabbed for his arm, pulling at him and was stopped by the door dragging as he tried to reach for the gun. The door banged against him, bruising his arms. Wolf had hold of the guard around his neck, Gunther shouted and threw something over them both as they struggled.

The other guard shoved Gunther aside and fired, finally getting a clear shot. Wolf bellowed as he felt the bullet go through him. He let go in shock, the guard dropped to the floor while Wolf clutched at his leg. The guard crawled away, red in the face and holding his throat.

"Shut the door and move back to where I can see you." They were back in control. Wolf stared for a few seconds longer until he was threatened again. Limping, Wolf did as he was told, snarling at the lost chance. The door was locked while the guard pointed the gun at him, flinching at the sight of Wolf's fangs. They moved back to their chairs further down the corridor.

Wolf looked at his leg and fought his inner self to calm down. It hurt. The bullet had scored along his thigh but it would heal. He sat on the bed, avoiding the dead cat. His clothes were wet, Gunther had thrown something over him. Curious, he tasted it. Water - holy water? It tickled his sense of humour and despite the pain, he started to laugh.

Chapter 14

The guards brought Tina back to the computer room. She'd been taken in for questioning several times, with long periods in between, where she lay in her room, staring at the blank walls and worrying. The lights were on constantly and she fell into a fugue, drifting between sleep and waking without being aware of time passing. Images pressed against her eyelids, some she recognised from the past, others were nightmares of the deep.

The computer room was empty and the desks were tidy. This time it had the air of work finished for the night. The scientist sat at the back of the room, the door still leant against the wall.

Concentrating through her foggy brain, she tried to start off on the right foot this time, "Thank you for sorting my arm out, forgot to say earlier."

He smiled back, "No sign of your boyfriend."

"He'll be coming, he won't stop looking for me. Can I have a shower? I must stink."

"No. Are you going to tell me what you were doing in that cellar?"

"I've told you the truth several times. I shouldn't have been there at all. I was told the code by a friend. I didn't realise anything else was there."

"So, is this 'boyfriend' a vampire?"

Tina took a deep breath, trying to work out how much truth she had to tell him without revealing everything. "Yes but he doesn't live in the cellar."

"Interesting. I have been doing some research on you Christiana Johansen." Tina looked at him and went cold. "Your accent is English and it is your preferred language, am I correct?" She replied in

Romanian automatically and he laughed. "Very good. But Christiana Johansen appeared on the records twelve months ago. Oh, it is very well done but when you begin to look properly, your internet footprint only started at that point."

"Not everyone has an internet footprint."

"True but most do. Those that don't tend to have a good reason for it. What would your reason be?" She kept her mouth shut and he smiled, "Given your accent I decided to look through records of missing people in the UK. There are plenty and I couldn't find you."

"I'm not missing."

"You are correct. You are not missing, you are dead." She froze. Feeling like a rabbit caught in the headlights, a disaster, unavoidable for the rabbit at least.

He watched her carefully, "Christine Johnson. There are pictures of you and your daughter. You died in a car fire, so sad. Don't you miss your daughter? What made you give everything up? Your 'boyfriend'?"

Tina shook, she desperately wished she wasn't here, that she was safe in the castle. Hell, even being with Consort was better than here. She tried to stop her voice from trembling, "You don't know anything."

"I know I could tell your family that you are alive. Would you like that? You could talk to them, see your daughter again, cuddle her."

She could see how he spoke with care, constantly watching her for the impact of his words. It wasn't fair, raking up old memories. She thought she'd sorted herself out, dealt with them. She'd sworn not to talk. Trapped, Tina closed her eyes, took a deep breath and said "I'm sorry. I can't tell you anything."

"Do you admit that you are Christine Johnson?"

"I can't say." She had to protect everyone, the only way she could was by refusing to answer.

"Why you? You say you were in Romania. Why did he take you from England? It's a long way to go to find someone." Tina stared at the wall miserably.

"Vampires drink blood. Is it something to do with that?" She rigidly controlled her face.

He nodded at the guard and he grabbed her, twisted her good arm and pushed her face against the table. The scientist rolled her sleeve up and took a syringe out of its packet. Tina struggled and was cuffed around the head for her troubles. Ear ringing, she stopped, her cheek pushed against the papers on the desk as she watched the needle go in and the blood pulled out, thick and red. He taped cotton wool to her arm, he didn't know that she would stop bleeding quicker than a normal human.

The questioning continued, him pressing her and her refusing to answer. Knowing she had to hold out but unsure how she could escape from this place. She was never sure what he would ask her next, she had to stay on her guard, trying to concentrate.

Tina sprawled on her bed exhausted when the guards left. What else could they do to her? She'd become acutely aware of the guard's strength while he'd held her down. If she held out much longer, any threat would become a reality. Her head hurt from trying to work it all out. She couldn't betray Kalmár but she'd never expected to be in this situation when she'd made that promise. How long did she have before the infection began to make her ill? She shied away from what might happen, she had to believe she would get out.

What about Jo? Would he let them know she

was alive, purely to create mischief? Had she dealt with never seeing her daughter again or had she simply buried her feelings? Tears leaked out. She'd not cried once through all this. Not through Consort stealing her, despite him frightening her, she'd stayed strong and stood up to him. Tangent had terrified her. She'd thought she would never get free of him, had thought that the next time she would see Kalmár would be at the ball, behind Tangent, being unable to disobey him.

The tightness in her head intensified. Jo was her vulnerable spot. She couldn't go back or could she? She was bound, under Kalmár's protection. The thought of going back, to explain she couldn't live with her daughter…to tell her that her mother was alive…

Tina rolled over, gave up being strong, gave up on dealing with what life threw at her and howled into her pillow at the unfairness of the world. How tall was her daughter? She missed cuddling up on the sofa, watching TV, talking with Jo. She wanted to know all the little things in her life. The things that couldn't be written down and sent to her on a computer file. Did Jo still bounce down the stairs, hopping from one foot to the other? Did she still pull her hair when she concentrated? She even missed the way Jo would cross her arms and glower when angry, a miniature mirror of herself. A dozen silly things, things that didn't register in day to day life but made all the difference when you weren't around.

Tina turned over after a while and stared at the ceiling, the tears still coming. Her blood. She wondered if the differences would be obvious to the scientist when he looked. She rubbed her wet face with her sleeve, smearing her face. It itched. She gazed at the ceiling and her thoughts folded around each other, repeating themselves. The tears leaked out, until exhausted, she fell asleep.

The dark dream rose to claim her with hungry fingers, then cleared and she dreamt she stood on the tall tower, watching the sunset, safe in the castle and knowing Kalmár would be waking as full dark approached. The height of summer and the night was warm and still. Kalmár greeted her and perched on the edge of the wall. He shifted so he could hold her, pulling her onto his lap.

She leant against his shoulder, wrapped an arm around him as he ran a finger down her neck and fiddled with the strap of her sundress, sliding it off her shoulder. His cool fingers chased chills over her skin. Within the warm security of the dream, Kalmár bent his head and brushed his lips into her neck. She sighed with his mind wrapping itself around hers and she drew away, kissing him, teasing him whether she'd allow him to bite. Impatient, he wanted to feed, not be teased. His lust growing, he pulled her tighter, tipped her head back and bit. She buried her face in his shoulder and shivered as the desire ran through her veins.

Tina swore as she woke, the shivers that ran down her body fading into nothing. She rubbed her hand through her hair and over her face to shake the dream out of her mind. Only a dream, the despair hit her again. A memory of a perfect evening several months ago, she remembered the crickets chirping in the long grass below, owls and bats overhead. Kalmár had been in an amorous mood. Not wanting to leave her alone, touching her, teasing her over the drop behind them and making her clutch at him as he shifted, close to the edge. A full moon lighting the mountains around them. They'd talked for hours, not going into the cool confines of the castle until early morning.

Another thing that was unfair. For a moment, in the dream, she'd brushed across his mind. Now she was back in her own skull, trapped. The feelings she had left were hollow and unconvincing shadows.

Chapter 15

Tina had spent the night crying, wiping her face, determined to stop and then crying again. Her eyes felt swollen and she was desperately thirsty. She'd been so exhausted she'd imagined all sorts. She'd dreamt of Kalmár, imagined she could feel another vampire around but the dim contact had come and gone at different times during the night and she could no longer tell. She could sense nothing now, it must be the tiredness. Desperation forced her to keep her eyes open as darker dreams lurked around the edges of her subconscious, a further trial. She longed for the breeze in her face, proper sunlight instead of the harsh bulbs and white paint. She was sure all her nightmares would fall into tatters in the light of day.

The meal arrived, she presumed it was morning. Sniffing, she ate under the eyes of the guards. When she asked for more water, one of them took sympathy and filled up her bottle again. They took her through the computer room and into a small office. The guards waited outside the door.

The man leaned back in his chair. He ignored the state of her face, certain she would break this time. "Christine." She nodded in reply, it wasn't worth arguing that point.

"Your blood is fascinating, did you know that? You appear to have some form of virus in it." She tried to look surprised through her exhaustion. He was enthused by his discovery, "I took some samples from the vampire we have. They show a similar virus. Did you know you're infected? We have other samples of blood, they may be similar. I am in the process of isolating it. It may take a while. What would happen if I injected it into an uninfected human? Would they turn into a vampire?"

"I don't know, I'm not a scientist." Tina shrugged, one shouldered.

"It would be interesting to find out. Was that why you were taken, from so far away? Is there something different about you? We are hardly over run with vampires, are we?"

He was getting too close with his guesses and she looked at the floor, trying not to give anything away. Her brain wouldn't work properly, she'd not had enough sleep, not enough food. "Look, I can't tell you anything, even if I did know. I've got someone looking for me. He'll be angry if he finds me here, he gets protective."

"He's not found you yet. How did he find you in the first place?" Tina kept quiet, she didn't know. He sighed as though it were a bother, her non-cooperation. "We will find out. Maybe you will have to help us in other ways before you tell us. We would have to make sure you are able to speak afterwards. Maybe we could put you in with the other vampire first. See what happens."

Tina wrapped her arms around herself, the best she could with the sling. What other ways did he mean? She doubted they would be pleasant. She'd been bitten by Consort and Vinceti. What would this other, unknown vampire be like – they couldn't be worse than Lord Tangent. Maybe they could help her get out. She tried to distract him, "Could I have a wash?"

"No. Not until you begin to co-operate with me. Then you will have more privileges." He waited to see if she would talk further, a calculating look on his face. "Would you like to speak with your daughter? I could arrange it if you wanted me to."

She closed her eyes. "I don't have a daughter," she whispered. She didn't, it was true. She no longer looked after her, she desperately tried to believe it.

He tilted his head as she opened her eyes again. "It states here that you do have a daughter. Jo, I believe her name is?" She stared at the wall, swaying. "I have pictures from the internet of you both. You have lost weight since they were taken but it is clearly you." His voice became kinder. "Why deny it? What difference does it make to admit this? It obviously upsets you."

"Every difference. I can't help you, even if I wanted to." Her head became tighter. Her stomach clamoured for food, making her dizzy.

"What hold does this vampire have over you? To make you like this?" He was insistent, leaning forwards.

"No hold, only a promise I will not talk."

"Some promises should not be kept." She turned her head further away. Only a promise, only to Kalmár. "Were you running away when we found you? Looking for another vampire?"

That didn't seem to be dangerous knowledge. "No."

"Why where you there?"

She took a deep breath and decided to tell part of the truth in the hope he would let her go. "I'd been kidnapped by another vampire. I'd escaped and was trying to get back to Romania."

"What was wrong with the vampire who'd kidnapped you? Surely they are all the same? They all want the same thing, don't they?"

Tina tried to smile, it didn't come out right. "Might as well say to a woman, all men are the same, so why bother looking for Mr Right?"

He chuckled, "Why indeed. So, why is it that your original vampire hasn't found you again yet?"

"I don't know." Exhausted, she felt on the edge of a deep pit, with too many questions being fired at her. A moment's madness that maybe Kalmár had given up and found an easier pet to deal with, one that he could swear to him.

"Then I don't think we have a problem for the moment. Why do you want to get back to him? Surely you'd want to go back to your family?" She stayed silent, the only thing she could do. He sat for a while, then sighed and said briskly, "I am sorry you can not tell me anything. Next time I bring you here, I regret I will have to use more persuasive means." He called for the guard to take her back to her room.

Tina lay quietly on her bed, exhausted and tried to stop her thoughts whirling, her arm over her eyes blocking the lights out. Several meals had come and gone, it must have been hours and she no longer wanted to sleep, frightened of the dreams that haunted her. She didn't know what was worse, the waiting or the questioning. The sleeping or the trying not to sleep. What was he going to do to her?

She became aware of noises began in the corridor, shouts from people running past her door. The rhythmic banging had started again, the vampire he said they held, it must be trying to escape. Tina leant against the door, trying to listen to the words from the agitated voices and failed. She thumped on the door and was ignored. Without any warning the lights went out, the darkness absolute. She shrieked, her voice catching. Nobody took any notice and the banging continued. She could hear gunshots and yelling, it sounded chaotic out there.

The noises and shouts trailed off, everything went quiet. Long minutes dragged by in the silence. She sat on the floor beside the door, empty. Had she been completely forgotten? Would she be left here to starve? Tina was reminded of being under the castle with Kalmár during the day. She stared into the blackness, unless someone came here, she had no chance of getting out. Time had no meaning in the dark and silence, only her heartbeat reminding her of her reality. She sat for what felt like hours, her ear pressed to the door, waiting to hear something.

She woke with a jump, not having meant to sleep, dis-orientated by the darkness around her that echoed her dreams. For a moment she couldn't breathe, not sure if she was awake or asleep. She had the feeling of being trapped underground, the pressure of rock above her and she felt vibrations under her cheek from where she'd slid onto the floor.

Her dull brain took a few seconds to register the measured footsteps, countered by her brain still hearing the slow drip of water underground. She could hear the click of the person's heel as it struck the floor, coming down the corridor, stopping to open doors, and check the rooms. Tina pulled herself up and banged on the door. It didn't matter who it was, only that she had a chance to get out. The footsteps came closer and the handle was rattled. Her heart sank, it was locked and she didn't know where the key was. She was about to shout when the lock clicked and the door opened. Small emergency lights were on in the corridor and she squinted, trying to see through the gloom.

The shadowed person in the doorway hesitated and stepped inside, "Little Mouse?"

This must be another dream, she sat on the floor, unable to move. She sagged in exhaustion, it wasn't real, she'd wake up shortly and someone would come with their methods of making her talk. She would talk in the hope they'd let her go afterwards and she swayed in the knowledge that they wouldn't leave her alone, the experiments would continue after she'd told them what she knew. Sooner or later she would die, either through dissection or the slow torture of the virus turning sour. A thought occurred that if she were with Tangent all she'd have to do was give in to him. It would be easy. A waft of air carried with it a scent of rosemary. These dreams were becoming more realistic, she waited for the lights to fade and the ceiling to lower, trapping her in her stone coffin. In desperation she held up her hands to the figure in the doorway, knowing he couldn't save her.

The figure swept her into his arms and she lay there in shock. Slowly she raised a hand to touch his face and felt cool skin under her fingers. He carried her over to bed and curled her up into his familiar embrace.

"Kalmár," she whispered and wrapped her working arm tight round his neck. He ran his hands over her as she started to shake with relief into his shoulder, unable to cry through the numbness of the few last days. She couldn't feel connected to him, could only feel his physical presence, barely able to see him in the subdued light.

He pulled her away from his shoulder, frowned and touched her plastered arm through her fleece. Confused, she let him inspect her in the dim light, still sniffing and swallowed back her upset. He picked up her wrist, smelled it, brought her close to touch her neck with his tongue and pulled back with a disturbed look on his face. "Why can I not sense you? You smell wrong, taste wrong."

It took a few seconds for her to process what he was saying, captivated as she was by hearing his voice so close. How long had it been since she'd heard him? She managed to stammer, "Consort did something to me. I don't know what. I've not been able to sense any vampires since I've been with him."

His face changed, anger replacing the disturbed look. Kalmár nodded curtly and carried her out of the room, into the shadowed corridor. Miserable and knotted up inside, she buried her head into his shoulder, smelling his herbal scent, desperate for this not to be another dream. He carried her past the computer room and stopped near the open bunker entrance.

"Stay here." Tina slid down the wall to sit on the cold floor and watched him leave. She shivered in the breeze and jumped as the main lights came back on.

Kalmár returned and Ansell stalked behind him, his movements tightly controlled. He squatted in front of her, pulled up her chin to look into her eyes and Tina recoiled. She'd not seen him like this before, ancient eyes burning in a face of a teenager. He had dried blood flaking down one side of his face and she was reminded of Consort reaching for her. On edge, Kalmár bristled as he reacted to her fear and Ansell snarled back at him.

"Calm down. You wanted me to look? Let me look. I'm not going to steal her." Ansell turned back to Tina. "You are frightened of me?" Tina nodded. "Contain it," he snapped. Swallowing she tried, looking away from him as he inspected her. She shook, trying not to flinch as he moved his face down her neck, smelling. He touched her hair and rubbed his fingers together.

"Look." He showed them to Kalmár. "Dust." Kalmár touched her hair and pulled some out. It clung to his fingers.

"I have felt this before. Old one."

Ansell turned to Tina, "Did Consort rub anything onto you?"

374

She shrugged. "I don't know. I fainted, he hit me with a knife when I opened the door to him. If I'd known it was him, I wouldn't have gone. I couldn't sense him." She looked at Kalmár "And I couldn't find you after I woke." She flinched, Kalmár's eyes had become a match to Ansell's.

Ansell spoke to Kalmár, "Consort must have kept back some of the dust from an old one. It appears to have masked her scent, prevented you both from connecting to each other." He rubbed his fingers absently together, "Interesting, I'd imagine Consort has done the same to hide himself." He stood, and said briskly, "Wash her, Sasha has fresh clothes." He looked down and asked, "Have you washed since Consort took you?" Seeing her shake her head, he stuck his head round the door motioned to someone outside and he continued, "I didn't think so. The dust will be engrained into your skin, it will take longer to wear away."

She managed, "I had a funny taste in my mouth, I thought he'd drugged me too."

Ansell grabbed her jaw, tilting her head to look into her mouth. "Hmm." He exchanged looks with Kalmár and let go.

"What?" She rubbed her chin, he'd not been gentle.

"Never mind." She clicked her mouth shut at the unfairness and saw Sasha come in. Ansell put his arm out to stop Sasha coming close and told her to get clean clothes when she went to hug Tina, exclaiming over her appearance. Shooting an irritated look at Ansell, Sasha did as she was asked, disappearing back outside.

"Come." Kalmár took her downstairs to find a shower room. The door to the computer room was partly open, a hand showed through the gap, the limp fingers curled.

Tina stopped or tried to, Kalmár kept her walking. "What happened?"

"They died."

"You killed them?" He nodded and opened another door.

"All of them?" A bedroom appeared, knick knacks, a few books, clothes inside - the remains of somebody's life.

Kalmár showed her the bathroom. "Wash yourself." He went to wait in the other room and she swayed feeling dizzy. How many? She'd seen maybe four or five each time she'd gone into the computer room. Her mind ran through the times she'd been in there, it seemed important to remember. She couldn't recall their faces, why hadn't she looked? Had they stayed at the same desks or moved? Had they killed all of them? Lives, finished, purely for being in the wrong place at the wrong time. Men and women, no mercy given. Tina felt sick. Soap and shampoo on the shelf, a towel, fluff in the corners belonging to somebody else. No longer alive. Tina closed her eyes, not coping.

The door opened and Kalmár leaned against the door frame, "You need to wash." When she didn't respond, he came forwards and unzipped her fleece. She brushed his hands away and began to undress herself awkwardly, turning her back on him.

He found a plastic bag, taped it round her cast to keep it dry and stayed, making sure she got in the shower. The hot water helped, sluicing through her hair, puddling into a dirty grey brown pool around her feet. She scrubbed everything she could and stood afterwards under the water, letting it flow over her.

He held a large towel out and wrapped it round her. Towel. Not hers. Tina could feel him in a distant way as though they shouted over a long distance. Her mind felt foggy. Sasha called through the door that she'd put the clothes out and Kalmár went to get them.

Again, he stood over her while she dragged them on. He helped her with the buttons and gently rubbed her hair dry. She could smell Sasha's perfume on the clothes, warm and comforting. The trousers were too long. She carefully folded them, each movement precise through her cotton wool brain. She couldn't cope with the shoes and socks, they were too big and she left them on the floor.

Kalmar pulled her close, smelt and touched her. "Better than it was. I felt you at points last night, that is why we investigated this place."

She looked at him bleary eyed and childishly said, "I asked but they wouldn't let me wash." His face tightened, the anger in it undiminished.

They met Ansell in the corridor, the scientist was talking animatedly at him. Tina shifted away and behind Kalmár, he must be the only person left alive here, why?

Ansell spoke to Kalmár, "This man says his name is Gunther and he was in charge here. One of those statements is correct."

Gunther turned to peer at Tina. "Your boyfriend has found you I see." He was bright eyed, he didn't seem bothered about the death of his staff.

"He took samples of my blood, said he had a vampire here, threatened me…" She trailed off, both vampires were ignoring her and watching Gunther. She cradled her arm, they reminded her of two cats stalking a small creature, working out which way it would run next.

"I can help you," Gunther went on talking to Ansell. "I've found out plenty of interesting information over the last few days, imagine what I could do for you with more time."

Kalmár's voice was quiet, "Which government do you belong to?"

Gunther shrugged, "I don't bother with governments, they get in the way, rules, regulations. I am a scientist. I do what I want."

Kalmár nodded and Ansell pointed out, "Gunther has been most helpful."

"Good." Kalmár stepped forwards and touched Gunther's face. He appeared transfixed by the cool fingers. "So, whom do you owe allegiance to?"

Gunther shook his head. "No one. I report to no one. Let me study you."

Kalmár's other hand joined the first on Gunther's face, stroking, long fingers settling themselves. His eyes burned, the anger contained. "You wish to help us?"

"Yes. You are fascinating, I could make you my life's work. Study you, find out why you are what you are." He became openly excited at the prospect.

Ansell leant against the wall, looking serene as he watched. Kalmár smiled and tightened his grip, slowly compressing Gunther's head. Tina registered at the same point as Gunther what was happening. She shook, watching the look of panic come across his face as he tried to break the iron grip. He appeared unable to make a coherent noise and he wailed as Kalmár increased the pressure. Tina turned away, her legs dropped her to the floor. She hid her head in her arm and held her ears, trying not to hear the muffled noises.

A step behind her and she looked up, her nose streaming, shivering as she tried to control her heaving stomach. Kalmár calmly wiped his hands on a handkerchief and brushed off the splatters on his jacket. His hands, the long fingers she was used to touching and caressing her, had just killed someone in front of her.

He bent to raise her to her feet. "Come."

She stared at him as unconcerned, he pulled her up. She desperately tried to keep her eyes away from the mess on the floor. Her ears heard a rushing sound and she fainted.

Chapter 16

Tina woke on the back seat of a car. He drove, his eyes on the road, his fingers tapping against the wheel. She watched his fingers, seeing them around Gunther's face, seeing the limp fingers in the doorway. She felt limp all over, so tired. She'd wanted Kalmár to come, wanted him to sort everything out and he had but in his way, not hers. A final brutal solution, no further problems.

She missed the contact they'd had, his way of wrapping his mind around hers. The warmth enveloping her, until she could think of nothing else. She fell asleep again, troubled by dreams of the last few weeks. She woke with a start as he shook her.

"Can you walk?" Tina nodded and pulled herself up. Numbly she got out the car in her bare feet and didn't notice the cold rough tarmac or the chilly wind. He opened the boot, took out a large case and a smaller one. Steering her towards a building, he booked them into hotel. She sat on the bed and watched as he took the cover off the large case, unfolded it into sections and assembled it to make a large box. If she'd been well, she would have been fascinated, made comments and teased him.

There was a knock at the door. He answered it and gave instructions to the person on the other side and accepted a large tray. He brought her to the table, sat her down and made her eat, one slow bite at a time. Tina stared at the wall when she'd finished. Containing his impatience, Kalmár steered her back to bed and tucked the bedclothes in around her.

He went into the bathroom, showered and changed his clothes. Tidy once more, he sat next to her and ran the back of his hand over her face. She gazed past him. Sighing, he rose, locked the door and drew the curtains.

"The staff will bring food, they will knock and leave it outside. The key is on the table. Otherwise, stay in this room." She continued to stare, the room dimly lit in the pre-dawn. He stretched and folded himself into the box, pulling the lid shut.

All was quiet. In the distance she felt him switch off with the dawn light. Slowly the tension unknotted and tears leaked out. She lived with a man that fed from her, a twisted normality. How much had she given up... how much did she really know him and why did she stay? He could kill without a thought, without remorse. She thought she'd recovered from the idea of giving up her daughter, maybe she never would.

She felt a shaky relief Tangent hadn't got her and she that wasn't in the bunker anymore. Her mind wandered listlessly, she was no longer a citizen with rights, she was a creature scientists wanted to study. She couldn't leave him, she'd die and have no protection from the rest of the world. She couldn't think. Limp and unable to function, Tina lay and watched the box with the vampire inside.

Kalmár sat her down to eat again when he woke and made her shower after. He pulled her close to smell and taste her skin. When he didn't bite, she asked dully, "Aren't you hungry?"

"I fed two nights ago." Her feelings plummeted further. He'd fed, not on her. He didn't want her, couldn't cope with the taste of her skin.

He folded the box into its flat case and made a phone call. Taking her out, he drove them to a small airport where a tiny aeroplane waited and abandoned the car. She dozed during much of the journey, resting against Kalmar. The dreams of hunger felt less urgent around him and she was unwilling, despite her anxieties to be apart from him.

It was in the early hours when they arrived by taxi at the castle. He carried her up the steps and into her rooms. Kalmár read while she lay tucked in her bed. The familiar surroundings comforted her, soothing her frazzled nerves.

"Will you kill Consort?" She managed to speak past the cotton wool. He put his book down and removed his glasses to see her properly.

"No."

"Why?"

"I would like to, for stealing you from me. You are mine, bonded to me. He has no right to you but if I kill him then we risk too much instability and the balance of power will change too far."

"There's something not right about him."

Kalmár nodded. "He should have been allowed to sleep many years ago. He is no longer entirely stable."

"Sleep?"

"He has never coped with the changes that living a long life entails. He should never have survived this long. Madame has kept him with her and refused to let him sleep, like the old ones, until he no longer wakes."

"What do you mean, survive?"

"What do you think it takes, to keep on living? Life owes us nothing. Living, year after year, decades, centuries." He paused, "It is not blind acceptance that keeps us alive Little Mouse. It is fighting. Refusing to give up, insisting that you will survive. That is why there are so few older vampires. So many refuse to change, to learn the ways of the world they move through."

Tina was quiet for a while and asked, "What if I chose to give up? Would you let me?"

Kalmár turned his face away, his deep voice soft, "I would allow you your choices." His fingers clenched, stroked the carved arms of the chair and tightened again.

She changed the subject to another hurt, "You fed from someone else."

"I can not live on empty air. I needed sustenance. I could not find you."

"You don't like how I smell."

"There is a coating to your skin from the dust. It is not pleasant to me, it will wear off in time."

She felt adrift, she had nothing to anchor herself to. The last few weeks had sheered her off from the strange life she'd settled into. She held out her hands. "Do these smell?" He nodded. She exposed her wrists, he took one and smelt, shook his head in rejection. She awkwardly pulled up her sleeve on her good arm to her elbow. "I haven't touched here that I can remember. Try this."

He bent, touched the soft skin on the inside with his tongue. "It is better." He stopped, held her elbow and stroked her with his thumb. "May I Little Mouse?" She nodded and turned her head away as tears welled. She couldn't feel the bond between them, she felt empty. He came to lie next to her, curled an arm around to bring her close and bit. It was uncomfortable. She hid her face in his sleeve, smelling his scent and refused to think further.

She lay and stared at the wall after he'd left. She'd always known what he was - a man centuries old and with different views of the world from her. Tina knew he'd killed before and without regret, he'd never hidden that side of himself. She'd always pushed it to one side, tried not to think about it, she didn't need it proven to her. What would someone make of her, if she survived, in a couple of centuries time? Would they consider her ruthless as well?

Single minded?

Tina woke with the traces of a different dream lingering. She'd lain deep beneath the castle, nothing remaining of her mind apart from the twin desires of feeding and sleeping as she gradually collected dust and mould. Above her, Kalmár read in the library, waiting out the years. Listening for her waking and allowing her to feed from him... She shuddered, he would look after her, in whatever form it took, he wouldn't let her go. She curled up in the warmth of her bed and tried to push the horror out of her head, the horror of them both trapped with no escape.

This must have been how Wolfie had felt before the ball, faced with the possibility of living, year after year. Suddenly it didn't feel such a temptation, the concept of an endless parasitic life was paralysing. The only other option she could think of was to walk off the top of the tall tower and end everything. Tina thought about the drop and the rocks below and her stomach lurched. She thought about Kalmár sitting alone in the library and her insides twisted in a different way. So many weights and responsibilities, she couldn't think. She tucked it away, she wasn't that desperate yet, but it would be for her to decide if she carried on. A decision no one could take away from her.

The sky was leaden when she got up, echoing her mood. She scrubbed herself in the bath, tried to find any traces of the dust and failed. Dead vampire, that's what she'd been covered in, she shuddered. Not pleasant Kalmár had said. She smiled wanly at his understatement and got herself breakfast.

Tina wrapped up warm and drove to the barn in the ruined village. Her driving was slow and deliberate. She changed gear as little as possible, thankful her good arm could change gear. She picked up the letters and parcels, noting the piles of boxes that had been delivered for the winter. The wind was icy as she left, whipping her hair around into her eyes.

As she got out of the car in the courtyard, a single snowflake drifted in front of her. She watched it float down and melt on the car bonnet. Turning, she closed the big gates and saw more flakes starting to fall in the valley below. The cars needed to be prepared for winter storage, on automatic pilot, she dealt with them, doing what she could, making a note to ask for help on the things she couldn't. Exhausted from the work, she went through the post and opened her own. New music books, information on courses, everything normal for her abnormal life. She left them in a pile and watched the snow coating the courtyard.

Chapter 17

She recovered her equilibrium slowly, the cold helped. She couldn't wander through the castle, she had to stay in certain areas to stay warm and this gave her a sense of safety and of being enclosed. A simple routine, keeping the fires going in various rooms and cooking food settled her further.

Tina spent most of her time in front of the fire, a book on her lap. Not always reading, sometimes just staring into the flames, her mind a blank. She flicked through her new music books, picked up her viola and put it down again, unable to hold it properly. She walked herself through the martial arts moves Wolfie had taught her, slowly at first, then speeding up, finding comfort in only thinking about her body.

During the long nights, Kalmár sat with her, reading voraciously and talked about what he read. He wanted to hold her more as the dust wore off. He fed but not as frequently as she knew he would like to. The dark dreams had faded with the dust and she started to sleep better. The times when she woke with her heart pounding and searching for him happening less often.

Curled up in his arms, head on his shoulder, Tina finally broached the subject that had disturbed her for weeks. "It would have been easier if I had been sworn to you when I was in the bunker, I couldn't have told him anything." She fiddled with his fingers, they were becoming his fingers again, the flashbacks to the bunker had been happening less often with time. "I didn't know what to say, I'd promised not to tell. He told me I could be with Jo. Threatened me with experiments if I didn't talk."

"If you had been sworn to me, Consort could never have taken you. My control over you would have been absolute, unless he had challenged me. You can always choose to break the bond and because of this you will never be completely safe. You are a temptation to others."

"I can't swear myself in that way, it's too much." He made a noise of quiet agreement, the cool breeze of his breath stirring her hair. "Lord Tangent nearly took me at the safe house." His fingers became still in hers.

"I had been informed he was there."

"I never thought I'd see you again. I didn't know how long I could hold out. He told me that he was looking forward to forcing me to swear myself to him. That he'd heard I was stubborn and difficult. I was so frightened at the thought of him having me, of making me swear myself to him." Her voice dropped, one of her worst nightmares, not having free will.

"I would have come for you, he would not have been able to keep your presence a secret. It would only have been a matter of time." He dipped his head to rest it against hers, "And your stubbornness can be appealing, in the right circumstances."

She smiled, smoothing his fingers out, still cool despite her holding them. The warmth of the fire made her drowsy. "That scientist, he would have worked with you, purely for the knowledge, nothing more."

"He acknowledged no one as master. No government. He would have worked for himself and when he had studied us enough, he would have betrayed us. We could not trust him."

"But you might have found out more information about your nature."

"Ansell informed me that when Wolf went through the computers, there was little other than folklore mentioned."

She woke up. "Wolf? Our Wolfie? Why him?"

"He was the vampire they had confined. He was in the bunker at the same time as you. They studied him during the day whilst he was helpless."

Tina sat up in his lap, confronting him for the first time in weeks. "Why didn't you tell me? I was worried about him. Tangent threw him against the wall, knocked him out."

He touched her face. "He is not who you remember. You knew the man not the vampire Little Mouse."

She sat back in his arms and refused to talk for a while. She should have guessed it was Wolf they'd held, it was an indication of her mindset at the time that she hadn't. Kalmár hadn't changed either, it was typical that he refused to tell her half the story until it was convenient to him. Tina dozed in the warmth of the fire. She woke to find him running his fingers through her hair. He stroked her neck and she stretched against him, allowing him the space to bite. He pulled her close and fed, lingering while he licked the wounds.

Tina asked, "Has it worn off?" He nodded and found his handkerchief, wiped his mouth. "Why can't I feel you properly? It's not the same. You are there but distant, fuzzy."

"You are holding yourself away from me, blocking the bond between us."

"Couldn't you do something about that?"

"Bonding means both sides give up part of themselves. It can not be forced." He returned to caressing the back of her neck as she stared into the fire.

Tina wandered into Wolfie's old rooms. Apart from tidying the clothes, she'd left them as they'd been. Everything was cold here. Wolf was a vampire with skin as cold as Kalmár's. Her memories of Wolfie were as a warm, tactile man, with a sense of mischief and a flashing grin that lit his face. She missed him, the old Wolfie would have brought her out of this far quicker, his teasing and poking, refusing to allow her to brood.

Despite the cold, she sprawled on his bed and gazed at the ceiling. In the corner, sat on top of the wardrobe was the old sledge they'd played on last year. Her gaze fixed on it. She dragged a chair across and pulled it down. Heavier than she thought, it pulled her arms down and she struggled to catch it before it hit the floor. She found some wax and carefully rubbed the runners.

Wrapped up, she went outside and pulled open the small door in the gatehouse. Dusk fell in the clear sky. Everything was still and cold, for once no wind. The moon rose, full and bright, lighting the winter landscape.

Tina took a deep breath, lined herself up and launched herself down the hill. A shriek burst from her as she skidded. She fell off at the first corner and she rolled, protecting her arm. Determined, she got up, brushed herself off and ploughed her way back up the hill. Tina remembered how Wolfie had leant over her shoulder, pointing out the directions. His warm breath on her cheeks, holding her. The kisses and laughter when they rolled off into the deep snow. On her third attempt she managed to get all the way to the bottom. Whooping with delight she looked and felt Kalmár watch from the top of the hill.

She had to make the decision to go on.

Tramping up the hill through the snow, she realised she loved life too much, was still curious and wanted to know what happened next. She could get out of the hole she was in. She might spend at least her daughter's lifetime missing Jo. Wolfie may have been right not to stay in contact with the children he'd had but she wasn't going to allow herself to regret having Jo or missing her, however much it hurt.

Kalmár had been stood on the battlements, he came to meet her by the door of the gatehouse. "Good evening Little Mouse." Breathlessly she greeted him back. He took the sledge from her and propped it against the wall. "It is a beautiful night. Would you like me to take you somewhere?"

Tina hadn't had that offer for a while. She shook her head, her arm ached. "I'm cold. My fingers must be as cold as yours." She took her glove off and reached to touch his cheek. He smiled and turned his face into her fingers. A trace of mischief ran through her and she asked, "Aren't you going to invite me in?"

He took her hand with a serious look on his face, "Come in and be welcome." He pulled her close and carried her into the library to warm up.

After that point, Tina made a determined effort to help herself. It helped when her arm came out of plaster. Gradually she strengthened it. As it became stronger, she picked up her viola and despite not wanting to play, she played it. She made decisions to learn more on her martial arts. Starting to look at courses for the spring, she tried not to think that she would be away from Kalmár. He took her out into the mountains, held her tight and talked to her about the books he read.

One late afternoon, approaching close to

spring, she went through her wardrobe and found herself pulling the ball gowns out of their covers to look at them. The rough silks, rich colours, nearly a year since they'd been made, months since she'd worn them. She picked out the green one and sat near her stove, stroking the fabric. Her mind elsewhere, the threads caught at her fingers and light spilled over it in a pool of sunlit leaves.

A decision made, she found the petticoats and corset that went with it. Tina spent time swearing over fitting them to her, trying to stay within the warmth of the stove. Her arm was back to normal, it just ached when she overworked it. Humming quietly, she put on a CD. She painted her face and put her hair up. Looked in the mirror and delighted with the effect, she turned to look over her shoulder at herself, moving with the music.

She'd become vaguely aware of Kalmár waking and moving around, he was in his dressing room, next to her bedroom. She bit her lip, closed her eyes and felt for him. The thread between them was insubstantial, it slid away from her when she tried to grasp it, she couldn't catch it. Opening her eyes she swore, she'd have to go and talk to him. Tina checked her dress one last time.

There was a knock at the main door behind her. She grinned and turned her back to it, pretended to fiddle with a hair grip, looking in the mirror.

"Come in." She peered over her shoulder at him as he entered, knowing she looked a picture.

He paused as he saw her dressed up and inclined his head, "Little Mouse."

"Your Excellency." She smiled mischievously and swept him a curtsey.

"You would like to dance?" He held out his hand and she took it, allowed him to pull her close. Tina could feel his delight as he danced with her and his growing hunger in the way he held her. She relaxed into him, letting her mind go as he whirled her around, their bodies moving together.

He picked her up and carried her to a chair, kissed her neck and stroked her face with his cool fingers. Her skirts swirled across his lap and onto the floor. She touched his face, the edges of his mind brushing hers. The pupils of his eyes looked huge, they swallowed the light and pulled her in.

He took her hand, turned it and delicately cut into the side of her thumb. Covering it with his mouth, Kalmár half closed his eyes and concentrated on sucking the blood that welled out. She put her head on his shoulder and watched as he did the same to her wrist, taking care not to slice into the big vein. He turned his head to use his canines. Sharp nips anaesthetized by the tendrils of his mind running across hers and she closed her eyes, following both mouth and mind. He moved up her arm and took his time biting gently as she started to shiver.

Her mind relaxed as it ran through old pathways, like water trickling down grooves in the earth after a long drought. Feeling his lust pull at her for the first time in months as warmth ran down her limbs, bite marks up her arm. Tina ran her fingers through his hair and pulled his face to her neck, wanting him to bite. He buried his face into her, unable to resist her invitation. She felt the click as his mind slid into its place around hers and sighed as both of their pleasure intensified with his feeding.

She stayed curled up in his arms afterwards. The thread was there and she could feel him wrapped around her. It balanced itself between them delicately and he held himself back, allowing her to settle. It was a start.

Kalmar touched her face, "I have missed you Little Mouse." She felt him breathe out long and slow as she brushed along the thread between them and saw him close his eyes.

Chapter 18

Wolf looked around at the other vampires and gazed at all the finery for the spring ball. He'd announced himself early and then had to wait and watch others go to the front of the room to declare themselves. He'd fought a number of other vampires to get his ranking in order. They didn't like him not being at the bottom. He grinned, he could imagine Yorgias making comments and shaking his head.

Ansell had also gone up early, ignoring all the whispers. Wolf grinned again, if anyone wanted to take advantage, not realising how old Ansell was, then he wanted to watch. He remembered walking away from the bunker, having cleared it of anything useful. Ansell had stopped by the car, a frown on his face which had cleared as a series of explosions happened underground. He'd caught Wolf's eye and smirked. Smoke had poured out of the doors as they'd driven away, Wolf was sure he could see flames licking out of the bunker's entrance in his mirrors. He reminded himself that getting on the wrong side of Ansell could be a very bad idea.

It had been good to be out of the bunker. He'd driven a van behind them, humming to the radio. They crossed borders into Russia, heading for Madame's residence. The nights had become cold, the frost hard, a promise of snow in the air. The heater in the van didn't work. He felt the cold as a sensation against his skin, one he found he could dismiss.

They'd had to stop outside the palace gates when they arrived. Fuming, Ansell had sent Sasha in to see if she could find anyone. She'd returned, shaking her head, it was all locked up. They'd had to wait for Madame to return with Consort. Wolf had experimented with the barrier at the entrance, fascinated, pressing his fingers into it. He couldn't get far, maybe a centimetre, the tingling growing harder until he couldn't cope. Ansell had eventually snarled at him in frustration, threatening to throw him in, over the wall, if he didn't stop.

Wolf had been here all winter. He'd gone through every computer in the palace, flicked through most of the books and he was bored. If he wanted to feed, he had to tramp to the nearest town, the smell of Sasha and Nikos tormenting him. Wolf had to watch himself, he could get seriously injured if either Ansell or Consort decided to take offence. Sasha appeared equally uncomfortable around him.

Wolf had seen Consort when Madame had brought him back. He'd been brooding, staring out the windows into the night and refusing to talk, at other points yelling until his voice cracked and throwing things. There'd been a horrendous argument between Ansell and Madame, with Madame eventually giving way to Ansell's insistence that Consort be allowed another companion. Wolf had been ordered – asked was not the right word – by Madame to help Consort to recover a new pet. The planning hadn't been easy, trying to arrange everything before the snows came down. Consort was now obsessed with Nikos. He appeared to have forgotten about stealing Mouse, becoming absorbed in his new pet.

The older vampires had started to go up. He could smell their pets and feel the jolt of wanting them. He noticed the other vampires watching and knew they felt the same. There was a gap in the crowd and over by the wall was the Count. He stood with his head bent, listening to someone talk. Wolf narrowed his eyes to see the threads of green pulse through his aura. Kalmár raised his hand to kiss the wrist of his companion, amused at a comment she'd made.

Wolfie stepped behind a pillar, ignoring the other vampires. The familiarity of the slim figure pulled him. He almost remembered... A flash of memory, of seeing her for the first time as Kalmár carried her into the castle. Bare feet, her head tucked into the Count's shoulder, vulnerable in her drugged sleep and being told he would have to look after her. He gazed wistfully for a few seconds and tried to remember more. Her smell intoxicated him, he could feel the call now. He remembered... being curled around her small body, talking. She'd liked him too, laughed with him in the same way. Unconscious of his fangs being down, he watched until the crowd moved again and he lost her.

Madame announced the dancing and everyone swirled away. Wolf looked again for the pair and couldn't find them. Instinctively he went to the piano. He'd not played since the last ball, his fingers twitched, he'd not had the chance to. He played for a few dances, loosening his fingers up and enjoying the chance to play with other musicians.

The music tugged at him and he decided to dance. He brushed hands with humans, passing them on. His only chance to get near them, to imagine getting closer. The contrast between warm and cold partners. Seeing others look on with jealousy when he had a warm partner to whirl around, lusting after those himself when he didn't. He didn't care who he danced with, male or female, all that the ranking meant was who led.

He went back to the piano, brushing past those lower than him with glee, avoiding the many who were higher. Someone made a small noise to the side. She stood there, her eyes huge, looking at him, hand over her mouth.

"Wolf."

Confronted by her, Wolf couldn't cope, he stepped back, shaking his head. Trying not to look, he smelt her and wanted her. Memories of them intertwined, her warmth and teasing fought with his desperation to feed. She stepped towards him, hand out, not understanding his conflict. He felt rather than heard the rumble, deep down and threatening and the other side of Wolf scrabbled at him to get away. The Count appeared. Wolf could almost see the air vibrating as he wrapped an arm around her and turned her towards himself. Her eyes flashed and she slapped Kalmár on the chest, angry at his jealousy. He paused to look down at her and thankful for the distraction, Wolf slid away, hiding himself behind the others.

He got to the hallway and stood, breathing hard. His eyes closed in relief. She'd expected something from him, he had a desperate need to remember. He failed. The veil was too thick to push through. He'd started to realise Yorgias was right. He was a baby, he hadn't re-established his personality yet. So much was lost through the veil. He couldn't reach it, he wasn't sure who he was supposed to be. He'd known once. Wolf sighed and shook the thoughts out of his head. Someone jostled him and he snarled without thinking. Turning, he saw Ansell and behaved himself.

"Thinking of leaving?" Wolf shrugged, caught. "Stay until tomorrow night, you can leave after you've done something for me." Ansell walked away, without waiting for an answer. Of course Wolf could leave but he'd end up being found at some point, Ansell wouldn't forget. Sighing he turned to go back to the ball, determined to avoid Kalmár and the woman he'd once known.

Chapter 19

Tina woke at lunchtime, starving hungry. She stretched and got dressed, tucking a knife into the back of her jeans. She'd not worn it since Wolfie'd left. Wolf - had he wanted to bite her last night?

Kalmár hadn't left her alone the whole time he'd been awake. He'd refused to allow her to dance with anyone else and refused to dance with anyone but her and his jealousy around the other vampires had been shocking. She'd tried teasing him to stop it getting out of hand, nobody would steal her at the ball. He'd refused to listen and told her that they would leave after tomorrow.

She sighed, it had been good to see Sasha again. Maybe Ansell could talk Kalmár out of leaving. Tangent had been there, he'd ignored both her and Kalmár. Strangely, she'd not seen Vinceti, he was normally nosing around somewhere. Consort was nowhere to be seen either, she'd heard he had a new pet to occupy him. She wondered what he'd be like with a new pet and how he coped with someone who defied him. She hoped he was happy.

Tina wandered down to the kitchen, sidling past a couple kissing in the corridor, she didn't know either of them. Ludovic ate at a table in the kitchen. She smiled and kissed the top of his head as she walked past, not expecting a hello. He flicked his eyes up and smiled back, watched her when he thought she wasn't looking. She sorted out her breakfast while she chatted to him, she got most of his responses by looking at his face.

"You're part of the presentation tomorrow?" Ludovic nodded. "How many this year?" He held up one finger and pointed to himself.

"How's that going to work? You've no one to fight."

He shrugged, not having much choice either way. At her concern, he put his arm around her and smiled, bending to kiss her, pausing to give her the chance to pull away. Instead, Tina wrapped her arms around his neck and his mouth became insistent, his hands beginning to explore. She sighed as he pushed her against the kitchen wall and kissed him deeper, enjoying the feel of his body.

"Hang on." Tina pulled away, twisting out of his arms and grabbed a tray, loading it with food. Ludovic leant against the wall and watched. She grinned at the disappointed look on his face and gave the tray to him, taking his elbow, "My rooms?" They only had today and that was half gone, she wouldn't allow herself to lose the chance as she had with Ivan. His eyes had a rare flash of mischief as she pulled him out of the kitchen.

She let Ludovic leave her room before dusk and blew kisses at him as he walked away. If he'd been any other vampire's pet, she would have kept him longer. Sasha had been right though, she smiled, she'd remember this afternoon for a long time.

Tina got ready for the evening, remembering last year and the fight and worrying about Ludovic. Kalmár appeared from his room and took her to an area where she'd not been before, refusing to say why. Ansell waited for them, sitting at a table in a large room with the curtains drawn. The lamps along the sides lit up the rich dark colours across the walls. Wolf appeared behind them to sit on the other side of Ansell. Tina stifled a sigh as Kalmár sat her next to him, away from the others.

Ansell started briskly, not bothering to greet

them. "I have spoken with Madame. After the ball, I will begin looking for Vinceti. He has not been seen since he was last at the safe house."

Wolf said, "I think I remember him trying to persuade Lord Tangent to sleep elsewhere. He wouldn't leave, just ordered Vinceti to get rid of Yorgias' body. I don't think Lord Tangent knew what would happen. I'm not completely sure, I wasn't thinking straight."

Tina stirred, having to speak despite not wanting to. "I remember," she said softly. They stopped and looked at her. "I remember that Vinceti did try several times to get Lord Tangent out. I don't think he would have stayed if he'd known. He killed a man who came to close…" She trailed off. She remembered the panic in Vinceti's eyes, he'd known something would happen.

Ansell nodded, "There was blood on the floor of one of the cells when we arrived. We can assume Vinceti was responsible for you being taken. We will need to know who else he has spoken to and how he arranged this. We can not allow ourselves to be studied in this way. Vinceti will tell us what we need to know, when we find him." Tina felt a moment of sympathy for Vinceti, his prospects were not looking good - Lord Tangent wouldn't be happy with him either.

"We also need someone to look after the safe house." Ansell continued, "Yorgias is dead. No one trustworthy wants it."

"What about Jon?" Wolf asked. "There are a couple of others around."

Ansell shook his head. "I would like you to do it." Wolf looked nervous. He glanced in her direction – once. Tina folded her arms in irritation as Kalmár casually leaned an arm across the back of her chair.

Kalmár commented, "Madame has also

indicated she thinks it would be a good idea. You impressed her in the way you handled retrieving Consort's new pet."

Wolf flinched, Tina didn't know if it was Kalmár speaking to him, or the mention of Madame's name. "I don't have any seniority. Yorgias complained I spent too much time fighting."

"You would not need the seniority. Once you are installed, you should have no problems. Any concerns you have will be dealt with." Kalmár's voice was cool. Tina wondered why she was here, she couldn't add anything else to this. Sasha wasn't here and she couldn't believe Kalmár would go so far in his jealousy as to not to want to leave her in her rooms alone.

Wolf looked at the table, his fingers picked at each other while he avoided everyone's eyes. Both the older vampires gazed at him, the pressure bearing down on him to do as they asked. She shifted, uncomfortable with the tension, wondering what would happen if he refused.

Eventually Ansell said, "If you will take the position, some seniority can be solved easily. You are already strong for your age, that is part of your problem. Here." He pulled his sleeve back and held his wrist out. Tina could see the greed tugging at Wolf. He glanced at Ansell and at his fingers while he tried to think. Bribery, Tina thought, she ought to be used to this from Kalmár. One way or another they would get what they wanted.

Wolf looked at Ansell, "How long?"

"Drink. If you do a good job there will be more at regular intervals." Tina saw him hesitate, unsure, then the flash of his canines as he took Ansell's wrist and drank. She stared as the sight finally brought it home to her what he was.

Ansell paused to collect himself as Wolf

finished. He swayed slightly and propped his head up, elbow on the table. "I believe that will take care of the seniority question. Jon has agreed he will support Wolf at the safe house. We don't need him having to fight through every decision." They'd arranged everything before they'd spoken to Wolf, typical. Wolf wiped his face, looking as though he was desperate not to lose a drop of Ansell's blood.

"The last thing," Wolf stopped as Kalmár spoke. "We wish you to wait until after the ceremony. It will not take long. You will take Ludovic with you when you leave."

"Why?"

Ansell sighed with irritation, "I do not wish Ludovic to be under Tangent's thumb again. Vinceti is in hiding. He does not dare show his face, either with Tangent or with us. We will pull Tangent's fangs with this. He will be without a trusted deputy or a source of information." Wolf nodded slowly and Tina's heart leapt. Ludovic would be safe, he just had to get through tonight. Wolf would look after him.

Kalmár continued, "He does not need to stay with you. Once he is away from here it will be difficult for Tangent to track him down."

"Transport?"

Ansell reached into his pocket and pulled out a set of keys. "Take these. They are the keys to the van you drove here. There are papers in the glove compartment." Ansell turned to Tina, "You have some unfinished business. Say goodbye to Wolf." She blinked, not expecting to be spoken to. "You had a strong bond with each other. It is unusual but you need to let him go, for everyone' sake." Ansell stood carefully and drew Kalmár away to the windows at the other end of the room.

They were left, staring at the table, not

knowing what to say. Wolf looking uneasy, came around the table and sat closer. After glancing over his shoulder, he left an empty chair between them.

Tina tried first, "Kalmár explained, I know you're not the same man as a year ago. It's difficult. I didn't expect to see you again, at least not so soon. I've missed you so much."

Wolf looked too aware of being left with her while the older vampires watched from a distance. He shifted in his seat and said in a low voice, "I can't remember what you were to me."

Tina crumpled inside. "You were my friend." Her voice choked, "My lover." The table swam in front of her eyes as tears threatened.

He nodded once, "I thought we had something. It's going to take time for me to sort myself out. I don't know who I am any more, I can't remember." His frustration while he struggled to explain was noticeable. "It's as though I'm a child, I've got to relearn so much but I don't think I will ever be the person you remember. I don't think I can be. Please, don't come near me again, it's not safe, for either of us."

She bit her lip and looked for Kalmár. He was watching her intently, Ansell's hand was restraining him and she could feel his emotions roiling across the room. "I miss you," she said again.

"Yes."

She wrapped her arms around herself, looked at her lap. "Goodbye Wolfie." It hurt as much as it had at the ball. He was still alive but she couldn't hold him, couldn't touch him, losing him like she'd lost Jo. Wolf reached out to touch her and stopped himself. He walked across to talk to Ansell and left the room with him.

Kalmár sat close by and held out his hand. Tina took it and let him pull her onto his lap. She could hear the murmurs of others, passing in the corridor, another world away. She allowed him to wrap her in the warmth of his mind while she let Wolfie go. Drifting off to a place where time wasn't important, held in his arms, secure. She became aware of him as he touched her hair and rested his chin against her head.

Collecting herself, she sat upright. "I'm all right," she responded to his unspoken concern. "It's not a weakness to get upset."

"You do not need to come with me tonight." Kalmár shifted her back into a more comfortable position, curled against him.

"Yes I do. I want to see what happens with Ludovic. If I don't go, I'll be left wondering." Kalmar wouldn't tell her everything if she didn't go, only what he wanted to. As she rubbed her face, he offered her his handkerchief. "I hope that's clean."

"Of course. I believe you would have noticed if it were not."

"Maybe." A streak of macabre mischief ran through her upset and she looked at him from beneath her eyelashes.

He caught her change of mood and ran a finger along her jaw. His eyes gleamed. "Shall I remind you?" She pretended to think as his fingers wandered down to her shirt collar, her hiccup turned into a gasp of laughter as his mouth followed and his mind started to wrap itself around hers.

"Kalmár, we're in public…" He grunted and pulled her tighter into him, refusing to let her say no, swamping her with his feelings. She let him bury his face into her neck and closed her eyes with a sigh as he touched her skin with his teeth, tasting her as he gathered himself to bite.

There was a nervous cough from the door, Tina jumped. Kalmár removed himself with reluctance and half turned, irritation on his face. "Yes?"

Clearly unhappy about interrupting them, the younger vampire said, "My apologies your Excellency. I have been sent to remind you, the ceremony is due to begin in ten minutes."

"I will be there." Tina saw the shadow waver against the wall and then disappear out of the room. Kalmár turned back to her, bent his head and brushed his lips against her neck. "Later," he promised softly.

Tina smiled at him and tapped his chest, "When you're hungry. Don't want you spoiling your dinner." He snorted, refusing to respond further.

She got up, stretched, took the elbow he offered and walked into the corridor with him. The hall was full. She could see Wolf. He was looking stroppy as he leant against a pillar and snarling at anyone who looked at him. The other vampires were sizing him up, somehow, she doubted he would have many problems. Tina watched Tangent walk into the middle of the room with Ludovic behind him. Only one new vampire this year. The room hummed, this hadn't happened for a long time.

"There will be no fight." Tangent's head jerked up at Madame's announcement, his eyes narrowing. The crowd murmured. No fight?

"In the past, the single candidate has fought a newly fledged vampire." Tangent's voice was confident, carrying through the hall. Tina twitched, he was expecting Wolf to fight Ludovic. She could see the others eyeing Wolf, smiles curling the corners of their mouths. Their bloodlust would be satisfied, Ludovic would have no chance. Wolf stared straight ahead, his feelings concealed. Ludovic, still very human, looked terrified in the knowledge that Wolf would kill him easily.

Ansell shifted from where he lounged, close to

the front and caught Tangent's eye. "After a long debate, we have made the decision only to hold the fight when there are a large number of candidates." Ansell blinked sleepily, "Of course, you are welcome to hold your pet back until the next time if you wish." Tina watched Tangent's face. He was no longer cool. If he wanted to wait so that Ludovic could fight, then he would have to spend at least six months with a pet he couldn't feed from and he'd have little chance of getting his hands on another human if he had Ansell watching him.

"We have always challenged those who wish to join our ranks." Tangent's face hardened and his voice rang out, sounding assured as he appealed to those around him. A ripple of agreement followed his words.

"That may be so however the numbers of suitable humans are becoming less, we no longer need to weed out those without the necessary will to survive. However,..." Ansell paused, his smile deepening. "Should you wish for a fight, I am happy to offer myself as a substitute. What do you say Tangent, to you against me?"

The crowd reaction was uproar. Tangent stood stunned, he'd been outgunned. Ansell hadn't challenged anyone for years and he'd offered Tangent the chance to fight in the same way Ludovic, a fight without a chance of surviving.

Tangent collected himself as the noise died down. His expression was furious. The audience's attention was now focussed on him, they'd been offered a better show than a mere human. It wasn't everyday they got to see those stronger than themselves battling. "For the sake of our community, let us not fight."

He bowed gracefully to Ansell, gritting his teeth through the words and loss of face. Ludovic looked dazed. Tina let out the breath she hadn't known she'd been holding and relaxed her grip on Kalmár's arm. She glanced up at him. Kalmár's face was impassive except for a slight curve to the corner of his mouth - he'd known. She suppressed her irritation, something else he'd not told her.

Madame gestured to Tangent to start and he pulled Ludovic towards him. A hesitation on Tangent's part, a gleam in his eye and Ludovic froze at the implied threat. Tina saw his chest moving, could hear his rapid breathing from where she stood. It would be typical of Tangent to rid himself of a useless pet purely to spite others.

Ansell pulled himself up from where he leant and walked over, "If you do not wish to, then I will."

His words carried, challenging Tangent not to complete the process he'd started on Ludovic. The hall was quiet, watching. Tangent had hesitated too long. He snarled, showing his fangs and sank them into Ludovic's neck. Ansell watched closely, making sure Tangent behaved.

Tina felt dizzy, no fight, no blood bath, no senseless murder for the sake of it. Tangent had been contained. Ludovic staggered towards the platform, pushed away after feeding by Tangent as though he were rubbish. Madame smiled and raised her wrist, the same quiet words that failed to carry. A subtle change in Ludovic's stance as he walked out, no longer under someone's thumb. She saw Wolf casually wander out after him. Ludovic would be safe, they both would.

A long arm around her waist. She smiled in relief at Kalmár as he took her hand, turning it to kiss the inside of her wrist. "Let us go home Little Mouse."

She smiled back. "Yes. Let's."

***